T0049298

The Late Rebellion

Mark Powell

Regal House Publishing

Published by
Regal House Publishing, LLC
Raleigh, NC 27605

ISBN -13 (paperback): 9781646034123
ISBN -13 (epub): 9781646034130
Library of Congress Control Number: 2023934860

Cover design by © C. B. Royal

Regal House Publishing, LLC
https://regalhousepublishing.com

Printed in the United States of America

for Joy, James, and Cliff

There is another world, and it is this one.

—Paul Éluard

The Tragic Prelude

HERE'S A LITTLE GHOST FOR THE OFFERING
(yeah, yeah, yeah, yeah)

She couldn't find her boy.

Rose Greaves had hoisted herself from her recliner to get an ice cream sandwich when she realized he was missing. She looked for him in the kitchen and the living room, and then went out to the front porch calling for him—*Teddy, honey? Are you out here?*—knowing all along that he wasn't because—she knew this only faintly, but knew it all the same—her son Teddy was dead. Nearly a half-century ago he had fallen from the fender of Anson's International Harvester down beneath the back right tire and through the broken teeth of the hay rake. Seven years old. They'd buried him behind the church, his Sunday clothes tucked into four-and-a-half feet of pine.

"Anson," she started to call, headed for the front porch, but her husband was dead too.

She knew all this. Yet it was easy to forget.

And because it was so easy to forget, because it was easy to imagine it 1969 all over again, Teddy still alive and their oldest boy Richard away at the Citadel, she often did.

"Teddy?"

Above her still-green yard and the still-leafed maple, above what pasture lay beyond the white fence and the graying barn, above the shaggy abandoned orchard past it all, the wind was just beginning to snip and pick. She could smell rain and mown grass, and looked up at the wash-water of the sky just as the first drops began to bang against the metal roof. A box fan was running and she bent to unplug the extension cord snaked beneath the screen door but the bend was too much, the effort too great; she stood stiffly, gripped the rubber handles of her walker, and began the slow process of turning from the porch back into the house.

By the time she made it inside the rain was falling in long slants of silvered darkness, barely six o'clock on the first

Thursday of October, and all at once it was like night had fallen. She made her steady, methodical way down the front hall past the photographs of her grandchildren—only children in their frames, grown now, parents themselves, out in the great wide world. She didn't know where her own boy was. Anson would know, if only she could talk to him. They had done everything together, and then he'd up and died on her. Pancreatic cancer winnowing him from a big-handed good-looking man in a silverbelly Stetson to no more than a scarecrow curled beneath the sheets of a rented hospital bed, the kind of thing you'd prop in the corn patch more out of spite than warning.

Don't you dare up and leave me.

Yet he had.

She moved from the laminate flooring of the hall to the carpet of the living room and this was always a tricky moment, raising the rubber stoppers of her walker the half-inch over the threshold, balancing, shifting. She wasn't supposed to be up. Yesenia—the sweet Mexican woman hired to sit with her in the afternoons—had just left. Her son Richard would come by around seven. She could have waited on him, sat in the giant armchair with the TV cranked so high the windows shook. The evening news or *The Price is Right,* some foolish Hollywood gossip she couldn't stand, as if the noise from the speakers equated to the noise of a life.

She could have called him.

But she had done neither, and now there was little she could do but stand there in the kitchen like the helpless thing she had become. Something old and perhaps loved, but more than that something to be run back and forth to this or that doctor, to be fed and changed and occasionally fussed over.

She paused now.

She had the front two stoppers on the carpet and wanted to rest a moment before attempting to raise the back two. It was like an expedition, this striking out across a house shuddering into darkness and the drilling of rain. Had she left the screen door open? Maybe, but she couldn't turn again. To turn would waste what little energy she had left, and before she started the long sojourn back to the chair she had to find Teddy.

She leaned forward on her walker so that her legs wouldn't shake. If she didn't hurt, it was only because so little was left to suffer—the sores on her gauzy skin, purpled with bruises; the construction of her brittle bones that had become a little more visible every year until now she lived with the topography of every ridge and swale.

She weighed—

She didn't know how much she weighed. No one did. Because what was the point in knowing? She was eighty maybe eighty-five pounds if you didn't count the orthopedic boot on her right foot. She had lost most of her hair and much of her hearing. She had trouble keeping her false teeth in place. She was ninety-four and dying, but not dead yet. Right then, in fact, looking for her lost boy, she was very much alive.

She started moving again. The burnt-orange shag of the carpet was safer, but also slower and she wondered if it might not be better to retreat to the living room and wait for Richard. Probably Teddy was hiding, tucked into his closet wearing an Eddie Munster mask and laughing.

"Anson," she again started to call, and, for a second time, stopped herself.

The chair was no more than twenty feet away, but she went not toward it, but toward the basement stairs. Richard would be here at seven, or maybe it would be seven-thirty or eight or even nine. She loved him but it was difficult to count on him. *Got busy, Ma. I'm sorry. I'm here now.* And he always was in the end, eventually he always came. But she couldn't sit two hours with *Inside Edition* playing at one hundred decibels while she prayed her boy was fine, just hiding, just playing, and not having fallen down the stairs or wandered down toward the old cow pond that got deep quicker than it should.

"Teddy?"

He wasn't in the bathroom. The door was open, the light on so that she saw the handicapped toilet with its plastic surfaces and metal rails. The amber phials of pills. The Metoprolol, the Digoxin, the Endocet. The bottles of ibuprofen and Sudafed. The ancient, jellied Nyquil the colors of sapphire and turquoise. The tinny urine smell she refused to believe was her.

She went up the hall toward the kitchen, past the old Christmas cards and get-well cards and Easter cards Scotch-taped to the pressboard walls. Past the old dining room breakfront, the forgotten china within. Into the kitchen with its cooked peel of wallpaper, the high corners just beginning to curl, a fleshy tube of paper and glue and the fading pattern of a thousand yellow flowers so faint that to properly see them you needed not vision but memory.

Out the window through a curtain of rain, she could just make out the dark shape that marked the barn, the wood almost blued with age, the door open on a gaping space darker still. Inside, rotted the old International Harvester, the hay rake with its missing teeth, the disc plow, the Bush Hog. All of it sitting where it had sat since that day in the field. Ossified tack nailed to the walls like the pelts of animals.

Beyond that stood the old homeplace, the one they had bought when Anson came home from Europe in 1946. They'd been living there when it happened, and even across the field she could feel the augers of that house, the memories soured like old milk. The brown patch where the stovepiping went into the wall. The corner where they'd put the Christmas tree. It lay a quarter mile away, beyond a window of double-paned glass, across a field of uncut fescue, but she smelled it all the same. It was no more than a shell of rotten floorboards and a brick chimney. Still, she tasted the pot roasts and new potatoes.

The field greens on the stove.

The cornbread and soup beans.

The smell of mornings, too, the shoe polish and shaving cream and—

A door shut.

Somewhere she heard laughing, Teddy laughing, playing whatever game he was playing. She turned to find an ice cream sandwich in the center of the table, melting to soup in the dull underside of its paper wrapper. Had it been there a moment ago? Had he left it for her?

"Teddy?" she called. "Come on out, honey. Your brother'll be here any minute." She listened for a moment, but there was no sound beyond the clatter of rain. "Teddy?"

Outside, rain fell through the porch light, a bright globe in an area of darkness.

"Teddy," she started, but there was no use calling. He was either playing hide-and-go-seek or he was dead and buried in the churchyard. Either way, he wouldn't answer. She turned to continue the long trek to the stairs. The door was dead-bolted and though it took her a moment, she managed to turn it, the satisfying thunk as it swung open onto the red-carpeted stairs, steep, with a turn at the landing two-thirds of the way down. There was a handrail, but she wasn't sure that was enough.

How to get down?

Backwards, it turned out. The frail ship of her body swung round, and she let her booted foot drift behind her, felt it find the grain of the carpet, and then the other foot, and then the walker, slower and harder than she had ever imagined so that halfway to the landing she was sweating, something she thought she had lost the ability to do, had forgotten, even, what it felt like. Turns out it felt good. It felt like her skin breathing. But all at once it didn't. All at once she was cold and tired, marooned between upstairs and down, and when she called for her boy it was weakly and without any real hope for answer.

"Teddy? Are you down here, honey?"

It was hard to believe he was gone. More like simply absent, like Anson had been during the war when the letters came V-Mail from England and France and Germany and finally from a little town in Czechoslovakia. Like her boy was traveling not through memory but some foreign country from which he'd eventually return.

She had once believed it.

For years, she had sat on the porch and waited to see him walking along the rail fence, laughing and coming on through the honeysuckle heat. He'd be eight or eighteen, older, but still her boy, laughing, apologizing. *I weren't really dead, Ma. Just gone for a while.* Later, she watched only from the perch of sleep, but still she studied that rail fence, knowing well the view had outlived its use but no less able to part with the vision. Like water kept in the vase long after the flowers are dead.

Moving—

She started moving again. It was barely perceptible at first, her backward crawl, but by the time she reached the landing she had found a rhythm, a woeful pattern of descent. The sound of the rain quieter, the smell of the basement all around her—the moldy clothes and cold concrete. It was only when she reached the bottom that she realized there was no way back up. There was the spring of panic, but Richard was coming, Richard would be here soon. He could get her back upstairs.

She reached for the light switch and the room revealed itself.

Block walls and cardboard boxes. Along the right the exposed studs of what had been a partition and then later wasn't, just the boards and electrical box, the gray curl of wiring.

She eased her walker around and moved forward.

Where was he? She wouldn't call to him. If he was playing a game, calling was the surest way to keep him hidden. She would have to find him, and moved right, staying close enough to the wall so that if she fell she might catch herself. Which is how her finger went to the frame, the cool glass with its particles of dust. Without looking, she knew it was Anson's company photograph. Two hundred or so young men in their wool uniforms. Company "C" Forty-Fourth Signal Regiment, Fort Lee, VA, it read. She could barely see it—the dim lighting, her failing eyes—and this was a good thing, there was a sort of enchantment in staring.

She had known, perhaps, twenty-five of the boys in the photograph, including her husband, including her brother, who had sat for this picture but no others, who had returned from the war in a container no larger than a hatbox.

She balanced her palm on the glass and moved on, one hand advancing her walker, the other gripping the naked wall studs. To her right sat a shopping cart stacked with glass bottles.

Brownie.

Kist.

Sun Drop.

Buffalo Drop—Buffalo Drop tasted awful, like Lieneman's, only worse—

Bireley's orangeade.

Mountain Dew.

Fowler's Quality Flavors.

They were in boxes marked BELTON BOTTLING COMPANY. Past them hung Anson's field jacket, the yellow stripes of a tech sergeant on the sleeve. There were boxes of old clothes and photos and magazines and empty Ball canning jars. A Whirlpool electric range and Pioneer Stove. Bags of Morton Rock Salt turned to bricks.

"Teddy?"

A vase full of umbrellas and a yardstick marked Jim Owens & Sons Fertilizer.

"Teddy, honey? Are you down here?"

He wasn't, of course, and she thought of turning back—Richard would pitch a fit, finding her in the basement—but then she heard him. Teddy was just around the corner, just beyond dim sight. He was laughing softly and she eased her walker forward, rubber stoppers on the concrete floor, nearer, closer. She was about to find him, and it occurred to her that perhaps he hadn't really died after all, perhaps he had simply been down here, hiding, playing, waiting on her to show up and now she had—

"Teddy," she said, "honey, why don't you..." and then she saw him, crouched there in the corner. He was wearing Jon Jons, a little boy squatting on his chubby little-boy legs, pink-faced and smiling, and it was the sight of him that did it, the sight of him that made her feet go out from under her legs and her arms and her everything, and she knew she was falling but knew it for only a moment. She started to speak.

"Teddy," she meant to say, but then her head hit the concrete.

And the earth shook.

Thursday

WHAT WILL YOU DO WITH YOUR FOUR MINUTES?

Yet somehow his ma's collapse wasn't enough to ripple the surface of her son's whiskey. His third—already—in case you were counting which, it seemed, his wife Clara was. Richard stood by the drink cart splashing Elijah Craig into his glass and sensed her just beyond sight.

"Celebratory," he explained, but when he looked she wasn't there.

He downed the bourbon and poured another.

"Celebratory," he said again, though quieter.

And it was, wasn't it? The first cool evening of October and all his children en route. Soon enough he'd have everyone back under one roof the way the Good Lord intended, even if it was only for a couple of hours. Tom, their youngest, was coming home from seven months in Europe doing God-only-knew what. His oldest, Jack, was driving over. His daughter, Emily, was already in the kitchen. Tom would land in—Richard checked his watch, and strange how the face seemed to blur so that he held it close, shut one eye, squinted. He'd land in—damn, he might have already landed.

"Tom's landed," he called toward the kitchen.

"Tom?" Clara called back. "Did he text?"

"No, I..."

"You heard from him?"

"No, I just..."

Just what? That was the question, wasn't it? But Richard Samuel Greaves—sixty-seven years old, president and founder of Mountain Empire Bank, chair of the board of Golden Corner Baptist, father of both the high school athletic director and the county solicitor, a Citadel man, a businessman, a man for God and Country and all that is good and right in the real America of hard work and prepackaged processed food—couldn't answer, and instead began to slowly pivot his body from the drink cart across the living room and toward the kitchen, past where his granddaughter, Lana, sprawled in a recliner, face lit by the screen of her phone. He touched the part in her hair as he lumbered by.

"Is your dad here?"

"What?"

"Your dad?"

"I don't know," she said, already looking back down. "He's at the game or something."

The game or something—of course. The game would be the JV football game.

"He'll be a little late, I guess," Richard said, but she seemed not to hear.

"Richard?"

His wife met him in the living room.

"Honey," he said, and tried for a moment to do something with his glass, put it behind his back maybe, hide it with his hands. Finally he settled on taking a drink, and then another, while his wife stood waiting, if not patiently then with at least a certain resignation.

"I'm think I'm gonna put the banner up," he said finally, tears in his eyes.

"The what?"

"The banner." The banner he'd picked up on his way from the bank, WELCOME HOME, NINJA!! in the big swirly comic sans that felt appropriate if somehow embarrassing. He'd ordered it three days ago when Tom emailed—emailed! not even a damn call—to say he was on his way back from wherever the hell he'd been and could someone please buy him a ticket? The banner Richard had very nearly forgotten about, coming, as it did, on the heels of what he was starting to think of as The Call.

"It's supposed to rain," Clara said. "Why don't you come and talk to Emily?"

"It's plastic."

"It's what?" Clara asked, and he realized he must have slurred his words.

"Plastic," he said with great effort. "The banner."

He wanted that to settle it and patted her head in genuine affection. She kept staring at him though, took a step closer and looked down at the nearly empty glass in his right hand. He couldn't help but stare back. Her eyelids shone as if worn, as if soon enough they would become as transparent as wings. Her neck was looser, a few brown splotches barely visible along her throat. She was aging.

"Richard?"

Yet she remained beautiful, and as for aging, she was managing it far better than Richard. He was a short squat man with the wide hands of a butcher and a face like a cut of meat. Yet it had taught him things, to be a meticulous dresser if nothing else. To match his socks to his tie, to wear the onyx Zegna cufflinks with the Chelsea oxfords.

"Honey, are you listening?"

He shifted his weight, his balance suddenly coming into question.

"I'll be quick," he said.

"Okay."

"Putting it up."

She nodded, nothing more, and he felt a flood of tenderness. Even after nearly fifty years of marriage there was a shyness about her still, as if she'd come into her beauty late, and as such never quite believed in its existence.

"Five minutes," he said.

"Okay."

"You haven't heard from Jack?"

"He said he'd be here." She took the glass from his hand. "He's still at the game, I would imagine."

"Right, of course. And Tom?"

"Knox is picking him up."

"Knox. Got it."

"Judson's with him."

Knox being Emily's husband, Judson being their son.

"It's all perfect," Clara said.

And it was, wasn't it? Standing there with his right hand now strangely empty, Richard felt a surge of pride somewhere beneath the slosh of bourbon and the weight of The Call. It was, well, maybe not exactly perfect. But surely the world was righting itself: Tom was coming home. Jack was running the athletic department. Emily was the county solicitor and though she'd spent the last several months on an extended maternity leave she'd be back to work on Monday, back on track, as Richard understood it. She would almost certainly be the next district attorney. She was smart, hardworking, and married to Knox Rhett, a filmmaker and son of a famous (if dead) South Carolina politician. It was cheering to consider and he danced his way into the kitchen, Clara behind him, hands clasped at her waist.

"Dad," Emily said, looking up from the counter.

"I'm here to make your life a bit happier, darling."

"You're here to help?"

"Even better." He raised his cell phone, hit the right-facing arrow, and winked at his daughter as the Beach Boys began to sing from the tiny speaker he'd had his grandson Judson mount in the corner. "Kokomo!" he said.

"So you're not here to help?"

"You love this song!" Richard said and danced his way back to the living room.

It really was cheering to consider—three grown children, each decent and upstanding—so damn cheering it made it all the more frustrating to feel whatever it was that he felt sitting, wallowing, fairly crawling around his gut.

"Richard," Clara called over the music, "I think it's about to—"

"I'll be right back," he said, and eased his way past his wife, back to the drink cart, and finally onto the porch. Rain? He saw no signs of rain. In the last hour the day had softened, sure. The yard, the trees, even the bare azaleas had grown dark, but the sky remained the thin blue of blown glass. He'd hang the banner and then run over and check on his ma. Her caretaker,

Yesenia, would have left and she would be looking for him.

"Celebratory," he told the evening, just as the first of the rain began to slant onto the expensive slate roof he'd installed in the spring.

"Celebratory!" he called to no one.

But it wasn't.

Of course it wasn't, Tom Greaves would have agreed had he heard and, more importantly, had he not been engaged in a rare bout of loathing not directed at himself. It was the people around him this time. The people watching the seatbelt sign as if it were an Olympic sport, the leaping up, the grabbing of luggage that may or may not have shifted during flight, and all for what? To stand in the Lufthansa aisle like lobotomized sheep while the plane unloaded not a second slower or faster than it would have otherwise? It seemed like a metaphor or a symbol or a something meant to represent his life of late.

The futility, the disaster, the—

The light flashed, the people jumped.

Everyone but Tom, everyone but patient put-upon Tom, who didn't budge because he was too busy remembering Prague because, Jesus, Prague had been a disaster. But then so had Budapest and Vienna. Split and Dubrovnik—all of it one endless mistake. As if he'd misled not so much himself as an entire subregion. His sins less mortal than geopolitical.

Instead of standing, he checked his phone. There were texts from his mom and sister but nothing from Ivana, not that he'd thought there would be. She'd said what she'd said and what had Tom done? Gotten a new tattoo—Leonard Cohen, not pretentious in the least—and then emailed his parents to beg a ticket home to the rebel flags and MAGA stickers, his mother's insistence on speakerphone, his father's reliance on all-cap emails…

They were starting to move now.

There was some disappointment in it, the movement, the inevitability of it all. If his arrival had ever been in question, it wasn't now: he'd be home in an hour, if *home* was what he was still calling it. His parents' house. His old bedroom with the same vaguely motivational posters advertising obscure running shoes and climbing harnesses, things he'd hung as a teenager not because people knew the brands but because they didn't.

He put his phone in his pocket and stood.

He'd always been the sort of person who lived without a TV. Only lately had he become the sort of person who made sure everyone knew it. "Social media," he'd sometimes catch himself saying. "I don't *need* it." As if the rest of the world did, as if dear sweet honeyed Tom with his hemp shirt and donations to the Rainforest Coalition would surely, just any day now, achieve enlightenment—and then wonder aloud why you hadn't.

All right, he thought, enough of that, and pushed his way into the aisle.

He had no need for the luggage carousel and walked out into the warm October evening, his stainless-steel canteen clutched like a safety blanket, his bag slung over his shoulder. Some clothes, toiletries, and one extremely potent edible. His expensive running shoes and a copy of *The Cloud of Unknowing* (again with the pretention). The Moleskine he'd picked up at the Atlanta airport seven months ago in preparation for his self-declared "pilgrimage" and proceeded to open not once.

"What the hell am I doing," he half-mumbled.

Two years prior Tom had been a season champion on the television show *American Ninja*. That, an endorsement deal with a failed energy drink, and—most importantly—a sizable Instagram following had made him into both a minor celebrity—an *influencer*, he reminded himself—and something of a joke, as if his life amounted to not so much his well-stamped passport and ability to scale a warped wall as his ability to curate such. But he was finished with that life. Saturday he was to be the guest on *SoulCast*, a podcast hosted by an LA guru of micro-dosing and sensory deprivation tanks. Tom had agreed to it months ago and, while he'd debated canceling, it seemed better to go through with it, let it be his last word, his goodbye to all that. He'd do the show and disappear into a life of—well, of what wasn't totally clear. Only that it would be something totally different from this.

It was just beginning to rain and he tucked himself under the awning to scan for his brother-in-law Knox. He was peering out into the line of headlights when he noticed the woman beside him.

"Nice threads," she said, and very nearly plucked at his sleeve.

"I'm sorry?"

"Even the stitching is popping," she said, in a voice that fell somewhere between flirting and mocking. He looked down at himself. He was, to be fair, wearing a Reiss tracksuit, the sort of velvety glove you could find in Berlin or London but certainly not here.

"Oh," he said. "Thanks."

She was smiling, mid-twenties, he guessed, tan and athletic with a shiny black brace on one knee.

"You're not waiting on an Uber, are you?" she asked.

"No."

"Silver Audi, you sure?"

"No, my brother-in-law."

"Ah," she said. "Devastatingly convenient. But I'm not so sure I believe you."

Her voice was most definitely flirtatious now, and he attempted to smile back. Tom looked like he had just stepped off a Wheaties box and, to his great detriment, knew it. She looked like a professional athlete in some obscure if impressive sport, someone who'd once cleared fifteen feet in the pole vault or taken the bronze in skeleton. He had an eye for it. In college, Tom had been a sort-of-athletic legend: a river swimmer in July, a trail runner in January. A doer of insane masochistic feats who'd taught Brazilian jujitsu and started a parkour club. This leggy blond who maybe played midfielder for a club team or ran ultras on the weekend—this was very much his métier. But the thing with Ivana, the way it was quickly coming to embody *The Greatest Moral Failing* of his life, the sort of mistake he imagined headlined across a Roz Chast cartoon in *The New Yorker*…

"So maybe if this so-called brother-in-law—" she started, but he cut her off.

"Actually, there he is."

"Oh, okay, I…"

He couldn't hear the rest as he hustled through the rain and slung himself into the passenger seat of Knox's Lexus.

"Whoa! Look here," Knox said, and grabbed his shoulder. "Odysseus come home!"

"Hey, Knox. What's up, Judson?"

His nephew sat in the back seat and swiped at his phone.

"Dad made me ride in the back."

"Heartache," Knox said.

"Like I'm five."

"Heartache and sacrifice," Knox said. "It's all I know. But damn it's good to see you, man. How was your flight?"

"Fine," Tom said. "Prague to London to Atlanta to good ole GSP."

"Odysseus indeed! Or is it Ulysses?"

"Odysseus, I think. Shall we?"

"Oh yeah, of course," Knox said, and edged away from the curb. "So what was that?"

"What was what?"

"The girl? Kneebrace over there."

"So, no small talk? No 'how was your flight?'"

"I just asked you that," Knox said. "But seriously, the girl?"

"Just some random girl."

"Some random girl who appeared into you. We could see it from here."

"All the way from the car?"

"All the way from the car," Knox said, and turned into the loop that circled the terminal. "Speaking of women."

"Were we?"

"I want some details, brother. This girl, Czech or whatever."

"What girl?"

"Come on, man. Like I don't see things."

"Oh, that," Tom said. "That was a mistake."

"Didn't look like a mistake."

"Believe me though." And Tom made sure here to shift to that wistful faraway voice he'd spent years perfecting. "Believe me, biggest mistake of my life."

Except it wasn't. It was Ivana. Tom had been so taken with her at the time, so taken with everything actually, that he'd made a few ill-advised posts with his arms wrapped around her. But then what had happened, happened, and he'd fled, taken a bus through Brno to Prague where he did his forty days in the desert thing and then woke one Czech morning sporting the Leonard Cohen tattoo. Which seemed a clear sign it was time to go home.

As for home—

"Hey," Knox said, "I'm sworn to secrecy here but I think you should know. Your parents are having a sort of surprise welcome home thing for you."

"You're kidding?"

"Like a 'welcome home, dear ninja' if you will."

"When?"

"Tonight."

"Tonight. Jesus. And who's going to be there?"

"Just family. Emily's there now. I think Jack's coming."

Jack. He hadn't talked to his big brother since January, since after their grandfather's funeral when Tom had declared himself ready for a "pilgrimage" and Jack let him know just what he thought of such. Not that Tom had ever been in the dark. If there was an ad for millennial self-indulgence Jack believed Tom to be the poster boy. Tall and good-looking with that slightly mussed hair that was carefully contrived to look as careless as possible—that was Tom. The CBD oil, the biohacking and "self-care"—all Tom. It would be nice to see Emily though.

"How is she?" Tom asked.

"Who, Emily? Oh God. Judson, how's your mother?"

"Manic," Judson said.

"Like normal-Emily manic," Tom asked, "or like—"

"Like next-level manic," Knox said. "Like she goes back to work Monday manic. No more extensions on the maternity leave, you know?"

"Ugh."

"Exactly. The real thing though is this case. Some sick motherfucker—excuse the language, son. But some sick motherfucker—this was right after you left—he tied his wife to the bed, soaked her in gasoline, and, no joke, set her on fire with a tampon. Happened right before Kyle was born."

"Are you serious?"

"I'm telling you, Tom. Your sister, she can't get over it." He shook his head. "Hey, on a brighter note, you still haven't met Kyle, have you?"

"Not yet."

"Well, tonight, my friend. Tonight."

Yes, tonight, Tom thought, and tipped his head sideways against the cool glass. He had to somehow survive not just the coming days but, more immediately, tonight. And then it came to him.

"Hey," he said. "Could you pull back by the terminal?"

"You forget something?"

"I'll be like sixty seconds."

"Yeah, no worries," Knox said, and merged back into the loop. "Like luggage or something?"

"Sixty seconds."

"No worries."

"Time me, Judson," he said, scanning the crowd. And then Tom saw her: Kneebrace, still waiting for her silver Audi.

"Hey," he called, window down and door barely open, showing that orthodontic smile that had always served him so well. "I think I found your ride."

"Oh, snap," Knox whispered. "You're nuts."

"I know," Tom said, his smile brilliant, false, and not so much as flickering.

Clara and Emily were in the kitchen with a dry chardonnay, Kyle marvelously asleep in the bedroom. It was time, or very nearly: the food was out on the bar, covered in tinfoil, and Clara had moved to the window where she stared into the black gloss of her reflection.

"I wonder where he is."

"He's coming," Emily said.

Clara startled, not having realized she'd spoken out loud.

"You mean Tom?" Emily asked. "Judson texted me. They picked him up like a half hour ago."

"Oh."

"Or did you mean Dad?"

"He went out to hang some banner and it's raining now and…"

Emily put her knife down on the cutting board just as the lightning broke.

"Why don't I go look," she said. "Want to just pop your head back and check on Kyle?"

"Do you mind?"

"Just make sure he's still sleeping. I'll find Dad."

"Thanks, honey," Clara said. "I'll just go check on him."

And she did, Clara did check on Kyle, who was still angelically asleep in his footed pajamas. It's just that while Clara was back there, since she was back there, it seemed to make sense to take one of the lozenges she kept in the Advil bottle beneath the sink, the one whose top she could barely remove, what with the way her hands were shaking.

As for Jack, his hands were steady, at ten and two on the steering wheel just like they were supposed to be. He had left the high school and was headed to his parents' when the lightning began to finger and crack and then, as if on cue, as if this unseasonably late October thunderstorm had formed for no other purpose than to exasperate him, his phone went off there on the seat where it sat next to the LBJ bio he kept meaning to finish.

Lord, he thought, already?

He had planned to stop and see his granny, alone since Jack's grandfather had passed in January, but all of a sudden the JV football coach was on the phone and the rain was coming down in goddang icy buckets and the coach couldn't remember the goddang punch code to the goddang locker room and here his boys were, down two touchdowns to Palmetto and shivering through what looked to be a substantial rain delay.

"I ain't gonna lie to you, Jack, I got parents yelling shit."

"At you?"

"Terrible mean shit like you maybe ain't never heard."

"Because of the door?"

"The door, the score, the goddang state of the universe seems like."

"Is Elvis not around? Elvis has a key."

"I ain't seen that mother-scratcher since kick-off."

"All right."

"Elvis has left the goddang building, I'd say."

"All right," Jack said. "First, clear the thing to 0."

"Do what?"

"The lock. Clear it to 0."

Jack talked him through the code twice but *I don't know, Jack. All this newfangled Chinese shit. Why can't they just give us a key?*

Jack, being the newly promoted athletic director at the newly built Germantown High, had a key, and rather than attempting to talk the coach through a third round of numeric failure he told him he'd run it over, it wasn't a big deal except for the simple fact that it was. His wife, Catherine, was at work but his daughter, Lana, was at his parents'. The plan was to swing by, say his helloes, and then exit with Lana before his brother arrived and Jack had to fake the whole welcome-home thing.

"I'm turning around," he told the coach.

"Hurry, Jack."

He pulled into his granny's drive and thought about running in to check on her. But there was no time and he got back on the highway and hit the gas. Anyway, his dad had probably already come by. For his part, Jack would make a point to ride over with Lana Saturday evening after the Clemson-Citadel football game, the future event that was pulling him through the obligations of family.

He put the wipers on intermittent and hit the gas.

"Somebody just threw a bottle!" the coach declared.

"Hold on," Jack said. "I'll be there in five."

"Think we could detour through town?"

"Through town?" Knox asked.

They were off the interstate now, ten minutes from the Greaveses', and Tom made the sort of shrug that would have embarrassed even his ten-year-old self. He was up front, Sherilynn—that was Kneebrace's name, *Share-ah-lin*—in the back with Judson. She'd leaned forward to tell them about herself—she'd finished an MBA at Furman in the spring, had just nailed ("God, fingers crossed") a job interview with a Southern California beach apparel company, and was home visiting friends. She'd been all effusive eye contact, but was now sunk into her seat, eyes on Judson's Minecraft.

"Just Main Street," Tom said. "Just to, like, see it?"

"Because it's changed so much, obviously."

"Obviously."

Knox smiled and gave Tom's shoulder another squeeze.

"You're like your sister, a true romantic."

And he was probably: romantic and confused, quixotic and deluded. Immature, too, since Tom was asking to see town simply to delay arriving home. But he knew Knox wouldn't mind. He was technically Tom's brother-in-law, but given the age difference—Tom was thirteen years younger than both his sister and her husband—Knox felt more like an uncle. Maybe something of a hero, too, ridiculous as it sounded. As a law student in Columbia, Knox had made *The Late Rebellion*, a documentary that tracked the fight to remove the Confederate flag from the grounds of the statehouse. The film had been on every "year's best" list, reviewed lavishly in the *New York Times*, shown at festivals from Telluride to Cannes, and for a while Knox had been the darling of the independent film circuit, the precocious genius appearing on panels at far-flung universities where he waxed eloquently on race and history, trading on his charm and talent until, a few years down the line and no new film made or even in production, there seemed little left to barter.

Lately, he had become the subject of the occasional "where are they now" article. There was occasional talk of another film, something that would be two decades in the making. There was speculation, hope. It would be magisterial, Ross McElwee for the twenty-first century, Werner Herzog in Southern seersucker. But Tom knew it was not to be, and that knowing, that sense that like him, his brother-in-law had been written off, was as magnetic as it was comforting. Knox Rhett was adept at disappointment, and Tom envied him.

"Voilà," Knox said. "Town in all its glory."

Which meant Arby's and McDonald's.

"This is where you grew up?" Sherilynn asked.

Which meant the wide expanse of Country Boy Tire and Brake by Little Tokyo Express and The Wine Cellar. German and American flags alternated up and down the street, and seeing them, Tom's flicker of confusion gave way to a rush of regret. That this was Oktoberfest weekend and that tomorrow Tom would be sitting on the dais with his father and Jack—guests of honor at the kick-off luncheon—was the least of his concern. His real concern was—

"Oh no," Tom said.

"There she is!" Knox said.

"Oh my God," Sherilynn said, "that's you?"

A sign erected at the corner of SC 28 and a Hawaiian Ice stand read:

Welcome home
Tom Greaves!
Meet Germantown's *American Ninja*
Saturday 1:00 p.m.
Sertoma Field

In a rush of guilt at having asked his parents to buy him a ticket home (nearly nine hundred bucks bought, as it were, at the last minute), Tom had promised his father to put on what he'd vaguely described as a "ninja display." Tom had thought nothing of it at the time. But it appeared his ninja display—whatever that was—would be happening after all, and no doubt all of Germantown would come out to gawk.

"I used to love that show," Sherilynn said. "I still do, actually. I just didn't know it was still on."

"Still on," Knox said, "still going strong. Isn't that right, Judson?"

"What's that, Dad?"

"*American Ninja.*"

"So cool," Sherilynn said, "so devastatingly cool, Tom."

But *cool* wasn't the word. The word was *embarrassing*, *ridiculous*. The word was *joke*. The child of privilege and promise who had thus far amounted to little beyond a talent for the "Salmon Ladder" and an endorsement deal with an energy drink the FDA had never quite gotten around to approving.

He checked his phone a last time—once again, nothing from Ivana—and looked at Knox.

"Thanks, man."

"That good?"

"More than good," Tom said. "Way more."

"All right then," Knox said. "Hey, Sherilynn, let's go find us a party."

Emily was out in the yard, a borrowed raincoat pulled over her head, searching not for a party but for her dad. She found him beneath the twin oaks, a large banner wet and limp on the walk at his feet. She called his name and when he didn't respond she approached him slowly, as if closing on a wounded animal.

"Dad, you're soaked."

"This banner," he said, and gestured, maybe, at the now ruined lettering gone limp in the grass but also, perhaps, at the larger world beyond the green pasture and white fence. "We need to hang it."

"I don't know," she said. "I think maybe it's past hanging."

"For your brother."

"Mom's worried."

"But Tom…"

"And I'm pretty sure Tom won't even notice."

"You don't think?"

"I don't, Dad. I'm sorry."

"No, you're right," her father said, so despondently she instantly felt awful. "Of course he won't."

"Though I'm sure he'll appreciate the gesture."

"Sure, certainly, the gesture," he said, and Emily realized her father was maybe crying? Or was that just the rain? Either way, it scared her, and either way they needed to go inside.

"Come on, Dad," she said, and began to coax him back toward the house, one hand on his elbow.

He stopped beneath the glow of the faux gaslight.

"You remember Annie Smalls?" he asked.

"Annie I work with?" Emily said. "Obviously, yes. Why do you ask?"

"I just thought of her. No reason."

"You just thought of Annie for no reason?" She leaned closer and took his elbow again. "Come on. We're both soaked."

"It's fine. We'll go in." He started again toward the steps, appearing older than she'd ever imagined him. "Hey, you remember renting *Splash*?" he asked. "It was your birthday."

"Where we going with this, Dad?"

"You must have been eleven or twelve? You had that sleepover. Annie was there, wasn't she?"

"Yeah, probably."

"I thought so. I thought I remembered her there."

She took the empty glass from his hand—when had he gotten another?—only to have him stop on the front steps and take both her wrists in a gesture that felt frighteningly formal.

"Honey," he said, "you just look so sad."

"Dad, I think you're maybe a little drunk."

"I'm worried about you."

"I think maybe you've just pre-gamed a bit too much here."

"Pre-gamed?"

"As the kids say."

She got him inside, toweled herself off, and stood by the front window, waiting on Knox and Judson. Normally she would have busied herself, checked on Kyle, made sure the food was warm, the glasses full of ice. But not tonight, not lately. Lately, a certain zero-sum ruefulness seemed to have entered their lives, and standing there, she felt it waiting on just the other side of the glass, this new life she'd gradually come to think of as That Which Cannot Be Named.

Partially, it was the fault of the woman in the burn unit.

Or no, not her fault, it was just that Emily had thought about her so frequently it had begun to seem like some sort of evil fairy tale she couldn't—

Lights—thank God.

She saw lights coming up the driveway and stepped back from the window.

"They're here," Emily called, just as her mom walked into the room carrying Kyle, both magnificently becalmed. And Emily too, Emily as calm as you've ever seen her, Emily a study in serenity as she walked out onto the porch and waved at her husband and son and brother.

They crowded around the giant dining room table, nine of them, Richard at one end and Clara at the other, which made her feel a bit ridiculous—they hadn't become *those* kind of people, had they?—but Richard was insistent, *It's how it's done, it's natural!* and she wasn't going to argue. She'd talked him into a quick shower, thrown his wet clothes into the hamper, even forced a cup of black coffee into his hand before she hurried back to greet Tom and Judson and Knox and *Oh, Tom, who is this?*

She turned out to be a girl Tom had met not on the plane but at the luggage carousel, you're saying?

"The curb actually, Mrs. Greaves," the girl said (she was a girl to Clara, they were all children). "We were both waiting on rides and we just..."

Just something, Clara supposed. Which would have been weird had the girl not turned out to be the sort of charming sweetheart Clara had been hoping for years her youngest would bring home.

"They gave me the tour," Sherilynn said. "Took me through town and everything."

"Hey, the tour!" Jack said, and Clara gave him a look that said *Honey, please don't* but he was going to, she could tell from the smirk. "Then I guess you know this weekend is dedicated to celebrating the prodigal son's return?"

"I wouldn't say 'celebrating,'" Tom said.

"Oh, I would," Richard said, louder (and drunker, Clara realized) than necessary. "I'm sure you've heard our Tom here is a star."

"An American Ninja," Sherilynn said.

"*The* American Ninja," Richard said, "at least so far as we're concerned."

"But that's not all," Jack said. "He's also something of a celebrity, at least in certain rarefied caffeinated quarters. What's the energy drink you endorse, Tom? Remind me."

"Jack," Clara said.

"You endorse an energy drink?" Sherilynn asked.

"Not exactly endorse—" Tom said.

"But would," Jack said. "If it wasn't for that darn FDA. Or is it the DEA?"

"Jack." This time it was Emily. "Knock it off."

"No, I'm just saying. What was it called, Tom? Whiplash?"

"Ripcord."

"Ripcord! That's it." Jack leaned forward, elbows on the table, and Clara tried to will him back. "What was the tagline? 'What will you do with…' What was it?"

"'What will you do with your four minutes,'" Tom said.

Jack spread his hands wide. "Because you get four minutes of pure energy before you go into cardiac arrest. And then the cap—it's marketing brilliance. You tear the cap off," he told Sherilynn, "like a ripcord."

"Hence the name," Richard said.

"Hence the name indeed. And inside," Jack said, "stevia and coca leaves as I recall."

"Coca leaves?" Judson said, suddenly aware. "Like coca known for its psychoactive alkaloid, cocaine?"

"Why would you know that?" Emily asked.

"Judson has an intuitive sense of the moral gray areas," Tom said. "I think he has a future as an arms dealer."

Emily looked at him.

"Why would you say that?"

Richard raised his fork.

"In fairness, Em," he said, "it *is* a lucrative field."

"I'm hoping it's a joke," Emily said.

Tom turned to their mother. "Unrelated, but you don't happen to have any beet juice, do you, Mom?"

"I'm hoping *that's* a joke," Jack said.

"Why?" Tom asked. "Because suddenly this family has no interest in antioxidants and inflammatory-fighting effects of flavonoids?"

"Ripcord, beet juice, and that's not all!" Richard declared, and Clara felt something clench within her. "You see Knox there? Knox is probably the most famous director in the country."

"No, he's not," Emily said.

"Definitely not," Knox said.

"Why don't we all go into the kitchen and fix our plates?" Clara asked.

Sherilynn looked first at Richard then at Knox.

"I made this documentary," Knox said, "years ago."

"*The Late Rebellion,*" Judson said, "'a small, searing masterpiece,' per Rotten Tomatoes."

"Wait," Sherilynn said. "About the Confederate flag and all that?"

"Ninety-eight percent on the Tomatometer," Judson said, "in case you're counting."

"It got an Oscar," Richard said.

"No, it didn't," Emily said.

Sherilynn was nodding dangerously fast. "I know that movie. I saw it in a film class."

"It was up for an Oscar," Richard said.

"No, it wasn't," Emily said.

"Nominated, as I recall."

"Why don't I go get the food and bring it in here?" Clara asked.

"It wasn't nominated for an Oscar, Dad."

Clara stood. "Maybe, Lana, if you and Judson would just help me."

"Well, you would certainly know," Richard said, smiling and pointing at Emily with a spatula and Clara thought: Where did he get my good spatula? And when did another bourbon appear? "She would know," Richard told Sherilynn. "She's just about to be the new district attorney."

"I'm the county solicitor," Emily said.

"For now. She'll be the DA by probably Tuesday, Sherilynn, trust me. And Jack here, Jack's the new athletic director. In fact, Jack might have some big news about the new basketball coach he isn't sharing with us."

"No, I don't."

"What's the news?" Knox asked.

Richard winked. "About the van Gundy boys?"

"Not true."

"Come on now. Old Elvis said—"

"It's not true, Dad. Elvis doesn't have a clue."

Elvis was a volunteer coach slash yard maintenance man

slash busybody. Jack loved him like a brother but he really didn't have a clue.

"Sure, it's true." Richard looked at Lana. "You believe your daddy?"

"Who knows," she said. "Mom says he's going through a thing."

"She said what?" Jack asked.

"Lana, Judson," Clara said.

Jack shook his head as if to clear it. "She said I'm going through—"

"A thing." Richard seemed to roll the idea around in his mouth, its taste much as he'd anticipated. "Sounds about right. How was the game, by the way?"

"Canceled," Jack said.

"Canceled?"

"You know, the rain, the lightning, the storm."

"What storm?"

"Same storm you got caught in, I'd imagine. Or maybe you were just soaked in Woodford?"

Richard waved it all away with his spatula.

"So you see, Sherilynn, besides my American Ninja, I've got the AD and the DA and—"

"I'm the county solicitor, Dad. That's all." She turned to Sherilynn. "I've also been on maternity leave for the last several months, so—"

"Here it is," Clara announced, Lana and Judson flanking her like disgruntled sous chefs. "Who's hungry?"

"Me," everyone said—everyone, Clara noticed, except Richard, who was too busy smiling, his spatula conducting an orchestra only he could hear.

They ate in blessed, relative silence, only Catherine missing, Jack thought.

He missed his wife but was glad she was elsewhere. *A thing?* What the hell was that supposed to mean? Sure, he'd made a bigger ass of himself than he'd intended. He'd meant it as good-natured ribbing—well, somewhat good natured—but his mother's brittle smile made clear he'd gone too far. As for his wife, she was probably driving home by now, though still on the phone with a client. They had met when Catherine was in law school at Carolina and Jack was half-assing his way to a master's in education. She was Emily's best friend, the two smartest L1s on campus, and it was a credit to Emily's charm that she had somehow managed to convince Catherine that she was not a rival but a friend. It was during their first summer interning at a firm in Columbia that his sister had half-mockingly half-seriously introduced Catherine to the Citadel's former star defensive end and now future educator of the young—ta-da!—my big brother, Jack Greaves.

Now Catherine was her own sort of star in a litigation firm in Greenville. She was the hardest worker he'd ever met, and if she wasn't married to her work they were at least entangled in a serious affair. He thought of getting up and calling her but knew he wouldn't. She would be abrupt, preoccupied, and then she'd regret it and he would regret it too.

"Hey, brother."

He looked up to find Tom staring across the table expectantly.

"Want to pass that along?"

"Sorry."

"No worries."

No worries indeed. He passed the grilled chicken, the zucchini and squash and microgreens, all concessions, Jack knew, to Tom's semi-precious diet.

"Lana," his mother said, "darling, how is school?"

He looked across the table at his daughter, who wore an oversized hoodie, so big she appeared elfin, an oval of pale face framed by a few wisps of blond hair. Face down, her phone on her thigh. As if it wasn't obvious.

"Hey, Lana?" he said.

"Yeah?"

"You with us?"

She looked at him and he could sense her restraint, how she kept her lip from sneering, and what he wanted to know was: What had happened? Life, Catherine would say. But Jack knew the real answer: Stinson Wood was what had happened. A boy with a name that sounded very much like a poorly named state park somewhere along the I-20 corridor, Stinson Wood was the single exception to Jack Greaves's theory that beneath the sulk and yawn, the anger and indifference, all kids were good kids. Stinson Wood was not a good kid. He was a senior, three critical years older than Lana. He wore a black Ramones hoodie and black skinny jeans and on one forearm was a field of intersecting parabolas of some intricate shape. Mayan, Lana had told him when he asked about the tattoo. It indicates gratitude. Jack suspected it indicated bullshit. Everything about the boy did, from his gelled hair to his droopy eyes. She wasn't dating him—she had told him this.

She—

"Oh, wait," his dad said, standing. "I've got a surprise for everyone. Where's my phone? This is for you, Tom. In honor of your arrival!"

"Here, here," Knox said.

"Richard," Clara said softly just as the Beach Boys started their chant.

"Honey, please," Clara said.

"Kokomo!" Richard pronounced.

"At 120 decibels," Emily said.

"Come on, pretty mama," Richard sang, and then—oh, Dad, please don't—put his hand out to Sherilynn to dance.

"Oh," she said. "Are we?"

"Of course, we are, darling. Tom won't mind."

Because Tom was suddenly made of stone, Jack thought, and put his own head down, hands over his ears. But not before he stole another look at Lana, who was turning a cheap ring around a finger. Likely something Stinson had given her.

We're just friends, she had told Jack. We just like to talk. But now a ring, seriously?

The Beach Boys sang but Lana didn't appear to hear them.

"School is great," she said over the music. "I barely ever see Dad."

Jack felt the sneer on his face now and felt someone kick him under the table. He looked up to find Emily staring at him.

Be happy, she mouthed.

But Jack didn't want to be happy.

Jack wanted his daughter back.

Tom wasn't sure what he wanted.

He was in his childhood bedroom, down on the carpet in—wait for it, he thought—child's pose. He'd gotten through dinner, which felt like a small victory. Survived the sitcom humor of it all, everyone gathered around the table and playing their part, all of it canned, all of it scripted. The Theater of the Banal. Right down to the drunken patriarch and angry older brother, the idealistic daughter and steel magnolia of a mother. The kids not even kids—the kids' appendages to their phones. Knox had offered Sherilynn a ride and they'd parted by the garage. Sherilynn, somehow charmed by it all, tapped her number into Tom's phone and kissed his cheek. He'd smelled her lip gloss: cotton candy. A child's scent, *devastatingly* so, he'd thought miserably. *I'll see you soon,* she'd said, and he hoped to God she wasn't right. But if she was, well, Tom had his own role to play, and picking up the hot girl in the crowd for reasons construed as bonhomie but masking a deeper self-recrimination was fairly on-brand. After all, they knew Tom as the eccentric athlete, the good-hearted if self-indulgent traveler. The guy who was never serious in quite the right way.

Tom had become a minor reality television star and then, instead of taking some lucrative role on a sitcom in Hollywood or becoming a personal trainer to the stars, went to Europe on his self-declared "pilgrimage," as if it was not so much a trip as the latest installment in the Indiana Jones franchise, delivered a generation too late. At least that was Jack's take.

But it was fine.

It was what it was, quoting either Confucius or Donald Rumsfeld.

They knew Tom as indulgent, narcissistic, and lantern-jawed.

But Tom knew himself as a seeker.

His family thought he'd spent the last two years loafing, skiing in Utah or swimming in the Pacific—documenting it all on Instagram—and while he had certainly done those things, he'd been doing something else too. In truth, he had spent much of his adult life searching for some moral absolute. The world was burning, the world was falling apart—and what stuck with him was that no one seemed to notice, or care, or consider doing anything about it.

There had been some prize money from his appearance on the show, some money from his social media posts, not much but enough, and he'd set out to find one single pure-hearted human being doing good in the world. In the spirit of his brother-in-law, Tom planned to make a documentary, to film it on his iPhone, to capture it—if only he could find these people. Yet he couldn't quit hashtagging long enough to focus. Then his grandfather had died, and Tom had gone on his "pilgrimage" where, yet again, he'd succeeded in not making a movie. Not that it mattered, because what he had discovered was that he couldn't actually do anything. Given MAGA. Given climate change. Given the plastic ocean and the dying everything, what could he possibly do?

Make a film—but why? To stoke the outrage? To throw tinder on the burning liberal anger of his own heart?

What could he possibly do?

If they didn't even believe—as his new Leonard Cohen tattoo put it—that there was a war everywhere, at all times, then what the hell was Tom to do? He wanted purpose, he wanted moral clarity. He'd gladly trade 10,000 followers for the Moral Equivalent of War! 100,000 for actual war! Just so long as it was good vs. evil, or, maybe, just so long as Tom could convince himself of the fact.

Again: stupid. Colossally stupid. How many guys his age

had celebrated their twenty-first birthdays living in a shipping container in Afghanistan? Still, what had Leonard said about giving me Stalin or St. Paul? Which Tom took to mean give me passion, give me violence if you must, suffering even. But most of all give me a cause worth dying for. And, yes, he knew too he shouldn't be living his life according to the wisdom of Cohen—at least he had that much clarity.

He sat up and exhaled deeply.

He was sweating, actually sweating, and took a deep breath. Having survived the evening, he now felt thrown back into all this. Not just being back home and not just Ivana, but the whole bullshit existentialist woe-is-me crisis that actually wasn't bullshit at all. At least not any more than it had been in Prague.

Prague was where he'd killed his precious social media accounts, rented a tiny flat in the Malá Strana, and for six weeks spoken to not a soul. It was a recipe for crazy, and he supposed crazy was what he had become. But with the crazy came clarity: he had to do something. And he'd done something all right: he'd fled.

He took his phone out.

He didn't know what he was doing, only that he was suddenly bringing up her name, suddenly typing. It wasn't exactly him but it wasn't exactly someone else either, his fingers on the screen, but not really.

He sent the message before he could stop himself.

It read: *What if I came back?*

Once upon a time there was a man—Emily strapped Kyle into his car seat, worked the belt over his right arm, over his left—*once upon a time there was a man,* and this man set his wife on fire with a bottle of Kingsford lighter fluid and a flaming tampon, and the woman—her mouth was gagged, her hands and feet tied to the bedposts. And oh! how the woman begged and cried through the sock duct-taped in her mouth, but the man was meticulous, the man was focused, and then Whoosh! the woman was burning, and Whoosh! the woman was a great pyre of suffering and light. And the man, her otherwise doting husband, watched her burn, and watched her burn, and then, perhaps having grown tired of watching her burn, decided to call 911 and out came the fire truck! and out came the police! out came the Life Flight helicopter that sat down in the street and the woman was off to the trauma center and then off again, weeks later, to the burn unit, and, and—

Oh God, she knew she had to stop, and slid the van door shut gently.

Why a tampon? she sometimes wondered, and buckled her own seatbelt.

But she knew why.

When everyone was gone, Clara sat alone on the couch and felt her heart do that impossible thing where it both dipped and rose. It had all ended well enough: they had loaded the dishwasher, wiped down the counters, everyone chipping in, everyone happy, or at least pretending to be until the kitchen was immaculate and the day was gone and Richard was offering everyone a nightcap and *no, honey,* Clara was telling him. *Let them go, they have school tomorrow, they have work tomorrow,* they have something tomorrow.

But what did Clara have?

She locked the front door and put a blanket over Richard where he had fallen asleep in the recliner, a football game on the TV. She'd get him up later, move him to bed, but for now she poured a cup of decaf and moved onto the screened porch.

She had met Richard the year she worked at Long's Country Junction. Punching keys on the old IBM cash register back when there was such a thing. Stocking the shelves. The price gun with its yellow tongue. It was the summer before her senior year of high school when Richard walked in, four years older, muscled and shave-headed from the Citadel and on his way to officer training in Virginia, and a part of her was there still, ringing up cans of Vienna sausages and sardines, the big forty-pound bags of sweet feed or marine pellets.

The store had belonged to Richard's best friend's parents but you would have thought it was his alone the way he was always lying and bragging and dancing and bouncing, trying to impress her, or himself, maybe. Bluster, a lot of bluster. But beneath it all such tenderness. It was the thing she'd fallen in love with and the thing she loved still. The way he used to sit at the table and talk with her mother. The way he held Emily's hand, both tucked beneath a blanket watching *Wonder Woman.* Playing catch with Jack or dragging Tom up to the Kountry Kupboard to show his boy off to his friends. She thought of it often. Less often, Clara would think of her parents. Her daddy dead before she finished high school. Her mama dying only a few years ago, sitting in her carport, cordless phone in her hand, right up to the very end.

But those thoughts were rare.

Mostly, she remembered her parents as young, before she was born, before she was even imagined. A poor farm boy and an equally poor farm girl sitting in the meadow off Whetstone Road. Working. Going to dances and revivals. Always working. The farm, the textile mill. Her father sent to Korea. Her mother sent to fits of depression and Levi Garrett snuff. Black coffee and sleepless nights. Clara cutting teeth just as her daddy came home to go back to work at the plant in town because who could make a living farming? He farmed nights, farmed weekends, plowed in the dark, plowed by headlight. Still, they remained poor, impossibly poor, though it had never occurred to Clara to wonder why. Poor but happy—that was the reason she never wondered.

Lately she'd been reading books by people who were dying, generally dead by the time the books were out. It was a new genre, it seemed. All these surgeons and saxophonists granted this great clarity as death closed. But since the pills, she'd had this detachment. Buddhist, maybe, the way the world appeared bathed in clear light, the way the world simply was. She wasn't sure if it was a good thing or not. Likely it didn't matter.

She knew she was being dramatic, defensive too.

Defensive when what she should be was grateful, her family home, safe, loved.

She got up, cut off the TV, and helped Richard into bed.

Gratitude, she told herself.

Be grateful, she told herself, while outside it rained and rained.

He'd given her the ring, given it to Lana.

Jack thought of it driving home, remembered giving it to her two summers ago out on the back deck. Remembered the way she'd slipped it on, so shyly, so bright-eyed, the silver against her tan skin, the way it caught the grain of the day's light.

He looked at her now staring blankly out the truck window.

He'd given it to her!

How had he forgotten that?

They staggered into the house, Emily carrying a sleeping Kyle, Knox shunting Judson before them and, no, he couldn't play Fortnite, and, no, he couldn't see what was happening on Slack, he could go to bed. It was, it was…

"It's not that late. Come on, Mom."

"Please, Judson," Emily said. "I'm exhausted."

And if it sounded like pleading, well, it sort of was, wasn't it?

She kissed his head and left Knox to make certain their eldest actually made it to bed. Meanwhile, she carried their youngest to his crib, swaddled him, kissed him, checked that the baby monitor was on high, checked that the ceiling fan was on low, checked that—

Enough, Em. Go to bed.

Which is where she found Knox, already beneath the sheets.

"Fun night," he said.

"Crazy night. My dad…"

"Ah, he was just happy to see everyone. You know how he gets."

"You mean drunk?"

"I mean overwhelmed, semi-ecstatic."

"He kept asking me about Annie Small."

"Annie Small you work with? He was just nervous, babe."

She smiled at him.

"You are a very generous man."

"Come to bed."

"Sometimes," she said. "Sometimes you are."

"Come to bed, Em."

"Let me brush my teeth."

Which she did. Brushed her teeth, washed her face, peed. The flossing, the eye makeup remover—all the rituals that signified night, that signified rest and restoration but also another day gone, another day washed beneath the bridge and not coming back.

The light was out when she crawled into bed. She rolled onto her side, away from her husband, then felt his arm snake out to encircle her waist, his hand on the bare flesh of her stomach. She wanted it, but also not. Wanted it but was also exhausted. But they were old hands, familiar in what tonight she understood as the best way: how he knew to put his fingers in her hair, his lips just behind her ear. How she knew to put her hand on his thigh. That was how it started.

It ended with her on top of him, both panting and filmed in the lightest of sweats. The kind of vigorous, athletic sex she associated not with middle age but the single year after law school when she and Knox had lived in his family's beach shack on Hunting Island. The way the sand threw itself at the glass door. The way their clothes scattered around the bed. He'd had some streak of boyhood athleticism back then, something only vaguely defined. She imagined, but never actually saw him shaking out his arms, rolling his shoulders, a half-second from some feat. Exuberant. At the time they had both been studying for the bar. But that wasn't what Emily had been doing, not really. What she had actually been doing was taking a leave from all things Greaves, from the grand sense of duty on which she was busy building a life. That year she'd been on sabbatical from herself, drinking white wine and becoming the sort of woman who always seemed to arrive with wet hair, happy and laughing in some strappy thing. But then the year ended, and they came back to Germantown, back to the vinyl siding and yard dogs, back to reality. Emily took a job not with some well-heeled white-shoe law firm, but with the domestic violence task force of the county solicitor's office and since then…

She let her body collapse onto his.

Knox kissed her temple.

"Jesus, Em, who are you?"

"I thought that was obvious," she said. "I'm Wonder Woman."

But she didn't feel like Wonder Woman. The line was pure bluster, the one thing she might say that would keep her together since, all at once, it wasn't simply her perception that things were falling apart; it was reality. What seconds ago had felt like great sex suddenly felt like break-up sex. Was she too old for the expression? And did it matter? What she felt was scared. What she felt was dirty, like deeply cosmically sullied. She felt like a fool. She felt like, well, she felt like a shower.

"This late?" Knox asked.

"It'll help me sleep," she told him, then realized he'd already rolled over and shut his eyes.

Emily grabbed the baby monitor and headed for the bathroom, and it was undressing in the half-light that she caught sight of herself in the mirror. Only it wasn't her. Only it was. She saw her reflection out of the corner of her eye and for a split second she didn't know who it was that stared back. She looked like someone else, someone sadder. Like someone who had realized she was about to be ruined but realized it too late to do anything about it. It was, perhaps, her older, future self.

She started to call out to Knox but instead started the water and tried to think through what was ahead of her, to make a plan. First, there was the school skit—play, be generous, Em—at the pep rally tomorrow. Saturday there was her high school reunion at which Emily, the long-ago president of Germantown High, would play host (though she dreaded it, she had managed to book the *oh my God best bartender in all the South!* according to Yelp). Between the two was Tom's ninja display. Emily had no idea what that meant, only that she was meant to be there because, quoting her mom here, *This isn't about Tom cutting flips or whatever and us watching, honey. It's about Tom knowing that we're proud of him, that we take him seriously, that we support him through whatever it is he's going through.* But what could Tom possibly be going through? she wondered. It pissed her off a little, his freedom, coupled, she supposed, with her total absence of such. Lately she'd felt the last grains in the hourglass of self trickling out.

Cliché, Emily.

Trite, Emily.

Yet real, Emily. Very real, since come Monday she would end her maternity leave and return to work. Only she was thinking of not going back. Only how could she not? She'd once wanted to be Rachel Corrie, after all, the American activist who had died facing down a bulldozer in Palestine. Ultimately, she'd gotten a law degree in lieu of martyrdom, and it hadn't felt like a compromise, at least at the time.

She stepped beneath the water.

She didn't want to go back. She knew it. But there is a way in which knowing ruins you, alters your shape in some irreparable way, like soap once wet. So how could she possibly even consider not returning?

Yet she was.

Which meant her career, like her marriage, was yet another thing flowing beneath the bridge of middle-aged uncertainty. Like the way she and her husband, Knox, were sexting more but having sex less. Agreeing on what new Netflix series to watch but never actually watching. Commiserating over Judson's bad/selfish/ridiculous/beautiful/altruistic behavior or the *absolutely amazing* way Kyle was beginning to roll over because both cared deeply about their children, but not for much else.

There was no talk of these larger issues.

There was much talk of phone plans (do we really need three lines?) and carpools and great strategic campaigns for "after"—after the end of her maternity leave—which was necessary, but also somewhat ridiculous. But ridiculous has a way of seeping into the everyday until it becomes the everyday itself. She was stuck in the past, stuck in memory. Except lately it felt less like memory than eulogy. A benediction ending their marriage.

Those were the good days.

On the bad days, she found herself wondering if maybe they never should have gotten married in the first place, that maybe she had fallen in love with the idea of Knox more than the man. His family was old-money, antebellum Beaufort money that had somehow survived the Civil War to fund the political career of Knox's Dixiecrat kingmaker father. Which meant Knox's childhood had been an exercise in managing public perceptions, from the clothes they wore (Ted Baker suits bought from nowhere else but M. Dumas & Sons on King Street in Charleston) to the places they vacationed (the family cottage at the end of Hunting Island, just before the channel opened and off in the blue distance stood Fripp).

She'd known all that.

She'd fallen in love with it.

But that had been two decades ago.

All this—the worrying, the crying, the second- and third-guessing—was now. It had come at the center of a great storm: her grandfather's death, Kyle's birth, and between the two, the flaming tampon that gradually evolved into the burned woman Emily now and then felt hovering above her. So maybe it had been circumstance, maybe it had simply been too much.

She shampooed and rinsed. Wrapped the towel around her and stepped from the shower.

She pulled her clothes on and was slipping into bed when she realized who it was that she had seen in the mirror. Not her older self, this woman on the edge of ruin, no. Who she had seen was the woman gagged and tied to her bed, this woman on the edge of immolation.

Richard woke at what time? At three, four in the morning?

He rolled onto his side and found the clock.

Four-forty-seven.

Four-forty-seven and his head throbbed and his throat ached and overnight worry had wormed its way into his gut like something that might kill a farm animal, some invasive species that lodged itself in the intestinal track of one of his Herefords. Fear, dread—if you could inoculate against such he would have done so months ago, back when the first issues with the money arose. But he hadn't, because you couldn't, and thus The Call.

He didn't need to think like this.

He needed to get up and get dressed.

And he needed to do both without waking Clara.

She was asleep beside him, the room grained in the failing darkness, and he eased from beneath the sheets to put his bare feet on the floorboards. The morning was cool, the late summer thunderstorm having settled into an early fall downpour, steady and unbroken.

He stood as gently as he could, shifting his weight, careful not to wake Clara, who lay on her side, breathing through a clogged nose. Not exactly snoring.

Grating the air, he thought. Shredding it.

He said a quick prayer for her—he could only ever pray in the dark—two fingertips resting lightly on her side, found her housecoat on the chair, and lumbered toward the kitchen. Started the coffeemaker and stared out the bay window at the back forty, the first intimations of dawn a single stroke over the trees, a lighter gray atop the slipping night.

They'd had a good time, hadn't they.

All the children back under their roof, happy, laughing.

When he saw his wet clothes in the hamper—he'd maybe had a few more than he'd intended, maybe got a little too loud—he felt a rising of shame. But it wasn't too hard to push it down.

Take stock, Richard:

Tom was upstairs sleeping, thirty-years old and back home, and that was a happy thing to realize, even if he'd spent the evening all moody and quiet. Here was another: it was Friday—the world was slowly articulating itself: day, time. More specifically: the Friday they kicked off the annual Oktoberfest, and in a few hours he'd be on the dais with his boys looking out at the crowd—that too cheered him. But here was the thing that didn't: While Richard was looking out at the crowd, the crowd would be looking back at Richard. Normally, this would have given him great pleasure. He'd worked hard all his life, took chances, believed in himself, followed every piece of advice from *How to Win Friends and Influence People* to *The 7 Habits of Highly Effective People* to the cat posters on the walls of the Chamber of Commerce, and part of his motivation—he wasn't afraid to admit this—was that he liked, craved, to be perfectly honest, the affection of others. And he'd always gotten it because Richard Greaves had led what could only be called a charmed life, even if charm had nothing to do with it.

But now there were issues with what he had come to think of as "the movement of funds," as if he were dealing with ocean currents, as if it all were something as natural as the tides.

Here was the worm in his gut—these issues.

Issues because they weren't exactly problems, at least not yet. What they were, were a series of complicated entanglements that seemed to be complicating faster than Richard could track. It all tied to Mountain Empire Bank, which meant it all tied to Richard because while the bank was vaulted money and online accounts and the proverbial brick-and-mortar of physical commerce, at its most essential it was Richard Greaves. Richard as founder and president, Richard as animating spirit.

When Richard had started the bank better than thirty years ago, it had been an outlier in the old-moneyed world of Germantown. The town's wealth was Southern and familial, the remnants of textile fortunes that had migrated south from New England before migrating on to Southeast Asia or the Maquiladora belt of Mexico. Everyone banked at the Blue Ridge Bank and why, by God, wouldn't they? Who was this upstart with the gall to found a new bank?

The upstart had been one of many, all young men at the time, or young enough. Thirty-somethings drawn together by both their age and their ambition. All Richard's friends had wives and children and pools converted from chlorine to the newer, much improved Baquacil. They were the New South, the Sunbelt South, not the men who had fought against the Nazis abroad and against integration at home, but the children who had lived through it, Cold War boomers raised according to the gospel of trickle-down economics as much as the Bomb.

They weren't exactly rich. None of them had inherited money but they all had the sense that the world was open and new if only someone would inform their fathers' generation. They sold burial plots and encyclopedias, and then graduated to insurance and cars. They sold and they bought, until, that is, the local bank—the local old-money, risk-averse, gentlemen's bank—began to refuse to fund their more ambitious schemes. Apartment complexes, office parks, strip-malls. A golf course, for God's sake? Why on earth would we want that in Germantown, son, when we—we being them, Richard remembered thinking, his father's generation, not us—are all members up at High Hampton in Cashiers?

Why? Because it makes money, you dumb son of a bitch. Because that is the future, and you are the past. Why? By God I'll show you why if you'll just give me a chance. I'll happily welcome you and your shareholders into the second half of the twentieth century. But no chance was forthcoming. No financing, no loans, no nothing, and don't go around thinking that's likely to change before these sons-a-bitches start dying in their sleep.

They were on their own, Richard and his friends, and the clarity of such was a long-running discussion, the source of constant commiseration every time they sat around the pool, drinking their Jack and Cokes, kids swimming or down in the basement doing God knows what—ping-pong? Making out to the sound of their 45s? *I can feel it coming in the air tonight, oh Lord*—wives off discussing whatever it was that wives talked about (they no more knew what their wives talked about than they wanted to know—blue-light specials at Kmart, Richard figured), bitching and moaning in Sansabelt trousers and Sperry boat shoes, Reagan on the TV, when one of them says simply, "You know what we should do, we should start our own bank."

Which would teach them, right? These old farts making eighty grand and still washing out their Ziploc bags. These arthritic dinosaurs still hating the Germans and straightening bent nails. Old men talking about "colored folk" while putting up their canning, as if the Great Depression weren't so much a historical event as a season.

They shook their heads in contempt. These men—their fathers—were ancient and embarrassing and somebody needed to show them, somebody needed to point the way to the future, to make them aware they were living in it.

"I tell you one thing, boys." Who said this? Was it Richard? In his heart, Richard believed it must have been him because it had been Richard Greaves who had set out and done it. "Starting a bank, that would show them."

"Hell, yes, it would."

"We should do it."

"We could."

"Of course, we could. I'm not doubting it for a skinny minute."

And then the rarest of silence, just four or five men out on the lanai, maybe barefoot, maybe semi-crocked on the margaritas Fred's wife was always making, but quiet to a man, because, by God, why not? We could hash the whole thing out before the kids came up to watch the Solid Gold dancers. Because weren't they the future? Weren't they the pillars, the new pillars of the new community? So Richard went and did it. Had to go all the way to Atlanta to get the seed money—which was its own form of local heresy—but he did it.

That now, thirty years later, Richard Greaves was likely to be charged with wire fraud, breach of contract accompanied by a fraudulent act, breach of fiduciary duty, and civil conspiracy was bad enough. That the charges stemmed from his good intentions made the matter particularly reflux inducing.

He sipped his coffee.

There was light over the field now, an actual morning organizing itself just above the trees. It was almost a relief—he hadn't realized he had doubted its coming, but he supposed he had.

It had started innocently enough.

Around the time a local businessman had taken out a $450,000 loan to build a complex of chicken houses down in Townville, Richard's longtime friend Jeff Duncan had come to him with a plan to open a textile mill right there in the county. It would make high-end merchandise, get crazy good press (Made in the US of A!), and, most importantly, reap a slew of America First! tax breaks. Duncan had gamed out the entire thing and he wanted Richard as his partner. Together they would become fantastically rich.

All they lacked was the starting capital.

Richard dropped in 300K of savings and sat back to await the riches.

But it wasn't enough and he dropped in another 300K, this time borrowed.

But then…then…

The damn thing just kept eating money—impact surveys, grading, permitting—and Richard kept borrowing it. He'd sought the help of his childhood friend, John Long, and if that had been disastrous it had also been inevitable. Richard had been floundering, mortgaged to his fluttering gills, absolutely overextended in every direction (he'd taken out a Belk's credit card in Clara's name for God's sake), doing everything and finding everything wasn't enough. He needed, what? A paltry 200K and he would be fine, he would be better than fine. The plant would go up and within a year he would be raking the money in, turning it—as his father used to say on the way to the market in Riverside to sell his eggs and sides of beef—hand over balled fist.

Yet he couldn't get a loan. President of a bank and he couldn't get a loan! True, he had a nine hundred thousand dollar note mill-stoned around his neck, but he was very obviously good for it even if—especially if—no one else seemed to realize as much. Ridiculous the lengths he went to, visiting every bank imaginable. Atlanta, Charlotte, Charleston—yet no one would float him a dime. Not the even the Chinese would make him a loan, and at the time the Chinese seemed to be printing money, making yuan out of the very air.

He needed another option, something more—the word that came to him was *nimble*. And then he saw it: when the payments on the chicken loan (as he came to think of it) came in, Greaves paid the interest and quietly shifted the rest to a secondary account. The idea was simple: so long as the chicken money kept servicing the interest no one would go looking for the principal, and by the time they did come looking—years down the line—he'd be making ball caps for Versace and the missing money would have long since been replaced. It wasn't stealing. It wasn't even borrowing. It was leveraging the bank's assets. It was fueling the engine of growth. Creating jobs. Building the local tax base. Good Lord—he should have gotten a medal for it.

But then things had started to go awry.

When Chick-fil-A failed to renew their contract (those bastards at Tyson were underselling them), the chicken man defaulted on the loan and the bank's auditors—Richard's bank's auditors—came looking for the money. Except the money was now tied up in building a garment plant that didn't exist. This was the area where things got sticky. Sticky, meaning a number of investigative services were now involved and so, too, it appeared, was the Financial Crimes Division of the FBI.

That was what Richard had learned yesterday, that was The Call, something so upsetting that he'd forgone stopping by to check on his ma—something he'd done every evening in the months since his father had died—and driven straight home for several calming glasses of Elijah Craig.

Annie Small, the acting solicitor during Richard's daughter's absence and, just as relevant to Richard, one of Emily's childhood friends, had called right at closing time yesterday to say that she wanted him to know—in the strictest confidence, Mr. Greaves—that the Feds had contacted her. On Monday, she told him, he, Richard Samuel Greaves, president, founder, and chief shareholder of Mountain Empire Bank, sitting at that very moment in his expansive well-appointed office with its family photos and prints of waterfowl and a numbered lithograph of Robert E. Lee astride his horse Traveller, would receive a raft of subpoenas requesting, it sounded to Richard, like everything from tax returns to his now-grown children's Christmas lists, circa 1983.

"I just wanted to give you the heads up, Mr. Greaves."

"Yes."

"Before it's public. And let me say, sir—" And funny because as she spoke he saw her not as a grown woman in a pantsuit and an Aeron chair but as a child again, eight years old and camping out in the basement with his daughter, that old 70s incarnation of laminate flooring and a drop ceiling, the VCR they had rented—rented!—from Electromedia down by the Winn-Dixie so that the girls could watch *Splash* and *Grease*, sleeping bags spread like petals in front of the screen and around the sectional couch— "may I say how terribly sorry I am about all of this."

"Yes. Thank you, Annie."

"Let me also say," her tone suddenly shifting, all professional assurance now, "that it's not unusual, Mr. Greaves, especially for a commercial bank branching out. Honestly, I don't think there's undue worry here. But I wanted you to know all the same."

He had thanked her and she had assured him that she would be in touch should anything actionable arise. "Though I can't possibly imagine anything would, Mr. Greaves. I don't see anything here to worry about."

But how could he do anything but worry?

How could he do anything but lie awake in bed at whatever

the hell time it had been when he woke until whatever the hell time it was that he felt justified in getting up?

"I wondered where that went."

He turned at the sound of his wife's voice.

"What?" he said.

Clara leaned in to kiss his cheek. "This," she said, and touched the lapel of the housecoat he'd forgotten he was wearing.

"Oh yeah. You want it back?"

"Absolutely not. You wear it well."

She said it with that lightness that often seemed to belong to her alone, that smile in her eyes. His wife. Yesterday's drunken assessment was absolutely correct: she was still a good-looking woman though he thought the word now might be handsome, elegant maybe. She had been raised poor by good hardworking people, country in the best sense. But it had been Richard who had lifted her up and shown her the greater world of wealth and she seemed never to have forgotten that. As if no matter how much they fought or argued over the years—no more and no less than any other couple, he thought—that she remained grateful to him.

At least that was what he had always told himself.

But standing there in a tattered pink housecoat, the hem hanging mid-thigh, the sleeves not reaching his hairy wrists, he wondered for the first time if perhaps that was pure projection, that if maybe he hadn't spent the last forty-five years bullshitting himself with the same unbroken focus with which she humored him.

"Tom up?" he asked her.

"Honey, it's five-something."

"Right, sure."

Richard turned back to the window. The gray above the trees was no longer gray but something brighter. It wasn't exactly light but he knew light was coming, and what had once had him nearly springing out of bed—action! promise! Not *what are we going to do today?* but *what are we* not *going to do today?*—now made him sink into himself, into his coffee and his wife's ill-fitting housecoat. Turned out, he thought, he didn't want the day to arrive so much after all.

"Today's the luncheon," he said glumly.

"What's that, honey?" She was in the fridge, removing eggs and butter.

"The Oktoberfest kick-off."

"Oh, that's right. I'm so excited for y'all. Jack's still coming?"

"He said last night he was."

"I'll remind him."

"I should probably get Tom up soon."

"Oh, let him sleep, Richard. Lord knows he needs to rest."

"Yeah, maybe wake up with a better attitude, sulking after having brought home that sweet girl Shannon."

"Sherilynn."

"He's damn ungrateful is what he is."

He regretted it as soon as he said it and regretted it more when she didn't deign to respond. Picking at her, at maybe his lone ally because, like the sun creeping over the trees, that was something else he was only now seeing: how the world was divided between those who were for you and those who weren't. Or more accurately: those who were against you and those who simply didn't give a damn.

Clara was on his side. Tom, yes, certainly Tom. Emily, of course, always Emily. Jack, sure. But about the rest of them, Richard Greaves didn't know, only that they were coming.

He turned his back on the rising sun.

Kokomo, he repeated silently.

They were coming, which—all right, let them come.

Richard Greaves was up.

Friday

THE WHOLE DAMN CIS-TEM IS CORRUPT

Nayma González was up too.

She'd listened as her abuelo rose before the sun, the dim necessary light of his dressing bleeding through the beach towel hung to partition the room, pinpricks dotting a seascape of balloon-eyed sharks and smiling flounder. Nayma kept her face in her pillow and waited. She knew her abuela was out on the stoop with a heating pad on her knees. She would be sitting in her chair, extension cord run under the screen, rubbing the nubs of her rosary and saying her prayers. But it wasn't her grandmother she heard. Through the pasteboard walls of the Germantown Motel, Nayma could hear the human moaning that filled the gaps of whatever cartoon was playing. But it was their fingernails that got to her.

The sound was like a dog scratching itself bald, but was, in fact, the couple next door—the early twenties man and woman and their ghost-like wisp of a daughter, all three brown-toothed and frail—the daughter haunted by malnutrition, the mother and father ravaged by the meth mites crawling in and out of their bones, an itch that signaled the impossible distance from one government check to another.

By the time Nayma got up and left her "bedroom"—you had to think of it like that when a worn-out Moana towel formed the limit of your privacy—both her grandparents were off to work for the Greaves family. Her abuela took care of the ancient Mrs. Rose Greaves. Her abuelo maintained her yard. Which meant Nayma was left alone in the kitchen to eat her Cocoa Pebbles and finish the last of her homework for Dr. Agnew's English IV. She was seventeen and currently first in her senior class. They were reading *The Grapes of Wrath* and, no, the irony wasn't lost on her. With the exception of eight hours of sleep and little more than a passing engagement with the four food groups, very little was.

She showered and ate breakfast in the kitchenette: an alcove with a mini-fridge, microwave, and the hot plate they had to keep hidden from the motel's owner and her crazy son, an Iraq vet who twitched with the same intensity as the couple next door. She spooned cereal and flipped pages. It was quiet now—the meth heads having fallen into some catatonic stupor—and she was grateful for the silence. A few minutes to collect herself before the walk down to the bus stop where she'd ride with two dozen kids half her age, the lone high schooler in a sea of children because what kind of senior doesn't have a car? What kind of senior isn't riding with her girlfriends or boyfriend or somebody, right?

This kind, she had thought, in the months past when she used to try to riddle out the why of her days. One cheek against the cool glass while outside grainy darkness gave way to the gathering daylight, back pressed against the torn pleather seat while they rolled past the Hardee's and the First Methodist Church, and Nayma just sitting there, books in her lap, trying to hear that small still voice that was all: how do you put up with this shit? I mean seriously.

There were other places she could be. Her parents were at home in Irapuato, but *home* was a tenuous concept. She was born in Florida, a US citizen—her parents and abuelo were not—and had spent far more of her life in the States than in Mexico. Her parents came and went, blowing on the wind of whatever work visa allowed them entry. But for the last two years they had been working at a garment plant in Guanajuato State. It was good work (relatively speaking), at a fair wage (again, in relative terms), and Nayma had the sense that her parents were finished with their cross-border migrations. No more queuing at the US consulate. The forms in triplicate. The hassles from ICE. The rhetoric of hate—*build a wall! build a wall!*—spouted by the same folks paying you three dollars an hour to pick their tomatoes or change their babies. When she had last visited her parents—last summer it had been, two weeks of mosquitoes and long days watching *telenovelas* wherein she experienced the sort of cosmic boredom that would later haunt her with a guilt so intense she smelled it in her hair—when she had last visited, she had detected a certain relief in her parents' eyes, a sort of bounce that glided them around the edges of Nayma's life. They were done with *el Norte.*

That her abuela was a housekeeper and her abuelo a gardener for the Greaves family, that they had *ascended* to these positions from the indentured servitude of migrant labor, that they were meant to be grateful for the condescension and hand-me-down clothes. That her parents had been rounded up by the federal government, held for a week on Red Cross cots in the city gym after INS raided Appalachian Quilting, and subsequently deported with the rest of the three hundred workers Appalachian Quilting had *recruited* to come in the first place. That she had said goodbye to her parents through a scattering of holes punched in a plexiglass visitation window at the county detention center, that both her mother and father had contorted their bodies in such a way as to hide the zip-ties binding their wrists. All this, *all this, mija,* would burn off in the fire of her success.

As a US citizen, as a brilliant minority student—relatively brilliant, Nayma thought again, glancing now from the graying milk of her Cocoa Pebbles to the papered wall behind which slept the meth heads—she would receive some sort of generous scholarship to some sort of prestigious university and from there she would go to law school or medical school. She would spend the rest of her life in New York or DC and make money in such ridiculous amounts as to assuage the decades of humiliations suffered by her family. That was her parents' plan at least. Their daughter would become rich, she would become a *blanco* by the aggregated weight of her bank account, and there would be no better revenge.

But first she had to get to school.

She rinsed her bowl and brushed her teeth, put her phone and the Joads in her backpack, and stepped into the morning. The night's thunderstorm seemed to have blown out the last of summer and in the skin-prickling cool it was disturbing to see so many children shivering in T-shirts and shorts. There were ten or so that lived at the Germantown Motel with their mothers or grandmothers or aunts or some elderly female they may or may not have been related to, each of them either fat on Mountain Dew and pixie sticks or emaciated with need, lean as the Hondurans she remembered doing the stoop work in the strawberry fields outside Tampa. That they were cold, that their noses ran, that their hair had been shaved to their skulls (the boys, at least) or matted around forgotten Elsa barrettes or Princess Sophia hair clips (the girls, especially the younger ones) seemed most days like the results of a referendum on human negligence, something to fill her with anger at the world's injustice. But today it just made her sad.

She stood on the concrete stoop, the motel L-shaped, the rooms opening onto an apron of parking lot. Down by the highway a sign read SOFT BEDS COLOR TV WEEKLY RATES.

"Hey, girl!" she heard a voice call.

The motel office was at her far left, a block building with a pitched roof and a neon vacancy sign. It was from that direction that the voice came, and she didn't have to look to know who it was. Elvis was the son of the hateful old woman who owned the motel. He cut the strip of browning grass along the filled-in swimming pool and on two occasions had unclogged their toilet when the septic tank backed up. He was of some indeterminate age—somewhere between thirty and fifty was her best guess—and possibly he was a decent guy trying to do right by his mother and the world and possibly he was an embryonic serial killer running on Zoloft and cognitive behavioral therapy at the VA. The brim of his Gamecocks ball cap was pulled low and his arms and throat were inked with assault rifles and an unsettlingly precise map of the greater Middle East, complete (she had noted one day as he ran the Weed Eater) with a legend denoting capitals, troop movements, and sites of major US battles.

She started across the parking lot toward the bus stop and

a moment later the pickup sidled up beside her, rattling and clunking, this ancient 1973 Ford F-100 with three-on-the-tree. This was Elvis on his way to work or maybe on his way to get his mama a gravy biscuit from Hardee's or on his way to any number of the errands and jobs that occupied his days.

"Hey, girl!" Elvis called.

Nayma kept walking, her books pressed to her chest as he wheeled down the window and hung an arm on the door panel.

"Hey, girl! You want a ride?"

"No." She didn't look at him. She didn't stop moving. That was her theory: no eye contact and no hesitations. Not that that deterred him.

"Why not?"

"Because I'm riding the bus."

"Well, I'm headed to the same place. You know that, don't you?"

She motioned in the direction of the children gathered ahead of her.

"Why don't you offer *them* a ride?"

"What, them kids? Can't do it. Liability."

"That's bullshit."

"Maybe," he conceded. "It's Mama keeps track of the legal stuff."

"Whatever."

"You know I ain't offering a ride 'cause I like you."

"How flattering."

"I'm asking 'cause you a human being."

"I know why you're asking."

"Because you a human being and you too old to ride the bus like some ten-year-old."

"You're a creep."

He gave the engine a small rev. "You got too much grit in your shit, girl. You know that?"

She started to tell him to go away and then realized he had, which meant Nayma, once again, was all alone.

She tried to read on the bus, if only to prove she wasn't.

But it was loud and somewhere ahead of her the window was down and a stream of air kept rustling the pages. Finally, she put the Joads away. She was ahead anyway—there was no rush. What there was, was a bus ride that took seventy-five minutes to cover the four miles to the school. That would be four miles via the direct route, but Nayma guessed they covered a good twenty of back road, stopping at every trailer park or block monolith of Section Eight housing where poor children clustered sleepily by mailboxes and stop signs with their backpacks and bulldogs. Bethel to Thompson to Tribble—back and forth over the bridges that spanned the wiggle of Cane Creek—East Broad to Sangamo to Torrington Road. There was the occasional watchful adult—a grandmother behind the screen door, a mother smoking on the stoop while inside *Mama's Family* played on MeTV. The old men sat in plastic chairs and stared or took great care not to stare, depending, she often thought, on their experiences with the South Carolina Department of Corrections.

The bus stopped first at the elementary school where the children bounced off, awake now, and then the middle school where they navigated blindly, faces fixed to the screens of their phones. When the bus pulled out of the middle school parking lot there was no one left but the driver and Nayma. The driver, for his part, seemed to have not the slightest notion she was there. He parked the bus in the high school lot and walked away without a word, earbuds plugged into his head as he lumbered to his car.

Nayma pushed the door open and crossed toward the school. She was up near the main doors, and down the gentle slope that eased toward the football stadium she could see people loitering around their cars, talking and flirting and generally ensuring their collective tardiness.

Someone was playing Taylor Swift.

Someone was playing old school Eminem.

Her classmates these people would be, already self-segregating into their American lives. There were jacked-up pickups with fog lights and boys in Realtree pants. The girls in Browning jackets of pink camouflage. There were stickers that read MAKE AMERICA GREAT AGAIN and WE HUNT JUST LIKE YOU—ONLY PRETTIER! and FFA jackets from the thrift shop—no one was actually *in* the FFA—and retro ironic trucker hats from the rack at the Metromont (MY HUSBAND THINKS FOREPLAY IS TWENTY MINUTES OF BEGGING). Beside them were seven or eight vintage Ford Mustangs—the Stang Gang with their bad skin and BOSE speakers, the bass dropped to some heart-altering thump. They looked to have eczema and a desperate need for haircuts. She could practically see the crushed Ritalin edging their nostrils. Beside them were the athletes, few in number but easily identifiable by the swish of their warm-up suits. The school's two dozen Black kids in football jerseys and Under Armor. Bulky redheaded linemen with arm zits and man-boobs. Cheerleaders with their fuck-me eyes. The rich kids—the lake kids—were all Vineyard Vines and secondhand Benzs. It was a mark of late teen sophistication: the '90s German engineering, the chatter about diesel versus gas.

There were no brown kids, or very few, at least.

It hadn't always been like that. There had been a moment, brief as it was, right before the great INS raid when sixty or seventy kids made a little Mexico out of the right quadrant of the parking lot. They were mostly older than Nayma, and she had watched them congregate and laugh and play the same pop you heard in el Distrito Federal. She had watched them go, too, all but a handful deported with their parents, and when they were gone, so too was the world they had made. There was no more gathering. The dozen or so who, like Nayma, had stayed in the States had drifted to edges of existence, a few quietly dropping out, a few graduating. All of it governed by an abiding sense of bereavement, a mourning so softly realized it hadn't been realized at all. Nayma hadn't been part of it, but she felt it then, and felt it still. Even knowing what she knew, knowing *what she was*—the smart girl, the girl with a future—didn't help. Knowing didn't make her happy.

That was the thing, maybe.

She could watch them—her classmates, she meant—classify them, dissect them, know them in her secret heart—her *real* heart, the one she kept tucked behind what she considered her public heart. She could mock their choices and dismiss their lives as sleepwalking clichés (like her analysis was anything more than a John Hughes movie replayed on TBS). She could recognize their inherent ridiculousness. But crossing toward the main doors of the school she was also forced to recognize their happiness, and placed against her own unhappiness, that galled her.

She entered the great stacked-rock cathedral of the school's foyer with its trophy case and barely noticeable metal detector.

Most days that galled her, their oblivious glee.

Most days it sent her into fantasies of returning to Mexico, but never Mexico as it was. What she dreamed about was some idealized homeland, some rainbow's end without the roof dogs and fireworks and the women holding posters showing their disappeared sons. In her dreams, there were no cartels. There were no street beggars or bag ladies with deformed feet or children dehydrating and lost somewhere south of Nogales and then not dehydrating and lost but dehydrated and dead, past tense. There was no room for that. But then there didn't seem to be any room in her dreams for Nayma either. She was always some ethereal floating thing, a gauze of veils hovering just above imagination's reach.

"Nayma!"

She turned to find Regan hustling down the hall in her giant tortoise-shell glasses and vintage corduroy. *Her*—so far as she knew, Nayma was the only one to grant Regan the pronoun. Regan was maybe five-two and thin as a rail, her hair cut like a pixie so that from a certain distance—the distance at which Nayma now stood—she appeared as nothing so much as an eleven-year-old pixie wearing an oversized sweater and carrying a Get-Along Gang Trapper-Keeper of mid-80s provenance. She was, biologically speaking, a fifteen-year-old boy, who identified as female.

"Nayma," she called again, "wait up. Almost missed you, girl. You all right?"

"Yeah, I'm fine."

"What's wrong?"

"Nothing. The usual."

"Well, it's all bullshit, okay? Don't forget that."

"I couldn't if I wanted to. What happened to your shirt?"

"Oh," Regan said. "This was Mr. Harvey's doing."

Her shirt read THE WHOLE DAMN CIS-TEM IS CORRUPT. Only the *a* and *m* of *damn* had been covered with masking tape.

"I like it," Nayma said. "It actually makes it more provocative."

"Really?" Regan touched the tape. "Thanks, I guess it kinda does. Hey, we still on for tonight?"

"Maybe."

"Not maybe, definitely."

"Definitely maybe."

"I've got to go, but text me later, all right? I'll see you at lunch."

The bell sounded and the languor of the hall began to fray, kisses, goodbyes, speed-walking to first period. Nayma turned and moved forward at the same inexorable speed. She was the senior assistant to Dr. Elias Agnew's sophomore English course and that was where she was headed.

Bullshit started early, she thought.

But also, more accurately: bullshit never stopped.

And here was the worst of it: Dr. Agnew had scooched her desk right up against his, like she was his junior partner, his little frizzy-haired brown sidekick, and together they could survey the vast sea of indifference that was English II at 8:15 in the morning. Maybe that was the worst thing—though admittedly her choices here were legion. For Nayma, there was a hierarchy of embarrassment, a sort of great chain of humiliation that she would sometimes finger when Dr. Agnew went on a particularly long and tangential rant about Keats or Sylvia Plath or white shoes after Labor Day or the way gentlemen no longer wore hats *and why is that, Nayma? I'll tell you, my dear, I'll give you a hint, it is linked—is it not?—to the decline of moderate political beliefs in the tradition of western enlightenment philosophy which has hitherto stretched from Copernicus and Francis Bacon to LBJ's Great Society and you, Connie Cayley, I don't know what you're laughing about, my dear, no ma'am I don't, why if I found myself giggling in peach culottes with a sixty-four-point-two quiz average and an apparent inability to comprehend the mere definition of allegory in the work of George Orwell I believe I might be inclined to seek if not sartorial at least ecclesiastical intervention, don't you agree, Nayma?*

She did not. But that didn't mean she didn't love the man.

A former minister, he had been the local community college's lone humanities professor until the local community college lost state funding and evolved into a start-up incubator slash pet-grooming salon with two tanning beds in the back. Now he was the overeducated, overweight chair of the English department. A long-suffering, put-upon Log Cabin Republican who was sarcastic and erudite and slowly losing a war with diabetes. He was overweight and—though Nayma had never seen him in anything other than a suit and a vintage NIXON '72 straw boater worn, perhaps, out of a sense of irony so overdeveloped it had become sincere—quite slovenly: shirt untucked, hair a mess, somehow barely avoiding tripping over his untied Keds as he lumbered into the room leaning on his four-stoppered cane and sighing contentedly, as if the only necessary supplements to truth and beauty was a charge account at Ken's Thrifty Pharmacy and Medical Supply.

Have you seen this year's line of Rascal scooters, Nayma? My Lord, they are sleek creations, compact and carbon neutral. I imagine them conjured in some modernist fever dream of glass and brushed steel, let us say the aerospace industry, headquartered in Orange County, circa 1953, whisking Baptists through the aisles of Walmart, baskets laden with Chinese manufacturing. Why it almost tempts a man to eat his weight in organ meat and simply be done with this bogus charade we collectively describe as walking.

Today they were discussing, or Dr. Agnew was free-associating on, Emma Lazarus's "The New Colossus." *A poem, my children. A sonnet. Fourteen lines following a strict rhyme scheme and structure. Sing it with me. Give me your tired, your poor. Come on, children, we all know it. Your huddled masses yearning to breathe free.* He cupped his ear. *I know you know it, my sweets.*

But if they knew it they were offering no sign. That much was evident from Nayma's perch at the front of the room. Equally evident was the deep dislike radiating off the face of Stinson Wood, a dislike that appeared on the verge of crackling like sparked dryer lint into full-blown hate. He was one of the rich lake kids, and had the shaggy salon-dyed blond locks generally associated with Orlando-based boy bands. In a class of tenth graders, he was the lone senior, not stupid so much as lazy, entitled into a catatonic stupor he broke only to thumb indifferently through his Facebook newsfeed. But today he was alert, today he was all smirk, all dismissive superiority and all of it aimed at Nayma. She got this, she did because:

A. In case anyone had failed to notice, she was decidedly brown in a decidedly white world, and Stinson Wood—who appeared to be of Swedish extraction, or perhaps of something even whiter (an Icelandic Republican from, say, East Tennessee?), should something whiter exist—didn't exactly come across as someone with what might be referred to by Dr. Agnew as an open mind bound to an open heart, and

B. She was ostensibly Stinson's peer, yet here she was seated at the front of the room, occasionally called upon by Dr. Agnew to provide the right answer after Stinson Wood supplied the wrong or, more likely, no answer at all.

It was surely both A and B, and just as surely didn't matter. What mattered was that he was staring at her with a freakish intensity that would have implied amphetamines were it not for his sociological preference for designer drugs filched from his mother's purse.

Dr. Agnew seemed to catch it too.

"Why, Mr. Wood," he said, "and top of the morning to

you, good sir. What a pleasure to find you both diurnal and present. To what do we owe this rare convergence of the twain? Were you, perhaps, musing on the possibility of encountering a mighty woman with a torch? Because I am here to assure you, my boy, that the likelihood of such falls just short of none, though I grant you that with some focus and persistence on your part it may yet approach not at all."

"What?"

"*What?* A Swedish diphthong and an interesting one—its interest is beyond refute. Though perhaps not terribly illuminative as to our current state."

"I'm just watching her," Stinson said.

"And to whom, my child, might you be referring?"

"Her," he said, and thrust his chin at Nayma. "Chiquita Banana there."

"You mean Nayma?"

"Whatever her name is."

"Her name is Nayma. Child, are you slow? Are you of addled mind? Did your mother pass to you some derivative of the coca plant, smoked, perchance, in a glass pipe, while you nestled in her womb? Mr. Wood? Dear Mr. Wood?"

But Stinson Wood said nothing. He just stared at Nayma with his lopsided grin, nodding so imperceptibly it was possible she was only imagining it. But she knew he wasn't. He was entitled. He was privileged. He was exactly the sort of person who hated people like Nayma. Hated the non-white, non-male, non-Southern, non-straight, non-whatever it was that Stinson Wood had been declared by the accident of his birth. It still went on, the hate, the bigotry, only it was softer now, it was subtle. It was patronizing and—the look on his face told her—it was smug.

Dr. Agnew didn't seem to notice.

Dr. Agnew was off discussing the poem again, a woman with a torch, he was saying, let's talk about this image, let's talk about this French woman standing in the harbor with her granite robe and patrician nose…

Stinson had gone back to his phone, but every so often he would look at Nayma and wait for her to look back. Then he would smile that smug smile and look away, like he couldn't believe how ridiculous she was there at the front of the room with her obese mentor rambling on about the world's most irrelevant shit.

She went back to the poem. *I lift my lamp beside the golden door!* it finished, and she imagined that golden door, that place at which she might finally arrive. Did it exist? The cynical side of her said it did not. But the truth was, she believed in it. By the standards of white-bread Germantown, she appeared as un-American as you could get. But she was more American than all of them put together. She was more American than all of them by dint of her belief, and by dint of her arrival, by dint of her parents' sacrifice. By dint of—

She sensed Stinson's head snap up with a reptilian quickness. He had the sort of gray eyes and pale skin that made her imagine him as cold-blooded in the actual biological sense. He was looking up again, but not at her. He was looking across the room at Lana Greaves, a freshman in sophomore English, and the daughter of the athletic director. That Nayma's grandparents worked for the Greaves family, that Nayma and her grandparents even existed, seemed lost to the Greaves. She didn't blame them. It didn't seem malicious, their ignorance. They were simply ignorant, just as she (Nayma) was simply invisible.

Lana looked up. She was cute and blond and appeared just barely old enough to gain entry to the high school. She sat, legs crossed, in her black tights, a worried look clouding her face. She had her phone in her lap and her eyes dropped to it: Stinson was texting her. She put the eraser of her pencil in her mouth and slowly lowered one hand to her lap where the phone was hidden. Not that it needed hiding. Dr. Agnew was holding forth at maximum velocity, all sweeping hands and grand declarations.

The girl texted back.

Stinson texted again.

The girl looked even more worried.

Then Lana's phone actually rang.

Dr. Agnew snapped around from the board where he was busy diagramming the Roman street where Keats had died, but now, but now…

"A cellular call! My, my," he declared. "Who is it that is calling? Who is it that fancies him or herself so wondrously and spectacularly important as to ring during a discussion of the world's unacknowledged legislators?"

Then Nayma realized it wasn't Lana's phone but her phone, the cheap Walmart Asus with its fifteen-dollar SIM card and factory-direct ringtone. She hadn't bothered silencing it because why should she? No one ever called. But now…

"Nayma?" Dr. Agnew looked both hurt and surprised.

"I'm sorry." She was up out of her desk now, the phone pressed to her stomach, not so much to mute the sound as to cradle some wound to the body. "Excuse me. Sorry, Dr. Agnew."

She hurried into the empty hall and flipped open the phone—yes, it was a flip-phone—to find her abuela yammering in Spanish, so frantic Nayma could barely understand her. Then, finally, she did: it was the Greaves woman, the grandmother. She was in the basement. She had fallen. There was blood.

Was she alive?

Yes, she was alive.

"Call the ambulance," Nayma said. "Call 911." Then she realized she would have to call. She got the address and hung up just as Dr. Agnew lumbered into the hall.

"Nayma," he was saying, "this is highly peculiar. I think perhaps—"

He stopped when he heard the voice on the other end.

9-1-1, what's your emergency?

"Oh Lord!" said Dr. Agnew and pirouetted on his four-stoppered cane.

It was like an elephant dancing and Nayma might have applauded had she not been reciting the address. The voice of the operator carried up the block hall.

Was she breathing?

(*Breathing!* cried Dr. Agnew.)

Yes, she was breathing.

Was she conscious?

(*Conscious! Oh Lord!*)

I don't know.

Please stay on the line, ma'am.

But she had already slapped the phone shut, louder than she had intended.

"Oh Lord!" Dr. Agnew said. "Child—"

But she cut him off with a look.

"Dr. Agnew," she said. "I need to borrow your car."

Late that morning Richard Greaves got another phone call, and it was both its news and the proximity to The Call that served to undo him. He was sitting in his office at the Mountain Empire Bank when the charge nurse on the fifth floor of Germantown Memorial called to tell him his ninety-four-year-old mother had suffered what was likely a stroke and was in stable but critical condition in the ICU. Yesenia had found her in the basement.

Richard Greaves had been too stunned to ask questions.

His mother? How could that be?

He had checked on her yesterday evening and—

Then he remembered that he hadn't. Acting Solicitor Annie Smalls had made The Call and he had been too stunned to stop by. He'd gone home and lost himself in several glasses of bourbon and Tom's welcome-home party. There was the rain and the soaked banner, something about the Beach Boys, and now, his poor ma…

He had to get to the hospital as fast as possible—but when he looked up again Jeff Duncan stood in the door, a bottle of Elijah Craig gripped in one fat hand, a fleshy smile spread across his fleshy face.

"Boo," he said, and took a step into the room. "You ready to go?"

"What?" Richard managed.

"To the luncheon." Duncan lowered the bottle. The smile was gone. "You wanted me to come by, right?"

"Yeah, I just—"

"You all right?"

"What do you mean?"

"I mean forgive my language, but you look like you just messed your britches. Who was that on the phone?"

"What phone?"

"The one you just hung up."

"Oh, that. I…I don't know."

"You don't know?"

Richard put his hand out toward the bottle. "Let me see that."

Duncan passed over the Elijah Craig and Richard twisted out the cork with a dull thunk.

"Well, goddang, Richard, you know that was meant as a gift for the congressman."

"I only want a swallow."

Richard took a quick fierce gulp, and then a longer, slower drink.

"I mean not that I don't applaud the mood," Duncan said. "Bourbon for brunch and all, but damn."

Richard corked the bottle and offered it back.

"You sure you all right?"

"I'm fine," he said, "positively fine. Give me thirty seconds here."

Duncan studied him for a moment and then tucked the bourbon beneath one arm like a football. "Well, don't sit forever. We got to stop by the goddang liquor store now."

Jeff Duncan was Richard's longtime business partner in, first, a series of low-income housing developments and trailer parks, and, more recently, the garment mill he and Richard had yet to build. As for the *aw shucks*, *y'alls,* and *ain'ts*, it was an act, though it was possible that Duncan had played at it so long he had forgotten as much.

"Thirty seconds," Richard told him.

"All right."

When he was gone, Richard reached into the back of a desk drawer and removed a Ziploc bag that contained a thin white bar, XANAX lettered down its length. He had grown up a child of the Cold War, groomed on the tactical nukes and U2 overflights, and one of the things that had always stayed with him was the memory of Francis Gary Powers, the downed pilot who had been captured by the Soviets. Powers had carried with him a suicide pill, a coin ringed with shellfish toxin. He hadn't used it, of course, and that had always troubled Richard, something about Powers's failure to commit that final act.

He put the pill on his desk. He considered the Xanax his own suicide pill, ridiculous as it sounded. Obviously, it wouldn't kill him. It would simply glaze the day. Likely, it would put him to sleep. It was ridiculous, but he thought of his ma, her thin bones arranged in some hospital bed, intubated and IVed, nose-tubed and heart-cathed. He needed to go to her right away, to skip the luncheon, to sit by her side. But then there was The Call. There was his coming arraignment, the depositions, and newspaper headlines. He couldn't skip the luncheon—he had to find out what people knew, if anyone was talking. He'd go sit on the dais and the second it was over head to the hospital. It was heartless, but it was the only way.

He could call Clara, of course.

But he wouldn't, no, not till he knew what was going on. He would wait. He would have to explain everything soon enough. Not just his mother's health but the movement of funds, the forging of signatures. Shuttling between the hospital and his lawyer's office. Everyone would want answers, and not just the FBI and the bank's reinsurers, but his wife and daughter and sons. There would be entire days to get through, clear-headed days, days seared white with revelation and shame. What was coming were the rumors, the stares, the attempts not to stare. What was coming was the systematic unpacking of his life's work.

They were coming for his job and his home.

They were coming for him, and knowing as much Richard put the pill in his mouth and swallowed.

Germantown sits in the first rise of the Blue Ridge Mountains, the county seat of a triangular wedge of hills giving way to mountains that was once known as the Dark Corner (for its predilection toward bootlegging and gunfights), but had long since been rebranded—thanks to the forward-thinking folks at the County Economic Commission—as the Golden Corner, an aspirational nod to its "beautiful lakes and rushing streams." It had been founded, as its name implied, by German settlers pushing up from the suffocations of class and heat that was Charleston in the 1840s. They came in wagon trains, on horseback, on foot, and what they found were forested slopes and rich bottomland that appeared nearly virginal.

It wasn't, of course.

But the Cherokee had pushed out or swallowed up the smaller tribes in the late eighteenth century, and white trappers and land agents had pushed out or swallowed up the Cherokee in the early nineteenth. So there it was: beautiful lakes and rushing streams, and all of it there for the taking.

They built a clapboard church with a white tower, a monstrous hotel, a lumber mill, and a string of boxy houses built on skids for easy transport should it all go bust. But instead of going bust, the railroad came through and the town prospered. Then outriders from Sherman's Army came through and the town burned. After that, things became dusty and weary and a lot of children wound up with rickets. Eventually people began to come down the mountain and off their subsistence plots to work in the mills. The war came, the big one, then desegregation, though it was by and large a white place and the idea of separate water fountains was mostly just that: an idea. Folks argued against it, though not with any real conviction. They built the courthouse facing south, but didn't seem to know why. Most people were relatively poor, but happy nonetheless.

That was the world of Richard Greaves's parents: the war,

and all the promise after. But for Richard, it might as well have been hearsay.

He was heir to Vietnam and Watergate and talk of a sexual revolution that was little more than rumor in rural South Carolina. An adult in the 1970s and what good had ever come of that God-awful decade, he wanted to know. *Hee Haw* and *Colombo*, he guessed, but what was that against the rest? The way the mills shuttered and left. The way the Mexicans were recruited and then deported. The '80s came, the '90s. They got a Walmart and a McDonald's on the bypass, but the local diner and hardware store had closed. Richard had gotten rich, true, but the Bee Gees were still on the easy-listening station out of Greenville. Richard hated the Bee Gees. A position, he believed, both morally and aesthetically defensible.

Mountain Empire Bank sat just beyond the reach of Main Street, situated right as the highway widened to four lanes and was lined not with the antique shops with their oil lamps and brass bedframes, or the bistros serving their heirloom okra and sourced pork chops, but with a muffler shop, a used car lot, and a prefab church offering childcare and Sunday services in both English and Español. If the downtown with its gaslights and charcuterie was the South as imagined by the Tourism Board, here was the South as it actually existed: poor and sprawling and rebel-flagged to the hilt. The timber and rock of the three-story bank stood marooned in the red clay like a misplaced ski lodge, the location as much about arrogance and defiance as it was cheap real estate.

It was Richard's baby. But it was also his middle finger to the world of old money and old ideas and now they were trying to take it down, now they were trying to take *him* down, and the crazy thing was, what bothered him most wasn't the impending charges or what they would do to his reputation or his family or his life. What absolutely galled Richard Samuel Greaves was the thought of the old men laughing. The Greatest Generation yukking it up. There probably weren't even any old men left, but he heard their ghosts, the old heroes with their three-piece suits and Negro jokes. He had built the bank away from Main Street as much to defy them as anything else.

"Goddang traffic," Duncan said.

He was behind the wheel of his black Excursion. Richard sat beside him, the Elijah Craig nestled in his lap like a sick child, watching what really was unusually thick traffic glide by as the bourbon and the Xanax began their first tickling forays out toward the neural receptors of his brain.

"Oktoberfest," Duncan said, and Richard grunted agreement.

He wasn't listening. He was thinking about his ma in the ICU. She lived alone—there was Yesenia, and there was Richard with his daily visits. Beyond that, there was a network of church friends and cousins and grandchildren who looked in on her. But it was completely possible that entire days could fall through the cracks. Richard was careful about these—this was his ma, he loved his ma—but it could happen. Hell, it *had* happened.

He felt something lurch, his heart dipping and leaking some viscous fluid that was surely love. He should be with her—to hell with the luncheon and goddamn FBI—and felt his hand go to the door.

He would get out right now, go to her, take care of her—

But Duncan was already gunning the Excursion past the oncoming traffic, making the left toward Main Street. Downtown was undergoing a massive renovation and the result was a confusion of detours and construction barrels and the smell of hot asphalt in the otherwise clear air.

Duncan made the left onto Catherine Street and pulled to the curb in front of Miss Lee's Wine & Spirits. He opened his door and paused, one foot on the road.

"You just sitting here?" Duncan waited for an answer, but Richard was mute. "Richard?"

But Richard wasn't listening.

Richard was time-traveling.

Richard was thinking about his ma, but his ma as realized

through a chemical veil, gauzy and unreal. His ma as memory. More specifically, his ma in 1967, it must have been. Riding up to Cherokee that Fourth of July weekend. That summer! The sun in their half-closed eyes. The wind in their smiling faces. His ma's hair tied in a kerchief like Jackie O, dead for half a decade or half a second because back then time had not yet been invented. That day! Most days his father seemed to have left his spirit behind him in Europe, but that day there was no silent brooding, no hunkered waiting in the Bastogne of his mind. His ma spent half her waking life on the edge of a nervous breakdown, but missing that day were the butterflies of her hands, flitting delicately as they attempted to wave away whatever savage memory had arrested her husband. His younger brother would soon die violently, but that day Teddy had not yet gone beneath the tire and through the teeth of the hay rake. Instead of a dead brother, there were Vienna sausages and sardines on Ritz crackers eaten on a concrete table by the river that parted the reservation. There was watermelon and then, hey, let's get the boys' picture made with the Indian chief over there, want to? Hey, Geronimo? Hey, Chief Wigwam, how much for one with the two boys?

His last great summer, as Richard remembered it. The next year his brother died, and the year after that Richard was too old to care about anything but himself, too much a bastard, a cadet at the Citadel sipping Canadian Club out of a waxed paper cup and chasing girls at the College of Charleston. By the time he realized how much he missed those family trips—the roadside picnics as they wound up toward Gatlinburg and the motel swimming pools, those sunny days and sunburnt nights—he was sweating his way through officer training at Fort A.P. Hill, wondering if he just might be the last man to die for a mistake.

It hadn't proven to be the case, of course—by '72 Vietnam was as good as lost and his mechanized infantry unit had never gone farther afield than the sandy expanse of Fort Irwin National Training Center. He had survived, gotten married, had children, had success after success so that eventually it became hard not to imagine some dispensation had been granted for Richard Greaves alone: amid all the sameness, he was special, and as such, the slings and arrows of outrageous fortune would not touch him. He was blessed. He was not afraid. It was a belief he had carried throughout his adult life.

It was strange to realize he carried it still, even as there arose a flicker of late-breaking regret, as if he'd misread the menu and realized it only on the ride home.

"Richard?" a voice said, but it was not his ma's.

"Hey, Richard?" but it was not his dead father.

"All right," Duncan asked. "I won't be but a minute."

The door shut—he heard it, felt it, even if he didn't exactly see it—and Richard was left alone in the hush of the car. Sun came through the window and he felt the bourbon and the Xanax and the dreamy sleeve of sleep, uncuffed and descending. His ma wasn't dead. It was his brother who was dead. More than that: it was his father. For almost fifty years it had been Richard's job to accompany and then drive his father every December 21 to North Carolina, where his father would spend the day with his oldest friend, Benjamin Harden, the two men, aging and then old, sitting around in quiet contemplation of the fact that they hadn't died in the Bulge. The Panzers coming through the snowy fog, ahead of them deer and a flight of silent owls. Goddamn bloody Bastogne.

The men talking quietly.

Christ, the smell that came from the aid station, the smell that came from the burning trees and the burning rubber and the burning bodies.

"Cabbage," Harden said once. "Like they were burning a thousand heads of cabbage."

Richard not listening, not really.

Richard down in front of the fire with a toy tractor.

Richard with a metal Farmall in one hand.

Lord, how he had loved those trips.

It had started when he was six years old with his mother's silent disapproval, started with the smell of his daddy in his

Chevy Impala: Colgate shaving cream and KIWI Heel & Sole. From the time he was six he rode with, and then somewhere in his thirties drove, his father north, late at night through the peach fields stippled with frost, and then paved over for Direct Factory Outlets. North across the state line to Cary, a hamlet with a textile mill and a post office until—like the peach fields—that too had disappeared, this time beneath the aggregated weight of retirees from the Research Triangle with their degrees from Duke and TIAA-Cref accounts. They buried the town in antique shops and meat-and-threes that kept showing up in the pages of *Southern Living* but Benjamin Harden didn't move and they kept going, year after year, and never did Richard mind. Never did he mind because right up until the moment his father died, Richard was waiting for his father to say something, to tell him something, anything. To talk about the war, to talk about Teddy. But he didn't and he didn't, and then he was dead and that *never had* was re-qualified as *never will* and how the hell was a man supposed to live with that? Sitting in one silence for sixty years only to die right into another, the second no deeper than the first.

He sat up, took a healthy pull from the bottle and then a second. He was so sleepy, but—

Someone was knocking at the window.

He looked up at the broad face of Blake Stevens, the local barber outside of whose South Cackalacky Cuts Duncan had parked. Stevens gave him a smile and motioned for the window to come down.

"Hey, Mr. Greaves. Y'all not going to eat?"

"Headed that way now. Just waiting on Jeff."

"Jeff Duncan?"

"He's in the liquor store there."

"Needed some fortification," Stevens said. "I hear you." He tapped the sill twice with his big ring, rectangular and golden and studded with green stones. "Hey, while I got you here," Stevens said. "What's Jack said about the van Gundy brothers? They going to be coaching the boys' team come fall or not?"

"I certainly hope so," Greaves said. "If Jack has any sense one of 'em will."

"Shoot, Jack's got plenty of sense."

"Maybe more than he needs."

"Nah, he's a good one, ole Jack is. Last of his kind. You ever see 'em in the bank?"

"Who's that?"

"The van Gundy brothers."

"Oh yeah," Richard assured him. "All the time. I mean, I haven't seen them myself, but I know they've been in. You know old Elvis? He's seen 'em a few times."

"That's pretty dang cool. Hey, I'm gonna ask you another day about my fool brother-in-law camping on your property. He keeps asking."

"To camp?"

"Just somewhere out of the way."

"Tell 'em to come on anytime."

"I appreciate it."

"Tell 'em tomorrow if they like."

"You wouldn't mind it? They got four-wheelers to ride in. I mean they dumbasses and all, but they wouldn't bother nobody. Probably just camp down by the creek."

"Tell 'em to come on. They can just come in through the back gate. It's unlocked."

"Tomorrow? Hell, all right. I will then. Seriously. I appreciate it."

"The back gate."

"Roger that. I appreciate it."

Richard waved him off as Duncan came out of the store holding a brown bag.

"Knob Creek," he said wearily. "Which is fine, I mean, but it ain't Elijah Craig. I had to get that in Greenville, Richard."

"You can still give it to the congressman."

Duncan shook his head in disappointment.

"I ain't giving him a bottle you done tapped." He got in and started the engine. "What's old Stevens want?"

"Nothing. Just talking."

"He's always talking. Let's go."

They turned around in the parking lot behind the old Harper's Five & Dime—it was subdivided now into a tienda, a pizza place, and a men's formal shop that stayed in business through some defiance of economic reality—and headed down North Catherine Street toward Sertoma Field and the luncheon. The streetlights were hung with flags, American and German banners on alternate poles. It would have killed Richard's father, had killed him in its way. *So we're flying the flag of the huns now? Drinking their beer, driving Jap cars. You tell me who really won the war.* But he hadn't been asking a question. He had been settling deeper into a silence already so profound it felt cosmic. It felt like the universe before creation.

"Your boys coming?" Duncan asked.

"Meeting us."

"Jack and Tom both?"

"That's what they said. I know Tom'll be here at least."

"He back in training?"

"I don't know what he's doing," Richard said. "He just got in last night. Went to Europe after Daddy died. Wanted to find the town he was in the day the war ended. Some sort of spiritual thing, I think. Then last night he shows up with some girl he met at the airport."

"Good looking?"

"Did I not tell you this?"

"You might have," Duncan said. "I can't remember a goddang thing anymore. Old age."

"We aren't that old."

"Well, old or not, it'll be good to see him."

Richard nodded: if Tom was something of a vagrant, he was also a sort of late-life gift. The pilgrimage to Europe—Richard hadn't even attempted to understand, but it didn't matter: Tom was a blessing.

"He back for good?" Duncan asked.

They were in a queue of traffic now, waiting to make the

right down to the parking lot that edged Sertoma Field, a police officer waving in a blinking trail of Germantown's finest.

"I don't know about for good," Richard said. "I guess he might start training again."

"His ninja stuff?"

"You know he built an obstacle course right in the pasture there behind the pool?"

"You're kidding me. And Clara let him?"

"Clara loves it. He could set fire to the woods and Clara would declare it bold and creative. Declare it performance art. You know how she is about Tom."

"He still making money online?"

"He's what you call an influencer."

"Influencing what?"

"Lord, Jeff, I don't know. It makes no sense to me."

They were moving again, pulling into the parking lot, an SUV to the right, a pickup to the left. Duncan cut the engine and held his Knob Creek against him as if Richard might snatch it.

"All right then, let's—" he started to say, but all at once Richard couldn't hear him.

Because all at once Richard Samuel Greaves was joyously and deeply intoxicated.

Nayma piloted Dr. Agnew's Oldsmobile into the parking lot of Germantown Memorial Hospital, her body hung over a giant steering wheel the size of a manhole cover, her butt slid forward over the beaded seat cover as rough as the corrugated motel roof where she would occasionally hide in plain sight. It was a little like driving a boat—not that she'd ever driven a boat, she'd never even actually *been* on a boat—but that didn't stop her from imagining the car as a giant yacht that rocked lightly as she turned at the traffic signal and eased nimbly around corners. She was going too fast and couldn't get the cassette of the Statler Brothers to cut off, but then she was going too slow and accelerated until she could feel the car bouncing on its shocks. She had driven before—she could certainly drive—but never in something this big and never over forty-five miles an hour.

She glided into the parking lot at sixty-five, fairly sailed over a speed bump, and braked abruptly to thirty, to twenty, to a lurching ten. A dashboard hula dancer bobbed wildly and across the purple leather seat; Dr. Agnew's papers and books fluttered and slipped. John Donne. Geoffrey Hill. Some ancient coffee table atlas of *Olde England*.

She shoved them all to the side and made for the main entrance, the glass doors sliding open onto the chilly foyer with its potted palms and new carpet. The hospital smell was barely noticeable here, though it got worse past the reception desk where the walls were lined with Purell dispensers and signs explaining the importance of sanitized hands. She took the elevator to the fifth floor ICU, more or less bouncing on her heels and wringing her bacteria-free hands.

When the doors opened the smell hit her: not so much the sharp of antiseptic as something heavier and more frightening: it smelled here, she realized, like death. That it was the sort of cliché Dr. Agnew would abhor didn't make it less true. She felt something inside her twist. Up until that moment she had worried solely about her abuela, but at that moment she felt her heart—it was definitely her heart—twist for the Greaves woman, alone here with the tubes and wheeled machines and that smell Nayma was starting to recognize as the aftertaste of human shit.

She found her grandparents in the waiting room, a couple of aged nervous children who fluttered to their feet when they saw her. Her abuela had virtually no English which made her, a woman who was otherwise a workhorse of devotion and faith, pathetically helpless. Her abuelo was fluent, educated, smart, and sarcastic. Or had been once.

He'd been expelled from the tomato fields of Immokalee, Florida, after attempting to organize what were effectively indentured servants. But the process of kicking him out—she suspected it had been more than simply driving her grandparents to the city limits and telling them to beat it—had cracked something in him, or widened a crack that already existed so that these days he was mostly silent. There were no more jokes, no more laughing. He worked. He smoked. He drank one Victoria every evening in a plastic chair on the indoor-outdoor carpet of the motel stoop. After that he lay in bed, hands crossed on his chest as if by arranging himself for death he would save a few dollars on the undertaker. Whether he actually slept or not she never knew. She didn't think he prayed. It was her abuela who prayed. Her abuela who kneeled on her swollen knees before the candle of the Virgin that Nayma had gotten her from the "Ethnic" aisle at Ingles. Her abuela who took Nayma to mass at La Luz del Mundo behind Hardee's.

But now they were both standing, silent, tragic.

She started to speak but something in their faces stopped her. They weren't staring at her, but past her, and Nayma turned to see Mrs. Greaves on the other side of the glass. She stepped closer to look, and then closer again, pressed her face to the glass so that it was all perfectly clear: Rose Greaves was dying, and she was doing it all alone.

Richard made it to the footbridge that spanned the creek through force of will, an intense focus on the act of raising and lowering his feet that made him appear no worse than any other arthritic man limping toward senescence. They all seemed to be waiting for him and he waded in, bravely at first. He shook hands, he smiled, he had his back slapped. He got a kiss on the cheek from the eighteen-year-old Miss Oktoberfest and, without intending, smelled the vanilla in her shampoo. There were jokes about the bottle of Elijah Craig he only now realized was tucked beneath his arm (he had drunk out the neck and shoulders) and for these he smiled and winked and even dapped fists—he dapped fists! something Tom had taught him—with what seemed the day's lone African American, a mortician from Seneca. It was all going just fine, he thought. Perched in the bridge of his self, the captain of the lurching but still upright battleship R.S. *Greaves* did a quick assessment and through the narrowing portholes of his eyes found the world to be bending and blurring, but on the whole, wholly manageable.

Tom wrapped him in a hug.

The mayor laughed and mimed drinking from the bottle.

The congressman initiated a two-hand clasp-hug that seemed to approach the genuine—*I'll always appreciate the dinner you and Clara hosted*—and then all of Germantown came forward to say hello. Richard dropped a twenty in the donations basket and meandered down the serving line, greeting the women ladling potato salad and pinching bratwursts. He was happy because the world had lost its sharp edge and he was happy because he realized how much of it was simply a dream. The two phone calls—his mother's stroke, his coming indictment—none of it was real. It was a product of anxiety, of paranoia, of whatever psychic weakness had heretofore afflicted him. But it was also over. His ma was home safe. His garment mill was built. It felt like 1984 all over again and there he was, back with his friends. Reagan was calling out the Evil Empire and their children were around the pool listening to Cyndi Lauper on a boom box. Their wives barefoot and drinking Blue Nun. The men laughing in their pastel trousers. How beautiful life was! It wasn't just girls that wanted to have fun!

It's a great day to be in Germantown! the mayor sang over the microphone.

And it was! It truly was!

Absolutely nothing could alter the day's perfection, except—

It was only when he was seated on the dais with Tom and the mayor and the congressman that Richard noticed the empty chair beside him; it was only when he realized Jack was not there—and wouldn't be coming!—that he felt the fantasy collapse. He had screwed over everyone and come Monday would be arrested for it. That his ma likely wouldn't be alive to see it was no consolation.

His ma! He had to go to her and stood abruptly, banging his knees hard enough to rattle the table and splash his tea.

"Dad?" Tom said.

"Excuse me for a minute. Gentlemen, excuse me."

Tom was at his elbow, easing him back.

"Dad, you okay?"

"Fine. Just forgot something." He looked at the mayor and the congressman, both staring up expectantly, not yet worried, but not far from it either. "Excuse me for a moment, gentlemen. I'll be right back."

"Let me help you," Tom said.

"I'm fine," Richard told him, but found as he said it that his son was guiding him down the steps behind the dais.

"Dad, how much of that bourbon did you drink?"

"You haven't talked to your brother, have you?"

"Did you ride with Mr. Duncan?"

"He said he'd be here."

"I haven't talked to him," Tom said. "But listen, why don't I run you home? I'll grab our plates and grab one for Mom. How about that? That work?"

He realized now his son was speaking in that slow-and-clear voice, the patronizingly calm over-enunciation used by the rational adult when speaking to the irrational child.

"Dad?" Tom said.

"I'm all right."

"How about I grab the food?"

"Yeah," Richard managed, "that's fine. You can text your brother? Call him or whatever."

"Yeah, of course. Why don't you go wait in my truck?" He held out the keys for his battered Chevy Luv that had spent the last several months in Richard's garage. "I parked right by the bridge. I'll get the food and tell Mr. Duncan you're riding with me."

"And tell those two—" Tell them my mother is dying, he thought. Tell them I lied and stole. Tell them—he motioned at the mayor and the congressman, now deeply and obliviously involved with their cased meat. "Tell them—"

"I got it. Just go wait in the truck and I'll be there in five."

Richard limped along the edge of the field, the grass long and laid over with dew. It was a retreat of sorts, but no one seemed to notice, all of them lost in the snow globes of their own lives. As for him, he was lost in the glass of the Elijah Craig bottle, which—and he congratulated himself here—he had remembered to bring with him. It was a good thing. He thought he could survive the inevitable trial and funeral, but getting to them was another matter. Oblivion would be his only solace.

Was this, perhaps, his father's secret? To hide inside silence was to *become* silence. It was what he had always resented in his father, that refusal to open, but now it seemed less spite and more a form of pain management. To live through the war only to drag your son through a hay rake. Forever Teddy, having lost the opportunity to become a Ted or Theodore or even a Theo. When he died, an old woman, a great-aunt it must have been, went through the house covering the mirrors and stopping the clocks.

Was that the answer?

To erase the image, to stop time?

Or was he just drunk?

He crossed the footbridge, the creek high and swift and folding the floss of grasses that lined the banks with the wash of last night's storm. The air was clear and bright and he felt autumn all around him, the change of seasons, the pure blue of the day. It was glorious. Yet somewhere in the midst of it, right around the time Richard was getting drunk and dancing to the Beach Boys, his ma's brain had grabbed at itself, clenched, released, and then failed.

He unlocked Tom's pickup and sat in the passenger seat. He had his phone out—when had he taken his phone out?—and was scrolling down through his contacts.

Where was Jack?

There was a shaker cup between the seats, the wire ball clotted with grainy green clumps of protein powder and oat milk. There were CDs stuffed into the console, a book called

Everyday Paleo, a curved gripping device meant to strengthen the hand. Richard slid the key into the ignition and on came the news. Brexit negotiations. A suicide bomber in Turkey. The goddamn news…He didn't miss the news, what he missed was Paul Harvey. Paul Harvey with *the rest of the story.* What had happened to Paul? Paul had narrated half his life and what was he now? He was dead, wasn't he? They were all dead, or would be soon enough. Francis Gary Powers had died in a helicopter crash in California. Ridiculous how he'd survived bailing out of his plane, capture and imprisonment, and being paraded on television by Khrushchev, only to die covering the rush-hour traffic in Santa Barbara.

Richard touched the screen of his phone.

Where the hell was Jack?

It was ridiculous to even care, but if it was so ridiculous why was he calling him?

But he wasn't, not really, and hung up on the first ring, pulled the door shut, wallowed his way behind the wheel and put his hand back on the key. Tom was coming across the footbridge exactly as Richard had imagined him, and he paused a moment to admire his son's gait. He was so fluid, such a natural athlete. He'd gone on that ninja show and owned it. Swinging and jumping and running like some jungle cat. Richard started the engine. *Dad!* he could see Tom mouthing. He dropped the truck into first, his foot on the clutch. *Dad!* Tom was coming faster now, the Styrofoam plates jostling. He was almost to the window when Richard hit the gas.

"I'm sorry," he said aloud to his son, to both his sons, and to his wife and daughter and his mother. He might have said it to his father too, had he not already been pulling onto the highway, gunning the engine toward home.

He needed to go see his ma.

But first he had to find Jack.

As for Jack, it had all started so wonderfully, so promising.

The day, he meant.

He had woken to the sound of his wife showering at some absurd hour, animated by some equally absurd optimism that had nothing to do with the fact that he had gotten in late from his parents' to find that Catherine had fallen asleep, *New Yorker* open on her chest, bedside light still burning. He'd gone up to tell Lana goodnight, knocking and entering quickly enough that she barely had time to hide her phone, and though she'd said nothing, Jack had gotten an angry vibe and retreated downstairs, lonely and disproportionately disappointed. Yet come daylight he'd been lolling on a mound of pillows, happy.

"Big day," he'd called from the bed. "Catherine?" And just like that his wife had stepped from the bathroom in skirt and bra, her blouse in one hand, all honeyed sweetness.

"What's that?"

"I said big day."

She'd looked at him for a moment, her face darkening, and when she spoke again her tone had changed.

"One second, okay?"

Her look might have reminded a less optimistic man of the *thing* he was purportedly *going through*, but he wasn't thinking of that. He was thinking of the football tickets Catherine had promised to get from one of the firm's partners, forty-five yard line, ten rows up. This weekend the Citadel, his Citadel, would play sacrificial lamb to the slaughter that was Clemson football. His old roommate Justin was coming. Once a year Justin bought three handles of good bourbon, put his Boykin spaniel in the back of his Grand Wagoneer, and drove south for a Citadel football game. Jack intended to be there too. More than that, he intended to be there with Lana. Not because he had any interest in the game, but because the Citadel now had female cadets, and he wanted Lana to see them. A part of him wanted her to become one of those female cadets, and why not? She was selfless and brave. Brilliant and beautiful.

"Jack?"

Was it really that absurd a wish?

"Jack?"

He'd looked up to find Catherine standing by the bed, dressed now, forty-two years old and incredibly sexy, this angular woman who appeared built from green tea and Pilates. She had saved his life a thousand times, most recently back in the spring with the simple act of changing his deodorant. For years he had worn a natural crystal: the aluminum of name-brand deodorants burned his skin and he couldn't bear the chemical smells, the MOUNTAIN BREEZE, the OCEAN SPRAY. But he had reached the point in life where a scentless hippie crystal no longer masked the odors of middle-aged sweat. Eventually, he had resigned himself to stinking like the old man he had become. Then Catherine came home with a tube of DUSK by Herban Cowboy. All natural, scented, but scented like leather and woodsmoke.

At eleven bucks a pop it was the kind of thing he never would have bought on his own and told Catherine no way, he would just go around smelling exactly like what he had become. Her response was to bring home ten tubes, the equivalent of at least a few years. He had fussed a bit, but inside, he felt alive, he felt young again—he was the Herban Cowboy!—and that energy, that youth, had carried through the summer all the way to the August week they had spent in a cottage in Blowing Rock. Just Jack and Catherine and Lana hiking, reading, cooking elaborate meals. Everyone had put their phones down, they talked, they listened, they played Monopoly for goodness' sake, and it had been Jack's dizzy misunderstanding, his failure to grasp the concept of vacation that had led him to believe that the week was not an idyll from their normal lives but their actual normal lives. Which made the return to home, the return to school—Lana's return to her phone and her friends—

"Let's talk for a minute about this weekend."

"Is there a problem with the tickets?"

"I'll get the tickets today. That's not the problem." She sat on the edge of the bed. "But maybe we need to think about what Lana wants."

Jack sat up here and solemnly took his wife's hands in his.

"I am. Lana wants to go."

"Jack."

"She really does," he said, and if there was a note of pleading in his voice there was also nothing to be done about it.

"She's fifteen, Jack. She has friends. She has a life—she *wants* to have a life. And yet—" and here his wife's hands had come forward to frame his face, a gesture that for a moment hung somewhere between affirmation and assault, before settling into gentleness. "—you're in this state, and that's okay, I understand. But maybe your expectations were a little, what?"

"I'm an idiot," Jack said, and all at once he was sick of himself and his big dumb optimism, the Labrador puppy enthusiasm that was all panting pink tongue and middle-age delusion.

"No," she said creamily, "just a dad. It's why we love you."

That was morning.

That was home.

But by seven he was at the high school, and by eight folks most definitely weren't loving him. Folks were, in fact, yelling at him, lined up outside his office and yelling; a cheerleading mom, a football dad—

Now I'm not one to complain…

Now you know I've never been one to fuss…

It was the bane of his working life, these otherwise satisfied God-fearing non-complaining parents of Germantown High's finest, suddenly struck down with the overwhelming need to bitch and moan, desperate to understand why their son was at right guard and not left tackle, the way the Good Lord intended it, or why that hateful woman whose daughter played second seed on the tennis team claps every time *my* daughter double-faults?

"You look me in the eyes, Mr. Greaves, and tell me that ain't the ugliest thing you ever heard."

Jack looked them in the eyes, but he didn't say much of anything, just stared back with what he hoped conveyed not only his boundless empathy but his quickly diminishing patience as well.

All right, Mr. Hot Shot Administrator, what are the chances we might get one of the van Gundy boys to coach the basketball team?

Oh Lord.

I'll not lie, Jack. I've heard the rumor.

Ah yes, the rumor! What was stalking Jack Greaves was a whisper campaign that the sister of Jeff and Steve van Gundy lived in a single-wide off Highway 28, and that the former NBA coaches (Knicks, Magic) turned announcers (TNT, NBC) were frequently in and out of their sister's underpinned abode, no doubt rebuilding the '57 Ford that had been up on blocks since the Nixon administration, just a couple of shade-tree mechanics, at least until they scoped out the local coaching opportunities and took over the boys' program.

There's no van Gundy woman, Jack would explain again and again, and no van Gundy brothers looking for a job, at least not around here.

You think maybe they just working on the Ford then? 'Cause open your mind, Jack. It ain't like they can't do both, right?

He granted the point, but assured the man they were far away in New York.

You sure about that? Old Elvis's seen 'em at least twice.

Elvis, good Lord, he wanted to say, but of course never did.

The last dad stomped out just after ten, and Jack Greaves leaned back from his desk, shut his eyes for no more than twenty seconds, and then picked up his phone to call his assistant, Carol, eight feet away but separated by a wall of cinder block and grief.

"Are there any more?"

"That's the last one. Your mom did call. Said you didn't answer your cell."

"I couldn't."

"That's what I told her."

"Lana didn't happen to come by, did she?"

"I haven't seen her. Should I have her paged?"

"No, no," Jack said. "I just thought maybe…"

"Sure."

"I'm going to get out of here for a few minutes."

"Remember to call your mom."

He hung up, ready to get outside but strangely immobile. His office, like the rest of the school, was brand new, and like the school it felt both overstuffed and empty. On his desk was the second volume of Robert Caro's biography of LBJ, which he hadn't touched since August, but he couldn't focus. At least until he found Lana. They had ridden in together, but had just as soon been orbiting different stars, Lana's eyes on her phone, Jack's on the road. He'd tried twice to get her talking but the angry vibe he'd gotten the night before remained.

His cell was in the drawer, flashing with a text from Emily reminding him today was the annual Oktoberfest luncheon—*I know Dad's looking forward to showing you off, Mr. AD.* Two missed calls from his mom, no doubt reminding him of the same.

She picked up on the first ring.

"I just wanted to check on you," his mother said, and he waited for it. "That and remind you your father is expecting you at the luncheon today. You can still go?"

"I'll be there."

"Tom is going, and I think your father has all three of you sitting on the dais."

"The dais?"

"I know, honey."

"Are you serious?"

"Just indulge him, all right? You know how he is."

"Hungover, I assume."

"Oh, Jack. Don't be like that."

But how could he be any other way?

The bell signaling the start of third period sounded just as he pushed the door open on the gym. Coach Groban already had his team circled around him at center court, everyone barefoot in shorts and helmets. Jack stood at the edge of the mass, sixty or so boys listening earnestly to the coach's earnest speech. And maybe that was what he couldn't take anymore: the earnestness of it all. He didn't fault it, and he surely didn't mock it. But somewhere along the way he'd started to feel exhausted by the seriousness of so much of living. It deserved it, surely life deserved it. But sometimes he caught himself wondering why. The striving, the hard work, the delayed gratifications—he knew this was the bedrock on which a good life was built. But also, he didn't really give a damn, not anymore.

"Coach Greaves?"

It was a feeling that came and went, but he sensed that the more he allowed it in the more it took root, the more it became *a thing*—

"Mr. Greaves, sir?"

There was a time he would have put his head down, focused, a time he would have worked assiduously to tear out the thought, to rip the undermining worry out by the roots, but now—

Everyone was looking at him, helmets turned like a field of sunflowers.

"I was just asking if you'd like to say a word to the boys," Coach Groban said.

It took Jack a moment to resurface.

"To the boys?"

"Maybe something about tonight? A motivational word," Groban said. "Or just whatever."

"A word," Jack said, reaching back through a lifetime of cliché but finding nothing worth the grip. But then he had something. "When I was in Iraq," he started. "I was in Iraq. Ramadi. This was a while ago. I bet most of y'all didn't know that. Y'all would have been babies, I guess. Kids. This was a while ago like I said, and what I'm saying to you now, about back then, I mean, is—"

He looked up at the earnest caged faces waiting for him to come to some sort of neat aphorism. They were children and had no idea what he was talking about. Not that he did either. He knew there was something there, he sensed something, but to articulate it—

Stupid to even try. But he needed to give them something.

"So I guess what I'm saying is," he told them, "hit 'em in the mouth, boys."

"Hit 'em in the mouth!" Groban yelled.

"Hit 'em in mouth!" they repeated. "Hit 'em in the mouth!"

The chant moved like wildfire and suddenly they had turned inward, back toward the center of the court, back toward their coach, who was shouting with them, *Hit 'em in the mouth, hit 'em in the mouth* as if this was the key to life, and who was Jack to say it wasn't?

Jack found Elvis down on the field, pushing the Grassline Marker over the crown from one sideline to the other, a perfect chalk stripe appearing as he went. Elvis was in a cut-off T-shirt that surely held the logo of some gun manufacturer and just as surely put him in violation of the district dress code. Not that Jack would say anything. You made exceptions for a man like Elvis. While Jack had spent his war in a National Guard hospital tent handing out Pedialyte to nursing mothers Shock-and-Awed into severe dehydration, Elvis had flown in a blacked-out C-130 to an abandoned airfield south of Najaf where, with the rest of the Fifth Special Forces Group, he had fought his way north, ahead of the advance of the Third Infantry Division. Some illegible tribute was inked on his left arm, a map, tombstone, and cross. Not the sort of thing you asked about.

Jack met him down near the end zone.

"I done asked you twice about bionutrients," Elvis said.

Jack motioned at the storage shed past the opposite goalposts. "You didn't see any in there?"

"You can get a Symbio Fulvic booster in ten-liter bags. Sugars and proteins. It's all online."

"I thought we had fertilizer?"

"Man, this grass ain't pining for no True Value shit. You see out around midfield? Nothing but skid marks."

"How's your mama, Elvis?"

"I ain't talking about my mama right now. She's fine—thank you for asking—but what I'm talking about—" He pointed down at the field. "What I'm talking about is right here beneath us."

"Just paint it."

"You can't paint mud, chief. I need you to take some pride in this."

"I thought that's what I had you for."

"Well, Christ, Jack. I'm a yard man. Not a magician."

Elvis shook his head and put his hands back on the push bar of the Marker. His shirt, Jack noted, featured the barrel of a .357 above the words IT AIN'T THE DOG YOU NEED TO WORRY ABOUT. He remembered a similar shirt the day Elvis's father had shown up in the yard on a ten-speed Schwinn, a Weed Eater balanced on his pumping knees, a Marlboro slung from his lips. He'd spent the day doing stoop work in Jack's mother's flower beds, Merle Haggard playing on a little transistor run off two AA batteries. When he came back the next time, he brought with him both a six-pack of Natural Light and his son. For the rest of their childhood Jack and Elvis had been inseparable. It was only in high school they'd realized they were meant to move in separate but parallel universes, one rich, one poor. It had come to both of them as a surprise. Apparently they made people uncomfortable, these two hulking kids anchoring the D-line. Apparently they made people stare. Sure, it wasn't the '50s, but it was still the south, and to Jack's great regret, they had drifted apart, though he'd continued to admire his friend from a socially acceptable distance. Elvis had been the meanest defensive end in the history of the Skyline Conference. Got a full ride to Carolina but lost his girlfriend to cancer and just plain spiraled. Got kicked off the team but eventually enlisted. He was honest. He stood up for the weak. He was sometimes mean, but only to those who deserved meanness. Jack found it hard not to love him.

"I'll take a look at the booster," he called.

"Well, you'll talk about it, at least."

"Hey, speaking of talking, could you please quit talking about the van Gundy woman?"

"Why? She say something to you?"

"How could she say something? She doesn't exist."

"Oh, you go to hell."

"You start these rumors and I have to deal with them. People expecting one of them to show up as basketball coach."

"So you're telling me one of Sarah van Gundy's brothers wouldn't be an asset?"

"I'm telling you Sarah van Gundy doesn't exist."

"Jeff van Gundy rebuilt the Knicks from scratch and here you think you're better than his own flesh-and-blood sister."

"I don't think I'm better than anybody."

"That's some arrogant shit is what that is."

"Maybe better than you."

Elvis shook his head. "I hope you go to hell with a basket of soggy fried chicken, you and your arrogant redneck bullshit backward ways," he called, halfway across the field now, middle finger of his right hand raised high.

Jack smiled and was headed toward the parking lot when his phone went off. He was determined to ignore both his mother and sister on principle—he was going to the damn luncheon, could they not take his word for it?—but it was his old Citadel roommate Justin. Justin was an obgyn in Maryland, having taken over his father's practice in a brick storefront in downtown Cumberland. Jack swiped the screen and Justin was yelling, *Jacky-boy!* before he could get the phone to his ear.

"You sorry son of a bitch, what are you doing?"

"How are you, Justin?"

"About three sheets to the wind, you silly bastard. Sitting over here in the bar of the Westin in Greenville. It's seventy bucks for two ounces of Pappy but I guess that's why I went to med school. You get those tickets yet?"

"Catherine's getting them."

"Good woman, your wife. What about that daughter of yours, she still coming?"

"That's the plan."

"Thank God all her genetic material came down the maternal line. The brains, the looks."

"You *are* drunk, aren't you?"

"You know how many babies I delivered this week?"

"Enjoy the day, my friend."

"The morning, evening, and afternoon," Justin said. "I intend to enjoy it all. It's rare I get loose."

"Noon tomorrow?"

"High noon, my friend," Justin said. "Oh, and I forgot to say, my daddy came with me. You want to talk to him?"

"That's okay."

"Hang on. Here he is."

"That's okay, just— Hi, Dr. Paulman. How are you, sir?"

"Old," he said. "Also decrepit. Is my drunk son bothering you?"

"No more than usual, sir."

"I'd cut him off but he's no better sober. He ask you how many babies he delivered this week?"

"He did."

"Damn him. That's my line. He stole that from me."

"He doesn't really have the delivery down. Not like you."

"Well, he's always been the stupidest of my children. Three lovely daughters and you're bound to get one like him."

He could hear Justin laughing and cursing in the background, his foul mouth begging for the phone back, and Jack thought: that. That's what I want. They were father and son, business partners, gentlemen doctors in a world that no longer allowed such. Yet there they were. They were as close of friends as he'd ever known a man and his boy could be. In any other circumstance, Jack would have been jealous. But all he could muster in this case was awe, a smooth appreciation of how rare was the thing he was witnessing, and a gnawing desire to have that same closeness with his daughter.

"Jacky-boy?" It was Justin back on the line. "Wake up, you sorry bastard. Listen—"

But what Jack heard was the bell going off to signal the end of third period/first lunch and the start of second lunch—his daughter's lunch. If he wanted to see her—

"Hey, Jack?"

"I gotta run."

"Just listen a minute."

"I gotta run. I'll call you later."

He hung up and started quickly back through the parking lot toward the building and into the crowded halls. It seemed louder now, livelier, and he hustled to the cafeteria where the lunch line had already formed along one side of the room. Boys, mostly. The girls sat at tables with Diet Cokes or expensive fruit-infused energy drinks.

He looped the room's perimeter, said hello to a few students, a couple of teachers on lunch duty. *You haven't seen Lana, have you?*

No, sorry, Coach. Want me to page her?

No need, no need. Thanks, though.

He was about to head for the library when he saw her coming in from the courtyard. She was in a faded Alice in Chains concert tee that had belonged to Catherine, the lettering no longer visible but he knew it, remembered it. She paused for a moment to thumb her hair back over her ear. It was the gesture even more than the shirt that put him in mind of Catherine two decades ago, and seeing it he felt a flood of tenderness that pressed from the corners of his eyes so that despite the risk of losing her in the crowd he looked away.

When he looked again he saw her standing with The Boy.

Jack didn't approach them. He just watched. They appeared to be in some sort of argument, The Boy coolly indifferent. His daughter plaintive.

Jack might have stood there all day had his phone not started to vibrate with an insistence that signaled a message from God. But it was only a text from his mother: *Have a wonderful time at the luncheon, honey!*

Tom Greaves stood in the gravel parking lot of Sertoma Field, three Styrofoam plates balanced in his right arm, and wondered what to do. He had already watched his father drive away, had waited for him to come to his senses, acknowledge his haste, his mistake, his *whatever*, and come back and pick Tom up. But Richard Greaves wasn't coming back. That much was clear.

His father was drunk and upset and—most relevant here—gone.

Tom looked back at the crowd.

He could get a ride with Jack, but Jack, naturally, was nowhere to be found either.

It was only Tom and the wet weight of the würst and sauerkraut that was just beginning to dampen his right sleeve.

He gave the horizon a last, hopeless scan.

Okay, Dad. Whatever.

He knew he shouldn't have come, shouldn't have agreed to the luncheon, the ninja performance, or the podcast. Shouldn't—if you got down to it—ever have returned from his European pilgrimage, even if the very word—*pilgrimage*, seriously?—embarrassed him. Yet he had. Stupid, Tom. Very stupid. But if he had come back to shake himself of any sentimental ideas of home, that he had certainly accomplished.

There'd been no need to shake himself of any sentimental ideas of himself.

He'd gone to Prague, waited, regretted, decided to return and then decided not to. Then, this morning, Ivana had answered his late-night email plea—*What if I came back?*—and the decision he had kept putting off could no longer be put off.

Now is the time if you are ever coming back

That was all it said. Not a word more. Not even a signature.

Not that he deserved anything more.

He was headed back toward the tent when he saw a woman waving.

"Tom Greaves!" she was calling. "I thought that was you."

It took a moment for his brain to fire but then it did.

"Evelyn," he said. "How are you?"

"Fine, late, running out. But so glad I caught you."

"Me too. How are you?"

"Oh my God. I don't know where to start. Selling real estate now. After the divorce—I don't know if you had heard about things with Brad's dad?"

Tom nodded solemnly. Brad was Evelyn's son, and Tom's classmate in high school and at Calhoun College. Brad was a trial lawyer now, like his father, Evelyn's ex-husband, apparently. Not a friend exactly, but as close to a hometown acquaintance as he still had.

"Hey," she said, "did I see your dad earlier or am I dreaming?"

"No, yeah, I mean you did. He just… How's Brad?"

"Wonderful. In town actually. Did you hear he's getting remarried?"

"Good for Brad."

"Hey, you two should get together. Catch up and all."

Evelyn gave a perfunctory report. She was in her mid-fifties, still slim and attractive, vibrant in the way one has to be who takes up a new career—a first career, Tom supposed—years past forty. She had always been on the philanthropy circuit—all the fundraisers and receptions attended alone while her husband was off defending Big Tobacco.

"So how are you?" she wanted to know.

He was fine, of course, he was dandy. He was inhaling some serious Schweinebraten, but truly, couldn't be better. Besides the stranded part, besides the whole adrift thing out of which he was making high art.

"So tomorrow night," Evelyn was saying. "I know Brad would love to see you."

"Yeah," Tom said, his right sleeve beginning to dampen. "Sure."

He gave his number and regretted it instantly. The point was to disentangle himself, right? But maybe it was also to debase himself, to go home and put on his ridiculous costume, to climb and leap and then, after the laughter, after the podcast, after—it seemed—drinks with Brad, to fly away, to salvage what he could of his life, to make it his own.

"Wonderful!" she said. "So glad to see you, Tom. Love to the family."

He smiled, hugged her, and was halfway across the footbridge when she called.

"Oh my God! I totally forgot. You're doing your performance tomorrow."

"Oh," Tom managed. "Yes, indeed."

"It sounds fantastic. I'm headed out of town for work but I will so totally tell Brad. "

And then she really was gone, and Tom stood alone at mid-bridge, smelling the honeysuckle and cut grass. Fall was the season of scent, a luxurious time, as if you'd forgotten in the intervening months what it was to smell the earth. First rains and ferns and mown hay in the evening cool, and then the cracked drying of the world, the particulates of autumn—the fallen leaves and scattered buckeyes—all crushed underfoot. Finally, the smell of fir and pine. For a moment he felt something flame in his body. He felt alive.

But then—

He shook the thought from his head and looked one last time just in case his pickup was coming back. Naturally, it wasn't.

"Whatever, Dad," he said aloud, but only barely, and took out his phone.

He was about to summon an Uber when someone called his name—*Mr. Greaves?*—and Tom turned to find a man approaching him, something extended from his right hand.

"Tom Greaves?" the man asked, as that something articulated itself as a badge. "I'm Daryl Abbott. I'm with the Federal Bureau of Investigation." He stopped in front of Tom. "Could I have a moment of your time?"

It was lunch by the time Nayma had dropped her grandparents off at home and made her way back to campus. The sight of the Greaves woman had upset her abuela so much Nayma had fairly dragged her to the elevator. By the time they got to Dr. Agnew's car her abuela was in tears and Nayma got it, she did.

The Greaves woman looked bad, her ancient tiny self a tent of bones pitched beneath a tangle of tubes and monitors. It didn't seem fair that she would die like that. But it surely didn't seem fair to have to go on living. Her abuelo just shook his head solemnly and went back to work: somewhere there was grass to be cut.

Nayma parked the Oldsmobile and headed for the front doors. You could sneak out of the school but you couldn't sneak in. The building was a well-concealed fortress of alarmed doors and hidden metal detectors and the only way in was through the entrance where, surely, someone would be waiting on her. They would suspend her, they would express their utter bafflement and complete disappointment in her and she could try to explain but, honestly, how? And why? The college applications had all been submitted, the essays written, the recommendations sent. In a few months she would leave Germantown and never come back. When the time came—when the *money* came—she would send for her grandparents. She would send for her parents, too, if they would come. Their plan, her parents' plan, was for Nayma to make enough money to *show* the gringos. Her plan was to make enough money to become a gringo. The money would make her untouchable. Her US citizenship and a bank account in the high six digits. That wasn't wealth—that was protection, that was stability. It was some foundational basement-like thing that most people so thoroughly took for granted they couldn't begin to understand why it was even a concern.

It was what she couldn't explain to the people who would question her in another sixty seconds when she walked through the front doors and confessed to having stolen Dr. Agnew's car (if she said he had freely handed her the keys, he would likely be fired and she wasn't about to let that happen). Why did you go, Nayma? If there was a family problem, why didn't you come to *us*? Why didn't you let *us* help you? Us…us…us…us… As if by the mere commingling of their white skin and good intentions they could unravel the messy knot of her life. As if skin pigment and evangelical hope would solve her problems.

The first world gallantly stepping in to save the rest. It was like a commercial of which you had to take immediate advantage: act now so that the white saviors, the ruin and solution to all your problems, can intervene and help you help yourself. Not a handout, Nayma. (How satisfied they would appear across their shiny desks or behind the ovals of their rimless eyewear.) Not a hand*out*, but a hand *up*.

Why won't you let me help you, Nayma?

Because you can't, she wanted to say.

Because how could you solve something you couldn't begin to understand?

And she wouldn't be blaming them. She would be attempting to explain to them.

Her life was a construction of wildly misaligned but nevertheless moving parts that were labeled individually as money, language, acceptance—or the lack of all three—and to tinker with one, to attempt to explain one, was to risk the others, and at this point, so close to her exit, so close to the end of her sentence at the Germantown Motel, so near the end of the next door meth mites clawing their open sores, so near the end of the creepy Elvis trying to lure her into his pickup, so near the end of so much, the last thing she was going to do was take chances.

Yet there she was.

She put her hand on the front door and took a moment to study herself in the reflection. But it wasn't her own face that caught her attention, but the face beyond the glass. It was turning away. The school receptionist was walking away from the reception desk and into the warren of hallways and offices behind her. The woman, Nayma realized, was headed to lunch. The woman, Nayma realized, was giving her a chance.

She didn't delay.

She pulled open the door and shot through, past the metal detector and the sliding second door that was—thank you!—unlocked before the bell could chime her arrival. Behind her she sensed the woman returning—*excuse me?* she heard—but

Nayma was already in the main hall crowded with lunch traffic.

She walked as fast as possible without running. The woman was still behind her. *Excuse me? Miss? Stop please.* But she wasn't stopping, not now and not ever. She rounded the corner and ducked into the girls' bathroom—okay, she was stopping now, but this was strategic. She went to the farthest stall, locked the door, and crouched on the closed toilet seat so that her feet wouldn't show. Behind her the main door swung open. A moment later it swung shut again. She was slow to lower herself, careful. But when she came out she saw that she was alone, which meant she was safe.

She took a moment to collect herself at the bathroom sink. Splashed her face, smoothed her clothes. She put her phone on vibrate and took Dr. Agnew's keys from her pocket. That was all that was left: to return his keys, get to her next class, get *through* her next class, her next day, week, month, and so on until she could walk. To where, it didn't matter. So long as it wasn't here.

Middle hall was less crowded. She passed the band room and the art rooms and turned right toward the English wing. A few couples were pressed along the walls, blowing little bubbles of privacy out of the otherwise wholly public. Girls with their shampooed hair showing their vulnerable throats, staring up at the guys who hovered over them. The guys were all lean. Elbows and knuckles and bristled hair. Eighteen-year-olds in lettermen's jackets kissing girls in cheerleading skirts. Resting their sweaty hands on hipbones. No one looked at her. She heard the guys whisper and the girls giggle as she walked past. Giggling in such a way as to let her know how different she was. Giggling to make certain she was cognizant of how ugly and brown and plain. That there was nothing of the strawberry to her, she knew this. No strawberry-blond hair. No strawberry sun-kissed skin. Never the right shoes or jacket or skirt, never the eyeliner that was oh-my-God-so-on-point. She felt the heat of it on her skin: the remarkable extent to which she didn't belong. Even if she did.

You're a woman with a torch, Nayma.

She tried not to walk faster.

You can do this, Nayma.

She tried to keep her head level, her eyes straight ahead. She rounded the corner—she was near the gym now, past the groping and giggling—and then heard something. Whispers. But not whispers directed at her. These were people oblivious to her presence, somewhere back within the chain-link lockers where the sports equipment was kept. They were arguing. She could tell that much. Two people—a boy and girl.

She peeked around the corner.

The hall here was long and dim and off-limits. Along one side were framed portraits of Germantown athletes who had gone on to play college sports. Point guards and goalies and fast-pitch catchers in jerseys that read Warriors and Tigers and Chanticleers, all hung in their 8½ by 11-inch frames. Along the other side was fencing, behind which were large, wheeled bins full of everything from shoulder pads to orange traffic cones. The voices, the arguing—it wasn't louder now so much as more intense—was coming from there.

She shouldn't stop.

She knew she shouldn't stop. This was an unnecessary detour, yet some part of her—there was no use not admitting it—really did believe she was a woman with a torch. Someone put in the world to light the way, to take care of others, be it her parents, grandparents, whoever it was now tucked back among the portable soccer goals and arguing very volubly for him to *stop, please. Please don't, Stinson* and she—

Stinson?

Then she knew why she had stopped: she had stopped because she recognized the voice.

Two quiet steps forward and she recognized the faces. It was Stinson Wood and Lana Greaves, both from English II. Stinson had Lana backed up against the wall just like all the other boys. But unlike all the other girls Lana wasn't kissing his throat or idly fingering whatever faux-gold chain he had hung around his neck. She was pushing her fingers into his blandly handsome face. She was begging him to stop.

Nayma had her hands on his jacket before she realized she was even moving. It was the white heat they talked about in books. The sort of thing that allowed mothers to lift wrecked automobiles off their trapped children. Except it wasn't a car she was lifting but what turned out to be a kite-thin boy who was mostly hair gel and lip—*fucking bitch!*—and a cloying cloud of Axe Body Spray. Possibly PULSE but also possibly SCORE. She pushed him behind her where he arranged himself, smoothed his hair, his clothes, all the while repeating to her what a fucking bitch she was. This declaration was prefaced by queries. Things like: What the fuck do you think you're doing, you fucking bitch? Or: Why don't you mind your own fucking business, you fucking bitch?

But Nayma registered it as no more than noise.

She had one hand on Lana Greaves's shoulder, the other extended toward Stinson Wood, palm raised like a crossing guard arresting traffic.

"Are you okay?" Nayma asked.

The girl—she was a girl, fourteen and lithe, a blond reed in running tights—nodded but said nothing. Then Stinson grabbed Nayma's hand and knocked it aside.

"I asked you what the fuck you think you're doing, Chiquita Banana?"

"Leave her alone," Nayma said.

"Fucking make me, how 'bout it?"

"Touch her again," Nayma said, "and I will." And with that she watched something terrifying take place: she watched his face morph from normal human rage to something approaching a mask of smug—that word again—comprehension. It was a look that said he was suddenly realizing this wasn't a joke, this fucking Mexican bitch was serious. That she didn't get it. Yet who the hell was *she* to interfere with *him*? Did she not know how this game worked? Then the bafflement was replaced by the sort of cruelty that only comes in very deliberate calibrations.

"I will have your daddy's ass on the banana boat back to fucking taco-town by sundown," he said. "You understand that?"

"Just don't touch her again."

"She wants me to touch her. Don't you, Lana?"

They both looked at the girl who said nothing.

"Don't you?" Stinson said again, but Nayma cut him off.

"Let her speak for herself."

She couldn't, or wouldn't, and this seemed to fuel something deeper in Stinson, some tertiary rage that had thus far remained buried.

"Fuck you both," he said, and straightened his jacket a last time. He started past both so quickly Nayma thought he was about to hit her and she jerked her head to the side where it bounced off a locker. Stinson paused, but only to smile and continue down the dark hall. Halfway to the corner he stopped and turned. "When you're ready to apologize you know where to find me, Lana," he called. "And you, you fucking illegal bitch. You will suffer for this. I promise you that."

And then he was gone.

Nayma turned to Lana and was about to speak but then she was gone too, all unsteady legs and bed-headed hair.

Gone up the hall.

Gone around the bend.

Gone, Nayma could only hope, anywhere but back to him.

Somehow, despite a chemical overload of Xanax, bourbon, and the quickly gathering shame of having taken, *stolen* really, his son's truck, Richard found the little Chevy straining its way up the last rise of Kings Highway, past the old green dumpsters, past the lawns of neighbors with swing sets and carports and concrete stoops crowded with couches and fans and box heaters until ahead spread the green expanse of home: pasture and trees and at the top of the hill's sweep, his two-storied slate-shuttered castle, all of it contained neatly within the fence, which he realized was past due for a new coat of paint.

He had made it the five miles from Sertoma Field by pitching his body forward, head leaned unsteadily above the wheel. That, and ignoring the phone that was steadily buzzing. He had intended to turn it off but had to achieve escape velocity as fast as possible. Otherwise, he risked falling back to earth. He hadn't so much made the decision to leave as been overcome by it: he had simply turned the ignition and dropped the pickup into first. The rest was in God's hands, or the hands of someone other than Richard Greaves.

He put in the clutch and slowed.

With the window down you could smell the hay, baled and drying in the field. You could see the front pasture, and that was the point. The land was meant to be seen, not touched. The land was meant to serve an aesthetic purpose. The land signaled safety and beauty, a wide buffer against the encroachment of the larger world of immigrants and infectious disease. His grass and trees and blue sky against their plastic shit. His feathery breezes against their suicide vests.

Then it occurred to Richard they would be coming for the land too.

But he wouldn't let that happen. Everywhere folks were selling their homeplaces.

Family farms poured over for another subdivision.

Pastures cut for modular homes.

It was the one thing he wouldn't let happen. He'd been wrong about so many things. It was possible he'd been wrong about everything. But about the land he knew he was right. You protected the land. You saved the land. Eventually everything quit you, eventually everything failed. But not the land.

He popped the truck into fourth and accelerated.

He wasn't going home.

He was going to see his ma.

But he had to make one stop first.

Long's Country Junction sat at the intersection of Kings Highway and Smithy Road. Of course, it wasn't the Long's anymore, hadn't been for the last two years, but it was difficult not to feel possessive. Richard had grown up working there alongside John Long, his closest childhood friend. Pumping gas and ringing up Cokes. Watching old man Long cut meat while his wife stirred the hotdog chili they served to the farmers and construction workers who would wander in each day about noon with their pouches of Red Man and their OSHA-approved boots. Long's Country Junction had become The Country Junction when the Longs were forced to sell it to a local family that staggered into church every Easter Sunday smelling like the debauchery of the previous 364 days. It became Metromont #17 when the Greens sold it to a conglomerate out of Atlanta. They—the conglomerate, whoever the hell they were—had cleaned out the fresh produce and moved in giant coolers of Budweiser and Red Bull. The old feed shed where the Longs sold everything from grass seed to marine pellets had been converted into a liquor store. The meat case held porn.

Richard was grateful John and Maggie Long weren't alive to see it, which was a way, perhaps, of assuaging his own guilt in the whole sordid affair. He passed the parking lot where the old Southern Bell pay phone had once stood and pulled into his ma's driveway.

He knew his disappearance would just be starting its ripple, Tom calling Clara calling Jack—he remembered his aborted call to his oldest son, remembered and regretted it. He fumbled out his keys and walked into the foyer.

"Yesenia?" he called. "Alphonse?"

He stopped when he felt his phone buzzing in his pocket. It was Jeff Duncan, still eating his brat on the dais for all Richard knew.

"What level of panic should I be at here?" Duncan asked.

"What's wrong?"

"What's wrong? By God, it seems like everything."

"What are you talking about?"

"Lord, Richard, are you serious? All I know is that I came back from lunch—and what the heck happened to you at lunch?—but I came back to find the FBI asking for documents."

"What sort of documents?"

"Bank statements. Loan information."

"What did you tell them?"

"What do you think I told them? I told them to come back with a subpoena and by God I think they are. One thing, Richard. Just tell me you didn't swipe that chicken money."

"Jeff—"

"Just tell me you didn't slide that money into another account like nobody was looking."

Richard put his arm against the wall.

"Nobody *was* looking."

"Oh Lord."

"What do you want me to say? You sure weren't asking any questions about where the money came from at the time."

"All right."

"You weren't complaining then."

"All right," Duncan said slowly. "That's fair, I suppose. We needed the money and I didn't ask. But what now? What are you thinking?"

"I'm thinking…I've been wondering all afternoon whatever happened to Paul Harvey?"

"Is he with the chicken houses?"

"No, Paul Harvey. The radio guy. Remember him? *The rest of the story* and all that."

"Paul Harvey?"

"Is he still on?"

"He's dead, I guess."

"You're probably right, you probably are."

"Richard, listen—"

But he wasn't, and pocketed his phone only to realize he was still clutching the bottle of Elijah Craig. He took the revelation as sign he was meant to drink, and he did, deeply and satisfyingly, gulping until he heard what sounded like someone moving in the basement. He corked the bourbon and planted himself at the top of the stairs.

"Hello?"

He took a step.

Could it be—

"Teddy?"

Teddy had fallen from the back of the tractor when he was seven, their father bumping through the field, the day's work complete. Richard had been away at the Citadel so it had come secondhand. But it wasn't hard to imagine: Teddy perched above the tire for the late summer ride to the barn when the tractor hit the slightest of bumps and he flipped forward, beneath the tire he'd been sitting on a split second before. It was a ridiculous way to die but that made it no less real, and Richard's brother no less dead. Their father had descended deeper into his silence then, and who, Richard supposed now, could blame him?

"Teddy," he croaked.

He came down the last few steps around the landing but instead of his brother, he saw a large rat retreat to the far corner. By the time he hit the overhead lights it was gone, rustling its way behind a cardboard box of old clothes.

Then he saw the blood.

It had pooled just beyond the toes of his wingtips, so glossy and black he had taken it for paint, spilled and dried in the previous millennium, back when Richard was a boy and nobody died and nothing could hurt him. But it was her blood, his ma's. He bent by it, extended his finger, but he didn't touch it. She had fallen here, cracked her head on the concrete, and this blood had run from the onionskin of her scalp. His ma's blood.

He looked around the shelves for something to clean it with, a towel, an old shirt, and that was when he noticed his father's company photograph. Two hundred or so young men on the bleachers at Fort Lee, Virginia. Anson Greaves was on the extreme right and what Richard noticed now was how soft he appeared, his father's nineteen-year-old face, the paunchiness only hinted at by the gathers in his uniform. Barely sworn in before he was shipped out, waving goodbye, a brass band on the quad playing Sousa, the girls waving. Two dead in France before you ever even thought to wonder about them.

Richard Greaves held the frame lightly, like a man unprepared.

His father had told the story only once, Richard just a boy.

How he had been in Bayeux for months, barely off the lip of the beach all that lovely summer and fall of 1944 when, just before Christmas, word came of the breakthrough near Bastogne. That day he was taking a jeep to town—everybody loved him in town—and then, right by the camp gates, he sees a guy he knows or knew, and he is flagging him down, arms waving. Let me in, turn around, get back.

Why? What's going on?

Buddy, ain't you heard? We're headed to the line.

And that night they did. The chaplain blessing them as they filed onto a waiting C-47. The man throwing holy water and right then you knew it was bad, the way he flicked it from his fingertips. The sting of it as they filed forward. Shuffle-step, stop. Shuffle-step, stop. Someone mooed like a cow but there was no heart in it. Everybody knew what was coming. His father lapsing then into silence while Richard sat on the carpet and pushed his metal Farmall from his knees.

He put the frame down and found a box of Morton's rock salt left over from the days his father would run the ice cream churn. It had solidified to a brick but when he knocked it against the block wall it cracked enough to sprinkle over the blood, to absorb it, the colorless crystals swelling into rubies.

Only when the blood was covered—it appeared a snow of granular iridescence—did he remove the papers from inside the Pioneer woodstove, a thick sheaf stuffed into a brown envelope and hidden in the grate. The papers were a record of every transaction Richard Greaves had made over the course of the last three years: the transfers, the forged signatures—everything he'd done to John and Maggie Long. Every move he had made regarding the garment mill—he'd recorded them after bank hours when he was alone. It wasn't so much paranoia as a sense of work ethic, a sense that certain things belonged on the clock and certain things did not. Once he made the copies or printed the forms he would bring them here, come by to check on his ma, and then slip down to the basement where he hid them in the stove.

He took out the envelope and tucked it beneath his arm so that he carried both the bourbon and his financial life, one seemingly no more important than the other. He would keep it with him, he would take it with him. He would take his father, too, and he slid the photograph out of the frame and folded it in with the documents. He would go to the hospital to see his ma. The rest didn't matter, and for a moment he thought about driving over and handing Duncan the file. *Here it is, partner. Do with it what you like.* Because what a fool he'd been, what an arrogant fool. He'd hand it over and laugh, hope for eight to ten at some low-security joint. Because it was coming to that. He saw her already, Annie Smalls, reading him his rights, tears in both of their eyes. Saw it, knew it, didn't care. The best he could hope for was a sentence suspended down to a few years of cutting grass in denim slippers. What was the worst?

The worst was the humiliation. Watching his wife and daughter cry. The judgmental smirk on Jack's face. The way Tom would stand by him no matter what. Facing those alive would be bad. But maybe worse still would be facing the ghosts, the old-timers like his father.

Maybe he would just skip it. Maybe he would turn himself in, save Jeff Duncan the trouble of turning state's evidence. But that was the Xanax talking, that was the alcohol, that was poor Francis Gary Powers with his suicide pill of shellfish toxin.

That was—Lord, Richard—that was Death talking.

That wasn't talk for his ma's house.

That was talk for the grave.

The luncheon was a city tradition dating back to the first

Oktoberfest ("first of the modern era," as the city's website put it) in 1965. The original Oktoberfest dated from the earliest settlers who founded Germantown in 1850 but had ended with the advent of the Great War. Apparently, it had taken the two decades between V-E Day and the weekend's return for the simmering anger to cool enough to unpack the bratwurst and potato salad. It had never cooled for Jack's grandfather, who had bled his away across Europe with Patton's Third Army, arriving in Pilzen, Czechoslovakia, with two purple hearts and a pronounced curl in his trigger finger.

Jack pulled into the asphalt lot at Sertoma Field. He was ten minutes late and only a few parking spaces were left. Walking, he saw the cars of greater Germantown, the councilmen and businessmen, the city managers and attorneys, the clergy and coaches. Jeff Duncan's hulking black Excursion was sleek and shining and impossible to miss. He was maybe fifty meters away though he would have to walk the length of the park to get to the swinging bridge that spanned the creek. The tent was better than an acre, white and centered in the grass, guy-lined and staked in every direction. Out of one end snaked a queue of Germantown's finest, donations in hand. He watched them enter empty-handed on the right only to exit with a plate of brats and kraut on the left. Styrofoam cup of sweet tea.

An oompah band was playing.

People wore lederhosen and felt hats.

There was a stand for iced coffee, a hot dog cart.

Jack felt his phone go off but didn't touch it. It had been going off, he realized, more or less constantly for the past five minutes. His mom, his sister. Maybe Catherine calling to say she had the tickets. Maybe Justin drunk at the Westin bar. Possibly Lana, *Dad, went by to see you…* But he didn't look. He stared at the tent. He watched the mayor go to the microphone and the sound system wheezed and cleared and the mayor said, very distinctly, *It's a great day to be in Germantown.* When he began to lead the crowd in the Pledge of Allegiance, Jack found himself walking back to his truck and turning onto the highway. He didn't know exactly what it was he was doing, only where it was he was going.

Arby's sat on Main Street beneath the sort of neon ten-gallon hat better imagined on the Strip in Vegas. It was mostly empty inside, a few senior citizens, a few construction workers, and Jack felt the sort of peaceful deceleration most associate with places of worship. The heat lamp. The bright tile. The yellow CAUTION sign propped by the newly mopped bathroom floor. It lent a strange sense of calm. Even the smells were healing. The highly treated and preserved beef. The fry grease. The chemical cleansers.

He didn't know the boy behind the counter—a smart-looking kid in his early twenties, sufficiently tatted, pierced, and bored enough to qualify as a respectable member of his generation—and he realized how long it had been since his last visit. Weeks, he guessed. No, months. The spring, though maybe it had been winter. January or February, but of this year or the last?

He ordered the five for five.

The kid looked at him.

The five for five being five junior roast beefs for five dollars—5.25 with tax (he had the quarter centered on the bill).

"I don't know what that is," the kid said.

"The five for five?"

"You have a coupon or something?"

"No, it's five junior roast beefs for five dollars."

"What?"

"It's like a deal you offer."

"You mean you just want five junior roast beefs 'cause I can do that?"

"You're saying you don't have the five for five anymore?"

"I'm saying I've never heard of it."

"You used to have five juniors for five bucks."

"Yeah, but the thing is I've never heard of that."

"No five for five?"

"You want me to ask the manager or something 'cause—"

"No," he said, eyes scanning the menu—and it was true: there was a dollar menu (when did they get *sliders?* and what respectable citizen of Germantown would be caught eating one?), but junior roast beefs were a—dear Lord!—dollar sixty-five each. So five juniors would be—

"Eight forty-six."

"I'm sorry?"

"That'll be eight forty-six. Or did you want a drink?"

"No. Water."

"One water."

"In a big cup, please."

"Big cup's a dime."

"For what, the cup?"

"The cup, ice, whatever." The kid touched the register. "Eight fifty-six. For here, right?"

Jack limped to the table, so out of sorts he arrived sauceless and had to get back up, pump three little paper thimbles with horseradish, and limp back over. It was like coming home to find the home no more, burned to the foundations, the ashes still warm. He unfoiled his first sandwich and imagined some soldier in the Civil War walking from Appomattox to find his family scattered. Was that dramatic? Well, not dramatic so much as insane. But he felt it. The little comforts falling away that signal nothing so much as the passing of life. Forty-four years old and though he was in the early autumn of his life, it was autumn still. And there was so much undone, and so much done poorly, and so much—he felt that same inner failing that caught just below the solar plexus, almost a hunger—so much that would remain undone.

He didn't taste a thing.

He ate five sandwiches and drank two cups—big cups, dime-sized cups—of water but it was sustenance, not pleasure. But that wasn't exactly right. The truth was, he did taste something: he tasted the chemicals, he tasted the falseness. The simplest of pleasures ruined, though he had no idea why.

When he got back in his truck, he checked his phone and

it was just as he expected: texts from his sister and mom, but nothing from Catherine. Justin had sent a photo of his right hand, middle finger blurry and extended. Then he saw the missed call from his father and that caught his eye. There was no voicemail—he hadn't expected there to be—but the mere fact of the call mattered.

He brought up the log: his father's name, his father's number.

He could call his father with the literal touch of a button. He could put his finger to the screen and there his father would be, present in his ear if not his life. He sat there for a moment, considering the possibility of dialing, knowing all the while he wouldn't.

Eventually, he put away his phone and pulled onto the street.

If it was important enough he wouldn't escape it for long. And if it wasn't, then to hell with it. He had a million things to do back at the school.

But more than anything else, he wanted to see his daughter.

Dr. Agnew's door was unlocked, his laptop frozen on a YouTube video of the soul singer Charles Bradley. But thankfully he wasn't at his desk. Nayma put his keys by a paperweight bust of Evelyn Waugh (Where on earth did you buy something like this?) and had turned to go when she heard him.

"Nayma, my dear."

It found her like a spotlight, his voice. One of those cartoon moments where the searchlight settles on the bandit escaping prison.

"Dr. Agnew," she said. "Your keys."

"Yes?"

"They're on your desk."

"My keys."

"Right there by Mr. Waugh."

"Mr. Waugh, my dear. As in *War.*"

"Right there by Mr. War."

"All right, dear," he said. "Thank you."

He cocked the great moon of his head and asked, "Shouldn't you be at lunch?"

"Shouldn't you?"

"Touché, my dear."

She was by the door when he spoke again.

"Excuse me, Nayma."

She stopped but didn't turn.

"If you ever want to talk about anything," he said, "I've been told I'm a good listener."

She said nothing. Her face was just beginning to hurt.

"I know what it is to need a good listener," he said. "I also know what it is to be an outsider, a stranger in a strange land. If that's not too saccharine a thing to admit. Realizing fully that perhaps it is."

She stood silent and still. He was moving, walking, but not toward her. He had exited through the back door into the materials room and she realized she was alone, and then she realized she was crying and couldn't stop. Crying for her mother and father and grandparents. For the scared girl in middle hall and the grandmother she did not yet know was dying alone. Crying for creepy Elvis, who was back from the war and lonely. Crying for Dr. Agnew, who was simply lonely. And crying for herself. These stupid tears.

These stupid, stupid tears she felt running down the copper of her robe, beneath her torch, past her book, and over her sandaled feet, these tears gathering in the vast harbor she suddenly realized surrounded her life.

Someone was cutting the cemetery grass.

Richard could hear the push-mower proceeding through the rows the moment he stepped out of Tom's pickup. He'd been in the process of heading to see his ma but then, somehow, he'd wound up not there but here, the graveyard of Golden Corner Baptist Church.

His father and brother were here, maybe that was it.

His old friend John Long and his wife Maggie were too. John had died eighteen months ago, two days short of his sixty-fifth birthday, and Maggie, displaying not so much the loyalty that defined their relationship as simple companionship, had wasted no time in following him, dying of loneliness—defined for her purposes as a cerebral edema—six weeks later.

Or maybe it wasn't loneliness.

Maybe it was shame.

Richard had the papers right there against his chest, after all. Embossed by Mountain Empire Bank and signed by Richard S. Greaves, his signature leaning and sweeping in a way that implied authority. The documents were countersigned by John, who wrote in the tiny block letters befitting a man who had lived not by silence, exile, and cunning, but by hard work and modesty. His old childhood buddy Richard Greaves, his old friend who had once worked side by side with him at Long's Country Junction, had persuaded John and Maggie to refinance their store in order to invest in his garment mill. That it was a scheme should have been evident from the start, but the Longs were cursed with an honesty and sense of trust as infuriating as it was beautiful. When things eventually went awry, Richard had foreclosed on the Longs, forcing them to sell the store at a ridiculous price. It must have been as embarrassing to Richard as it was to the Longs, and in choosing discretion as the better part of valor, both died rather than cause a scene.

He knew he should be ashamed to be here.

Yet here he was, Richard Samuel Greaves among his dead.

He approached slowly, waiting for the man running the mower to make his turn toward the far corner before he walked the few steps to the family plot. The cemetery was no larger than a basketball court and there, occupying one neat section, were the graves of his father, Anson, and his brother, Teddy. There was space between them for his mother. There was no space for Richard. His life, always so entangled, had, through the most basic process of living, become separate.

He took a knee by Teddy's grave and felt the sheaf of papers and the photograph of his father crumple against his gut. Poor Teddy. Richard had spent his childhood riding soapbox racers through the pasture on which the basement of the new house had eventually been dug. Soapbox racer. Even the name felt antique, but at the time it had been something sleek and daring. Richard and his friends would build them, these roughhewn things consisting of little more than axles and wheels salvaged from old Radio Flyer wagons, all of it bolted to the frame of a packing crate. No way to steer or brake beyond dragging a foot or simply throwing oneself into the passing grass. It was dangerous, or dangerous enough, and they had used Teddy as their unwitting test pilot, their four-year-old Chuck Yeager.

Teddy never said no, but he never said yes either. He simply stood there, green eyes wide in his ghost-white face, mouth open in fear or disbelief or whatever it was he was feeling. Richard reckoned it was fear, but also the fierce loyalty Teddy attached to his older brother. Without a word, he would climb in and they would push him off the slope, the cows lowing and trotting out of his way until the racer lost a wheel or hit a dip or barreled through a stand of poke salad and Teddy was thrown from the wreck to roll on down the hill of his own accord.

Richard had been what? Fourteen, fifteen. Certainly too old for such. A few years later he'd be a cadet at the Citadel and Teddy would be right here, buried, dead, frozen in deep time. Yet what had seemed tragic at the time—Teddy's death—now felt defiant. That Richard had gone on living, and not only living, but living well, happy. Those days when he was home from the army on leave, engaged and waiting for his discharge. Both he and Clara immortal that summer weekend he drove all night from Fort Polk down in mosquito-ridden Louisiana to arrive at dawn and collapse on the couch. She woke him at midday, the sun climbing and her parents away so that they walked slowly, wordlessly through the house back toward her bedroom, hands joined in a knot of complicity. They had moved so deliberately through that weekend, through that entire decade, that he remembered it now as a sort of swimming. Sun dogs and damp sheets. The window AC kicking on in the night.

He heard the mower cut and looked up to see Alphonse wiping his hands on a bandanna and walking toward him.

"Mr. Greaves," he said, and raised one dirty hand.

"Alphonse." Richard felt a disproportionate joy, having felt so alone, and yet… He started to rise but then, failing at such, lowered himself fully onto the ground. Alphonse sat across from him. "How are you, Alphonse?"

"I'm well, Mr. Greaves. How is your mother?"

Richard hesitated what felt like a beat too long.

"Better, I think. On my way to see her."

Alphonse nodded.

"Hey," Richard said, "I owe you and Yesenia." And without thinking felt his hand go to his wallet. "The trouble y'all went to."

"No, no." Alphonse stayed him with a hand. "You needn't."

"Well, I'd like to—"

"I'd rather you didn't, really."

"Well, okay, but I'm grateful. I always will be."

"And she's okay?"

"Stable, yes. That's what they tell me."

"Good, good," Alphonse said, and there was something in the way he spoke, Richard noticed. It was perfect English, intelligent English, formal and nuanced. Had he always spoken this way? Could it be that Richard had simply never noticed?

"I'll tell you the truth," Richard said. "I think it was a miracle."

"Do you?"

"The absolute hand of God."

"Divine intervention."

"Exactly."

"And you believe such is possible? Divine intervention."

"Well, I mean…don't you?"

Alphonse plucked a blade of grass and studied it. "Do you know Paul Éluard, Mr. Greaves?"

"He's the man runs the fish place in Seneca?"

"He was a French Surrealist."

"Then, no, I don't believe I do."

"He said—he was a poet, and he said, 'There is another world, and it is this one.'"

"'This one.'"

"Yes."

"So two worlds," Richard said. "Like heaven and hell?"

"Maybe. Though I think sometimes, perhaps this one and the one you touch through memory."

"That's just one world though."

"Perhaps so."

"But what about heaven?"

"What about it?"

"I mean…I don't know, I just…if you mean…"

"If you mean do I believe that when I die that I will go on being me in some celestial realm, then I don't know, Mr. Greaves. But I doubt it."

"I wish you'd call me Richard."

"I wonder if I would even want that."

"To go on being yourself?" Richard said. "Yeah, I understand. It might be easier to just disappear. But then sometimes I think about when my children were young…"

"Memory."

"Yeah. What did he say again, this poet?"

"There is another world, and it is this one."

"That's a kind of confounding thing to say. Damn confounding actually. But still, no hand of God? No intervention?"

"In this world?"

"In any world. In *my* world, I guess."

"I don't know. I've seen moments when divine intervention would have been most appreciated had it transpired. I think if God intervenes, he has a strange sense of timing."

"I guess he does."

"Or maybe I mean humor."

Richard nodded. "Talking about humor. Francis Gary

Powers," he said, staring off at the trees. "I been thinking about him lately. You know who I'm talking about?"

"Does he run the fish place?"

"No, no. He was a pilot. Got shot down?"

Richard looked back into the distance and back at Alphonse.

"Hey, can I show you something? I want to show you this."

Alphonse nodded and Richard reached beneath his hoodie and shirt, removed the sheaf of papers, and fanned them across the grass between them.

"What are we looking at?" Alphonse asked.

"Evidence of my grand malfeasance."

"This is your bank?"

"Maybe was."

"Past tense?"

"Maybe."

"Should I read them?"

"No." Richard began to gather them. "No need. I just needed to show someone."

"You're in trouble, Mr. Greaves."

"I really do wish you'd call me Richard."

"You're in trouble, Richard."

"Yeah, Alphonse," he said, and packed up the papers. "I believe finally I am."

Jack had just made the left off the highway into the student parking lot when he heard the horn and felt his head jerk up, wary and suddenly alert. He expected some disgruntled father ready to ram him, the logical expression of frustration over one's son playing second-string JV ball. But instead of a frowning parent he got his sister, smiling.

Emily's minivan was parked in a visitor's spot and she stood beside it, Kyle on her hip.

"Well, well," she said. "Back from somewhere other than the luncheon, I presume?"

"Dad call you?"

"Tom."

"Tom, shit. Well, I hope you didn't come all the way over here to give me a hard time."

"Who, us? I don't think so. I mean we didn't come *only* for that, did we, Kyle?"

"They were sitting on the dais, Emily. In front of everybody."

"So you skipped out?"

"Went to Arby's."

"Arby's? What are you, twelve?"

"They got rid of the five for five."

"Wait, that's some boy band Lana's into, right?"

"It's a combo meal they used to have. I've only been ordering it since maybe the fifth grade."

"Wow. End of an era."

"It *is* the end of an era."

"Oh no. I was afraid of this. Kyle, we've got to get out of here. He's about to get all *nostalgic* on us." She looked at him. "You're not going to start explicating the lyrics of some obscure Pink Floyd song, are you? Digging deep into the catalog?"

"So you did come to give me a hard time."

"Maybe, but—hold on." She dipped her head to her son. "Kyle says that was only part of the reason." She lowered her head and nodded thoughtfully. "Actually, he's changed his mind. It's the only reason. I told him there was also the skit we had to rehearse—"

"Ah, right."

"Yes, right. But he feels that's tertiary, at best."

"What does he feel is secondary then?"

"I don't know, honestly. He can be somewhat coy at times."

"Five months," Jack said. "I think that's the coy stage."

"Yep, I remember it from *What to Expect When You're Expecting*. Five months is coy. Around six months they go all meta on you."

"How long are you going to be here?"

"We rehearse fifth period. Then the pep rally is sixth period, so the rest of the day."

"Come by the office if I don't see you before you leave."

He pulled around to the athletic wing and parked. He had forgotten about the skit. For years Emily had volunteered with the school drama club. This year she was helping with the homecoming skit, a twenty-minute stroll through local history that would be performed at the day's pep rally.

Inside, his assistant was eating a plastic dish of paling iceberg lettuce from the cafeteria. She handed him a sheaf of messages and he took them into his office and shut the door. He had been hoping Catherine would have called already. He had a couple of hours before the pep rally. After that, would come the physical setup: the traffic cones and ticket booths. By five, the parking lot would start to fill up with tailgaters and parents, and at best he would be in crisis-management mode. If he was going to talk to her, now was the time. Of course, he told himself, calling was the not wisest of moves. He should trust her. She said she would get the tickets and she would. And he did, he did trust her. But also—

He touched her name on the screen before he could think about it anymore, half-expecting his call to go straight to voicemail. To his great surprise, she picked up immediately.

"I have them, honey. Didn't I promise I would?"

"I knew you would. I was just—"

"I know, it's fine. Really. But listen to me for thirty seconds, okay?" That was the point he began to worry: her continued calm, her intent soothing. "I know this is important to you, I do. But I wonder if *maybe* you haven't built something up in your mind here and the reality *maybe* isn't going to match up. I know Lana—"

"She's excited to go."

"I know she is, and I know she'd love it. But she texted me."

"Texted you what?"

"She's fifteen, Jack. All her friends will be at the Oktoberfest, hanging out."

"Really she could do that anytime."

"Really she couldn't. You know Tom has this performance everyone is going to."

"Oh my God."

"It's ridiculous, I know. I just want you to be prepared if she doesn't want to go to the game, and know that it isn't you or the actual game, it's—"

"They have female cadets now."

"Jack."

"Like 10 percent of the corps."

"That's great. It really is. Yay, progress. I'm just saying you can't take anything personally with a fifteen-year-old."

He knew that too, he thanked her, he loved her. His teenage daughter was what? A teenager. A daughter. Big deal, right?

For the rest of the afternoon he was all motion. He checked the field, he checked the concession stand, stopped by the music room where in their giant acoustic cavern the band was playing "Smoke on the Water." Coach Groban was in his office, eating Tums and watching game film.

"Misdirection," he said when Jack sat down beside him. "Look at this." He ran the tape back, the players in blurry reverse. "Watch their I-back. Everything they do is misdirection. I worry about our linebackers overcommitting."

"They know what to watch for."

"Watch their quarterback's feet."

"They've seen the tape. They know what to watch for. It's just execution at this point."

He kept popping Tums like Sweet Tarts, his tongue chalked white.

"We need this win, Jack. We need it bad."

"You've prepared them. They're fired up, right?"

"Oh, they're ready to run train on them sons of bitches. No doubt about that."

"Then just keep 'em focused," Jack said, standing. He put his hand on Groban's fleshy shoulder. "Coach. Listen to me. You've got this."

And then he was off again.

Fifth period he stopped by the auditorium to check on rehearsals. The stage was full of pioneers and pinafores, Cherokee braves, soldiers kitted out for a half-dozen different wars. Emily stood by the footlights, a clipboard in her hands, a pencil behind one ear.

"A cast of thousands," he said, sidling up beside her.

She kept her eyes on the stage.

"You again."

"Where's Kyle?"

"Asleep in the wings."

"Seriously?"

"I've got Strom Thurmond's second wife, three suffragettes, and like twelve Southern belles watching him."

"How many people are in the cast anyway?"

"I'm not sure at this point, maybe fifty?"

"In twenty minutes. Jeez, Emily."

"Hey, we've got two hundred years of history to cover here."

"How about the CliffsNotes?"

"This *is* the CliffsNotes." When she finally looked at him it was with the same withering dismissive look he remembered from childhood, a look that signaled not so much disdain of Jack as complete immersion in the skit. "Did you need something? We have like five minutes to rehearse the Great Depression to Watergate."

"You're doing Watergate? As local history?"

"Did you want something, Jack?"

"I'll see you at the pep rally. Break a leg."

By the time he got there, the pep rally was in full swing.

While one of Groban's assistant coaches stood at center court introducing the seniors who came jogging through a veil of smoke and Metallica, Jack looked for Lana. It hurt him to think she would be among the bored, but he wasn't surprised to find her there. Up near the bright windows, beneath the banners for this or that regional championship, she sat beneath the long part of her hair, staring wistfully at the boy who had paid her absolutely no attention.

Stinson Wood.

The son of a bitch.

It was all Jack could do not to climb the bleachers three steps at a time and do…do what? Jerk a knot in his ass, his father would say. And yeah, that would be satisfying, fulfilling in the most reptilian way. Instead, Jack just stood there, his own arms crossed, a scowl on his face: a six-foot-three and rapidly aging likeness of his daughter's dissatisfaction. How strange that he was both deeply pleased that the boy was ignoring her but also insanely pissed off. His worst nightmare was Stinson Wood paying his daughter attention. His worst nightmare was Stinson Wood *refusing* to pay his daughter attention. The pep rally wasn't over, but he decided he'd had enough and slipped out the side door, nodding to a few no-doubt jealous teachers as he went.

It was better outside. The day appeared honeyed, the air softening. He surveyed the parking lot and athletic fields that extended to the line of pines. Around them rose the mountains, blued with haze and distance, long shadows beginning to spread down the velvety slopes. He was preparing for one last stroll past the practice field when the bell went off.

Lana!

He surveyed the parking lot. She would come out the side doors and he needed to be in the best possible position to intercept her without appearing to intercept her. Should he be standing there? Should he be casually walking and then *Oh, hi, honey!* or maybe he should hustle past indifferently and then turn at the last second? He reminded himself he was a grown man, an athlete, a veteran. An authority figure, for goodness' sake. Then he decided the casual approach was best.

He positioned himself at the bottom of the parking lot so that he could look up the slight grade (a 3 percent fall to facilitate drainage—he'd read the specs himself). The plan was simple: keep an eye on the door and the moment he spotted her begin walking briskly toward her. Pretend to be occupied, be looking at—

At what?

He found a flyer in his pocket, a schedule actually. Be

pretending to look at the schedule. Walk quickly—you're important, after all, busy. If his timing was right—and much of his athletic career had been built on timing—he would meet her around the second or third light pole, just past the crush of the outrushing crowd. It would be perfect: a little eddy of calm in which they could speak for a moment and Jack could put to rest his fears and Catherine's warnings about Lana's indifference to the Citadel game.

In fact—and here was genuine insight, here was bold thinking—in fact, he could move preemptively, offer the tailgating, but not the game. *Hey, honey, you know I was thinking about tomorrow. And I know we talked about the game, but I was thinking what if we drove over. Hung out a little for the pregame and then got you back in time for the Oktoberfest. You could see your friends. And I know Tom is doing some sort of ninja thing that's supposed to be way cool.*

(Should he say that, *way cool*?)

But, Dad, she would say, *we had planned on the game.*

I know, honey, but maybe we can sort of do both: go to the game and make it back to the Oktoberfest.

But I don't care about the Oktoberfest.

You don't?

Of course not. I just want to go to the game with you.

Okay. Ridiculous. Back up, because she wasn't going to say that. It would be more like: *Are you sure? We talked about the game.*

And Jack, swollen with magnanimous grace, would be all: *Honey, you're fifteen. You need to see your friends too. Right? And your dumbass uncle* (no drop the *dumbass*) *your uncle would love to have you there so why don't you ride over with a friend.* ("Riding with a friend" was something he, normally speaking, actively discouraged.)

Well okay, Lana would say. *If that's fine with you.*

Hey, it's my idea, right? It's absolutely fine with me.

Then—oh crap—he realized he hadn't been watching the door. Or had been, but not with the sort of intensity required of the act. Maybe thirty kids had barreled out. A quick scan revealed that Lana wasn't among them and if his heart didn't exactly settle, it at least eased back to something approaching overdrive. He slapped the flyer in his hand, watched the door harder. A couple of times he actually twitched forward thinking he saw her but not yet, not yet.

And then there she was!

She was out, she was heading—where was she heading? She was speed-walking down the sidewalk, almost as if involved in her own game of casual intercept, and then he saw that coming toward her was Stinson Wood, actually appearing bashful, actually appearing to possess emotions Jack thought two or three evolutionary stages beyond him. Jack stopped to watch them, stopped to watch his daughter hesitate, to try and act as if she was anything other than interested in this boy. And without meaning to, he found himself actually pulling for her, willing Stinson Wood forward and he came! He actually came! When Stinson Wood chastely kissed the cheek of his daughter Jack felt a wave of relief, and then a wave of something else. Not anger, not rage. It took him a moment to place it. Then he realized what he was feeling was sadness.

He decided to walk away.

And then he did, turning toward the stadium.

When he saw Emily come out of the gym and scan the parking lot for him, he ducked behind the press box and walked the long way back to his office where he proceeded to shut the door and pull the blinds. He wasn't hiding, of course. He would never hide. All his life he had tried to do the opposite of hide: he'd tried to set an example. He worked hard at his job, loved his family. Cut his parents' grass and quoted Robert E. Lee without irony. When his National Guard unit was called up, he had hated the thought of going to Iraq, hated the thought of leaving Catherine and infant Lana, hated the thought of being complicit in someone's death. But he'd gone because that was what you did in life: you did what you were supposed to do and you didn't complain about it.

Jack wasn't exactly a devout man, though he believed nominally in all the things he'd been brought up to believe. But something had changed in Iraq. He'd started to pray, to really pray, to *beseech the Almighty*. He became religious because in some sense, at least in that place, it was impossible not to be. Only he realized it wasn't God he was praying to. Jack was praying to America, because that, it turned out, was what he believed in. America as both ideal and idea. Except lately he'd realized he no longer did believe, and maybe never had. It was, he supposed, why he was so adamant that Lana see the female Citadel cadets. Because were she to become one, Jack knew a part of him would be restored, his faith, his belief, or at least his ability to pretend to believe. There was a growing sense that just maybe everything his life had been built on, from the Citadel to that week he'd spent with Catherine and Lana in Blowing Rock, wasn't some grand consecration of some grand principle. It was simply what had happened to him, past tense.

That seemed like a revelation, or whatever comes just before revelation. He was breaking open, changing, he had only to stay open to whatever was next. Instead, he'd become scared, become the sort of person who dispensed advice, who said things like *you only regret the chances you don't take* or *hard work is always the right answer*, which was true enough, but not the person he thought he'd become. But maybe that was answer after all: we never become the people we think we will, we just stand there shivering as the pipes go past, the flags, the drums, the pennants, stand there as they are going by, and then keep standing there, long after they are gone.

Now he heard something: someone was knocking at his door. He raised his head from his hands. The knocking was intent, but he thought if he just sat still enough long enough it would go away. It didn't, and eventually he got up and opened the door on Emily.

"Caught you," she said.

"Caught me? I'm in here working."

"With the lights off and the door locked? You're in here hiding."

He gave a little shrug of surrender and moved back from the door.

"You want to come in?" he asked.

"Kyle's in the car. Just came by to say we're taking off."

"Okay."

"Hey. Did you see it?"

It took him a moment to realize she was talking about the skit.

"Yeah, it was great."

"Come on. You didn't even see it."

"Yeah, I did."

"It's okay," she said. "I know you've got a lot going on."

"I'm sorry. I missed it."

"I can see the sorrow on your face."

She poked at him. Jokingly, he realized.

"Hey," she said. "I saw Lana. Who's the boy?"

"Stinson Wood."

"Wow. Does he live up to the name?"

"Afraid so."

His sister stood in the doorframe, her nod somewhere between commiseration and a muscular tic.

"She's fifteen," she said.

"People keep telling me that, her age."

"Well, people are right. Don't lock yourself in here in the dark, all right? People will start to think you're—oh, I don't know—let's say depressed."

"I'm not depressed."

"Of course, you aren't. All the more reason you need to get up." She stood there, waiting. "In lieu of my standing here all day would you please offer some sign of life? Perhaps as a consideration of shared paternity?"

"I'll see you later, Emily."

"All right then, later," she said, and then she was gone and he was back at his desk because he wasn't depressed because how could he be?

He looked out the blinds at the still-mostly empty parking lot. The JROTC kids were putting out orange parking cones. Soon enough the first tailgaters would arrive and Jack could either hide out in his office and sink deeper into whatever it was he was sinking into, or he could get out and move. It wasn't really a choice at all—which made it all the more troubling to realize he was treating it like one. It was actually possible to disappear for most of the night, to lock the door and not come out, to—

"Goddammit, Jack Greaves, you sorry son of a bitch." Jack jerked his head up to find Elvis in the door. "Get up and get out here already."

"Elvis."

"You're goddang right Elvis. Now get your lazy ass up."

"What are you doing in here?"

"Getting you out the door. Your sister said you were in here all hiding and depressed."

"I'm not hiding."

"She said you'd say that."

"I'm not depressed."

"Said you'd say that too." He grabbed Jack beneath his arms. "Get up, you bastard. And don't you dare hug me or some such crybaby shit like I'm your mama, God bless the woman." He gave Jack's arms a tug. "Come on now. You're spoiling my good mood."

They marched down the darkened hall beneath the emergency lighting and out into the softening day. It was nearing five now and if dusk hadn't yet drawn near enough to whisper, it at least no longer needed to shout.

"Jack," Elvis said.

Then he remembered the missed call from his father, the strangeness of it.

"Coach?" It was Elvis again. It was always Elvis. "I got to mind the field. You gonna be all right if I leave you alone a minute?"

"Just go mind your grass."

"'Cause I give Emily my word I'd keep an eye on you."

"Just go play with your tractor or something, all right?"

Elvis slapped him on the back.

"Hell, yes, that's the spirit. Get mean. Get angry."

"Just go."

"Roger that, boss."

Elvis trotted across the parking lot and down the slope toward the stadium, laughing. Jack watched him go with a pang of nostalgia not only for their youth but for youth in general, youth lost, youth unrealized. People would say about their children: I wished they'd stay that way forever. *That way* being that age, or that sweet, or that innocent. But Jack never said it. It seemed such a facile thing, as if there had been anything more interesting and beautiful in his life than watching his daughter grow and learn and change. But then there were days he could nearly weep at the thought of never seeing Lana again at four or seven or any other of the ages that were forever in the receding past. The bedtime prayers, *I wished for everyone to have a good night and for no more wars,* the family portrait she once spent days drawing only to soak in milk, the way she sat in his lap in the mornings in her fuzzy footed pajamas zipped to the hollow of her throat. The smell of her Surf's Up Suave Kids shampoo and conditioner. The way she kissed his hands.

The air had gone muzzy with sentiment and he wiped his eyes.

Somewhere behind him the band was assembling—he could hear them through the block walls—and any moment they would come marching out for a last practice stomp on Elvis's well-groomed field.

Jack found his golf cart and drove away.

Clara Greaves was folding clothes when her phone went off. It was the hospital, calling to say Richard's mother was in intensive care, and had been all day.

"Dear Lord. Why didn't anyone call?"

"We did call. We talked to your husband, Mrs. Greaves."

"My husband?"

"This morning."

"Oh," Clara said. "I see."

Though, of course, she didn't. What she did do was call Richard immediately. He didn't answer and she left him a message. Hung up and dialed Emily but at the last second decided not to tell her. She decided not to tell Jack either. There was nothing he could do until the game was over. Why make them both miserable? She decided she would go to the hospital first, figure things out. If things were urgent, she'd call them right away. There was no sense spreading panic. But she needed to tell someone, and that someone turned out to be Tom.

She sent him a text and headed for the hospital.

Nayma rode the bus home, her morning commute in sad reverse. The butterfly of her day crawling back into its chrysalis, she thought, and then laughed so hard she snorted and the little foundlings playing with their secondhand phones and DS systems all looked up at her and snarled their peanut butter-and-jellied faces. Not that she cared. She watched them slag down the bus steps into a brilliant fall afternoon, the sun high and clear, the breeze light. The sort of day that called for tennis or baseball, for lounging on metal bleachers feeling happily exhausted and very American.

But Nayma didn't feel anything but tired.

She waited for the last of the children to exit and followed them into the parking lot of the Germantown Motel, unlocked the door, and threw her bag on the table. No one was home, and though she could hear the television playing through the wall at maximum volume, the meth heads no doubt having found their fix and now blissed into chemical nirvana, it was relatively quiet.

Her face hurt from where she had hit the wall.

It wasn't anything terrible, just a dull throb that beat like a reminder of something she'd rather forget. So what to do? She didn't know, and she finally poured a bowl of Fruity Pebbles and sat down to spend a half hour staring at the same paragraph, the sad Joads in slow transit. The citrus groves and starvation, the constant unavoidable nature of suffering.

How the world was bricked out of such.

Suffering atop sacrifice atop more suffering still.

She wanted to be moved by it but somehow wasn't. At least not today.

Get up, she told herself, and walked to bathroom to find her face beginning to discolor.

She broke her funk with mascara, and why shouldn't she? Showered, dressed, actually *decided to play an active role in her grooming and appearance* (her mother's plaintive words). Foundation, eyeliner, lipstick. She made a kissy face in the mirror and looked ridiculous, but also looked, maybe—could she say it?—cute? She had to layer the right side of her face, but by the time she was finished the half-moon of bruise was completely hidden.

So… It was after five now and she knew the high school parking lot would be beginning to fill with all the people who were not exactly her friends, but the people closest to such. Everyone her age would be there, and while she hadn't made a practice of attending, she had been a time or two, roaming the edges of the stands with Regan, and she'd had fun. She could admit to that: the fun.

She sent a text to her abuela and another to Regan.

There was no response from her abuela but Regan said she'd meet her by the concession stand at seven and Nayma texted back *yeah, cool, c u then* even if she only half meant it. But that left her with time to fill and she didn't think she could stay in the cramped apartment with *All My Children* bleeding through the drywall.

For a while she just sat on the concrete stoop. Beyond the parking lot was Blue Ridge Boulevard, which was actually little more than a median strip of kudzu and the shells of a few collapsing shotgun houses. To her far left was a Free Pentecostal Church and to her far right the rear of a Burger King from which the smell of cooking meat and fry grease (truly one of life's loveliest smells) carried.

She wished she had a drink.

It was a strange thought.

By and large, she didn't drink. Okay, she totally didn't drink with the exception of one afternoon back in Mexico when, driven by boredom and the unending glare of sunlight, she had gotten into a bottle of ancient brandy and spent the afternoon so lethargic on the couch her mother had threatened her first with chores and then with a trip to see the doctor. One other time too: with Regan, in solidarity, the night and early morning after the Pulse nightclub shooting in Florida when Regan had shown up teary and drunk, one false eyelash dangling in the sort of slow-legged peel Nayma associated with caterpillars clinging to the windshields of moving vehicles. They downed peach-infused vodka and Regan had eventually passed out on Nayma's damp shoulder, leaving her alone with her headache and the night's slow lurch.

She stood out of the beach chair, the plastic cross-straps impressed in the back of her thighs, and straightened her shorts. Inside she found her abuelo's beer, nine cans of Victoria ordered neatly in the back of the mini-fridge. She popped the top and drank off the suds. Mexican beer. Cheap Mexican beer, actually, which was probably why he drank it: it was canned nostalgia.

She took a deep pull, the beer cold enough to ache her throat, and already could feel it going to her head, the temperature as much as the alcohol.

She checked her phone—just after six now—and surprised herself by realizing the beer was gone. She was even more surprised when she found herself holding a second.

The third beer didn't even register.

She brushed her teeth and started giggling at the sight of her foamed mouth, the plastic brush wiggling. It wasn't really funny but also it very much was, and she knew, good as she felt, she needed to get a handle on herself.

And she did, maybe she did, though next thing she knew she was in a taxi headed for the stadium so, okay, maybe she didn't. Either way, she got out by the highway and, like three thousand of her fellow Germantown citizens, found herself walking toward the gate, student ID pulled from her pocket.

She was waiting to enter when Regan materialized beside her.

"Oh my God," she said. "Your eyes."

Nayma thought for a moment she was referring to her shiner, the great blue contusion that ringed her right eye. Then realized she was admiring her makeup.

"Love, love, love," Regan said, and squeezed her arm.

Nayma felt a little tug of such, of love, of acceptance. So much so that she was actually smiling as they entered the stadium and passed the concession stand already crowded with excited white people.

They went down the bleachers and started around the track that encircled the field.

Love, she was thinking, love, and was thinking it right up until the moment she realized someone was following them, and that someone was Stinson Wood.

Richard parked on the shoulder, two wheels abutting the drainage ditch still thick with wildflowers and weeds, two wheels on the highway's edge. A string of cars stretched a quarter mile down to the stadium, which from where Richard stood appeared as a well-lit bowl, the band on the field, the stands full. He took out the Elijah Craig and held it so that it was backlit against a distant bank of floodlights. It was almost gone now. How much left? A third—which was maybe a generous estimate. Four fingers, he thought, and took a swig. Three and a half fingers now, and he decided to take another swig, 'cause why worry with the fractions?

He planted his feet and drank.

Three then, and he tucked the bottle inside his windbreaker against the bank file and the photograph of his dead father so that it pulled the tight fabric tighter still over his left shoulder, a sagging square appearing where his heart should have been. It was fairly low-rent, staggering around with both a sheaf of indictment-worthy papers and a bottle of liquor flush against his gut, but at least he felt fortified, at least he felt ready.

He steadied himself, left hand on the truck, and waited for the dizziness to pass. When it did, he found he was in the uncut grass, hidden behind Tom's pickup while out on the highway people passed, families and couples and packs of teenagers filing toward the gates. He let them go, touched the bottle again through the nylon of his windbreaker. It was bulging just beneath the twilled embroidery that read MOUNTAIN EMPIRE BANK and that seemed significant though he couldn't say why exactly. Heart of glass, maybe. Something new there, or maybe something that had been there all along, but he had only now noticed. Age. The heart's calcification.

When he turned forty he'd had a brief encounter with the urgency of age. It happened one morning when putting on his socks he discovered a strange thin bone along the bottom of one foot, nothing painful or even sore, but something so tenuous and seemingly fragile that he recoiled. Then he checked his other foot: it wasn't there. There was some asymmetrical thing happening here, something loose or misaligned, and it occurred to him it wouldn't fix. Whatever was wrong would stay wrong. He would live with it, and he would die with it.

But before he did, he had to find Jack.

He put both hands on the still-warm hood of the truck.

The plan was simple. Get to Jack and then get to the hospital and see his ma.

What he would say to Jack he didn't know. Only that he would say something, or perhaps nothing. Perhaps he would just stand there and confirm that his oldest boy was all right.

It seemed like enough.

He began to wade through the shin-deep grass, five or six cars past Tom's truck before it occurred to him that his pants were likely covered with beggar-lice and why not walk on the road, Richard, you old fool?

But even that was an effort. Something about the level ground made him too self-conscious. On the grassy slope it was normal to stumble; his sloppy ramble seemed more than necessary—it seemed morally correct. But out on the shoulder he felt exposed, like he was giving off light, glowing with guilt and incompetence. The same light that had surely radiated from him at the luncheon if only he'd had the sense to notice.

But no one else seemed to notice either.

The parking lot was full of tents and foldout tables, tailgates lowered and covered with blankets and there was your buffet. There were your boxes of chicken from KFC or Bojangles or Ingles. Plastic tubs of coleslaw. Biscuits. Tea. Bottles of liquor and Solo cups of beer even though alcohol technically wasn't allowed on school grounds—you just had to be subtle about it and not act a fool. There were Germantown War Hog flags and pennants, and the mascot, a great upright razorback who appeared as a gray horse but for the tusks, was hugging kids and posing for photographs. Radios played sports talk out of Greenville or Classic Country off Sirius XM or Bob's Country Diner from over in Toccoa.

He passed the line of latecomers easing through the traffic barrels, waving parking passes at the JROTC kids, backing into narrow spaces. Horns. Voices. The band down on the field switching abruptly from "Smoke on the Water" to the "Emperor's March."

He kept walking.

The Rotarians had a tent, the Lion's Club, the Chamber of Commerce with a table of promotional literature, chatting lazily about absolutely nothing. All of them calling out to Richard. *Hey, Richard. Hey, brother, come here a minute,* and he smiled and waved and nodded, but never did he stop. He had momentum now, a head of proverbial steam, and if he stood at just the right angle, tipped back to his right a bit more than normal, the outline of the bourbon was barely visible beneath his windbreaker.

He fished the tickets from his pocket, same seats for the last thirty years because civic duty is what it was.

Now, let's see—

Where was Jack?

Down on the field warming up, he guessed—from where he

stood he could see the skeleton offense in the far end zone—then, no, Christ, Jack wasn't playing. It wasn't 1992. He was likely on the sidelines though. He was the AD now, not the tight end.

He handed the ticket to the boy by the gate. The boy tore it and handed him the stub.

"Welcome to the new stadium, Mr. Greaves."

And, yes, of course, it was the new stadium, the new school, the new everything. Except his poor dying ma—there was nothing new there.

"Help," the boy was saying. "Mr. Greaves?"

"What's that?"

"Do you need any help finding your seat, sir?"

"No, I don't think so. Same place as always, right?"

The boy smiled and Richard stumbled on. He was seeing things now, new eyes, fresh eyes. What was that thing in the Bible about the scales falling away? The Veil lifting? His ma would know, his wife would know. Hell, Emily would know. The one thing he had done right, maybe the single thing: surrounding himself with these wise, patient women. Maybe—surely—the only thing…

But then he felt himself sliding into self-pity, that wallowing trough in which he'd be mired if he kept this up, so he let the thought go. Lots he'd done right. Wasn't Jack running this show, the AD, the boss of it all? Count that as right. Put that feather in Richard Greaves's cap. And Tom—where was Tom?

Tom was not a subject he wanted to consider at the moment. Abandoning his son like that. Taking his truck—

"What can I get for you, sir?"

The way he'd driven home, huddled over the wheel, and then at his ma's house, her blood—

"Sir?"

He looked up.

Apparently, he'd somehow found his way into the line at the concession stand.

"Sir?"

He scanned the offerings.

"Yes?"

"What can I get you?"

"Maybe...how about a Coke, large."

"A large Coke, yes, sir."

"And a box of those M&Ms."

"What else for you, sir?"

What else?

"A pennant?"

"Yes, sir."

"And those sweatshirts. How big are those sweatshirts?"

"The hoodies? They come in small, medium, large, XL, maybe double XLs back here somewhere. I would suggest the XL for you."

"One of those too then."

"The purple?"

He nodded. "Let's do the purple."

"All right, sir, that will be. One moment here. Forty-eight even. Out of a hundred?" Had he passed over a hundred-dollar bill? "Let me make sure we can break this." He held the bill up to the light, squeezed one eye shut. "All right, great, I've got, let's see, fifty-two coming back to you, so that's..." He felt the Elijah Craig sagging his jacket and leaned back, shoved the bills in his pocket, and stood upright. The man was staring at him, grinning idiotically, waiting, and Richard realized the man was waiting on him to move, to walk away so the next customer could step forward and Richard did, he walked away, found the bathroom—they were grand and clean with two long troughs where everyone pissed together like true red-blooded Americans should—and unleashed a torrent of browning urine, dehydrated but fortified, dehydrated but not afraid.

He pulled the hoodie over his windbreaker (should have gone for the XXL), locked himself in a stall and poured half the Coke into the toilet and what was left of the Elijah Craig into the cup. He refitted the lid and left the empty glass bottle propped in the corner like a little shrine where he might offer up his own shame.

Yet he was happy—bourbon and Coke!—how could he not be?

There was something about drinking it through a straw—he was walking to his seat now, pennant tipped over one shoulder—the acknowledged good-hearted silliness of it. That first summer with Clara when it was clear he wouldn't be sent to Vietnam and clear she loved him, that they would make a life together. That this beautiful, graceful woman somehow loved this redheaded fireplug. Lord! *That* had been life through a straw! Sucking it up and loving it, knowing how ridiculous he appeared but not caring either. Life spread before them like a banquet table, something for just the two of them and all they had to do was sit down and eat.

He was walking, sipping, waving…

Hey, Richard!

What say, Mr. Greaves!

He found his seat, lowered himself down, careful with his drink, took a sip, another.

"Hey, man."

He remembered those summer trips to Garden City, pulling into the sand yard with its patches of grass, the house itself up on big pylons, giant telephone poles lifting it like the lunar lander they'd watched just a decade prior. Sitting on the deck, drink in hand, wicker chairs, Clara smiling at him while inside the children lay sleepy and sunburned and watching *Voltron.*

"Excuse me."

"Hey, brother. Excuse me, but I think you're in my seat."

He looked up into the gigantically bearded face of a gigantically red and fleshy man. A larger less evolved version of Richard, he stood there with his Yeti cap and Mossy Oak jacket, a box of popcorn in one hand and the hand of a young boy in the other.

"J 17," the man said. "That's my seat."

There was a long moment of incomprehension. The man

looked like something that had come out of the forest, having spent the last few years living in a cave. Who was this guy? What did he want? He was talking, pointing, and it dawned on Richard that he wanted Richard's seat and it dawned on Richard how insulting this was. Hadn't he had the same season tickets for thirty dang years, hadn't he supported the program through thick and thin, the lean years when they could hardly win a game, made a donation when they needed new uniforms, coughed up another thousand for the stadium fund, hadn't he always—

Now Richard was talking, yelling actually, though even sitting up in the bridge of the listing battleship *JS Greaves* he wasn't quite sure what he was saying. He could feel the spit flying from the man's lips, he could feel the hands grabbing at him from behind, trying to pull him away.

"I don't give a shit," the man was saying, and Richard was being lifted and then—just as suddenly—Richard was seated again. It was a curious situation: had he sat down of his own accord?

Had the man pushed him?

Had someone pulled him?

All three options were in play.

Then he looked up, not into the face of the beefy redneck hermit but into the face of Elvis, good ole Elvis.

"Let me just help you up here, Mr. Greaves," he was saying. "That's right. Come on. I gotcha." They were moving down the aisle, Richard realized, and then up the steps. "No worries here, partner. Come on now."

"Why, Elvis."

"Yes, sir."

"That man. He thought I was in his seat."

"There was some confusion."

"He thought—" And Richard had just enough wherewithal to bring the two tickets from the front pocket of the hoodie, just enough wherewithal to realize he *had* been in the man's seat. They had moved the seats! Jack had! Jack had tricked him, Jack had—

Elvis eased him into another seat. Forty-five-yard line, a third of the way up. Better seats, actually.

"There we go, Mr. Greaves," Elvis said. "All set now."

"My seats…"

"Jack wanted to surprise you with an upgrade, looks like."

"Jack did this to me?"

"Want me to send him up?"

"Jack tricked me like this?"

"I'll just get him up here for a minute. Let him say hello. You sit tight, sir."

Richard watched him go down the steps toward the sideline, watched him slide through the chain-link fence and walk toward the end zone. He was going to get his boy, to get Jack, and it occurred to Richard that was the one thing he couldn't countenance.

He hefted himself up and started back up the stairs for the gate, passing again the well-wishers.

Hey, Richard!

What say, Mr. Greaves!

Somebody asking about the van Gundy boys.

Is it true?

And Richard calling back, *You better damn believe it's true. We'll wind up with both of them as coaches before it's all said and done. Jack won't let us down!*

And one fool punching the other on his fool shoulder. *Shit, I told you so. Happy days are here again.*

You better damn believe they are, Richard called.

Called, but never stopped.

He had no time for that, because it had suddenly occurred to him what time it was.

He headed out the gate and up the road, back toward his son's stolen truck.

At last, at long last, it was time to go see his ma.

The hospital cafeteria was subterranean and somehow green. Multi-hued but all green. The walls, the floor, even the kiosk coffee Clara Greaves carried to the Formica table beneath the fluorescent lights had a sickly tinge. But the coffee was hot and black, and though it scorched a forest of taste buds when she drank, she kept drinking, feeling the heat run through her like something approaching comfort.

She had just come down from sitting with Mrs. Greaves, and while sitting with her she kept thinking—wondering, hoping, fearing, but only a little—Richard would find her there. But he had never come, and eventually, the charge nurse had knocked at the glass and Clara felt her head pop up. She'd been dozing, but perhaps not for long: her cheeks were still wet from her tears.

"Time to go, ma'am."

"Okay."

"I'm sorry not to let you stay longer."

So she'd taken off the mask and gloves in the hall, used the dispenser that spat foamy hand sanitizer with a mechanical flush, and walked to the bank of elevators where, without really meaning to, she found her way not to her car, but to this green cafeteria that smelled exactly as cafeterias always did, overheated and vegetal, all of it carried on an industrial cloud of dishwasher steam. The room was mostly empty. Just a few scattered folks at the scattered tables with their coffee or peach cobbler or plastic-wrapped muffins doing exactly the same thing as Clara: killing time. Not ready to leave, but not ready to go back either.

She took another sip of her coffee.

She really had thought she would find Richard already there. Sitting with Mrs. Greaves, she had felt at peace, but that peace, she realized, had derived from the inevitability of her and Richard meeting outside his mother's room, sitting together there, quietly assembled in what would start as nervous waiting but gradually evolve to acceptance and then actual peace.

This would happen.

She'd felt certain.

Richard would spend the night angry and raging against the

universe but come Saturday he would begin to feel the exhaustion that came before resignation that came before everything else. God would see to it. She felt certain of this too. That God's hand was on every moment of her life—yes. That the larger world, the invisible world, was as real as what was seen—she believed in this. She believed in the invisible. The invisible was everywhere.

But where was Richard?

He must have found out at the luncheon, panicked, and fled.

But where was he now?

She had no answer, and sitting there, Clara made herself think about the war because to think about the war was to realize that however tenuous things might be at the moment, they had once been much worse. Though it was a time in her life she avoided, she tried to conjure it now, to finger her way back through all her old fears, to be ready. As if at any moment the rotation of the earth might reverse and time would spin back on itself to that exact moment Clara had stood in the upstairs living room vacuuming the carpet while *The Today Show* played silently, only it wasn't Matt and Katie but something else. They had cut away to—

The second plane.

She'd seen the second plane hit and thought immediately *Jack*, though Jack was nowhere near New York. Jack was, in fact, just a few miles away at the high school. But then they showed it again, and again she knew, just absolutely *knew* that her boy was going to war.

And then, just like that, he was gone, first to Kuwait and then Iraq, and she spent a year in weepy fear, on her knees constantly, begging God in one moment, threatening him in the next. There was a stream of emails from Jack assuring them of his safety, but she believed it not for one second. He was over there with the bombs and the sand and the way they cut the head off that poor boy right there on camera. Begging *Lord, please bring my boy home to me.* And then, seconds later, demanding *Lord, bring my boy home to me RIGHT NOW!*

And he had come home, of course, he had.

She took another drink of her coffee.

She could feel the burned spot on her tongue, blanched and rough, and pushed it against the roof of her mouth until what was the slightest discomfort became actual pain.

There were tears in her eyes again, a certain dizziness in her head, and she relaxed her tongue. It was ridiculous, sitting here like an angst-ridden fifteen-year-old, making herself feel pain so that she'd feel something. What a cliché that was, and yet she went and did it again, and was about to do it a third time when she thought she saw someone standing by the door.

Her hand went up immediately and Tom cocked his head, found her, smiled, and walked over.

"Honey," she said, standing to hug him. "What are you doing down here?"

"I got your text." He looked around. "Just you? I figured everyone would be here."

"I couldn't find your father," she said. "I didn't want to bother Jack and Emily and—"

"What are you doing down here, Mom?"

"I came to check on your grandmother, honey."

"I mean down here in the cafeteria."

"Oh, guess I just thought… Do you want to sit?"

"Not really…" He looked around and then, as if settling something with himself, sat. "Is it me or is it green down here?"

"I thought you were at home."

"I was, but then when I got your text I just thought…"

"Yeah."

"So no Dad?"

"No."

"Where'd he go after the luncheon?"

"I don't know. I left him a message and thought he would be here. Upstairs or somewhere, but apparently…"

"So you're waiting on him?"

"Yes, no. I don't know. Maybe," she said. "Did you get to see her?"

"Through the glass." He shrugged. "Visiting hours."

"They made me leave too."

"Shouldn't we call everyone?"

Clara nodded. "I will," she said. "Soon. Just not yet. Until I talk to your father I—"

"Listen, Mom. Do you know anything about Dad's work?"

"At the bank?"

"I guess, yeah."

"Like what he does all day?"

"I don't know." Tom shook his head. "Never mind."

"Is something wrong?"

"No, I just…never mind."

He shook his head a second time and they sat for a moment. They were alone now but for the distant voices in the kitchen and the buzzing of the overhead lights.

"I really liked the girl last night," she said. "Sherilynn."

"Come on, Mom."

"She seemed sweet."

"I'm sure she is."

"But you aren't interested?"

"No."

"Then, honey, why did you bring her home?"

"Speaking of," Tom said, "I should probably go. In case Dad's at home."

She stood to hug her son and watched him go. She thought she would go too, but instead she sat back down and took out her phone. It was a number she hadn't dialed in weeks but had thought about every hour of every day.

Too long, she thought. I waited too long.

But she wasn't waiting any longer.

She sent a text and then, sooner than she wanted but longer than she could bear, she called the number she'd memorized months ago.

But he didn't answer.

Oh God, she thought.

But not even God seemed to be answering.

In the hours between the end of school and the arrival of the first tailgaters, Jack was too busy to think about Lana or his father or anyone or anything else. He got another text from his mom checking in and a call from Emily he refused to answer. Justin called and Jack's voicemail was graced with sixty seconds of what sounded like static and distant laughter. Then a text from Justin: *Oops. I butt-called u.*

And then another: *u butthole.*

Classy as ever. But by now the parking lot was starting to fill up and Jack drove his golf cart around the checkpoints delivering the same message to the JROTC kids. *Somebody is going to show up claiming they have the right to park here. They forgot their parking pass or I said they could or whatever. Just let them. It isn't worth the fight.* And then remembering, just before he scooted away: *Thank you. Thank you for doing this.* The band marched back to the band room and Jack wheeled back to the school where the DJ had now assembled speakers and strobe lights and a giant projection screen onto which he would project God only knew what at the post-game dance.

Did he have everything he needed?

He did.

Jack thanked him.

The tables and chairs were stacked and pushed to the sides, and out in the center the cheerleaders were going through their dance routine, makeupped and smiling and jumping and twirling in their glittery skirts to the sound of Pharrell. (They were all so happy! And how could they not be on a high school Friday night, and with such music? Even Jack knew the words.)

Then it was down to the stadium and into the concession stand and up to the press box, checking on everyone, thanking everyone. His security officers—they paid the county for the services of eight deputies every game night—were set to arrive and so he drove down to the service entrance to make sure they had supper—fried chicken and green beans from the Steak House in town—and, of course, to thank them. They were expecting a capacity crowd. A win would keep Germantown in the playoff hunt and, with luck, even give them a shot at the conference title. *But we all know Palmetto will come in here with five hundred screaming fans and we know how they get,* Jack told the deputies. *People will be fired up, kids especially. Be on the lookout for fights. Some of the boys from Palmetto will be looking to get—*

"Buck ass wild," one of the deputies said.

"Wild like a buncha soccer hooligans," said another, head shaved and INFIDEL tattooed on his throat. "Ain't nothing in Palmetto but the elderly and the addicted, and the elderly done all up and died on us."

Jack left it at that.

A moment later, the high-power LED floodlights quaked to life. The sound system crackled. The parking lot was packed, and when they opened the gates Jack was standing there to welcome and—what else—to thank everyone filing through the turnstiles in their purple sweatshirts and windbreakers and hats. He shook hands with the men, hugged the wives. He knew most everyone, and everyone, even the nastiest most self-serving of the parents, seemed to be on their best behavior.

Big night, Coach. The boys ready?

Oh, they're ready. I can assure you of that.

Coach Groban got the boys fired up?

They're champing at the bit. Trust me.

Playoffs, Coach. Tonight's the night.

Tonight was indeed the night, he thought. Though it was difficult to say for what exactly.

He waited at the gates for a full half hour, longer than normal, hoping to see his father and Tom. Last season they had come in together to commandeer their fifty-yard-line seats, his father a little bleary with his thermos of old-fashioneds, Tom smuggling a shaker cup of protein isolate beneath his jacket. He intended to find them, but was called up to the press box and then down to the sidelines and then the team was tearing out through their paper banner to the strains of "Enter Sandman" and it was game time.

It wasn't pretty.

Palmetto was clearly over-matched on the field but almost immediately things started going wrong for Germantown. A fumbled punt. A broken play that should have been a tackle for a massive Palmetto loss but somehow exploded into a seventy-yard Palmetto touchdown. Palmetto led by two touchdowns at the end of the first quarter and you could sense a restlessness in the crowd. They were still cheering but it could turn at any point. Another score, another fumble, and out would come the boo-birds, the chants of *Groban must go!* as ugly as they were premature.

Germantown rallied in the second quarter. A long drive and a two-yard dive into the end zone. A good defensive stop and another field goal. They were at midfield and driving when the half ended, down 14-10 but the momentum had swung. Another time out and a little better clock management and they would have scored again. But that was okay. Palmetto looked tired, Palmetto looked beat. Down on the sidelines the halftime shows began to assemble: the band, the homecoming court. They announced the king and queen, the band played "The Emperor's March," and all of sudden the teams were jogging back onto the field.

Germantown was driving again when he was paged up to the press box.

He climbed the iron steps where one of the student assistants, binoculars hung around his neck, stuck his head out the door.

"There's a woman that needs to see you, Coach Greaves."

"A woman? You mean Lana?"

"No, sir." He pointed to where a tall, red-haired woman stood alone by the edge of the concession stand. "That lady right there."

"Who is she?"

"Don't know, Coach."

"She didn't give you a name?"

"No, sir."

Jack walked back down, the steps ringing with his descent. The woman looked up at him and came forward. He was trying to place her—she looked too young to have a kid on the field—when she produced the badge that identified her as an agent with the FBI.

"What's wrong?" His first words, blundering out before he could think. Except he was thinking, thinking of Lana, thinking of Catherine, thinking of some released prisoner attacking his sister, thinking of the million horrible acts waiting, always, just past the edge of awareness. Only she said *your father*. She was looking for his father.

"You haven't seen him?"

"Not since this morning. What's wrong?"

"Why don't we walk for a moment?"

Jack looked around, suddenly aware that he was having a very private conversation in a very public place.

"We need to talk to him," the agent said.

"About what?"

"That's what we're trying to determine."

"What does that mean?"

"It means when you see him, please have him contact me."

"You can't say anything about what's going on?"

"Mr. Greaves—"

"You show up, produce a badge, and can't say a word about why?"

"Coach Greaves, please just—"

It was at that moment one of the deputies came hustling up, breathless, meaty paw extended. "Coach," he said, putting his hand on Jack's shoulder. "Been looking all over for you. Sorry, ma'am. But, Jack, I think you want to have a look at this."

"Right now?"

"I think you better. Got some kids fighting."

"Serious, or just kids being kids?"

"Serious enough. I think you better have a look."

"Okay," he told the deputy. "I'm coming. Can you give me three minutes here?" he said, turning to the agent.

"That was really all I needed."

"I'll be right back."

"Thank you for your time, Coach Greaves."

"Right back!" he called.

He followed the deputy down the grass slope that ran past the stands into a dark area tucked in the shadow of the locker rooms. They were almost there when Germantown scored and the crowd leapt to its feet. A few fireworks shot from the scoreboard and in the sizzling flashes of red and silver he could see several deputies had corralled someone. It looked like the usual nonsense—a torn shirt, a bloody nose—then he saw two EMTs were bent over a smaller shape that had yet to move.

"What's going on here?" Jack asked.

"This one," the deputy said, pointing to the boy, who was now zipped-cuffed. "He was beating the shit out of that kid over there."

"He okay?"

"He's mangled, but okay. Got the hell beat out of him though."

"That piece of shit—" the zip-tied boy yelled.

But the deputy cut him off.

"You say one more word, son, and your ass won't see the magistrate till morning. You understand me?"

"Fuck you, piggie," the boy said.

"I'll let that slide this time," the deputy said.

The kid grumbled and it was only then Jack saw that it was Stinson Wood.

"He was fighting?" Jack asked.

The deputy smirked.

"That's your goddamn ringleader right there, Coach. There was two more but they ran off. This one wouldn't let up."

Jack walked not to Stinson but over to the smaller beaten shape of a kid he recognized from Lana's class, a ninth grader. He was sitting up now, conscious but battered, with split lips and an ugly gash across his forehead.

"He okay?" Jack asked.

"He'll need stitches," one of the EMTs said. "Likely concussed too."

"We can take him in the patrol car," one of the deputies said. "Leave the ambulance here."

Jack knelt down in front of the boy, who was fourteen or fifteen but appeared ten.

"You okay, son?"

"I'm a girl."

"I'm sorry?"

"I'm trans. I'm female. It should be daughter, I guess."

Jack nodded. "Sorry. You okay?"

"Yes, sir."

"What's your name?"

"Regan."

"What was this all about, Regan?"

She sniffled. She had a small crimped face and the indentations on her upper nose that indicated eyeglasses though they were nowhere to be found.

"I don't know, sir."

"He pick on you before?"

"I don't know. Yes. Sometimes, I guess. But he wasn't after me."

"Who was he after?"

"He was following my friend."

"Why?"

"I don't know. Because he's a racist homophobic asshole, probably."

"And your friend?"

"I made her run. She didn't want to but I kept telling her."

"That was brave of you."

She shrugged, suddenly shy.

Jack nodded and stood.

The deputy who had led him down was waiting for him.

"There's two ways we can handle this," he said. "You can handle it as an issue of school discipline."

"What does that entail?"

"That entails me cutting off the plasti-cuffs and escorting him off the premises. Otherwise it's on you to do as you see fit."

"What's the second way?"

"Second way is we put him in the tank."

"You arrest him?"

"We'll keep him out of gen pop, but yes, sir, we arrest him. It would be serious business. Like I told him, he wouldn't go before the magistrate till tomorrow at the earliest."

"What do you think?" Jack asked.

The deputy looked at the girl, at Regan, who was standing now, her face already beginning to purple and swell.

"He beat a defenseless boy—"

"Girl."

"Roger that. Beat a defenseless girl and wouldn't have stopped had we not shown up. He's plenty old enough to prosecute. I believe I'd lock his ass up, Coach. If it was my call."

Jack walked over to Stinson Wood who scowled, twisted up his face, and looked away as if in disgust. He appeared to be on something, his eyes brittle-bright. But what Jack kept seeing was the look on his face when he had kissed Lana's cheek, the softness there, the tenderness. Had he imagined it?

"Tell me what happened here," Jack said quietly.

"Fuck off," Wood said.

"I'm trying to help you, son."

"I ain't your son."

Jack looked at the deputy who nodded his head like *you can't talk to entitled shit like that.*

"Tell me what happened here and maybe I can help you."

"I don't want your help."

"Yeah, but I'm thinking at this point you might need it."

"Fuck off, Greaves."

"Coach?" the deputy called.

"Stinson," Jack said patiently, "let me help you. Look at me."

"Fuck you."

"Stinson, look at me—" And suddenly he was, Stinson

Wood was looking directly into Jack's eyes, and then he was speaking in a voice perfectly controlled.

"Hey, Greaves," he said, "fuck you and while you're at it, fuck your uptight daughter's uptight pussy. You want to do me a favor, how about you do something to help that?"

Jack felt something tighten inside him, a spring compressed. He'd felt it on the football field just before the snap, felt it later in Iraq when the siren went off to signal incoming mortar fire. He was about to explode. He'd made a life's work out of exploding. There would be a situation and then there would be Jack. Jack would tear the situation apart because sometimes the world needed that, sometimes the world called out for it. But now the only one calling out to Jack was Jack. He'd explode out of the sheer pleasure of exploding. He already knew what it would feel like: that part of him already had his hands around this boy's skinny neck, choking the air out of his body. Lock his ass up? Jack would put him under the jail, the anger he felt building. Jack would put him on the goddamn No Fly list if someone would just show him where to sign. Jack would put him in the ground.

And then he just let it go. He let it go and turned to the deputy.

"Coach?" the deputy asked.

"Lock his ass up," Jack said.

"Yes, sir."

"Lock his ass up and throw away the key."

"Be my pleasure."

Jack turned to go but the deputy reached out to stop him.

"Hey, before I forget," he said. "Congrats on the van Gundy boys."

She wasn't at home, his ma.

Hadn't Richard known this? He had, he supposed. Yet somehow he had left the game with his pennant and his drink and his Germantown hoodie, got in Tom's pickup, and wound up here. Was this another of Jack's tricks? He couldn't be sure.

Standing in the dark living room, the house silent and settling, he couldn't quite be sure of anything. He was on his way to see his ma. Of that he was certain. Yet she was where? She was in the ICU at Germantown Memorial, of course. Which was where Richard had intended to go. Yet some homing instinct had taken over. Some inborn impulse, the kind of thing that pulls migrating birds from one continent to another and then back again.

He walked through the darkened house, feeling his feet sink into the pile of the carpet.

Were the Feds watching the house? They couldn't be because why would they? He felt the papers against his chest, his father's photograph hidden within them. He kept one hand there, pressing, securing. *Where are you, Ma?* Not here. But also here, he thought, still here, and for the second time that day he started down the basement steps.

This time he didn't bother with the lights.

At the turn in the stairs he put his hands out for balance and when he brought them back to his chest, his feet now planted solidly on the cold concrete, he no longer felt the papers or the photograph. He no longer felt them because all at once, he was home from the Citadel, dressed in his parade whites with the starched collar and blue shoulder boards, a golden SC pinned to his throat, home and walking through the dim labyrinth of boxes stacked throughout the basement, calling, *Ma? Where are you, Ma?*

And Ma not answering; Ma answering, *Go and find your brother. Your brother's down there somewhere, Richard. They have him. Find him, Richard. Please. Your father's away at the war where it's snowing and they're dying but your brother, he's alive, he's there. You have to find him, darling!*

And Richard answering that he could do that.

He could find his brother.

Just as soon as he got up.

Because Richard was—he realized—down on the carpet in front of the fire, Benjamin Harden's fire up in Cary, North

Carolina, plowing a furrow through the shag with his metal Farmall. It was 1956, maybe 1957, which meant Teddy wasn't even born yet. So how could he be dead? Which meant time had failed, time had turned back on itself, just as Richard had always suspected it might. And in its turning the past had swerved. The tractor had swerved, it must have. The great cleats of the back right tire must have shifted to miss the cavity of his chest, the teeth of the hay rake must have failed to claw his ear and nose and catch in the soft give of his lip, his face torn to the same pink you found inside a dog's ear. Some other world had been restored, some other not-quite-realized thing. Richard's life but without the dying. Richard's life but without the loss. The soapbox racers. The ice cream you ate with the wooden spoon. The way you could *taste* the wooden spoon and how Richard would suck on it until it was no longer cold. Restored!

The Merita bread.

The Cheerwine.

All of that returned to him, but also Teddy not dead, Teddy simply hiding. All of that, but also his father talking and laughing, having had his good war on the beach in France, never seeing the frozen hell of Bastogne. Was this possible?

Find him, Richard. Please!

It must be.

Which meant there were no bank auditors, no subpoenas, no acting solicitor Annie Smalls calling to say, *Honestly, I don't think there's undue worry here. But I wanted you to know all the same.* Somewhere stood the cathedral of his garment plant, his textile kingdom turning out T-shirts and shorts and vast sums of money, all of it Made in the US of A! Somewhere, Jack was on the dais with him and Tom. Somewhere, Emily was being sworn in as the new district attorney.

Find him, Richard!

Of course, he could do that, he *would* do that!

He put one hand down inside the great pockets of his Germantown hoodie (he was back in the hoodie) but didn't feel the bottle. Then he remembered he'd poured the Elijah Craig into his drink and left the bottle in the men's room because why did he need the bottle when the actual Elijah Craig was in his blood? He couldn't even feel the papers anymore, the transfers and transactions, the lies. His father's company photo buried with them. He couldn't feel them because they no longer existed. The panic, the fear—none of it existed! He thought of Francis Gary Powers and what it must have felt like. The S-75 Dvina cracking the fuselage of his U-2. They'd fired fourteen missiles, one of them hitting their own plane, a MIG-19, killed their own man but couldn't kill Powers even if it must have felt to poor old Francis not unlike dying. The spin, the inversion, the tail-first dive. But in this new world the missile had missed. Powers had landed safely with his reel of aerial photographs. It was just another day, just another mission.

Richard opened the basement door and exited into the cool night.

Powers was fine, Powers was happy.

Still, what would it have been like to fall backward? To fall and not see?

The barn was ahead, a gray shape in the graying night. Stars overhead. The yawning mouth inside of which sat the International Harvester with its hay rake. Sat *still.* Unmoved since that day in the field. But something different had happened. He knew that now. Teddy wasn't dead but wounded. Teddy was—it occurred to him as he hefted himself over the fence and into the pasture—caught in the teeth of the rake, waiting patiently for his big brother to come home from college and remove him.

He drank the last of the bourbon and Coke. Forced the straw into the corners, the melting ice, everything diluted and sweet. When it was gone, he tossed it down toward the old feeding ring, an iron circle that had largely disappeared in the unmown grass.

The barn ahead.

The stars above.

That toy tractor in his hand, and how it would warm when

he forgot it in front of the fire, the metal of the chassis gloriously painful to the touch.

The real tractor was ahead. Iron seat. Flat tires. He could barely see it but managed to hoist himself up behind the wheel. It smelled of hay and rust. An ancient crosscut saw on the slatted wall. Nests in the high corners.

He put his hand to the ignition.

The key!

It was there still. He felt his fingers form around it, damp, cool, and then those very fingers were turning it and—miracle of miracles!—the tractor started, the engine choked to life. He could barely believe it himself, and yet there he was, already backing it into the field and turning up the slope of the pasture into the abandoned apple orchard.

But was he?

There was a moment of doubt. There was a moment when it felt very much like Richard Greaves was doing no more than sitting there, the cold of the seat bleeding through his pants, the world unchanged. The thought left him as he came out of the rowed trees and over the crown of the field, the engine sputtering, the rain cap on the exhaust bouncing. Here is what had happened: the old Bible-thumpers of his childhood, sitting straight-backed in their hard-backed pews, had talked about the Veil, the Lifting of the Veil, and now it had been: lifted! revealed! The Mystery exposed not as life everlasting but as life simply lasting: lasting because it was good, because it was right. Because the terrible thing from over there *stayed* over there.

Now ease off the brake, son. That's it.

He was moving toward the homeplace now, the house where he'd grown up, the house where his father had grown up, the house no one or no thing had entered in decades. He brought the tractor to an idle there on the cracked macadam beneath the dead oak tree. The asbestos siding. The missing shutters. The peeling paint. Inside there were raccoons or rodents, an owl, maybe. If he hoped for anything he hoped for an owl.

The engine went silent and he stepped down. The smell of

diesel in the air. A distant car moving along the distant highway no more than a vapor of light. The seat of his britches damp. His father had left from here, gone off to war in the summer of '42. He hadn't come from money. Not that he had come from the absence of it either. His daddy, the grandfather Richard had never known, had thirty acres of bottomland and who knew how much pasture. Enough to break your heart come time for bailing, which came again and again. That *again* being part of the reason Anson Greaves left. Part of the reason he came back too, that sameness, that predictability. The horny heads in the creek. The way the tractor engine at night kept rattling around inside you, caught in the ear like bathwater gone warm.

Honeysuckle and hush puppies.

The 3-in-One oil on his daddy's fingertips.

Machine oil frying, the smell of it, a big truck burning all the way down to the tires and nobody doing a damn thing about it. But wait. Wait—

This is Belgium Richard is seeing. This is the war. They walk past it, straight out of the belly of the C-47 that has brought them. His father, Ben Harden, all of them. And there goes his dad, got his food in his mouth, Luckys in his pocket, cartridge belt around his neck. The rounds he doesn't know what to do with yet. December 1944. Hasn't fired a gun in near a year but recalling now all the useless shit he learned back at Fort Jackson. The M1 Garand. 5.2 pounds unloaded. 5.8 with sling. They walk through the night, past a priest slinging holy water, walk and walk and then dig into the frozen dirt. The artillery starts at dawn. The dying starts at dawn. The remnants of the 44th Signals Regiment in their foxholes. The 88s bursting in the trees and bursting in the snow and they get that *thwick* sound of a shattered tree. Splinters the size of your forearm. Men so prickled in death they appear olive porcupines, quills raised. Men punctured. Men split in halves and quarters and smaller fractions not to be considered. Sometime after dawn, the barrage having finally stopped, Anson Greaves and Ben Harden claw their way out of their hole to survey what is left of their ravaged line. And nothing is left. Just Anson and Ben, standing up to stretch, their backs cramped, their fingers wrapped around their cartridge belts, all those bullets they have yet to fire, all those prayers they have yet to pray. Not yet knowing it is five months and four hundred miles to Berlin.

But in this new world none of it happens.

In this new world, the Panzers do not come through the sticks just after breakfast. No one runs, no one retreats. The winter sun coming through Ben Harden's living room window two decades later does not give his father's eyes the appearance of tears. This world is different.

In this new world, Clara doesn't walk into the kitchen, Jack four months old and finally asleep, to say, *It's too late to drive up there tonight. Go in the morning.*

And you do not say: *We always go up late. Get there at dawn.*

It's ridiculous. These words never leave her mouth.

So you never have to say in response: *It's how we've always done it.*

And she doesn't lose her temper, she doesn't level her eyes and say: *For God's sake, Richard. He barely says a word to you. He barely acknowledges you or your mother or his own grandson for that matter. And still you run around like you're his chauffeur, happy if he so much as looks in your direction and spits.*

And you never, ever say back: *But he's my father.*

None of this happens.

The Veil has lifted. The Mystery explained.

Standing outside the homeplace, having ridden over on the tractor that did not kill his brother, wearing clothes made from his garment plant, his family happy and content, Richard Greaves inhabited a world where such was not even imaginable, let alone possible.

Something moved in the house.

He saw it.

A curtain, some stiff window covering slipped back.

Could someone be in there?

Could it be his dad?

It seemed impossible. The doors not just locked but boarded.

And yet… He was cold. It came to him all at once. His damp pants having seeped through his underwear and against his skin. He was cold and exhausted and it was time to go. He looked for the tractor but couldn't see it in the dark. When he stepped forward, he couldn't feel it in the dark either. It was back in the barn, he realized. It had never left. The dampness he felt up and down his legs came from walking through the thigh-deep grass, his pants covered in beggar-lice and a single tangle of briars wrapped like barbed wire. He thought he had smelled diesel but, no, not anymore. Growing up, the smell of diesel exhaust made him think of work, of progress. The smell of diesel was America, yet he didn't smell it anymore. Where had it gone? Atlanta, maybe. Charlotte? Because it was sure as hell no longer here.

It was many places, perhaps, but it wasn't here.

Nothing was. He'd imagined every last bit of it and knew he should go. The Veil was descending, coming back down with the house lights that had lit this world of *almost* and *not quite* and *then again*, and he needed to get to the hospital while he still could. Yet that movement there in the window… What was inside the house, moving that curtain, was his parents' world, the world of his childhood. Biblical. Full of miracles and damnation and fish fries down along the Little River. The Veil was lowering all around him, but he had the sense that if he got inside, everything would change, everything would go back. But there was the equal sense that he wasn't welcome there.

He barely heard the man slither up beside him, Jack's age maybe, lean as a rake with a bushy white beard.

"Hey, now," the man was calling. "Hey, Pops."

Richard stopped and turned, hands in his pockets, everything wet.

"Do I know you?"

"I don't know where you do or don't, Pops." He looked at the house and back at Richard. "You waiting on somebody or something?"

"No, I'm just… That was my parents' house. I grew up in that house."

"House right there?"

"Me and my brother."

"That house old."

"You're not living in there, are you?"

"In that shit?"

"I haven't been in there in years."

"Ain't nobody, looks like." The man nodded at the trailer that sat almost hidden across the road, a dirty single-wide beneath a security light. "I live over there with my lady friend and her grandyounguns. I saw you out here. Don't never see nobody out here." The man waited. "So you waiting on something?"

"I don't think so."

He removed a toothpick that Richard only now noticed. "You don't know a thing, do you, Pops?"

"No," Richard said, "I don't suppose I do."

He followed the road back. No more than a quarter mile but it seemed longer, as did the day, as did his life. All the energy was gone. All the hope, too, and walking, he thought of all the memories he had, the good days and holidays and birthdays, his children, his friends, his grandchildren, and he wondered if it all was enough. But enough for what? Enough for a happy life, he supposed. Though why, he wondered, as late as it was, did it matter if it was happy or not? It made no sense. Yet also, perversely, sadly, belatedly, it did. The night of his father's visitation, the night before the funeral, the great Anson Greaves tucked into a gunmetal gray coffin, his old friend Benjamin Harden had sat in his wheelchair, VFW cap on his bald head, Combat Infantryman's Badge pinned to his dark suit, and wholly unattended, wept.

He started Tom's pickup and sat for a last moment staring at his ma's house. What would he do when she was gone? Sell it, he supposed. Sell the house, sell the land. All his bullshit about saving the land was, in the end, exactly that.

He pulled onto the highway, back past the fields in which he'd wrecked his soapbox racers and the fields in which he'd baled hay, back past Long's Country Junction and on toward his own home.

He remembered one night, his father dying in his chair, the living room La-Z-Boy, gray and threadbare, the arms browning from too much touch. Semi-reclined. The afghan across his legs. The feeding tube beneath the old V-neck Hanes. Pumping the milky Glucerna from the syringe into the tube and then one night missing, slipping, blasting that viscous goo all over his father's pale flesh. How he had jumped. The sudden intake of breath and Richard's apologies and his father just lying there, stoic and silent and goose-bumped the length of his cancered torso.

Tom had taken it hard that night, that night and every night. His youngest adrift. But he would be all right because Richard knew the answer. Richard knew the thing to do. The thing to do was to put Clara in charge. Let Clara love the world back into some semblance of shape. Meanwhile, old R.S. Greaves would sit quietly in the back, swallowing his Xanax and drinking his way toward blessed oblivion.

Clara...yes...

Clara was his only hope.

He would go to Clara and explain everything, get down on his knees and beg her forgiveness, and then—when she had forgiven him, because she would, of course she would, how could she not?—he would beg her to go with him to the hospital, to see his poor dying ma and this too she would grant him. Come Monday morning, renewed, reborn, he would rise up, put on his best suit, and hand the bank file over to acting solicitor Annie Smalls. *Here it is, Annie. Tell the Fed they don't need to bother with the subpoenas.* He'd face the music. He'd take the blame. Going not to Aruba or Jamaica but Broad River Correctional where he'd watch a lot of cable news, maybe make a billfold in the leather shop.

Simple as that.

He came over the last rise and pushed in the clutch, topped the hill, the truck gliding, clicked the turn signal, his boy's truck coasting. Forgiveness was just ahead. But he knew he wasn't ready for it, not yet, and knowing as much, Richard clicked off the blinker and gunned his son's little truck, headed now not for home but for the hospital where he knew his ma, intubated and tubed somewhere in the ICU, lay dying and dreaming and—most of all—waiting for her son to appear.

Jack kept moving for the rest of the game, never stopping, not for a moment while the Germantown quarterback kneeled down to exhaust the clock and preserve a 24-14 win, not for a second while people spoke and reached out to slap his back or shake his hand. *Playoffs, Coach!* somebody yelled. *Groban had 'em ready!* said another. But it slid off him, nothing attaching, not words, not sense. It was all Jack-in-motion, clomping around the stadium as the cleaning crew began to sweep the bleachers and folks shut down the concession stand and the lights flashed and then, like dying stars, began to rapidly dim. The FBI agent had been gone when he returned from the fight. He'd called his father but the stubborn damn mule hadn't answered. He tried to suss the thing out and came away unsure how concerned he should be. So instead of thinking on it he kept stalking up and down the concrete steps and back around the concourse.

He was headed toward the locker room when he saw Elvis approaching. "Hey, hold up a minute," he was calling. "Stop for a second. Goddamn, Jack, can you not be still a minute?"

"I want to catch Groban before he runs into the parents."

"Groban ain't going nowhere. Listen a minute." He was panting. "Let me catch my breath."

"Walk with me."

Elvis grabbed Jack's arm.

"Let me catch my breath. Your daddy—" Elvis stopped to wheeze. "He got in the wrong seats. Could hear him all the way on the sidelines. I tried to sit him down but he wandered off looking for you."

"There was a fight I had to see about."

"Well, he was looking for you. I think he'd had more than a few."

"Like drunk?"

"I'd say he was pretty damn deep in his cups."

"Was Tom with him?"

"I didn't see Tom. Like I said, he got in the wrong seat and got a little confused."

"No, no," Jack said, and took his cell from his pocket. Added to the missed calls from his mom and sister were now two missed calls from his wife. Catherine picked up on the first ring.

"I've been calling."

"I must have had the ringer off."

"All evening?"

"What's wrong? Is Lana okay?"

"Lana's fine. It's your grandmother. Apparently she fell."

"What?"

"She's in the ICU. Tom called."

"When did this happen?"

"They found her today so maybe late last night, maybe this morning."

"Oh no."

"There was some kind of confusion or something. No one knew until just a little while ago. Or maybe your father knew, I don't know."

"Is she—"

"She isn't good. Also your mom is all upset because she can't find your dad. Apparently, he got drunk and left the luncheon. You need to call her."

"All right."

"And, Jack," she said, "I'm sorry."

He hung up before he thought to mention the FBI.

He thought of calling her back, but to say what? It was clear now: His dad must have known about the fall, got upset, got drunk. Whether he knew about the Feds Jack had no idea. But either way, he'd head to the hospital.

"Your granny?" Elvis asked.

"She fell."

"Goddamn. I'm sorry to hear that. She's a good woman." Elvis put his hand on Jack's shoulder. "Look, you get on and I'll see to things here."

"You sure?"

"Ain't nothing left to do no way. Just start the laundry and lock the gate, right?"

"I appreciate it."

He made it to his truck before he remembered Lana was likely at the dance in the cafeteria. He'd find her and either drop her home on the way to the hospital or let her ride with him. She was old enough to decide for herself.

He pushed through the doors and nodded at the student government kids taking up the five-dollar cover at a foldout table, the reel of tickets, the handstamp. The gym was packed with bodies and noise—music, but it didn't sound like it. A purple strobe light pulsed. On the projection screen were what appeared to be celestial shapes, gas clouds or nebulae or whatever they were, forming and shattering and then reforming in a giant astral kiss. He guessed probably two hundred kids were in the room.

"Have you seen Lana?" he asked the boy at the table. "My daughter."

"Yes, sir. She was dancing."

He patted the boy on the back and snaked around the edge of the room where he'd spotted a few boys from Lana's class. "You fellas haven't seen Lana, have you?"

"Yes, sir. Want me to go find her, Coach?"

Jack nodded and the boy disappeared into the crowd. A few minutes later he came back and touched Jack on the arm. "Coach Greaves?"

"Yes?"

"You might want to come back, sir."

The back hall was overlit, or at least appeared so, stepping as Jack did from the darkness of the cafeteria. A few kids were leaning against the walls, glancing up and double-taking at the site of Coach Greaves hustling toward the door marked WOMEN.

A small crowd had gathered, a few boys, a few curious girls, interested but prepared to not be, phones poised just below their noses. Jack waited a moment for the crowd to scatter before he knocked on the bathroom door. There was no answer and instead of knocking again, he opened the door slightly and called blindly for Lana. It opened a moment later on Christie, one of his daughter's oldest friends.

"Christie," he said.

"She's pretty upset, Mr. Greaves."

"Is she okay?"

"I don't know. I mean I guess in the grand scheme of the universe she is. Like, you know, cosmically. But…"

"Gotcha."

"She had a fight with a boy."

"Stinson Wood," Jack said.

Christie shrugged.

"Thank you, Christie. I'll just—" and Jack opened the door slightly. "Lana?" he called and opened it a bit more. "Lana, honey, could we talk please?"

"No," came the voice from inside.

"Lana?" he called. "Please, honey."

"No."

"I have to talk to you."

"I already talked to Mom."

"If you don't come out, I'm going to have to come in."

"Don't you dare," his daughter called.

He turned to Christie. "Is anyone else in there?"

She shook her head and Jack nodded. *I'm going in,* he wanted to say, but it felt so theatrical, so contrived, he just swallowed and stepped forward. But then even the swallow felt like an act, something one part of him had informed the other it should be doing, swallowing, nodding. Playing at dad instead of being a dad.

"Lana?" he said from inside the dim tile.

"Oh my God," she said, but quieter now, softer. Her voice wet with tears, but wet in the ways trees are wet after a storm, dripping, yes, but also brighter for it. "You aren't supposed to be in here."

He could see now that she sat on the floor against the far wall, the stall door swung to partially obscure her but not enough that he couldn't recognize her shape. She sat on the ground, her legs spread before her like a rag doll. The screen on her phone was blue and then it went dark.

"Your granny fell," he said. "She isn't good."

"Mom said."

"I don't want to ruin your night."

"You aren't ruining anything."

He was still across the room from her, over by the foot-activated sinks and jet-air hand-blowers but sensed in her voice that he might draw nearer. He took a step tentative step forward.

"I have to go, honey, and I want you to go with me," he said. "I can drop you at home or you can go with me down to the hospital."

"We had a fight, Dad."

"I'm sorry, honey."

"I know you hate him—and please don't say you don't, all right? And I know he's an awful guy, and I know I shouldn't even care with Granny hurt and all," she said. "But still, you know?"

"Yeah."

"He isn't answering his phone and I guess that's for the best, really."

Jack didn't say anything. Then he found himself speaking without intending it: "He's not going to answer either, honey. He's…" He let it die in the space between them.

"He's what?"

"He got in a fight. He's—"

"A fight?"

"The police came."

"A fight? You saw this?"

"There was a boy. Regan—"

"Regan's a girl."

"Right, yes. But there was a fight and—"

"Did he hurt her?"

"Not too bad."

"And he's—? Actually, I don't want to know."

"I'm sorry about it. I just—"

"Please, Dad," she said.

He heard her stand, saw the screen of her phone glow through the denim of her front pocket where she had placed it. She stepped toward him as if in surrender, hands out, palms up.

"We can go out the back through my office," Jack said. "And about Stinson—"

"Please," she said in a voice Jack was only beginning to recognize, "don't talk to me."

He dropped Lana off at the house, not bothering to get out, not bothering to cut the engine—*seriously, Dad? You're not even coming in?* He'd told her to go on, he'd be home soon, and she'd rolled her eyes and lurched across the walk and into the house. At the foot of the driveway, he stopped and sent a text to Catherine. Lana was home. He was going to the hospital. Don't wait up. He didn't expect a response but it came almost immediately.

Come home, sweet man.

He texted back. *Lana make it?*

She's right here. Please come home.

Soon, baby.

Jack turned his phone off before she could respond and pulled onto the highway.

Ten minutes later, he was in the hospital parking lot. The front lobby was dark and what traffic there was gathered around the emergency entrance. Even if his grandmother was in a regular room—and she wasn't—they wouldn't let him in. But he'd come in late on enough Friday nights to visit boys with concussions and torn ligaments, lying on gurneys in their pants and cleats, grass stains still on their elbows, to know his way around.

He sat for a moment collecting himself. He knew his mother would have a peace about his father, a calm. What Jack had was the exact opposite. What Jack had was the sense that they were all on the verge of falling apart. Or they had already fallen apart but were only now realizing as much. It seemed preposterously unfair. That this life had perhaps ended the day he and Catherine and Lana had checked out of the cottage in Blowing Rock, his LBJ unread, his family unreconciled. Yet it seemed so close that if he only turned around quick enough he would catch sight of it. And if he could see it, he could catch it. If he could catch it, he could never let it go.

His father had called, he hadn't forgotten as much. But there was no use considering it right now and he opened the truck door. He was almost to the ER door when he saw Tom coming toward him. They shook hands there beneath the lights. Their granny wasn't good. Their dad was AWOL.

"No idea where he went?" Jack asked.

"The game maybe. You didn't see him?"

"I heard reports."

"Drunk?"

"What I heard. Still, you think he'd call Mom."

"I don't know. He was pretty upset at lunch. Remember lunch, Jack?"

Jack shook his head and looked up at the building, a few windows aglow with—was it too much to say?—suffering. "So," he said. "There was a lady at the game tonight, looking for Dad."

"She didn't happen to be with the FBI, did she?"

"Shit, Tom. You know about this?"

"I met another agent, Daryl Abbott, after you skipped out on the luncheon."

"Why didn't you say anything?"

"Why didn't you?"

"I *am* saying something. I'm saying it right now. Does Mom know?"

"I don't think so."

"We should call Emily, I guess."

"And tell her what?"

"I don't know," Jack admitted. "That the FBI is asking around about Dad and could she please do something? I guess you don't know anything else?"

"Like what?"

"Like details. Like is this about him *specifically*, or just tied to the bank in general?"

"He *is* the bank. Add to that the fact that he pals around with sleazy Jeff Duncan."

"Yeah."

"You don't have to imagine that hard."

"No," Jack said, "I guess you don't."

He went into the ER but avoided the check-in desk. Ducked into the men's room when a nurse came down the hall. Walked out and then walked right back in when he saw another. It felt a bit silly, a bit like a game of human frogger, the in and out, but when the second nurse passed he quickly skirted the triage area with its curtains and rolling carts of equipment. He passed through two doors and was in the dim corridor that led to the main lobby where an elderly man ran a buffer over the tile floor. Jack gave him a half wave and the man looked him over and went back to his buffer.

It was easier on the fifth floor.

He simply walked briskly, eyes forward, until he saw GREAVES in all caps by room 519.

Inside, the curtain was pulled to obscure his granny. But when he stepped around it, he saw that light poured through her body. She was arranged in the inclined bed, but only just. There was so little left of her was the thing. A skeletal system. A nearly bald head cankered with scabs. She had an IV port in her neck. She was intubated.

"Granny," he whispered and touched the parchment of her right arm. "It's Jack. I'm here with you."

It wasn't even papery anymore, her skin. There had been a time when it had dried, bunched at the wrist and elbow. But that time was past. She was translucent now, a web of blue-green veins visible through the skin.

The respirator sucked and hushed and after a moment he sat down in the far chair, close enough to the wall that he would be invisible to anyone peeking in. He hoped Lana and Catherine were asleep. He had some regret about Stinson Wood. Not about sending him to jail—Jack suspected the boy had been steering toward incarceration for years—but about what it had put between Jack and his daughter, about what it had taken from them. About how fragile it all was, how fleeting. How in losing something you might realize you had never possessed it in the first place.

The glass behind him was cool and he tipped back his head. His eyes had adjusted to the glow of the machines and he could discern the curve of his granny's tired head. She appeared to have been piled into the bed, dumped there. Not so much an animal wounded as an animal exhausted. He was drifting into the lightest of sleep when the door opened and the room was momentarily flooded with the light from the hall. Another figure was in the room, moving clumsily forward, a nurse. The light was off and the nurse knocked against the various wheeled machines.

Then Jack realized it wasn't a nurse.

He recognized the shape, the angle and gait. Something in him knew before knowing and he leaned forward and spoke in the softest whisper he could manage. Jack Greaves leaned forward and said, "Dad?"

SATURDAY

A WOMAN WITH A TORCH

No matter how early Emily Rhett woke, it never felt early enough.

Somehow, bless her, she always felt behind.

Somehow, bless her, she was always catching up.

Like the way she'd brought Judson home from the football game, late and happy and so distracted she'd failed to register the missed calls and texts, having learned only in the wee-est hours of the morning that her grandmother had fallen and was in the ICU at Germantown Memorial.

Behind—yet again.

So here she was on the penultimate day of her maternity leave, behind the wheel of the family Caravan, Kyle behind her occupying both his car seat and a state of listless bliss, his eyes heavy-lidded, his lips formed around something halfway between a first word and a kiss. Emily was headed to the hospital, worried, almost praying, definitely hustling, pulling onto the highway and crossing Lake Keowee just as the sun broke over the placid water. She'd spent the last two hours on the back porch, waiting for visiting hours, alone, or least as alone as she could be these days since everywhere she went she carried both her son and the burned woman who seemed to float just above Emily's head, tethered like a balloon.

The question was *why*?

She had spent her leave sitting on the porch riddling out the *why*, as if such a thing just might exist. Gathering herself: reading Brené Brown, thinking, praying, or at least intending to. Though having to remind yourself to pray instead of just praying—maybe not such a great sign? Either way, she now realized how much those quiet mornings meant to her. Those little moments of solace before Kyle stirred or Judson demanded Eggos or Knox came requesting whatever it was Knox needed—it ranged from ironed shirts to assurances that his ever-expanding bald spot wasn't expanding and, in fact, wasn't a bald spot at all.

Come Monday it would all end. Which meant she would hand Kyle over to her husband, exchange him (and the quiet mornings, and the coffee, and the reminder that she should be praying—all that *gathering*) for the DUIs and the domestic abuse and the woman still in the Toccoa burn unit.

Only she was thinking of not going back.

Over those months holding Kyle, it had occurred to her that she could have been something easier, something calmer, the executor of estates, the writer of wills. Now there seemed the opportunity for some return, the possibility of a world in which quiet mornings with her family, coffee on the porch, and actual prayer were not a reprieve from the everyday but the everyday itself.

"But first!" she announced to no one.

First there was the hospital. She pulled in and headed across the parking lot, Kyle a warm bundle against her shoulder. It was unmistakably day now, the sun up, the air crisp and cool, and she took a deep breath just as she spotted the figure step through the sliding glass door and raise a hand in greeting.

"Emily!" it called. "Hey, good morning." It was Jack, or at least a rumpled, dirty version of such. He came toward her wearing, she realized, exactly what he'd been wearing yesterday when she'd caught him in his office. Hair matted. Shirt untucked. Had it not been for the goofy smile he would have appeared irrevocably old, and Emily would have been sadder for it.

"You've been up to see her?" Emily asked.

They were stopped just beyond the drop-off lane, Jack's smile having faded not a watt.

"You won't believe it," he said.

"She's bad?"

"Just go up."

"You're not going to tell me?"

"Just go up and see. She's sitting up, she's talking."

"Are you serious?"

"It's kind of amazing," he said. "Actually, it's completely amazing. Like miracle amazing."

"That's great, I was afraid—"

"Yeah, it looked that way for a while."

"When did you find out?"

"Last night. I figured someone would call you. I stayed the night with Dad."

"He's up there?"

"Mom too. Just go up. It's really something else."

And it was.

Her grandmother was sitting up and laughing. *Laughing.* Emily's mother, perched by the edge of the bed, held a cup of ice chips. Her father was piled on the couch, hair disheveled, pants covered with beggar-lice, dressed in a War Pigs hoodie and breathing through his clogged nose, rumpled and reeking of alcohol, but no matter. Her parents stood—*Emily! Good morning, darling! And you brought Kyle!*—her grandmother clapped her hands in excitement. There were hugs and prayers and more laughing. What a scare it had been. They had thought broken hip, they had thought stroke. But turns out she just fell, she just hit her nearly bald but somehow astoundingly resilient head. Another round of hugs and then her father crashed back into what Emily saw now wasn't so much a couch as some sort of strange recliner, and seeing it all Emily felt her eyes tear, which was maybe her dad's smell, but more likely the miracle of it all. She passed Kyle to her mom and began to fan her face.

"Oh, darling," her mother said.

"I'm sorry!"

"Oh, honey," her grandmother said.

"It's okay!"

Her father sat in one part confusion, one part emotion, bourbon fumes atmosphering around him.

"I'm crying because I'm happy," Emily said. "It's okay. I just came up here thinking…you know…I was so worried."

Of course you were…sit down, honey…it looked so bad last night, but then…sit, honey, sit…

And she did, fairly collapsing onto the strange couch/recliner/upholstered thing beside her stinking and gentle father. Kyle was awake and cooing and her mother danced him around the room while her grandmother smiled.

"You just missed your brothers," her father said.

"I saw Jack outside."

Her father stirred now, leaned forward, and planted his elbows on his knees.

"He say anything?"

"Jack? Just that I wouldn't believe this. Was Tom here too?"

"I meant about me?"

"Not really," Emily repeated. "He was mostly just smiling like some happy fool."

Her father nodded at this, squeezed her knee, and lumbered into the bathroom.

"So Tom was here?" Emily asked again when the door had latched shut.

Last night, her mother said, but he would surely be back later though she'd told him not to.

"He has such a busy day," her mother said.

"The ninja thing?"

"The ninja thing, and then he's doing—what did he call it, Mrs. Greaves?"

"Some sort of radio program it sounded like."

"What radio program?" Emily asked.

They heard the toilet flush.

Her mother was bouncing Kyle on her lap.

"It's like what do they call it," her mother asked, "where they interview you? Except you get it through your phone."

"Like a podcast?" Emily asked.

"That's it," her mother said. "Something from California. *SoulFast*?"

"*SoulCast*?"

"That's it. After his ninja thing. Have you heard of it?"

"Maybe," she said. Actually, she subscribed to it, though she would never admit as much. *SoulCast* came out of San

Francisco and was very acai berry meets Silicon Valley meets intermittent fasting with a side of positive thinking. Brought to you by purveyors of CBD oil and meditation apps. It was so Tom she thought she might vomit because really, now that their grandmother was okay, why not be petty?

"You have a big day too, don't you, honey?" her mother asked. "Your reunion."

Emily could only nod. Her reunion being perhaps the thing she needed least in her life right now, but, as the long-ago president of Germantown High, was obligated to organize. And if Emily believed in anything, it was the obligatory nature of *obligation.* Even if it did make her want to cry, even if—at least lately—everything did. When her father came back from the bathroom, she put her head against the seat back and shut her eyes. She felt exhausted, out late last night, up early this morning.

Maybe that was it.

Maybe she was just tired.

It was barely eight by the time she pulled up at home but Judson was already in the hallway, already dressed, hair gelled and upswept in a little cresting wave of ambition, his eyes sparking in the way of children who know themselves to be not just intelligent but made sleek by such.

"Hey, honey."

"What are you doing out?"

"I went to see your great-granny." She could see the rectangle of phone in his front pocket. "She fell yesterday?"

"Is that a question?"

"What do you need, baby?"

"You look sad."

"Sad? No, honey. Tired, maybe." She eased him from the door. "She's fine, by the way. You want French toast?"

"I've already had my milk. You bought the Fairlife SuperKids."

"And that's the wrong one?"

"The one with added DHA. It doesn't taste right."

"And you don't want the Fairlife?"

"No, I want the *regular* Fairlife. Not the SuperKids."

"Because it cost like twice what regular milk cost."

"I *do* want the Fairlife, Mom, that's not what I'm saying at all."

"Besides, I think your father bought it." She guided him into the kitchen where the chocolate milk—wrong kind or not—still sat on the counter, several dark splashes beaded around it. Normally she would make him *clean this up, be responsible for yourself.* But not today. Today, she poured him a bowl of Raisin Bran and smiled, refusing to even consider That Which Cannot Be Named.

And why should she consider such? Her son was well, and would be, at least until the day he wasn't. Until the day he was gone out of their lives, or she was gone out of theirs. She put the cereal back in the pantry and focused on her breathing. This was a thought that intruded more and more frequently of late, how at some point something awful would happen. A wreck, an illness, a phone call announcing death or disaster. You could count every day that it didn't happen a blessing, a little miracle of sorts. But you could also—she thought of this making sure the pantry door was properly shut—you could also understand it as pure probability: that every day the worst failed to arrive, the statistical likelihood of its coming the next day only increased. Life burning like that poor woman in her accelerant-soaked bed.

She had told it all to Knox, these thoughts, and he had performed all the necessary acts of marital comfort. Held her, soothed her, talked logic to her—*these are normal thoughts, honey. Especially when you're home all day with Kyle.* But she had detected the perfunctory, the man playing the role of strong-jawed husband to the woman who played the role of weepy sensitive wife.

Did she really look sad?

Tired, sure. Tired she could have lived with. But sad?

Guilty, she knew that one.

Occasionally she would take a sleeping pill and every time felt guilty for it. She told herself it was a physical thing, her guilt. She shouldn't take it because it did damage. It made some obscure heart valve leak, some rarefied lobe deep in the prefrontal cortex degrade. You'd die fifteen minutes sooner for having taken it. But it wasn't that. It was the way she hid it in her hand, the way she swallowed it when Knox wasn't looking. That she needed it meant something was wrong with her life, that something wasn't quite in place. Otherwise, given the manic twitching of her day—the driving, the nursing, the cajoling, and considering—shouldn't she sleep at night of her own exhausted accord? But she wasn't sleeping, and the not sleeping part, did it signal sadness? And not just a personal grief but some sort of larger cosmic thing? There were days it seemed her family was coming apart, that something had come unhinged. Other days it felt fine.

Judson poured another glass of chocolate milk, apparently no longer caring that it was the wrong kind.

"Honey, hurry up and go brush your teeth."

"Now?"

"Yes, now."

"Otherwise," Knox said, having just entered the room, "we try you as an adult. Good morning." He kissed Emily's temple and raised the note she'd left him. "She okay?"

"Amazingly, yes."

"That's wonderful," Knox said when Judson was gone. "Big day today. The reunion."

"I was thinking maybe you could take Judson to Tom's ninja thing at the Oktoberfest? A father-son sort of thing?"

He shook the chocolate milk. The truth was, she was the one who had bought it.

"Yeah," he said. "Sounds great but you know I can't. I've got the thing with the house in Beaufort. Remember?" And then he smiled so that it wasn't quite so loaded. "You forgot, didn't you?"

"No, no, I just—"

"It's okay. I just can't really miss it."

"It's a showing or something?"

"I'm meeting the realtor."

"What for again?"

"Something with the air conditioning," he said. "No Freon, maybe."

The house was an antebellum mansion that had belonged to Knox's family since the 1950s. Three stories of Greek Revival, glorious if now a little shabby and moldy and in need of five figures of rehabilitative attention; it had been the field hospital for the 54th Massachusetts during the Civil War and then (was the word *irony*?) home to one of the South's most obdurate segregationists, Knox's father, the late Dixiecrat Senator Augustus Rhett, known toward the end of his life, thankfully, as much for fathering Knox when well into his sixties as for fighting desegregation in the fifties. The house had been for sale for the last two years. Overpriced, because Knox didn't really want to part with it. Overpriced, because they didn't need the money.

"And you have to be there?"

"Henry's mom is going to take him. I'll drop him by on my way."

"Henry's mom?"

"You know, the kid in Judson's pre-calc?"

"I know who Henry is. I just didn't know you had arranged things."

He shrugged, smiling, but not exactly at her.

"I'm going to hit the road right after dropping him, all right?"

"And Henry's mom is fine with this?"

"Completely and totally."

She nodded, though what the motion signaled she had no idea.

A few minutes later they were all assembled in the kitchen and then rushing out of the kitchen into the garage, Emily calling goodbye and Judson calling back. Knox kissed her cheek. He had his overnight bag with him, and she could see how anxious he was to get out the door so okay, go ahead, don't let me stop you.

It was only when they were gone that she reminded herself to pray.

Elvis Carter woke Saturday morning with the sort of hangover that generally kept company till on about dinner time. It was the neurological equivalent of some second cousin once removed who glommed onto you at a family reunion and then wouldn't quit talking, the kind of persistent and dumb relative you can't quite get used to, but can't seem to get rid of either. He lay on the bed and analyzed the thing inside his skull. It wasn't the wet throb of a whiskey hangover—he hadn't touched a drop in two decades, no sir, not since those ugly days after he'd lost his girl to the Monster—but the sort of collapsing sense that your dehydrated brain, concussed one too many times on the football field or the battlefield, was shrinking. The kind of hangover that signaled stupid shit, even if you couldn't remember what.

Maybe especially if you couldn't remember what.

He filched along the floor for a glass of water.

What Elvis did remember was staying late at the game. He'd left the laundry unwashed and would have to head back to the school to finish, but first he needed to check on his mama.

He got a swallow of tepid water, spilled a little on his bare chest, and sat up with the measured tentativeness of a groundhog emerging for what may or may not be spring. The room was cool, the heater off, the windows open. He rolled himself off the mattress and stood sectionally, unfolding his legs and then his torso, his neck and shoulders. Stiff and dry-eyed with a hitch in his lower back and a crick in his neck.

The room dim.

The room a mess.

But here such welcome coolness. Sometime during the night, fall seemed to have arrived, so there was that.

He got dressed, brushed his teeth, and stood at the toilet for a good half-minute before the urine flowed. He was a big man, bigger than he had ever been playing ball or in the service, and standing there in front of the mirror there was a scary quality about him, something that betrayed the fact that he lived in his mama's cheap hotel, or maybe reinforced such.

How the hell was he supposed to know?

Either way, he looked gigantic, piled up in a way that didn't necessarily please him. But didn't exactly upset him either. It was like the morning headache, which, in its way, was just like everything else here on God's green earth. Like the war he'd fought and the girl he'd lost—it just was.

He unlocked the office of the Germantown Motel, still dusk, still cool, and put on the Folger's that was meant for any of the folks who were by and large permanent residents but was inevitably consumed by no one but Elvis and his mother. He drank his first cup fast and poured his second, drank it slower, standing outside where he had an uninterrupted view of the Burger King drive-thru, already busy, the day smelling of biscuits and fry grease and the diesel exhaust of a big Ram pickup waiting on its orange juice.

Weekdays the parking lot would just be starting to fill with kids loitering around where the bus met them across from the Shumpert Farm Stand and the Escape the Fire Church of Living Water, both shuttered as far back as Elvis could remember. Maybe twenty kids. Poor white kids living with their meth-head parents. They came and went with such frequency he couldn't keep up, didn't even try to anymore. Just one wispy underfed ghost after another. Open-sored and sad as the music his mama played. He knew the Mexican kids better, or recognized them, at least. They were, generally speaking, longer term, and now and then he tried to strike up a conversation with one. Just like *hello, how are you* was all he meant. He didn't want to debate religion or free trade or US immigration policy, for Lord's sake. He just wanted some simple human interaction. But they were afraid of him. That was always evident. The big piled-up white man running the place. Keloid scars and one arm tatted up with a map of Mesopotamia. The TBIs from the IEDs.

He took a sip from his coffee and started walking.

His mother lived in a brick ranch three blocks down and he walked with the warmth of the coffee in his hand. The street just waking, lights on in kitchens, cars easing toward where the road met Main Street at an angle. His mother was likely still in bed, awake but under the covers, waiting, though on what Elvis could never say. Him, he supposed.

He'd lost his dad to lung cancer back in high school, the Monster's original manifestation. His mama had remarried twice more, older men, but Elvis had hardly known numbers two and three, having been dismissed from college and away in the service at the time, both dead and buried by the time he was out. She had a boyfriend now, but at eighty he doubted she'd be marrying again. He thought of her frying salmon patties and going to the Church of God behind the Dairy Queen, how you could still smell the canned fish when you came home from the evening service.

He lifted his coffee but didn't drink. Goddamn memories. At eighteen, Elvis had been outside the Magic Attic, Senior Week in Myrtle Beach, shirtless and huge, drunk and belligerent, wearing nothing but Kmart swim trunks and a puka shell necklace. At nineteen, barely a year later, he'd lost the only girl he would ever love, thank you very much. So it was just the two of them, Elvis an only child, a mama's boy, though she was a hell of a mama to have.

He went up the front steps of her house, calling for her as he shut the door behind him. He waited, and when she didn't answer he went down the hall. Standing on the threshold, his mama buried beneath two quilts, it appeared for a moment she was dead. He felt the heat of the coffee in his right hand and thought, *Mama?*

But she stirred, her gray head came up.

"You ought to be ashamed. Walking in on a poor defenseless widow woman."

He walked around to her side of the bed and looked down at her.

"You many things, but you ain't defenseless, lady," he said. "You want some coffee?"

She sat up in her floral pajama shirt and hairnet.

"Is it that that awful Folger's you brew? Smells like roadkill skunk," she said, but took the cup. "How are you, baby?"

"I'm all right. You sleep okay?"

"I don't know. I took two pain pills when the news come on and don't remember much else."

He sat on the side of the bed and petted her right hand while she sipped coffee with her left.

"You ain't supposed to take but one. Dr. Hamad said—"

"I don't give a damn what no Dr. Hamad said. Dr. Hamad ain't the one hurting."

"No, ma'am."

She passed him the cup, and he put it on the nightstand beside the pistol he only now noticed.

"You shouldn't have this out," he said.

"You don't need to worry about it."

"This is—" He took the pistol, a snub-nosed .38 that had belonged to her second husband. "Jesus, Mama, this is loaded."

"You watch how you talk."

"I don't want to see this out. This is crazy."

"You watch your taking the Lord's name like that. I'll put up with a lot, but I draw the line at the Lord's name."

He opened the cylinder and pressed the ejector rod, collecting the bullets in his palm.

"Don't you do that," she said.

"You don't need to have no loaded gun sitting by your bed."

"You telling me you don't?"

"I ain't the one taking two pain pills at night."

She said nothing to this, just sat for a moment working her jaw and settling her dentures.

"I need to get up. Help me here," she said, and he reached down and helped her stand, catching, as she shifted her feet from the bed to the floor, how swollen were her lower legs, the varicosed ankles and calves, fat and nearly purple.

"I'm swole up," she said. "My feet especially."

"How much salt you had?"

"Not more than a shake or two on a tomater sandwich."

"You know Dr. Hamad said—"

"You say 'Dr. Hamad' one more time and I will, by God, put them bullets back in my gun. Now help me get down the hall before I wet myself. I'll limber up here in a minute."

He started another pot of coffee and sat at the Formica table for the ten minutes she was in the bathroom. Outside the day was brightening, traffic picking up. When she came out she was dressed. Still in bedroom shoes, but heavy with QVC jewelry and everything she hadn't yet bothered to return to Jared's. She looked regal, tall and silver-headed.

"Want me to get you a biscuit?" he asked.

"I just want some cereal."

She poured a bowl of Lucky Charms and a cup of coffee and sat down at the table. Sort of heaved herself, falling the last two inches. He thought she might have hurt herself but then the spoon was headed up to her lips. Green clovers, blue diamonds. When he saw a pink heart, he stood and walked to the front windows, his shoes folding the grain in the blue carpet.

All her life she'd been a good-looking woman and you could still see it in her face. But you could see the age too. And seeing it, Elvis suddenly felt mournful. He didn't know what to do for her besides the daily minding of her needs. He supposed that was enough, and that it better be because that was all this life allowed. Still, it felt like there should be something else, something to signify that here is a life, lived hard and well, and in a few years it would be gone and how could such a thing disappear with such goddamn ease? When she was gone, something irrevocable would be lost. When they buried his mama, they would bury the only America he'd ever known, the only people left, a bunch of infantile adults with their Wordle scores and Snapchat.

"What?"

He looked at his mama, her eyes fastened on him.

"Why you looking at me like that?" she wanted to know.

"Like what?"

"Like maybe you about to eat me."

"I ain't looking at you like nothing."

"You want to eat something you come over here and eat you a bowl of cereal."

Instead, he dug his feet into the carpet. The entire house was carpeted, bathroom included. He'd put it all down himself years ago, but could see that against the front wall it was beginning to fray, to come loose in the corner by the door. The whole house was beginning to come loose. Hairline cracks in the drywall. Larger cracks in the masonry around the fireplace.

This was who he had become, a man quietly watching his aging mama eat breakfast cereal in her aging house. He didn't mind it. He was forty-four years old and had worked hard all his life, going to work cutting lawns with his daddy or hoeing the corn patch with his grandma, canning, plowing, dropping the fry basket at McDonald's when he wasn't but thirteen. Chopping and stacking wood. He'd played three sports in high school and never did less than his absolute level best. All-region, All-state, started at strong-side linebacker as a true freshman at Carolina. Not that there was a happy ending. Instead of any sort of fuzzy final sequence, there was the Monster. The great maw of its open face—that was always the way he saw it, wide-mouthed and swallowing not so much his daddy and the girl he'd loved, not so much so many of his buddies in Iraq, but Elvis's entire life, every molecule of being traveling down the pipe of its throat.

First thing his girl had told him was you got pretty eyes.

Second thing was I got breast cancer.

Monster didn't care, and why should it?

Why should the Monster recognize the mechlorethamine of her chemo if it failed to recognize her good health? Her youth? The summer internship with the six o'clock news (NBC affiliate, Myrtle Beach/Florence market) she'd worked her way into? That had been the thing with the Vicodin. How, after the funeral, he'd swallowed three and wound up driving along the shoulder of I-26 Elvis thought he'd never know. The highway patrol had understood. *Mr. Carter? Can you hear me, Mr. Carter?* Everyone had understood. He'd suffered not so much as a harsh word, let alone a booking photo. Just two cups of black coffee while he waited for someone from the athletic department to drive him home.

The second time they'd had no choice. He'd forced their hand. *Goddamn it, you've forced our hand, and nobody hates it more than me.* He acted contrite but it was what he'd wanted. He was dismissed first from the football team and then the university. The state suspended his driver's license. His picture appeared on the front page of the newspaper. Star linebacker dismissed after drunken assault. There followed everything it didn't say: girlfriend dead. Hope lost. Drunk and disorderly and, finally, Tasered into compliance right there in the breakdown lane, cheek to the rumble strip. Lucky, he supposed. Had he not once made thirteen tackles against Clemson, two for loss, he suspected they would have shot his ass. He was big and tough and scary, and they weren't. In the South, that entitled you.

But he'd gotten back up, gotten on his feet. Walked into a recruiter's office and told the man his story. If you can get your shit together, we got a place for you. The recruiter saying this, a staff sergeant with a combat patch and a faraway look. If not, well, what the hell are you waiting on? I understand grief, son, but not this self-indulgent bullshit whimpering.

The sergeant just shook his head.

And it was that part, the self-indulgent part that had rattled Elvis. The possibility that his grief was unearned, that he had somehow taken a greater share than what had been granted. He could take a lot of shit about being a drunk or even throwing his life away—his mama, his stepfather, even his old preacher had thrown all that at him—but the idea that he was somehow unfairly cashing in on the Monster. Well, what the hell are you waiting on?

He'd worked hard at basic training and pretty much all the

advanced training the US Army could throw at him: jump school and ranger school, the Q course at Bragg. He'd worked hard because he'd had to, but more than that because he always associated something uniquely American with hard work—the pioneers, dirt under your fingernails, Springsteen on the radio.

He'd climbed into planes because they'd told him to, and then he'd gone and jumped out of those very same planes when some old master chief gave the word. He'd killed men, and not to sound all high-handed about it, but he'd killed men and watched men die, knowing that in that moment he was a hairsbreadth from such, that in the next moment he might actually be there, gutted on the rug of some godforsaken concrete hovel, a nineteen-year-old dumping QuickClot all over his chest while someone ran an IV into the stump of his arm. It hadn't bothered him because he had believed then and believed still he had been doing a very nasty and very necessary job.

He was poor by the standards of the Great American Economy but he didn't lack for anything. He didn't hate anybody, either. What other folks did, Black or white, gay or straight—it didn't matter to him so long as they didn't try to hurt him or his mama. Just let people alone being the basis of his worldview. Try to do some good. Barring that, don't screw things up too much.

He had other thoughts too.

He liked football, though you couldn't get a thing on the rabbit ears anymore.

He didn't pray anymore, but when he had, he'd meant it.

He wouldn't take a burger from nowhere but Hardee's.

The only biscuits he ate were his mama's and since she'd given up on cooking he'd resigned himself to go without.

He had guns but had no intention of aiming them at anyone—he'd done enough of that overseas to last several lifetimes. He had guns because he'd always had guns and because holding a gun you were reminded of what everyone worked so hard to forget: that decisions had consequences.

So it came as a shock to him when he saw people take his

measure and turn away, or take his measure and screw their face up with what they surely imagined was the proper response. Walking up a sidewalk in broad daylight when some petite fancy-dressed woman pushing a five-hundred-dollar stroller suddenly drops her eyes and hurries across the street like she's just realized the place she was headed was *there*, not here. It was surely a tiny sliver of what a Black man faced, but it hurt him, and kept hurting him long after he had grown accustomed to it.

It was why he kept offering the girl Nayma a ride. It had started out of sincerity, out of sympathy, but then something changed. He saw how she hated him, the cut of her eyes, the way she cocked her head like *we'll see*, and he thought, *Damn, girl, we will see. You'll be something in life and I'll be sitting right here, snaking a toilet and changing the heating element in the laundry room dryer.* Because offering her a ride hadn't started as an aggressive act. It wasn't meant to be charity either. *You get where you don't even feel human,* he wanted to tell her. *Me I'm talking about. But you too. You telling me people don't stare at you? People don't judge you? 'Cause they sure as hell judge me, so all I'm saying is if you'd rather not walk the two miles to the Dollar General then get in.*

He wanted to say that.

But he never would.

Ole Elvis wouldn't say a word. But he didn't know how to take it, either. Not that it was really a question of taking it or not taking it. No response was required except to admit, now and then and only to himself, that it hurt him. They wanted him to be a bully, a thug, someone looking to go out queer-stomping on a Friday night, and when he wasn't it didn't compute.

They wanted a box to put him in and it was the one thing Elvis could not and would not give them. Which seemed like a good response until he just realized the world would do it for him. One Sunday morning he was watching *Face the Nation* when a professor of finance came on talking about economic collapse and its silver lining of "creative destruction." It had taken a moment for Elvis to realize that tenured son of a bitch was talking about him, the destruction of his life, silvered or not, and a moment more to realize he was talking not just about Elvis but pretty much everyone Elvis knew and loved. All the folks too poor, too uneducated, too backward to matter. Talking about him and his mama.

Still, it could have gone so much worse, their lives.

He wasn't dead yet.

He was still right here.

And so was his mama.

"I'll come by at lunch and check on you," he said. "Anything you need? Groceries or something?"

"All I need's a bed and a bible, son."

It was an old joke between them, a line from Mayberry, and for the first time all morning she smiled.

"Come here," she said, and when he bent to her she pulled off his ballcap and kissed the top of his bald head.

"I love you, Mama."

"I love you too, boy."

Emily's twenty-fifth high school reunion was to be held at the old Germantown auditorium, a castle-like red-brick monstrosity of keeps and crenellations that had served the first half of the twentieth century as the town's jail, and the second half as the town's high school, the joke being you couldn't really tell when it switched from one to the other. It had sat dormant for a generation, but a few years ago several civically minded retirees had founded the Germantown Auditorium Restoration Committee and, between the bake sales and state grants, raised enough money to restore the building to all its pre-Depression glory.

Having left Kyle with her mom, Emily arrived at the auditorium to find a pallet of alcohol centered in the banquet hall. Boxes of Yellow Tail wine. Coolers of Sierra Nevada and Bud Light. A smiling, well-dressed man came out of the wings pushing a hand truck of Turning Leaf.

He stopped when he saw her and walked over, hand extended. He had a high-watt smile and clear blue eyes. Emily was tall, but he was way taller. Tan and slim, he was in a charcoal blazer and jeans he appeared to have pressed.

"Barry Read," he said. "I'm early, I know. But I like to *be* early. Get everything to the venue and so forth. Be prepared being the thinking."

"Like a good Boy Scout," she said, taking his hand. "I'm Emily Rhett."

"The Emily Rhett. Nice to put a face with the emails."

He smiled wider, and all at once, the breathless reviews on Yelp made sense.

Barry was such a gentleman!

Barry is hands-down the best bartender in the South!

"Mind if I go ahead and set up?"

"Of course. May I help?"

Turns out she couldn't. But what she could do was sample the product. He had the beer in the cooler and had opened a bottle of Yellow Tail to let it breathe.

"Does it matter, really, if a five-dollar bottle breathes?" Emily asked, flirting, stupidly, but unable to stop herself.

"Folks like that sort of thing," Barry said. "'Let the wine breathe a little.' 'Don't be afraid to put your nose right in there to smell it.'"

He laughed and Emily laughed with him.

"Not a fan of Yellow Tail?" he asked.

"Should I be?"

"You know we have a package that's slightly higher end."

"What does that run?"

"Thirty-seven dollars per person, more or less."

"Nope."

"Too rich?"

"For our blood, absolutely."

Emily had paid fifteen dollars per person and knew Barry would run out of Bud Light in the first hour while taking home at least half the wine.

"I understand." He laughed and, once again, she laughed with him. "Out of curiosity, you want to see what we offer?"

She hesitated, thinking for a moment this was some sort of pickup line, feeling equal parts panic and excitement.

"I mean if you're busy," he said.

"No," she said, "not at all. I've got a few minutes, though it is, like—"

"Early. I hear you. But like my sweet grandmother always said, *It's dark under the house.*"

They walked to the parking lot where he opened the side door on a delivery van, reached past coolers and cases, and came up with a bottle of Clos du Caillou Cotes du Rhone.

"Here we go," he said, passing Emily the bottle.

"This is the good stuff?"

"So far as a catered event in upstate South Carolina goes, yep, that's the good stuff. How 'bout a taste?"

Except instead of a taste, they drank the bottle. More accurately: Barry sipped from a plastic wine glass while Emily drank three generous pours.

To be fair, Kyle was with her mom and Judson with Henry's mom.

To be fair, the wine hadn't hit her until she got out of the van at Sertoma Field and felt the ground lurch. There was a moment of shame at having driven, but then she hadn't felt a thing until that moment. But she was feeling it now. Her neck flushed, and then her face flushed, and instead of shame all she felt was happy.

Then she thought of Knox and it all dissolved.

Knox: it had come to her only recently that he was a selfish man. For a long time she had thought him a serious man, focused and self-contained, the sort of single-minded artist who lived in an attic garret and ate off a hot plate. Now she saw that what she had taken as artistic vision was no more than lazy self-interest.

She laughed out loud, put the phone in her pocket, strapped the empty Baby Bjorn to her chest, and crossed the footbridge.

Sertoma Field was crowded. A good three hundred people had gathered on the soggy field by the giant beer tent with its stage and folding chairs, all of them with their funnel cakes and hot dogs and sauerkraut from paper boats. All of them turning to stare as Emily entered.

She was looking for her mom while everyone else looked at her.

Or so she thought.

But the wine, the general disorientation of the day…

The sense that the woman in the burn unit was floating just above her…

Don't be paranoid, Emily.

Her dad had likely been talking about this performance for weeks and the looks were no more than high expectations. All the insane acrobatics his boy would perform. *I invite y'all to imagine a goddang flying monkey with giant Tarzan muscles and a bellyful of Red Bull doing exactly what he loves.*

"Ninja!" someone yelled.

She passed the idle bumper cars, the stand for funnel cakes. Somewhere Judson was with his friends.

"Ninja time!"

Behind her, families piled out of minivans and a rank of Escalades and Tahoes and F-150s.

She found her mom—who refused to pass Kyle over—*let me hold him just another minute*—and saw the mayor waving to her across the field from where he stood with Tom, who was dressed in—dear Lord, what was he wearing?

She waved and walked over.

Tom nodded, his green cape suddenly catching the breeze and billowing behind him, exactly, she supposed, as it should.

The mayor looked nervous, fidgeting in his Germantown windbreaker and lederhosen.

"Emily Rhett!" he called. "When you coming back to work, woman?"

"How about never?"

"Never?" The man looked around in a comically wary gesture, beer on his breath and mindful of Baptists. "But seriously," the mayor said, "say hello to our beloved ninja."

"Hello, beloved ninja."

Tom fingered the empty baby carrier.

"You maybe lost someone?"

"No, he's—oops," she said—she seemed on the verge of laughter, amused, delighted. Then she realized she was simply buzzed. "He's with Mom."

"Where's Mom?"

"I don't know." She tossed a shoulder. "Over there somewhere, grazing."

"Grazing?"

"I mean not grazing. Gazing. Wandering. Enjoying the festive day and all."

"Well," said the mayor, angling his way back in, "that's all just great. Hey, so glad to hear Miss Greaves is fine. That was a scare—whew." He wiped his brow. "And tell that husband of yours we'd sure love to see him around city hall sometime."

"I will certainly tell him, Herr Mayor."

The mayor was looking around again. "He isn't here, is he?"

"Who, Knox?"

"That would be the one."

"Beaufort, I'm afraid," Emily said.

"Beaufort?"

"His parents' old place. Something with the air conditioning."

"The air conditioning?" the mayor said, as if encountering the concept for the first time. "Very important in the low country, I'd think."

"Critical."

"Critical," the mayor said. "An imperative for living."

Emily nodded thoughtfully. She wasn't the only one drunk.

"That's what he tells me too," she said.

"You mean Knox?" the glassy-eyed mayor said.

"I mean Knox. Regarding Freon."

"Well, fine, fine," said the mayor. "That is all just fine and dandy. Now." He planted a meaty hand on Tom's shoulder. "So tell me, Mr. Ninja, what are you going to do with your four minutes?"

Tom adjusted his green felt mask.

"You see that pole, Mr. Mayor?" he asked, pointing to the outfield lights. "I think I'm going to climb it."

And then he did.

Tom jumped, ran, swung, pumped his fist, and, finally, he climbed. The light pole was metal, the width of a telephone pole but without handholds so that he had to shimmy the seventy feet to the top. It was crazy and stupid and very impressive, and people were howling, clapping, cheering until—wait for it, Emily thought—they were being drowned out by the voice of Clara Greaves—furious and frightened—telling her boy to come down.

"Thomas Richard Greaves!" she yelled, and the place went silent. "You come down from there this minute."

He did that too.

To laughter. *His poor ole mama had to tell him to get down!* Their mother apologized when he was on the ground. *I didn't mean to yell like that, honey,* and Tom apologized back—*no, I was showing off, that was stupid.* Judson was slapping five and jumping around and some teenage girl passed over a Sharpie and asked Tom to sign her arm (which he did) and then her friend asked him to sign her décolletage (which he did not). The mayor was pleased, and all at once the Ferris wheel was turning and the bumper cars bumping and there was a line back to the porta-potties to buy tickets.

They walked together around the rides and tents and back across the footbridge, folks hooting and cheering and shaking Tom's hand. Emily was sober now, absolutely stone-cold sober, and strapped Kyle into his car seat without a word. Judson was begging Tom to come back to the house—*Mom's going to her reunion thing and we can just hang*—and Emily was nodding encouragement when she felt her phone go off.

It was Knox. The AC in Beaufort was going to be just fine.

Great, she typed. *Coming home?*

Of course she knew he wasn't. That was the reason she had asked, after all.

Not sure, he texted back. *All ok?*

All was okay, all was fine, all was just dandy, Knox. Life was wonderful and grand, you selfish son of a bitch.

She felt weirdly buoyant, pissed at Knox for his absence, but pissed with the sort of anger that could animate, the sort of anger that gave purpose. But then she remembered the mayor talking about her return to work, about Monday, and she felt herself collapsing, her spirit, her life; and falling into herself, she let herself ask the one question she'd spent the past few weeks not quite willing to pose: what would happen if she simply didn't go back?

It was the wine talking, the Clos du Caillou Cotes du Rhone 2013, the high-end package starting at thirty-seven dollars per person, but it was also Emily.

It was very much Emily.

What would happen if she simply didn't go?

She stood there by the minivan, Kyle buckled, Judson piling into the back, and let herself be enveloped by the possibility. It wasn't a financial question. She was reluctant to admit as much, but they would be fine financially. It was more about duty, it was more about could she face the woman in the burn unit? Could she face any of them? The women beaten with extension cords. The thirteen-year-old stepdaughters molested by their fifty-year-old stepfathers. The broken-hipped grandmother knocked to the ground by her grandson, stealing Oxy from the bathroom medicine cabinet.

"Mom?"

She realized she was deeply, soulfully pissed at Knox for not being here.

"Mom?"

She realized someone was talking to her.

"Hey, Mom!"

She realized that someone was Judson.

"Are we going?"

"I'm sorry?"

"Like leaving?"

"Yes, of course, honey. Just one second."

She slid shut the van door and began the long trek around to the driver's side.

She realized she was angrier with Knox than perhaps she had ever been, and it turns out it wasn't an anger that could animate—what the hell was that? It was a deeper hurt that felt suspiciously like abandonment when what she needed most at this moment was to sit down with him on the back porch overlooking the rusted swing and the scattered Nerf darts and talk this out. *What if I just didn't go back?* she would say, and he would nod thoughtfully, take her hand. *What if I told you I just don't think I can do this anymore? What if I said it wasn't one thing but everything, all that suffering, all the meanness in the world. What if I just stayed here with Kyle? What if I said I've done my part, even if I don't believe that's possible. What if I said it would be like failing, but I'm ready to fail?*

Knox?

Knox?

It was good she was having this out, she thought, though maybe preferable to do it in a place less public, without her boys in the van, Judson now tapping the window trying to get her attention. Still, still... *He set her on fire with a tampon. He duct-taped a sock into her mouth. He soaked her in lighter fluid, for God's sake.*

She smiled at her son, which meant she smiled at her own reflection, and held up a single finger. One second, she mouthed, and hurried behind the trailer selling funnel cakes, where she proceeded to cry her eyes out.

By early afternoon Lana had sent Stinson at least twenty texts and knew she had to stop, or should stop, or something, not that she was going to. She'd already made what was probably a terrible mistake, several of them actually, but they were the sorts of mistakes that made her feel awake in a sort of way she wasn't certain she had ever been. Alive, tingling. Then, all at once, she felt something shift, and all she felt was regret, regret and her complete overwhelming stupidity.

She'd slept through—pretended to sleep through—texts

from Christie asking if she was coming to Tom's ninja display. Slept through—or tried to sleep through—her mom knocking on her door and quietly sticking her head inside, Lana an amorphous lump of bedding and gloom.

"Honey?"

"I'm asleep."

"I know, babe, but it's after eleven, and I thought if you wanted to go to Sertoma Field this morning with your friends then—"

"Where's Dad?"

"Dad left for the game."

"I'm sleeping, Mom."

But she hadn't been sleeping. She'd waited for the door to close but only just, sliding her phone out from her body and sending the first text to Stinson, a guilty, cryptic, open-ended *hey*. He hadn't responded and she'd hurriedly sent a second *r u ok?* and a string of emojis—so adolescent, Lana!—she immediately regretted. Thereafter followed a third, then a quick shower taken in order to prevent the sending of a fourth. Which she sent, of course, before her body was even dry. She went downstairs for coffee and found her mother curled onto the living room couch with a book.

"Your great-grandmother's fine, by the way?"

"What?"

"Your granny. It was a false alarm."

"Oh," Lana said, "that's good."

She was guilty about that, that she had completely forgotten about her granny, but the guilt was no more than a tickle against the pull of her phone, intentionally left upstairs by her bed. Lana had been the absolute Last Person On Earth to get a phone, and back in the spring when she'd patiently explained this to her parents—how she was always asking, borrowing, *begging* someone for theirs *just to get a ride home!*—her mother had looked up from her own phone just long enough to say *drama much?* Which—Lana got the gist. But did that even make sense? As if she was the dramatic one, asking for what was basically a tool, a logistical necessity in her world, but that brought her back to the real problem. That being, her parents couldn't acknowledge that her world had changed: she wasn't a child anymore, no matter how hard they wanted her to be. Still, she kept waiting for them to release her.

It was on vacation last summer in Blowing Rock that she'd realized she would have to release herself, that if she wanted her parents to acknowledge her as an adult, she'd have to force their hands. No more babying them, her dad especially. How many times growing up had he spoken to her about the importance of character, of independence and courage? But sitting across the Monopoly board, the Blue Ridge Mountains visible through the cottage's great bay window, she saw that he'd become this needy, clingy thing, and maybe had been all along.

When Stinson had started paying attention to her—on her very first day of high school!—it had felt like a lever, let's say, something she could use to pry open some space between little girl Lana and, well, whatever Lana came next. She was all whatever about Stinson, but then she'd started to like the attention, like *really* liked it, like gotten hooked on it maybe, and when he kissed her that first time—first time she'd ever been kissed!—there on the edge of the parking lot where no one was watching but anybody *anybody!* could see—it was like that lever had suddenly caught and that fissure, that hairline crack, had erupted and through it poured this brilliant blinding light.

"What are you doing?" her mom called, which was so like her mom, seeing as Lana was trying to escape.

"Nothing."

"Want to do nothing down here with me?"

"Um," she said, and left it as a placeholder as she shot back to her room only to find nothing indeed. That was the point at which she called Christie to ask if Stinson was there at Sertoma Field. He wasn't, but everybody was talking about last night, the fight, the arrest.

"So apparently like your dad had them haul his ass away."

"Oh my God."

"Like it was your dad's call or something. At least that's what everyone's saying."

"But have you seen him?"

"He was in some juvie thing and apparently his aunt had to go down and sign a bunch of papers to get him out."

"He's out?"

"That's what everybody's saying."

"And he has his phone?"

"I mean I guess."

She'd texted him again then, texts five and six, and it was then that he'd finally responded. *Blowing up my phone*, he said, and then *u know where I been right?* Lana had typed back furiously *I am so so so sorry about everything. pls tell me u r ok?* What had followed was a more or less normal conversation, Stinson laughing off the arrest (*ha ha doing time*) and then laughing off the fight (*no big thing*). Lana knew she should be angry, knew, in fact, that she should be disgusted, but the jolt of reconciliation was too strong. She felt a flood of sentimentality, of forgiveness, of—it made no sense but she felt it all the same—gratitude. That *he* forgave *her*, thank God, because somehow she had gotten it into her head that she was the cause of it all. What had happened in middle hall, how she had made way too much out of what was just affection, and then how Dr. Agnew's senior assistant had shown up to intervene or interfere or whatever. It had all just gotten so tangled and out of hand when all he had really wanted was to have a little something to look at.

She paced around her room, phone in hand, half self-loathing, half joyous. When her mom came up to ask if she wanted to go for a walk—*I mean since it sounds like you're about to walk through the floor*—she took off the silver ring her dad had given her and put on Alice in Chains, one of her parents' old CDs filched from the basement and perfect accompaniment to her frame of mind. She was working herself up to she didn't know what, though in fact she did.

I'm not just sorry abt last night, she wrote. *I'm sorry about in the hall too. I should have just relaxed.*

She waited and typed again, *we could meet later?*

Then, *So sorry*

how sorry r u? came the response.

She turned the music up, moody and dissonant, so that she could somehow drown out the greater thrumming inside her head.

Let me show u

Where r u now?

My room

She hit send and had to put the phone down for a moment, walked to the window, walked to the bathroom sink where she stared into her own eyes, came back to find his answer:

Why don't u show me right now

And hereafter came her mistakes, but, again, the kind of mistakes that made her shake with something that might have been excitement but might also have been the absolute terror that's easy to mistake for excitement. He'd started asking yesterday in English class, badgering, bullying—but God, only a little—the incessant texts that had built to their confrontation later that day in the hall. *Go to the bathroom and send me a little something k?* slowly escalating to his attempt to take a photo himself, pulling at her shirt, her skirt, until Dr. Agnew's assistant had stumbled into everything and everything had just fallen apart.

Mistake.

And she knew it. Still…

The first mistake was just Lana on the bed, hair splashed across the pillow, phone held just above her. She was in a tanktop and her face had that puffy sexiness she associated with morning after scenes in movies.

Cute, he texted. *And…?*

In the second mistake—though you couldn't really call it a mistake yet, mistake was aspirational—she slid her shirt up a few inches, nothing scandalous, just a few inches of her stomach. But why call it a mistake? It was what everyone did, wasn't it? Those who could, she meant, and here a little pride, a little swell of ego: those who were *desirous*. That was Stinson's word: *you're so desirous, baby* and had she ever been called anything approaching that? Cute—here he was with cute, but she'd been cute all her life. Smart, sweet, pretty—she got pretty all the time too. But desirous—the very shape of it in her mouth felt adult, the soft slide of it, as if it were less a word than entrée into some new kingdom.

Very cute. And…?

She had to check the door then, check the downstairs for her mom, who was apparently still out walking (still!), check for her dad, who was apparently still at the football game (still!). *And…?* she read again, and then fell into that *And*, back on the bed, sliding her shirt up farther, and then, without realizing what she was doing, taking her shirt off, like she was drunk, which she sort of was. Feeling like the day she'd had two double shots of espresso (oat milk, extra whip) and her body began to hum. She'd sent three photos like that, *desirous*, lying in bed, sitting up in bed, leaning forward toward the phone's tiny glass aperture, and was considering a fourth when the shift happened and it was all Oh my God, what have I done, now so thoroughly gaslighted that the smell of herself made her eyes water. She made a motion that signaled some intention to pick up her phone. Yet she didn't, not for a moment at least. Then, fingers trembling: *Hey Stinson. Hey baby. Would you delete that?*

Delete what?

Maybe all of them, or just the last three?

Ha ha. They r all for me

Stinson? Feeling her blood run so completely into her face she could actually feel the heat in her ears.

Right here

Pretty pls?

Tell u what, daddys girl

What?

u and your daddy can both fuck off

Tom Greaves had a run in his tights.

It wasn't a big thing, just a streak of tension up the back of his left leg, but still, there it was. He was back home, back in his childhood room, the humiliation of the ninja display behind him when he saw it. He'd accepted the laughing, the half-snide congratulations, the honking horns as he drove home; but a run in his tights!

That was just…

He slid them down to his ankles—eighty-dollar Under Armour compression leggings, snagged, he guessed, on one of the rungs of the light pole—and sat there on the bed with the green fabric gathered around his bare feet. He didn't need them anymore, of course. It wasn't like he was planning to wear them again. But to know that everyone had stared up at such, that his costume had been compromised! They were an integral part of it, after all—felt hat, green cape, and *tights*—and he was of the old maxim in for a penny, in for a pound, which should apply, he reckoned, as much to a ninja outfit as anything else. And at this point in his day, his journey, the branching decision tree that was his *life*, Tom was in for way more than a pound.

He pulled the tights back up and studied himself for a moment in the floor-length mirror.

Was it noticeable, the run?

He twisted left and right but all that was immediately visible was that he was thirty years old, alone in his boyhood bedroom, and more than a little ridiculous.

He didn't care.

Or, more accurately, he cared very much.

But it was behind him now and there were other things to worry about.

Not his grandmother—his granny was fine.

But how about the FBI agent looking for his father? At the time, Tom had been looking for him too, of course. So it wasn't like he could help the man. *We just want to talk to him*, the agent had said. For what? *We just have some questions.* The man had handed Tom his card.

When you see him, he said, nodded, and walked away.

Tom wasn't sure what to think. Not that it was hard to

imagine what his father had been up to. He'd heard a story a couple of years ago about his dad and his dad's childhood best friend, John Long. They had played ball together as boys and later worked together at Long's Country Junction as high school students. The Longs had run the store for nearly four decades, always making a point to finance their deals through Mountain Empire Bank. But somewhere along the way—so went the story—Richard had screwed his oldest friend out of a substantial sum of money. Tom didn't know the details. He hadn't understood it. What he had done was dismiss it.

But now—

He pulled off his shirt—white, cotton/polyester/elastane, a winged foot over his heart—and then the hat, a little felt number, *jaunty* you might call it, with a gaudy yellow feather he'd had to bobby pin to keep in place. It was meant to be a Bavarian look—*the Bavarian Ninja!*—but it looked more like a disco Peter Pan.

He took out his phone and looked again at Ivana's email—*now is the time*—and might have sat there forever had his phone not gone off.

It was Brad, Evelyn's son, texting to invite Tom out for a drink. *My mom said you were in town and I thought maybe Plums around seven? Let me know if you're free and of course if you aren't...* But of course he was, and it struck him that this was exactly what he needed: a reason to get out, to have a drink, to be in the world since—he fingered Agent Abbott's card—he had the feeling the world was about to implode.

He texted Brad back—*looking forward to it. See you at 7*—and tossed his phone down by his expensive Hoka running shoes. Picked it up, looked again. *Now is the time if you are ever coming back.*

Sadness was the proper response, shame. But it was laughter that almost came. He almost laughed at the absurdity of being back home, at the absurdity of his drunken father stealing his pickup, at the absurdity of his drunken father somehow drunkenly stumbling directly past the FBI. Of his granny, near death, but also completely fine.

He needed to shake whatever it was he was feeling. He had the edible he intended to eat, but not yet. After the podcast but definitely before meeting Brad. Yet he needed it now. The drive home had been five miles but also at least fifteen disappearing years, which sank Tom firmly in late adolescence and all its attendant ills.

This was not the Tom he wanted to offer to the world of *SoulCast* any more than it was the Tom he wanted to offer to Ivana, or the FBI. Yet it seemed to be all he had. The problem as he saw it was that he had always believed life to be a very serious affair. To be responsible. To make a difference. The need to do demonstrable good in the world—he believed this was important, adult stuff. And it was, yet it made him joyless, this seriousness.

A little less than a year ago Tom had come home to watch his grandfather die of pancreatic cancer, a process that was both slow and, all at once, very sudden. He was not even in the ground yet when Tom decided he would go to the old Czechoslovakian town of Pilzen, where his grandfather had been on V-E Day. He could film the entire thing, get Knox's help editing it. A first-person documentary shot on his iPhone: listless grandson returns to the spot where his grandfather stood the day the war ended. It would be about family and generational change. About the absence of meaning in our dying world. But with hope, with a glimmer of hope. It seemed worthy, revelatory, a pilgrimage perhaps?

Well, obviously, yes—a pilgrimage!

He declared it such and left immediately.

And how could he possibly not?

The word alone seemed to justify immediate departure.

He had explained it to his mom two days after the funeral.

"He was in Pilzen when the war ended," he told her. He had the map of it up on his phone, a little blue star tacked against a series of wavy lines meant to indicate mountains. "Look here. The old Czechoslovakia. Wouldn't it be something, to go there?"

"I mean it would, but—"

"To stand in the same spot where he stood the day the war ended? Like an homage."

"I think it's truly wonderful. But, honey, right now? So quick?"

But it had to be quick or else it threatened to fall apart, to reveal itself as exactly what it was: sentimental but silly, well-intended if lame.

He got online and found a ticket.

He got online and found Gerri.

Lufthansa carried him from Atlanta to Prague, but it was Gerri who carried him the rest of the way. Gerri being the guide he had found online who offered *shuttle from Prague to Bratislava and*—italics here trailing off into imagination—*so much more…* The "so much more" was of less interest to Tom than the 150-euro price tag, by far the cheapest rate he could find. It was only when he was airborne that he began to wonder if Gerri even existed.

Yet there Gerri was, small and red-faced, waiting for him just beyond customs, smoking a Marlboro and nursing a cup of kiosk coffee, and when Tom saw him, it became real. He was doing this. It was an actual thing, had to be, because there was Gerri.

There he was indeed.

He would have been an Irishman except he wasn't. Red hair, smushy face. Maybe five-five *with* the tweed golf hat. Some sort of tribal band of interlocking triangles on his neck, on his bad skin, his flushed skin, his skin like he had just shaved for the first time and made a mess of it. He was Czech and bored and apparently unfazed by the rain that was falling all over him.

"Thomas?"

"Tom."

"The American?"

"That's me."

"Fock yeah. Come this way, mate."

Tom walked to the Mercedes van and loaded his single bag

into the cavern of the back. The carpet was vacuumed, the wheels shined. There in the gray rain of the gray day, past the gray concrete of the terminally gray trees, the white shell of the van appeared a bit absurd. Tom figured it was stolen.

Gerri stubbed out his cigarette. "Where's the rest of your shit?"

"What shit?"

"Like your luggage and shit."

Tom motioned at the leather bag. It was no bigger than something you'd carry to the gym, but carried, he thought, just what he needed. Some clothes, his journal, a few photographs of his grandfather leafed into the pages of a copy of Bruce Chatwin's *The Songlines.* There were six of them, including one of his grandfather smiling shirtless in fatigue pants and combat boots. V-E Day in a square in Pilsen, Czechoslovakia. Which was where Tom was headed.

"Just the one?" said Gerri. "I like that." He lifted the bag but paused mid-air. "Hold on a focking second. I know you, mate. You're the four-minute guy. What is it?"

"I don't know."

"You bloody well do. I seen you on my phone, yeah. What will you make…no… What will you try?"

"What will you do," Tom said, with great resignation, "with your four minutes."

"Aye, that's focking it. Ripcord! Get in, mate."

That was the point Gerri started speaking, and then it was like he couldn't stop, hands like birds, window cracked to let out the smoke from the cigarette he kept burning.

He told Tom about the war, the Nazis, the Soviets, about his parents in Prague in '68, about girls. Did he want girls? Is that what Tom was after?

He was not.

Drugs?

No.

Boys?

No.

Well, what then, you skeezy bastard?

Tell Gerri and Gerri will find it, all right?

They were driving through fields, irrigation ditches, clusters of small houses. There was some color now but everything was so wet, the fog so thin and ever present, that it wasn't so much color as the idea of such, the possibility, the kind of thing that might grow up to be green or yellow or red if only it stayed in school and ate right.

Where was he going? What did he want? What did he *need?*

Pilsen? Gerri repeated. Do I know Pilsen? The fock I do, mate. I know it well. Little town in the mountains. I can take you to Pilsen. I know a girl, her family still lives in Pilsen. The Tatras, high mountains like your—what is it?—your Stone Mountains?

Maybe Rocky?

Your Rocky Mountains, right. I'll take you. You and me. Pay some glory to your dear dead grandfather, yeah?

Tom was all *No, thanks, just Bratislava is fine* but he was also sleepy, exhausted by eighteen hours of travel, and looking back he suspected that in his fatigue he must have shown some weakness, some crack into which Gerri wriggled his fingers.

They crossed the Danube and Gerri took out a bottle of *slivovice* and a moment later the van pulled up by a large gray—Jesus, the gray over here!—boat that appeared once to have been some sort of ferry meant for hauling cars down the river.

"Where are we?" Tom asked.

"Where are we? Earth, the world, the glorious Slovak Republic."

"I mean here." Tom gestured at the boat. "I mean this."

"This?"

"This focking boat."

The *focking* fell right out of him.

Gerri didn't seem to notice.

"You said Botel Gracias."

"Yeah."

"This is Botel Gracias. A riverine hotel."

"Riverine?"

"You see the sign right there?"

And Tom did: BOTEL GRACIAS A RIVERINE HOTEL scripted in four languages. Reading it, he remembered a moment in his mom's kitchen, three days ago though it felt like months now, when, scrolling through TripAdvisor he had come across the listing and thought to be sure to avoid that floating mold factory. But he had been in a hurry and now—

"Na zdravie!" Gerri said, and Tom found himself taking a shot of plum brandy.

A moment later, he was on the street, or the dock, more accurately, and Gerri was pulling away, smiling, horn beeping twice, big goofy grin, big goofy wave. Tom went to his room and passed out.

When he woke six hours later, the room was dark and seemed to be moving. Where was he? Oh yes, at sea, or docked, at least, along the Danube. The Botel Gracias. A circular porthole letting in just enough filmy light to see the shape of his tiny room.

He dressed and made his way up the hall—the carpet was damp, how had that happened?—past the desk clerk, and down the gangway onto the promenade that paralleled the river. There was still a pervasive grayness and the lightest of rains was not so much falling as hanging about his ears. But the lights of the buildings were on, the lights on the bridge, the ghostly streetlamps; and the city was beautiful, crawling its way up the hillside in a series of bright necklaces.

He felt cold and wet and, for the first time since his grandfather's diagnosis, happy.

He decided to walk until daylight, at which point he would fill up on coffee and find a car rental to head into the mountains. He would have made it too, had his stomach not started to rumble. It was after three by then, some of the bars having closed, but some—judging by the EDM bleeding through the walls—clearly having not. He found a quiet place with a brass Buddha. It was maybe a bar but maybe also a restaurant and he was eating pad thai and drinking a five-dollar Singha when a loud group came through the door, pushing aside the polite Asian man offering menus. Maybe seven or eight of them, like British soccer hooligans only they were speaking a mash of what was surely Slovak. He put his head down until one said, *Tom? Is that Tom focking Greaves?*

It was Gerri and something, that glimmer of happiness maybe, or the warmth of food and beer in his stomach, something compelled Tom to go along with them and soon enough he was drinking Jameson at an Irish pub—they really were soccer hooligans—and at some point after that, now thoroughly drunk, he was studying the map Gerri had drawn on a cocktail napkin. *Pilsen?* Gerri kept saying. Also *my sister* also *your grandfather* also *you have some money, yes?* which was the point at which Tom realized he must have been talking about his pilgrimage, drunk, yes, but still hoping to God he hadn't used that word.

He woke in his room, his porthole a wash of morning light, no clue as to how he got there until he saw a figure crumpled on the floor, snoring through his mouth. He was careful not to wake Gerri when he took his bag and left to find whatever breakfast would help ease the way out of the great circus cage of his hangover.

He found an urn of coffee and drank it hot and black, two cups and then a third, while out the fore windows he watched barges lumber through the brown water, the sun an area of light rising between a distant skyline of concrete monoliths. His own brain was rising too. And hangover or not, it was hard not to feel a certain optimism. Morning running around the edges of things, implacable. All of it with a purpose, including Tom. Purpose! That was important to keep in mind, otherwise the overwhelming feeling was a keen sense of how ridiculous he had become. He thought to perhaps make some note in his journal, a proclamation of sorts. It was a new journal, a Moleskine picked up at the Buckhead Barnes & Noble.

He had the journal out and yet…

Yet he knew he wasn't going to write in it.

Still, it was a step further than he'd gotten with his phone, having so far failed to film anything. Maybe one more cup of coffee, he thought, but also, maybe not. It was past ten now. Even in languid Eastern Europe, a rental agency would be open by the time he found it. His eyes ached and the first caffeine jitters were arriving as he hit the street. The chill air pulled the skin of his face tight. But he was here, he was going, he was happy.

He started toward the crosswalk when he heard the horn.

"The fock you going, Tom? Eh, Tom?"

It was Gerri, of course, in a Skoda knock-off of a VW Golf. Like that was the car you'd knock off, Tom was thinking. Not: Gerri? What's he doing here? Because Tom was open to everything, including, he now remembered, whatever it was Gerri had drawn on the cocktail napkin the night before.

My sister, he'd said.

The Skoda pulled to the curb. It was slightly larger than a bathtub but it was just the two of them and Tom had only his bag so why the hell not? he thought, and climbed in.

The sun came out in Austria, so bright it seemed to roll off the green hills and follow them through the fields of sheep, giant wind turbines turning above it all.

They stopped at a station for petrol and strawberry kefir, Tom paying for both.

They were headed south and south wasn't the direction that would take them to Pilsen.

Tom didn't have to say it because Gerri had already offered a long justification that took the form of a filthy monologue. *So my focking sister, Sarai, she's in focking Slovenia, so my mum sends me to pick her up and guess what, mate? She isn't focking there. She's left. Croatia, they tell me. Her friends do. Some football asshole she's been focking on the side. She's beautiful, my sister—half-sister, same mum, different dad—but she's a whore and she goes off to Croatia to do I don't know what. Now Mum hears she's back in Slovenia so my mum tells me...* The road ran through farms and hills, tunnel after tunnel cut through the mountains, a clear stream tracing the road before veering toward the ruins of a castle. The windows down and the air full of diesel and the smell of hay drying in ricks. Tom had lost the thread of the conversation and had never followed the logic of it. It didn't matter. The gist of it was that they were going to find Gerri's half-sister Sarai somewhere in Croatia and bring her with them because:

A. Gerri's mother had told him to, and, more pertinent to Tom's story,

B. She knew people in Pilsen, she knew, in fact, everyone in Pilsen—*likely slept with most of them, mate.*

It appeared all Tom had to do was pay. He was fine with that. He had money and, more importantly, had given himself over to the journey. If he was being used a little, well, he could stomach it. If he was going out of his way by days, possibly even a week, what was the real hurry? The point, he was coming to realize, was motion. The journey rather than the destination. The square where his grandfather had stood had been waiting for seventy years and would still be waiting in a few days' time. Besides, what was he going to do after? Didn't arrival signal an end? Didn't said end necessitate a new start?

They arrived in Ljubljana that night.

The next day they found Gerri's half-sister Sarai.

The next day Tom met Ivana.

Now he sat on the bed and looked at his meager possessions. He was leaving, and he would travel light. He needed to tell someone, though. Not his family, of course. Not his mom or dad, definitely not the host of *SoulCast.* Most definitely not Jack. He'd thought of telling Emily, but no. While he loved his siblings, he had long known he needed to live his life in a different manner. This had come to him very early, around, say, the time he refused the natural progression from five-year-old T-ball to six-year-old coach's pitch, and followed him up through his refusal to attend the Citadel—*first male Greaves not to go,* his father's words, whispered—through his long sojourns abroad—*first male Greaves not to get a real job,* his brother's words, yelled. Let it be said, however, that he wasn't trying to piss anyone off or even to be openly defiant. It was just that the only path he saw open to him was the path that ran in the opposite direction from that taken by his brother and sister (*big* brother, *big* sister). His conscious life ran from 9/11 to 11-fucking-9—it was the only world he'd ever known. He had a theory that it was different for Jack and Emily. They had known a previous world, animated by the Clinton administration and Microsoft Windows. A world *with* living coral reefs but *without* Twitter. What was bedrock to Tom was anomalous to his siblings.

That was everything.

That *changed* everything.

That he would eventually arrive at the far shore of Responsible Adulthood he took as an item of faith.

He would get there.

He just had to get there on his own terms.

The largest obstacle was his parents, but he had a plan from the very start: he would do his best to disappoint them early and often. The problem was, everything he did, every outwardly defiant act, only seemed to please them all the more. That his intentional defiance—because it became defiance, eventually it did—only seemed to make them love him more signaled trouble.

That they were thrilled by his matriculation at Calhoun College rather than the Citadel—trouble.

That they were delighted he eschewed graduate school or a "real" job to train for *American Ninja*—trouble.

That they believed Ripcord!'s rejection by the FDA to be a sign of chemical genius—definitely trouble.

It was all trouble because he loved them, and they loved him, but he knew that somewhere down the line he would do something that would drain their love for him. And the fall would be catastrophic. The fall would wreck them all.

Yet he couldn't help himself; he kept climbing higher.

Then came the near mythical pilgrimage, the disaster of it, the humiliation.

The fleeing to Prague and the eventual flight home.

Now he was beginning to wonder if he hadn't finally found something that would not only disappoint his parents, but break their hearts, as if he might last-straw himself right into memory. He'd been searching for it all his life, but now that he'd maybe found it, all he could think about was how to make it right. He walked to the bathroom, walked back to the bed.

Shower, he thought. Move. Something.

But what he needed was to talk to someone, and eventually, his mind had settled on his old English teacher Elias Agnew. Tom had hoped for a moment he would be at the performance, knowing all along he wouldn't.

But what would he actually say?

He imagined big sweet Elias Agnew leaning forward in that earnest manner of his.

Dearest Tom, are you all right?

Yes, I'm fine, thank you. I appreciate it, but I'm just fine. Just proving to be an absolute failure at navigating life. Just waiting for my father to confess whatever white-collar crime he's committed. But otherwise, sure, yeah, I'm dynamite.

"Honey?"

The voice surprised him: his mom on the other side of the bedroom door.

"You all right in there?"

"Yeah, about to shower."

"Okay." Yet he didn't hear her walking away and he waited for it.

"Are you sure?" she asked after a few necessary seconds had passed. "Maybe you want to talk for a second?"

"No, thanks," he said. "I'm fine."

She must have been nodding slowly, an affirmation Tom could only imagine.

"Okay. I've got to run out for a minute. Sure you're fine, honey?"

"I am," he said, and walked to the bathroom and turned on the sink just to prove it.

There was no reason to replace her abuelo's beer, but it gave Nayma a reason to get out, some purpose besides sitting inside which, she realized, she was in danger of spending the rest of her life doing. She'd already missed two calls and three texts from Regan. But she wasn't ready to talk yet, the previous night still too sharp. The EMTs had taken Regan away. The police had taken Stinson away. She'd seen it all from the shadow of the end-zone restrooms, Regan having screamed, *Run, Nayma,* and Nayma had. She wasn't sure how she should feel about it. A part of her wished she hadn't, a part of her was ashamed. But another, larger, part of her was exhausted. Running was what she never did. She was of the "stand your ground" school of thought, and that was what she had done again and again. Her entire life was made up of standing up against assholes like Stinson. But all of a sudden, around the time Regan jumped in front of her, Nayma had realized it wasn't sustainable, the way she was living.

All she wanted in that moment was to run.

And that was exactly what she had done.

She took a Dr. Chek from the mini-fridge and thought of her parents in an Irapuato weave room, the air fuzzed with fabric dust while they turned out seven-dollar T-shirts for J. Crew, or of her abuelo, whipped with a silver antenna before being locked in the airless moving truck that would carry him out of the tomato fields of Immokalee. She thought of the dying—the possibly now-dead—Greaves woman. This was all very real, and yet completely not. Which, Nayma thought, was maybe a sign of depression, but also, maybe, a sign of honesty, a sign that she was paying attention.

Consider this: what if all the things that screened you from *real life,* consumer decisions like the new Droid versus the iPhone 6, or the petty grievances playing out on Facebook, or even, say, memories and longings to see her parents while simultaneously wanting to get even farther away from her parents—suppose all of these things that kept you from *authentic* life (they'd read Camus' *The Stranger* in Dr. Agnew's class) actually *were* what was meant by an authentic life? That in trying to live outside of these conventions, in trying to live outside what seemed so petty and every-damn-day, you wound up with no life at all?

She sipped the tinny soda, one sip, two sips, and then held the can to her face. Surely this had all been thought out before, articulated with great precision by some German theorist with a starched collar and vaguely racist leanings. She should probably ask Dr. Agnew for a reading list, and she knew she would, eventually. But at the moment she just didn't much care to do anything beyond stand at the sink with the TV pouring through the drywall and the meth heads twitching their meth dreams and her grandparents working and her parents working and the world, so far as she knew, turning steadily on the great slant of its axis.

She stretched out on her bed. The Moana curtain/towel was pulled back, but that felt wrong—she never slept like that—so she pulled it across the wire line, closed herself in.

Felt a throb radiate from the ridge of her right eyebrow and shifted the still-cold can.

Her face was swollen—maybe purple—not that she was bothering to get up and look—and very much a badge of honor. Her *Red Badge of Courage*, just to keep with the whole US lit theme. Tender and swelling. She pressed two fingers against her temple until a white light burst behind her eyelids and she realized that was pain, the flash, the sweat that suddenly studded her scalp. But she was glad. She was proud.

She shut her eyes and let the warm quiet of the room sink around her.

There was always something poignant about cheap hotel rooms. She didn't always think like that, of course. Mostly this was home, mostly this was an insufficient stand-in for home. But it was always there, that sense of American timelessness. Like it was 1950 or 1970 and she was in Los Angeles or New York, smoking a cigarette on her back, unemployed and listless. That Edward Hopper romanticism. Earth tones and empty windows. Proof, she supposed, she'd spent too much time listening to Dr. Agnew. She was tired. An almost cosmic fatigue was falling now, lying over her, accumulating like dust. Her mother had taught her English from Arnold Lobel's *Owl at Home*, or maybe not taught—that wasn't exactly right. Read it to Nayma when Nayma was just a child, read and re-read it again and again, and she remembered well the story of Tear-Drop Tea, the lonely things, the broken pencils and mismatched silverware. John Steinbeck was on the floor beside her on the gray or graying indoor/outdoor carpet, so add that to the list of lonely things: thick paperbacks, yellowing on a dusty floor. Add to the list Nayma herself, lying alone atop her bed on a fall day, feeling all at once a lifetime of exhaustion so that it wasn't Nayma reclining on the bed so much as her sorrows.

Another name for me, she thought: My Sorrows.

But that was just a little too indulgent, despite the copper light parting the curtain.

That was just a bit too much.

She lay there until her grandparents came home, both dirty, sweaty, and exhausted. Meanwhile, she thought, here's Nayma, clean, rested, and depressed. She decided to walk it off, decided to replace her abuelo's beer, and in the late afternoon stepped out onto the concrete stoop, a wadded ten in the front pocket of her jeans.

"Nayma?" her abuelo called. "Where you going?"

"Nowhere," she told him, and turned in that general direction.

Clara parked not behind but beside the green dumpster, a subtle shift in arrangement that registered like the end of something. She'd always taken care to hide her car when meeting him but today, she didn't know about today. She'd left Richard at the hospital, left Tom in his childhood bathroom. Left the nose of her Lexus edged out, visible, cracked the window, cut the engine, and dug her fingernails into her palms.

The thing was, the day had started so well.

Tom's ninja display had put her in mind of those years when

the children were young, which made her happy, or at least she meant it to. Those had been the best times, when the children were little more than babies. Sun kissed, those years with the children. Such nostalgia was meant to comfort her. But in truth, it only made her more anxious. To be happy in a world of suffering, my lord, what kind of monster can be legitimately happy knowing what everyone knew?

Richard, she knew, was more than willing to accept the wrongness of his happiness, to accept anything so long as he didn't have to forsake such contentment.

To just be wrong.

To be wrong, but also happy.

That's how you do this.

This being life.

This being the only one given.

But Clara was less sure.

The sound of the boy knocking against the dumpster made her look up. He had that awful look on his face, smug, self-satisfied, a forelock of brown hair down beneath his skullcap and licking his eyebrows. He came forward like a dance step, a slide, a nod. She thought she might vomit.

"Hey, Mama," Stinson Wood said.

She tried not to look at him. The exchange should have taken seconds yet he dragged it out, arms folded on her door, smacking his gum. *Hey, Mama,* he kept saying, *you know a silver honey like you*—and she kept not looking at him, handing over the rolled bills, taking back the Advil bottle filled with the lozenges. *You know me and you.* And still she wouldn't look, eyes forward, palms on the wheel. *We could call...* She'd just put a hand to the ignition when he said her granddaughter's name, when he said, *Lana...* No idea of the context, just that single word floating out of a cloud of disregard, emerging through a fog of regret so that it was felt more than heard. *Lana,* he said again, and there on the screen was a photo of her granddaughter, and how Clara managed to drive the claws of her left hand into his still-smiling cheek, those nails that just a moment ago had been dug into her own palm, how she did it she had no idea. Only that he was yelping and staggering back, holding his face and calling her a bitch.

She shifted her car into drive, a sudden and decisive movement that required not so much as the turning of her head.

"You shut your white-trash mouth," she said, in a voice she barely recognized as her own.

But also, very much did.

They'd found Gerri's sister in Ljubljana.

Tom thought of it as he moped around the house. In another hour he would put on a headset and Skype in to *Soul-Cast* and was trying to collect himself, to prepare for the sort of questions Nick Handle would ask, questions about *mind mastery* and his *creative headspace*, about celery juice and the benefits of intermittent fasting. But he was alone, and Tom alone meant Tom lost in thought, Tom lost in memory.

Which meant Tom staring at the edible.

A purple cube wrapped in cling wrap and slumped by body heat and three days in his front jeans pocket, it was four or so gummies of good Serbian THC, Gerri had said. Artisanal and whatnot, so maybe cut it in, you know, maybe thirds.

But instead of cutting it in thirds Tom ate it in a single rank bite.

Ridiculous but also, whatever.

Now, he thought, back to Ljubljana.

Which was where they'd found Gerri's sister. Tall and dark-haired with those impossibly high cheekbones. She had a flat in the Neboticnik building, the city's lone skyscraper. Tom sat on a plastic lawn chair in the cramped living room with Sarai's roommate, Ivana, while Gerri and his half-sister yelled at each other in what passed for the kitchen. Ivana the roommate appeared shy, sitting properly on the couch. Pencil skirt, hair up in a bun, all secretarial. Saying not a word in English or any other language, but looking, nevertheless, invitingly ergonomic in way that made Tom aware of his hands.

Gerri came out of the kitchen scratching his head with his thumb, Marlboro between his fingers.

"We can't stay here, mate," he told Tom. "Spatial concerns."

"Were we planning to?"

"We'll get a place nearby. I may have to drug her to get her home." He shrugged. "Five hundred milligrams of Thorazine. Put a diaper on her. Stuff her in the trunk." He paced to the balcony and back. "I'm joking, of course. But Mum, she's upset."

They Airbnb'ed a room, and that evening sat at a café that overlooked the Ljubljanica, the table crowded with Heinekens and an untouched basket of pita bread. The ashtray gray and full, the river more smell than shape, an onion curl that wound through the buildings and market of the Old Town.

"My own focking sister and she treats me this way," Gerri said. "Mum would drag her over the coals. You liked the roommate though, Ivana?"

"We didn't speak."

"She has eyes for you."

"We didn't exchange a single word."

"They're meeting us tonight, you know. I think she wants you."

Tom sat very still to let the sweat run over his face, then pulled out his handkerchief and wiped himself clean, a careful gesture, moving along the brow, both sides of the nose. He intended the movement as solemn, the sort of thing he would record in his Moleskine, were he ever to take it from his bag. The sort of thing he would film, were he filming anything.

Meanwhile, Gerri had started singing something by Genesis.

There was more beer as the sun dipped toward the mountains. At some point Gerri lit a spliff and took a great luxurious puff. "Should you?" Tom wondered aloud.

"It's good Serbian shit."

The air was skunked with it.

"But in public—"

"Tom, really. Focking take it. You're uptight and here Ivana loves you so much."

Tom took it from him and a moment later felt the ground going out from beneath him, a sensation like standing barefoot in the outgoing tide, the water pulling the sand between the toes. Getting dragged out to sea. It was the point of the trip, he realized. The *theme.* Eventually, he'd write it down. He'd write everything down.

Meanwhile Gerri had moved on to Phil Collins's solo stuff.

Tom thought of this hours later, the idea of a *theme*, a *purpose*, while dancing with Ivana. They'd met Gerri's sister and roommate in a warehouse in a neighborhood of Stalinist apartment blocks. Walked past the Fiats and Mercs, the gangs of teenagers milling around skate parks. The buildings cluttered with satellite dishes and external wiring.

It was a busy night.

Prostitutes.

Children throwing rocks at dogs.

Men selling falafel and orange soda from carts.

Tom danced until sunrise and woke in the rented pension much as he had woken in Bratislava: hungover, with Gerri asleep on the floor. He went out for coffee and a box of fried chicken they ate with their hands. A tin of aspirin. The tap water warm and metallic.

"She wants you, mate. Sarai said as much."

They were seated on the floor, paper box holding the gray chicken bones.

"I'd say last night you were wanting her back," Gerri said.

That night they did the same thing, beer and pot, dancing with the girls. Following Sarai and Ivana through the crowd. The clutch purse holding their mobile phones and what proved to be a bump of cocaine Tom and Ivana shared in the bathroom. The world a dazzle after that. Dancing. Kissing. Clothes sweat-stuck and the music throbbing in his neck. Waking the next morning to find the sequins of her skirt all over his hands. Her body glitter on his face. He took a cold shower, realizing he hadn't done so in days.

"We should just go over there," Gerri said.

And strangely, they did just that.

"We'll just be going," Gerri said, and amazingly, he and his half-sister did just that as well, leaving Tom and Ivana alone in the tiny flat Tom was coming to think of as not so tiny after all.

They stood there facing each other.

It felt very cinematic, the way they stood, the way the afternoon seemed caught in the folds of the curtains.

"What do you want to do?" she asked him.

Her English was slow and studied, but not in any sort of caricatured way. She just seemed to be thinking, to be actually asking a question he should actually consider answering.

"I don't know. What do you want to do?"

"We could maybe," she said, "the bed?"

"Okay."

"It folds out."

They folded it out. Sat beside each other, lay on their sides, fully dressed. It felt so tender. He ran one fingertip along her forearm and she shivered. He could smell her hair, her shampoo. It was apple. The light in the curtains was amber. It felt so gentle. When he kissed her, he wanted her badly, needed her, and thought *to need someone, to want someone.* Desire being one more old friend, forgotten but now returned.

It was evening before either spoke again. The light gone, the room overheated.

"You are rich?" she said.

"What?"

"Gerri says you are an American TV star."

"Gerri said that?"

"He says you are a rich TV ninja with a powerful drink your American government will not allow."

They were naked and filmed in the lightest of the sweat, the sheet thrown over them.

"Gerri said I'm a rich TV ninja?"

"Much money he said."

"And it's really just the FDA, not the entire government."

"Very much money he told me."

You weren't supposed to say these things, though no one seemed to have informed her. Tom couldn't help but be charmed.

"Some," he said. "Enough, I guess."

"Do you like me?"

"Do I like you?"

"I like you," she said, and he thought: so here's where this is going, here comes the shakedown. Here comes the hustle. But he thought something else too, he thought, *Why not?* At that point, he still believed he was on a pilgrimage, and didn't that imply some circuitous way, some wandering? Again: the journey more important than the destination?

"Yes," he said. "I like you too."

"Then we should go somewhere, together."

"With my ninja money."

"Yes, exactly. Let's take a trip."

"Where do you want to go?"

She said, "Everywhere."

In lieu of everywhere, they rented a car and drove down the coast to Opatija, a seaside town that terraced to the palms and boats and cafés open to the Adriatic. Got a room at the Grand Hotel Palace by the jewelry stores and giant dogs in silver collars. The St. Bernard's and Mastiffs. The third husbands for the aging countesses. The caviar and late-night dinners consisting of nothing but vodka and quartered limes.

They walked along the promenade, her feet in straw flats, her fingers ringless.

On their balcony they ate tinned sardines and drank white wine, and Tom thought: I am falling in love. This is what it feels like.

And for a while, it did.

For a while, he was exactly right.

For weeks, he basked in it, reveled in it. He made a few Facebook posts that he would come to thoroughly regret, but right then, right there? It was pure. It was love.

Gerri had left to drive his sister back to Bratislava. He offered to take Tom, but Tom wasn't yet ready to leave. So instead of Pilsen, he and Ivana followed the coast to Split where they took a room in the old quarter, halfway up the hill with a view of the harbor and Diocletian's marble palace. Outside were terra-cotta roofs and flower markets, giant stands of bright fruit and Italian cigarettes.

Then came cloudless days, days they would kiss for hours.

They found a club in an abandoned bus station and for three weeks they went at her insistence. The androgynous boys. The kohl-black eyes of the underfed girls. When she danced he watched the spot in her throat where her heart beat. At dawn he led her home, the tablets of ecstasy lingering so that they kissed through a dreamy haze. He would wake to find her in the bathroom. He realized she was hoarding soaps, tiny hotel soaps, as if they could be eaten.

They slept and kissed and Tom felt his body going slack. Had there been more than a single meal a day he would have gained weight, but instead he grew leaner. Ivana seemed to thicken, barely noticeable on her spare frame but he noticed, and what it seemed to him was luxurious. Her breasts and waist. He woke one morning with his hand on her stomach, tip of his index finger nested in her navel. It was inexcusably intimate, yet he couldn't bring himself to move it.

In April, they bought tickets for a cruise on a massive catamaran that left the harbor as the fog lifted. The sun burned white and everything arrived in perfect focus, a molten clarity so that Tom imagined seeing every grain of sand, the feathers of every passing bird. They cruised toward a green dewdrop of island. The hostess had a microphone and a bottle of Jack Daniels with a pour-spout. The bar was open, the crowd young. Twenty-something Germans. Italians in soccer shorts.

They dropped anchor in a clear inlet, a few mountain goats watching them from the scruff of land. People jumped off the sides or clamored down the ladder fixed to a pontoon, drunk and loud and happy.

Tom followed Ivana over the side, the neoprene clinging to

her hips, her hair smoothed in a single motion. Sailing back, they dozed on the trampoline netting. You could feel the sun above and the spray beneath, the mesh embedded in the soft of their shoulders. Almost three months they'd been together. He knew it was love.

"There's something I have to tell you," she said, but she didn't, and the next day Gerri returned, and they all three left for Pilsen.

And it was in Pilsen that he decided he would finally write something in his precious Moleskine, something, he thought, about happiness, about finding one's way. He would film his hands moving. The film would start there, after the fact, after the pilgrimage was complete. But before he did, he took the six photographs of his grandfather, stood in the central square, and tried to orient himself. Gerri smoked, while Ivana slouched on a concrete bench, sullen since Gerri had returned. Tom held up first one photograph and then another. But something wasn't quite right.

"Been seventy-odd years, mate," Gerri said. "You didn't expect nothing to have changed, did you?"

He didn't. Shops, trees, even roads—he could account for those. What he couldn't account for was why that mountain was *there* when it was supposed to be *there.*

"Let me see that," Gerri said, and began to nod, stubby finger pointed at the handwritten caption on the back. "Well, there's the focking problem, Tom. Pil-zen, not Pil-sen. Zed versus S, mate."

And that was when it hit Tom: he was in Pilzen, Slovakia, when he should have been in Pilsen, Czech Republic. He was in the wrong goddamn country. He wasn't in love either. He was simply, and thoroughly, a fool.

The humiliation, the frustration, everything concerning this colossal disaster that felt less geographical than metaphysical was just beginning to crash over him when Ivana walked over to tell him she was pregnant.

Knox Rhett was in Columbia by ten in the morning.

He hadn't intended to be. His intention had been to take his sons to the Oktoberfest in the afternoon and accompany his wife to her high school reunion that evening. He had agreed to go months ago, and then, standing in the kitchen while Judson drank his designer chocolate milk, he had changed his mind.

And you have to be there? Emily had asked.

He'd shrugged, smiling, but not exactly at her.

And how she'd said nothing.

And how he'd said, *Sorry, Em*, and then left.

That was around eight.

By now she was—

Actually, he thought, pulling onto Gervais to park two blocks down from the statehouse, he had no idea what she was doing or even where she was. And where was he? He was in Columbia, just beyond the reach of his father's shadow. Big bronze Augustus Rhett up on a concrete pedestal, glowering like he'd just been informed by Robert Penn Warren himself that he hadn't got the part in the latest movie remake of *All The King's Men*. They'd erected the statue a few years ago and Knox, despite, or maybe because of, his complicated relationship with his famous father, had spoken at the ceremony. At the time, his father's scowl had served to amuse him. But now, realizing its permanence, it only made him sad, particularly in light of what Knox was doing.

He paid the meter and walked once around the grounds of the capitol, knowing before he was halfway that he had made a mistake. He felt his father's sculpted head following him, as watchful as ever, and by the time he was near the gates to the Horseshoe he knew he should turn around, abandon whatever it was he was doing, walk directly to his car, and go home. Yet he kept going.

Thirty minutes later, he was back at the car.

For his troubles, he felt sweaty and self-conscious.

For his troubles, he felt twelve.

Yet he managed to get back on the interstate, merging into

the southbound traffic, before he began to cry. It wasn't a big thing. He wasn't sobbing. More a misty-eyed regret, though who could say for what? Everything and nothing. A sort of emotional version of cancer of the unknown primary. Which was, he knew, insanely melodramatic, the sort of hyperventilation he normally loathed. But it also felt right. Everything he had told Emily that morning had been correct, so far as it went. He really *was* meeting the realtor about a problem with the air conditioning at his late parents' home. What he hadn't told her was that none of it was critical. Just an excuse for leaving, he knew.

Emily knew the same, of course.

Lately he'd been bracing for a *serious talk*. He could feel it coming like weather. Her maternity leave was about to end and Knox knew she was torn about returning. Torn about everything, really: Hated her job, but needed it. Sick of him, but, yeah, needed him too.

He felt himself on the edge of weeping.

That he wasn't with the boys or Emily—that was part of the tears, he supposed. Not because he was actually missing the events of the day. It was more that he had the desire to miss the events. He wanted to say the *need* to miss, but then where was he but back at melodrama, and he liked to imagine all the melodrama existed in the past.

Yet driving south, he felt it return, because driving south felt like time travel, the act of becoming a previous self. He'd made the drive, north and south, a thousand times since childhood, riding with his father, his mother, his father's driver or aide or page or counsel. Going to the statehouse, to college, a Carolina football game, a wedding, a party in a field somewhere in Laurens with a giant bonfire and a collection of vodka bottles they threw into the flames. He'd driven it early and late, hungry and hungover, dreaming, crying, to see Emily or with Emily, his right hand thrust down between her thighs, or—more properly—both hands at ten and two, Judson behind them with his picture books and then chapter books and then, later still, MP3 and iPhone.

He knew the highway intimately.

The highway comforted him.

Down along US-17 were signs for kale and field peas. Seasons' Best. Can after can on billboard after billboard and surely this was a good thing, advertisements for vegetables, something fibrous and moral. He needed that. There had been a moment of discomfort when I-26 intersected I-95. Beaufort lay down 95. This was his exit. To stay on 26 was to wind up in Charleston and there had been that moment of hesitation, that moment of confusion. He had thought all morning of making a side trip to Charleston but knew better. In the end, he stayed on I-95 and made for home.

A visit to Charleston would be—how to put it? He didn't know. Only that it felt off-limits. Knox wouldn't go to Charleston because he wouldn't go near Mother Emanuel church. He couldn't. Those eight souls, ascending, shot dead with their Bibles in their laps. To some unquantifiable degree, he was to blame for what had transpired there, the evil, the hate—wasn't that his father's legacy? Despite Knox's progressive politics and pro bono work, despite his unstinting financial commitment to the Southern Poverty Law Center and his progressive activist film—Jesus, how he'd come to hate his film—wasn't it his *family's* legacy? It wasn't logical but logic had nothing to do with it. He had made a study of race and poverty and injustice from the very start. He had *cared*, he had taken it all very seriously. But in the end, he hadn't taken it seriously enough. No white person had, and look what had happened.

He had once thought it would be different. What was amazing, actually, was that he'd once thought he was starting a revolution, or at least a conversation. *The Late Rebellion* would change things! He would lead the New South out of the darkness of his father's past! Oh yes, he would!

What he had actually done was take a few meetings, spent a few nights at the Chateau Marmont. Made provocative statements about Southern plantations and the "slavery-tourism economy." Used the expression "the New Jim Crow." He saw his errors now, the vanity, the hubris. He'd been so self-righteous, so *certain*.

And look what had happened.

Look at the world.

So. No Charleston.

Instead, he was in Beaufort, turning through a series of narrow lanes until he was parked outside his childhood home, the realtor's car already in the cobbled drive. The size of the house never failed to stun him. Three stories of white clapboard and black shutters. The grand balcony. The tidal pond in the backyard. The house was in the center of downtown Beaufort yet it appeared as some rural mansion, hemmed by live oaks and azaleas. The Spanish moss might have been hung by set designers filming some Civil War epic, which, of course, is exactly what had happened. Denzel Washington had stayed in the third-floor bedroom during the filming of *Glory*. The house had served as Union Hospital No. 6 and it was here that casualties of the all-Black 54th Massachusetts had recovered, and died—thirty-three of them—after their attack ("ill-fated" as it was usually described) on Fort Wagner in Charleston Harbor.

As for the movie, Knox had been witness to none of it, away, as he was, at the state Governor's School—his father's decision. He'd had absolutely no desire to shut himself away with two hundred well-meaning, ambitious nerds. Yet it was there he had met Emily.

The realtor Evelyn Walters was waiting in the kitchen.

"You didn't have to drive down, Knox." She came forward to put one hand on his chest and kissed him slowly, deeply. "But I'm glad you did."

They wound up in one of the upstairs bedrooms, the windows up but the room overheated by the time they were finished, sheets as damp as the still air.

"Did I tell you I saw your brother-in-law yesterday?" she asked. "At the luncheon."

"Jack?"

"Tom. He's doing some sort of ninja thing."

"Right."

"Like jumping and swinging and whatever. He seemed a little…"

"Yeah."

"I told him to call Brad."

Brad being her son, Knox knew. Brad getting remarried, having, post-divorce, landed on his angry, oversized feet. Knox knew all about that. Evelyn had landed on her feet too, post-divorce. It was only Knox, post-nothing, who seemed to be crawling.

"You okay?" she asked him.

He nodded and watched her slim figure rise naked from the bed to disappear into the bathroom. A few minutes later they began to move around the house, Evelyn back in realtor mode, as if it were she who had grown up here and not Knox, pointing out what had been repaired or painted or updated. There was an offer on the house, but Knox was starting to think he wasn't going to take it. In fact, he was considering moving in, a bit of information he had admitted to no one.

"And the air conditioning?" Knox asked.

"He should be here at two. Something's leaking Freon. The coil, maybe?"

"Is this a big thing?"

"Does it matter?"

"I guess it doesn't."

"One point four mil, Knox. If you have to spend a couple of thousand on the AC it's an acceptable price."

She stopped on the stairs to look at him.

"You are going to take it, aren't you?"

"I'm still considering things."

"Please, Knox. This is seven figures we're talking about."

"I know."

"This is serious money."

They wandered through the upstairs bedrooms and back down the stairs. The rooms were mostly as they had always been. Heart pine floors and bright walls. A fireplace of crumbling masonry at every turn. There was a pencil sketch by Holling Clancy Holling, and a number of paintings, including a John Singer Sargent that belonged in a museum, not a humid coastal mansion. Evelyn was talking now about a portrait of some aging cotton planter. She'd met Knox at a Calhoun College art gallery event two years ago. He had asked her advice on the house and despite the distance she had taken it on as a sort of special project through which she had come to possess an encyclopedic knowledge of its history, the artworks and the period furniture, this or that dignitary who had spent this or that night. Knox liked hearing it, even if he had difficulty paying attention. It was an alternative history, a narrative other than the one he was otherwise living. That being, the suffocating presence of his dead parents, who never quite seemed dead when he was here.

His hadn't been an unhappy childhood, more like a stressful one. Rewarding, interesting, often exciting. Full of trips and guests and lavish birthday parties. But those moments were extracted at the cost of great vigilance. As if he'd spent his first sixteen years sitting in a straight-back chair.

"What are your plans?" Evelyn was asking, or had apparently asked some time ago. "Knox?"

"My plans?" He reached for the hand she'd pulled away. "You know my plan."

"I meant today. The air conditioning."

"I'll wait for him. He's coming at two?"

"I've got some errands. But I'll see you this evening, all right?"

When she was gone he sat in the living room and pried open one of the windows that overlooked the backyard. The tide was coming in, an overripe smell he associated with illicit sex, something damp and mossy and not quite to be acknowledged. He put his face to the window, a book of Sally Mann photographs in his lap, and closed his eyes. His plans were to keep the house. He'd ask Evelyn to move in with him. Crazy, but why not? The affair had been an accident, he supposed. Driving down to meet her and then spending so much time together picking out wainscoting or interviewing painters specializing in historic preservation, and it was the wine or it was the heat or who the hell knew. All he knew was that he'd done away with any notions of due diligence and dove stupidly and irrevocably headlong into the thing. She couldn't quite take him seriously, though. Go back to your wife, she didn't say but surely thought. An affair is an affair, Knox. That's all. But it wasn't all.

When they'd started dating, Emily's serious do-gooder ways, her *convictions*, as Knox thought of them, were one of the first things he had fallen in love with. To care about the poor and powerless—it was hard to imagine a greater rebellion against the entitlement of his family. What diversionary fun, he'd thought, and watched his elderly parents squirm. It was tough at first, but he imagined that given time he would grow out of his casual expectations of money and privilege. What he'd actually done was grow into them, his sense of entitlement groomed by the knowledge that he'd given it away freely and, perhaps, foolishly. But okay, whatever. He'd thrown away the country club life, but that didn't mean he couldn't someday get it back. He'd put his time in, work hard, do good, and somewhere nearing the middle of life's way, he and Emily would take their feet off the social justice pedal and drift into a hazy afternoon of money and leisure and three o'clock cocktails. But it hadn't proven to be the case. Emily had only become more strident, more obsessed (though she no longer talked about it) with the life and death of the activist Rachel Corrie. Her maternity leave had been something of a reprieve, a safe, if shallow, harbor. That she would be back at work on Monday seemed dangerous. As if her life was teetering and the slightest movement might bring her down.

He put the book back on the coffee table and stood.

He'd heard something.

Someone was in the basement, and he walked down to find the repairman, another old family friend—*Hey, Mr. Knox, didn't know anyone was here*. It was indeed the Freon, the hose leaking, an easy fix. He wrote a check for two hundred dollars.

"Not too bad, actually," the man said. "Old houses like this you never know. All that history."

"Yeah."

"Stories, you know?"

He did, but he didn't want to talk about it. Instead, Knox saw him out and sat down on the basement couch and sent Emily a text.

Got off easy with the ac. 200 bucks.

Not that she cared. But including her somehow made it all feel a little less suspect, like he was doing the family some great service for which she would be grateful. The response came a moment later.

Great. Coming home?

Not sure, he texted back. *All ok?*

All good, was the answer, and he left it at that. No *Luv U*, No *Miss U*. It would be easy enough to solicit such. If he texted Emily that he loved her, no matter how annoyed she was with him, she would text the same right back, and mean it. Only to do so felt manipulative, *was* manipulative, and he had enough of that in his life right now.

He wasn't going to text her.

He put his phone on the end table and thought of the way his bronze-headed father's shadow had followed him in Columbia. They were tearing down statues all over the South and it came to him that they would be tearing down his father soon enough. He suspected he would be asked to attend whatever ceremony accompanied its removal, just as he had been asked to attend the ceremony that accompanied its unveiling.

He thought of his father blocking the door of a high school.

He thought of his father on what had proved to be his deathbed, here in this very house. What about the fact that his father, the champion of segregation, the kingmaker of the militant South, had died in the same room as soldiers of the 54th Mass? The men shot to shreds on the sand ramparts of Fort Wagner. It was one of those accidents of history, one of those ironies. A question for *Jeopardy*, if *Jeopardy* was still even a thing.

This US Senator and longtime champion of states' rights died in the same house in which African-American soldiers in the Union...

That was true. But also so unsatisfying, so inadequate, that it was reduced to trivia.

What it came down to was more basic.

When his father was dying, this proud titan of a man who had both stormed Omaha Beach and screamed defiantly into the face of LBJ, had told Knox that he wasn't afraid, and in that moment, there in his inclined bed, his father a skeleton with eyes, Knox had believed him. But he didn't believe him anymore. How could he?

He almost turned to ask Emily but Emily was where?

No, he definitely wasn't going to text her. It was clear she wasn't texting him either.

The basement was stifling, but the AC was humming now, and he could feel cold air just beginning to pour through the vents. Oh, Emily, he thought, what happened to us? Only he wouldn't let that thought actually arrive. That was the one thought that had to be suppressed.

Somehow.

Then he saw how.

Across the room was a giant armoire that sat tipped forward on the uneven floorboards, appearing to Knox, as it had since his childhood, like a fat man about to vomit. Inside was a VCR and television combo, a giant thing from the early nineties, surrounded by VHS tapes and the occasional DVD. He found *Glory* in its padded coffin and inserted it in the player. It flickered to life and there was Ferris Bueller done up in epaulets and soul patch, there was Denzel in his homespun and brogans, and there, thought Knox, was life, and just like that, he was crying again.

That he had pretty much lost his shit wasn't up for debate. Even if both the host and producer of *SoulCast* had assured Tom that he'd actually given great content—*living content, open and vulnerable*—that would be edited to convey the nuances of his thought, rather than the rage that had overtaken him, Tom knew, all the same, that he'd made a mistake. Which was maybe the edible he'd eaten, but more likely was simply Tom being Tom. He slipped the headphones down around his neck and looked around the basement—the quietest, calmest place he could find.

A mistake—he could feel it just beginning to articulate itself: regret, self-loathing. But then again, maybe not. Maybe he'd just spoken his mind, though wasn't *speaking his mind* rather than enacting his curated self the essential mistake?

Probably.

Almost certainly.

If you were angry, you must be right. If you were offended, you were correct. That was the current credo, he reminded himself.

He clapped shut his laptop and unplugged the headphones. It had started well enough. He'd sat silently through the long lead-in that sounded like a discussion of exercise habits before revealing itself as a well-disguised ad for an outrageously overpriced fitness-tracking app. That was followed—seamlessly, it should be said—by another pseudo-discussion/advertisement for a meditation app that led to—again, the transition was seamless—the host, Nick Handle, introducing Tom to his listeners. There was lavish praise for Tom the Influencer, reckless regard for Tom the Athlete. Even Ripcord!, Tom's failed energy drink, came off sounding like a magic elixir. It was all glorious and complimentary, and Tom wasn't above hearing it. It was only when it dawned on him—was everything here concealed or was he just that slow?—only when he finally, *finally* became aware that the show was a sort of "whatever happened to…" deal that he felt the flicker of panic that steadied itself into a flame of absurdity. The gist of it all seemed to be: *this once rising cultural icon is now a has-been, but there's life after ruin, right, Tom? Right?*

Q: So talk to me about the peace you've made with renunciation.

A: Renunciation? As in renouncing what exactly?

Q: I'd love for you to articulate that, Tom. The idea of finding meaning in obsolescence. The desuetude of human purpose, if you will. I know we'd all love to hear your thoughts.

A: You realize I'm thirty, right?

Q: Exactly. An intelligent, compassionate human in what should be the marrow of his life and yet you've elected a different path, one of obscurity, of an almost corporeal anonymity, as if your facelessness has a smell. You were a cultural darling, perhaps the preeminent influencer in the field of twenty-something longevity-seeking holistic progressive athleisure humans, yet here you are. You aren't out scaling mountains with Bear Grylls or making commercials with Simone Biles. You aren't on social media. Up until today you haven't given any interviews—

A: Well, I—

Q: It's antiquated. It's almost religious, your level of withholding. I think of monks and desert holy men. I think of shamed politicians caught in blackface. Only you have chosen this path freely. You have chosen to cross this public Gobi on your knees. Talk to us about that, Tom. About your conscious withholding. Can you give us your *thing*?

A: My thing?

His thing was that why did it have to be a *thing*? Your interests, your beliefs, your lifestyle—God, how he hated the idea of lifestyle—why did all of it have to have a name, a following, a hashtag, a "meet-up" for "like-minded" individuals? Is it, he wondered (stupidly) and very much aloud, that I've decided my values needn't be performative? That maybe the act of virtue-signaling signaled not virtue but the absence thereof? That maybe I take issue with the fact that you don't actually have to believe in anything and you sure as hell don't have to do anything so long as your Twitter followers can clearly label you as woke or MAGA or whatever the relevant category? That you can spend forty Gs on a new kitchen while half of America starves, or buy your children's way into Yale while employing not two but three tax lawyers to make sure you don't have to support public education for a dime more than necessary, and it's all just fine so long as you speak the language of critical race theory or the flat tax? You just have to pass whatever purity test is currently en vogue, Nick.

A: Interesting, yes, I see, I see…

Why just yesterday he'd read an article in the *New York Times* about the "consciously sober," which, turned out, was just folks who didn't like to drink. So why couldn't they just not drink? Or drink? Or do whatever the hell they wanted without it being a *thing*? Did it all have to be advertised, a brief flicker of ego only to be forgotten a moment later? The world had always run on disposability, but only lately had disposability acquired such frenetic speed. The universe was cold and indifferent. God was dead and you paid student loans into your sixties. Yet here I am, tagged in this Instagram feed yet again! Can you imagine Tarkovsky on Instagram? How about Simone Weil on Snapchat? It was the neediness of it all that he couldn't bear, the naked pleading to attach oneself to something, to anything. It should have filled him with sympathy (wasn't he an influencer after all? one of the best and brightest? one of the worst?) and probably would have, were it not for the willingness of people to turn themselves into yet another commodity, sold on the market of public opinion in exchange for an endorphin rush of acceptance. Entire households making TikToks to 80s rap, thus turning families into consumer brands.

And it wasn't just people!

Driving around town over the past few days he had noticed just how much had changed. In place of mills and warehouses and the sort of shit-kicking pool halls that had existed just a generation ago were bakeries and coffee shops, home decor and hiking stores, boutiques, doughnuts, ice cream. Noodle shops. Crepes, for goodness' sake. The Americana band busking on the sidewalk while a flock of girls in sundresses window-shopped.

A: I'm not sure what to think of this, Nick.

But actually, he was.

A: I'm happy, but it's a happiness tinged with the sort of

sadness I recognize as two parts nostalgia and one part bullshit. This is progress, and of course I want it. But there is also this sneaking suspicion that in paving over so much of the past we've lost anything remotely authentic. That's the nostalgia part. The bullshit part is that we need, and need still, Nick, *we need still* to bury so much of that last authentic culture because so much of that last authentic culture was a racist, homophobic patriarchy.

But hear me out: there used to be a bar in Pickens County called Bob's Place, better known as Scatterbrains. You didn't go into Scatterbrains, you didn't go *near* Scatterbrains unless you were a biker or at least fancied yourself badass enough to handle one. Then, before it burned, it started showing up on various lists of the South's best dive bars. It started showing up on Pinterest. It became, through no fault of its own, a caricature of itself. A place where retirees in Land Rovers could drive over from their gated communities—they're every-goddamn-where now—have a two-dollar Bud, and then dine out with their HOA friends on the story of their night slumming with the good ole boys. Somehow this infuriates me, the way in which the things that still exist have become commodified, served up as "authentic" Southern, all of it grits and field greens and scored to James Dickey's banjo.

Q: I so admire your intentionality, Tom. But I'm hearing anger too.

A: Hell yes, you're hearing anger. But let me tell you, I'm infuriated at my own anger. I'm also, when I'm completely honest, afraid of it. Lately I've been thinking about that "you also had some very fine people on both sides" comment made, you remember, in regard to protesters and counter-protesters at the Unite the Right rally, remember? Charlottesville, remember?

Q: I—

A: It's a repulsive comment—on one side were white supremacists and white nationalists, Nazis. On the other side were, well, everyone else. Then I think of all the people I've loved in my life, people I believe were indeed very fine people, but were also racists. Not Nazis, of course, but folks who were—as some people used to say—"products of their time," and I start to worry that my frustration at witnessing so much of the past disappear is, in fact, nothing more than some deep-seated unacknowledged evil, something that as a Southern white man I am neither more nor less than my cultural inheritance.

Q: I had the feeling that in your endorsement of Adidas you were perhaps trying to say something about race—

A: I am. I'm saying I don't want this.

Q: So what is it you do want?

A: I sure as hell don't want online self-flagellation. I want to be critical of my country while also loving it. To acknowledge the evil of slavery without throwing out the entire project of enlightenment thinking.

Q: And, of course, you are a Southerner?

A: I want that too. I want to love the South without being implicated by it. I want progress but I want it surgical. Take secession and Strom Thurmond, take Bob Jones and his university, take the racism and the guy wearing the sandwich board, all bad-eye and venom, and leave me the Chattooga River, leave me my grandparents on the porch, leave me the fish fries and Ronnie Milsap and the old man at Open Arms Church who played the dobro so lovingly you swore he was cradling his child. Leave me the South, leave me the *world*, Nick, the one I knew before I actually knew anything. Leave me the world I grew up in, only make it better. We don't have to burn this place down. We can love it into something better. That's what I really want: I want it both ways.

Which is what makes me Southern. It's also what makes me American.

There'd been something more after that, he supposed. He knew there had been, but his heart rate had been too elevated to comprehend much else other than the assurances of Nick Handle and his producer. That, and the regret. He sat with the headphones around his neck and let his blood pressure drop, eyes shut until he heard his mom's feet on the stairs. A lamp burned in the corner.

"Tom?"

"Down here, Mom."

"Can I come down? You're finished?"

"Yeah, I'm off."

She came into the room and sat down across from him.

"How did it go?"

"I think I just canceled myself."

"Canceled yourself from what, honey?"

"Nothing. It went okay."

"I'm sure it went great," she said, and reached out to squeeze his hand. "But don't stay down here, all right? It's so—"

"Yeah. I won't. Remember Brad Walters?"

"Your old friend, of course."

"Well, maybe not exactly an old friend. But I'm going to meet up with him."

"Oh, that's wonderful. I'm so glad."

"Unless you think— Did you see that?"

"See what?"

The lamp in the corner had begun to glow brighter, he noticed. Softer, yeah, but definitely brighter, as if someone had shaken it, woken it.

"See what, honey?"

"Nothing. I just meant like with granny."

"She's fine, Tom. I promise you. She'll be home in the morning. Go have fun."

He slipped off the headphones and noticed his mother was dressed to go out.

"Where are you headed?" he asked.

"Over to your sister's to watch the boys. I think Judson is having some sort of party."

"Maybe I should just go with you."

"Tom, go. Have fun."

"It probably won't be any fun."

"Oh, honey." And here she placed one palm lightly on his cheek. The light behind her was blinding. "You don't have to be so serious all the time, you know?"

He nodded, even if he was incapable of being anything but.

"I'll see you tonight, Mom. I love you."

He waited until she was up the stairs before he took out his phone, so radiant with the glow of THC it almost hurt his eyes to look.

Still, he managed to message Ivana.

At precisely six p.m., Elias Agnew drove downtown for his fried chicken. The school week was complete—the classes he taught, the lunch duty he refused, the pep rally he skipped—and here was his reward, a tradition that dated back to his childhood. His father had been the last country doctor in the county, a pure soul who martyred himself to the whims and whooping coughs of his patients, but no matter how many house calls there were to make, no matter how many patients sat in his waiting room reading *Highlights* or *Field & Stream*, come Saturday evening he met his wife and young son at the Steak House on Main Street. His father worked ten hours a day, six days a week, but for seventy-five minutes, he belonged to Elias and no one else. Those had been, perhaps, the best moments of his life. After his father had passed, Elias and his mother had continued to go. Then she had passed and Elias supposed that should have been it, but of course it wasn't. It couldn't be. He was too far along, too deep in the grooves of life's making to change course now. And he sure did love his chicken.

He nosed his Olds up to the meter and lumbered out into the cool afternoon.

The Steak House was an odd place in that it served fried chicken and biscuits, candied carrots and chocolate chess pie, giant glasses of tea so sweet as to set the teeth singing in their sockets, but red meat—the *steak* in Steak House—was nowhere to be found. The owner was Lebanese, a jolly man beloved by Germantown's white-bread hyper-conservative lawyer-and-doctor class who made deals and weekend golf plans, arguing real estate and tee times and Clemson football over plates of creamed corn and Arabian Rooster. There'd been some brief disquiet when the owner had posted a few anti-Israel fliers during the First Gulf War but such was life, Elias supposed, in a thriving hotbed of multicultural sentiment. Ultimately, not even End Times theology and the conversion of the Jews could compete with that light breading and juicy breast meat. Ultimately, all was forgiven because the Steak House was not so much a restaurant as an institution, at least according to *Southern Living*, though Elias, forgive him, had always found *Southern Living* notoriously pedestrian.

Not that he preferred any of the shameless purveyors of the New South, all dandified and upmarket with their handcrafted pocketknives and né-plus ultra-artisanal jams. Their "Ten Best" lists selling everything from bars to patio furniture. He'd spent years riding with his father on house calls, and the South he knew, the South he loved, was earnest and blue-collar, devout and hardworking. They loved Elias—good to see your boy out with you, doc—though he knew had they not known him as the son of Houghton Agnew they would have hated him. Bookish and obese, poisoned-tongued (though only to those who deserved such), sexually indeterminate. They voted Republican and read—if anything—the *Left Behind* novels. Elias would sooner have cut off his swollen feet than do either. But then again, pulling wide the front door and hobbling into a wall of air conditioning, some overeager surgeon would no doubt be cutting off his feet soon enough.

He moved left along the wood paneling as heads began to peek up and call *Dr. Agnew! Professor! Reverend!* (the only one that hurt). They were his friends, to the extent that he had friends, which was to say not at all, not if you got down to it. They loved him, but loved him the way you love a pet that behaves so strangely it seems to be begging for its own YouTube channel, loved him for no more than the anecdote that could be wrung from his life. *You should meet this guy. Sweet guy, fat son of a bitch, but sweet. And queer as the day is long.* That he was mocked by the acolytes of Small-Town Capitalism, devotees of Chamber of Commerce mediocrity living their *Purpose Driven* lives, made it, almost, bearable. Their Dale Carnegie smiles, yucking it up while their overweight wives (wearing too much foundation, and don't even start on the hair spray), elbowed their bald husbands in the region once defined as the ribs. *Stop it, Ty. He is a sweet man. I remember his daddy giving me my measles shot.*

He took a tray and silverware wrapped in a paper napkin.

What he'd learned was to give them what they wanted, that so long as he was high-strung and fey, so long as he was swishy and erudite on the outside, he could be himself—whatever that meant—on the inside. Masks. Secrets. He'd learned that during the George W. years, a time that had seemed perversely dark, though that past darkness now seemed no more than the lightest of fogs against the Trumpian present. His ability to hide himself inside himself was a trick he played on himself, as childish as it was embarrassing. But it had also kept him alive. He had thought to teach it to Nayma, then realized one day she knew it far better than ole Elias ever would, the smart brown girl taking up American jobs/oxygen/space.

He slid his tray down the metal tubes of the buffet while behind the sneeze guard a series of smiling Mexican women nodded and plated his chicken, his creamed corn and candied carrots, his *Yes, a biscuit, please, I don't particularly care for that sweet cornbread, darling, I'm sorry, but my mother raised me to abhor cornbread better suited for the pastry case than the cast iron and I won't chance the possibility of meeting her on the other side of the pearly gates, only to have her accuse me of such gustatory behavior.*

The chocolate chess pie.

The sweet tea.

Nine dollars and sixty-four cents at the register. A bargain, he thought. Ten dollars for the feast he should avoid altogether or at least limit to chicken and vegetables, the tea and the pie sugar bombs that would shortly go off, sending his insulin spinning and spiking and crashing. But then he thought—as he so often did—of his dead parents. He thought of the world outside the plate-glass windows covered with circulars for cancer benefits and church concerts and how little of that world he still recognized, and how much less he cared to recognize, and how what he carried toward his booth—*his*, the same booth he'd sat in since he was nine months old—represented one morsel, one taste, of what his life had been before everyone who loved him up and died on him, and he was left among the ones with passionate intensity, the worst, exactly as Yeats had understood them to be. He thought of all that, and he ate.

He would eat every bite.

When he was finished he would go home to the deep harbor of his study, the books flush to the shelves' edges and arranged by subject—theology, history, poetry, fiction. Within those divisions they were alphabetized by author. It was his mother's sense of order—control what can be controlled, because so much we cannot—and it was comforting. He had loved her for many reasons; not least of these was her ability to order the everyday. He had come to believe it was what people needed most: a sense of order, a firmness. To be looked in the eye—it was the most human of acts—to be affirmed. That had been his belief as a pastor: you stood up there in the pulpit and looked them in the eye. You told them they would be all right. It didn't matter if you believed it. It didn't even matter if they believed it. He needed to say it as much as they needed to hear it. It was what they gathered for, it was the reason for the church, that blessed assurance.

He hadn't always known this.

He had once thought his role as the head of the church was prophetic. He would read and pray, and in silence he would wait on the small still voice of God. It would come on the wind or it would come in the thunder or, perhaps, out of the whirlwind. But however it came, *when* it came, he would listen intently, bent toward mystery, knowing shortly he would rise up from his knees or his desk or from behind the wheel of his Oldsmobile, straw cross around the gearshift, and speak to his wandering flock. What wisdom he would impart. Poems and parables. Much talk of the mustard seed and the faith of children. The Kingdom of God is like this or like that—he had only to sit and wait.

So he had sat, and he had waited; he had cupped his ear to heaven. Only God in his infinite wisdom had chosen not to speak. God in his infinite wisdom had chosen to define himself with silence. Yet, for a long time he kept getting up before them, his congregants.

Then one day he simply couldn't, not anymore.

One day he surrendered.

He gave up and came home, took a job first at the community college and then, after it was closed following state budget cuts, the local high school.

In the end he realized his role as a teacher was not terribly different from that of pastor.

It was contingent.

It was to ferret out needs and meet them.

For the Stinson Woods of the world, he was there to break their certainty, to bring an awareness that the world was larger than the new Benz on the sixteenth birthday, or the vacation in Aspen. The fooling around with prescription pills and fourteen-year-old girls.

For the Naymas of the world, he was there to channel, to assist, to midwife them into that larger world out of which he had fallen.

That he was a figure of derision, a running joke with his cane and his diabetes and his Nixon boater—he could live with that. He had returned to this world by choice, after all. He'd had his chance to run away and what had he done with it but run home? He could live with that. What he couldn't live with was the thought that someone else might not get the same opportunity.

"Hey, Dr. Agnew! Hey, Elias! How are you, doc?"

He looked up into the pink face of Kenny Dunn, an

insurance salesman in golf attire, a mask of blood pressure puffed around his eyes. The rodent-like face of Ben Barnes appeared beside him.

"Elias!" Ben announced.

"Mr. Dunn." Elias wiped his mouth and followed his napkin into his lap. "Mr. Barnes. To what do I owe the pleasure, gentlemen?"

"We just saw you over here and thought, hey, can we sit a second?" Kenny was asking, but Ben was already squeezing into the booth opposite. They faced him, damp forearms planted on the table, both jowly and flushed and leaning in with what was surely known in less genteel quarters as shit-eating grins.

"Well, gentlemen?" Elias let it hang there, a little ring of verbal smoke they allowed to dissipate before elbowing each other and giggling.

"We's just wondering if you heard about Richard Greaves—" Ben started.

"If you'd heard about his mama?" Kenny asked.

"You mean Rose Greaves? What about her?"

"She fell or something."

"Or something?"

"Hit her head, is what I heard."

"Oh no. How is she?"

"She's in the hospital," Ben said. "But that ain't what we came over to tell you."

"Yeah, sorry," Kenny said. "That's something else entirely. It's Richard—"

"But is she okay?"

"Who?"

"Rose Greaves."

"Yeah, I heard she's fine, but listen, at the luncheon yesterday—"

"This would be the Oktoberfest luncheon, I presume?" Elias asked.

"You'd presume correct, doc. The whole town saw it."

"Saw her fall?"

"What? No."

"So how is this related to—"

"It isn't.

"You really didn't hear?"

Elias shook his giant head. "I'm afraid you two envoys from the greater Germantown social circle will have to enlighten me."

And enlighten him they did: Greaves drunk, Greaves stumbling over the footbridge to steal—*like a common dang thief!*—his own boy's pickup and disappear, off to Lord only knew where.

"This would be Jack's truck?"

"Nah, his youngest," Kenny said.

"The strange one," Ben added for clarification. "The one off that game show."

"I see. And was this an incident of isolated inebriation brought on by an excess of autumnal fervor, or do you two gentlemen suspect something larger is afoot?"

Here the elbowing and good-ole-boy guffawing reached new heights.

"You better dang believe something is afoot," Kenny said. There were rumors that Jeff Duncan had been accosted by the FBI, some sort of bank shenanigans and you better believe if Jeff's in it up to his hips, Richard Greaves is in at least to his knees. "They're both of 'em thick as thieves and dirty as pigs in slop."

"The FBI?"

"That's what everyone's saying."

"I see," Elias said.

"They screwed over ole John Long years ago and he was their friend. Something's starting."

"Better buckle up, doc."

"Yep, something's starting up for sure."

It was only when they were gone Elias began to wish it wasn't so. Not a passing wish, it should be said, but a fervent desire not to see something else solid and dependable—a family in this case—torn apart. He knew Jack from the high school, knew Emily socially. Tom Greaves—the strange one—had been one of Elias's first and finest students after Elias came home to Germantown. Rose Greaves had long been a friend to his parents.

It was an effort to go on eating but go on he did. He ate his chicken with his fingers, allowed for his tea to be refilled a first and then a second time. *Don't let it put you off your feed, son.* His father's injunction. *No, Daddy, I won't.* He kept eating, evening now, another day moving toward completion. A life moving toward completion. Except don't be morbid, Elias. Don't be so damn existential. We are all moving toward death, and while Elias was in no hurry to die, he was in no real hurry to live either.

He cut into his pie, and as the fork found the crust Elias felt something form inside him that he might have identified as sadness had he not been years past feeling anything. Still, he had to drain half his glass of tea to swallow it down. The rest of the pie he ate quickly. He wanted to go home. He wanted to go home and open his laptop and watch the soul singer Charles Bradley sing "Changes," no more than three times, then he'd sit on his deck and watch his goats, the way you could see them in the dusk, light shapes in the grainy darkness. There was a lesson in it, he thought. The way you could see them and then, all at once, they were gone. That they were still there, that *it* was still there, the world, even when you couldn't see it. This greater accounting of the invisible, yes. That was a trick, wasn't it, Elias thought. That was *the* trick.

Only it wasn't a trick.

Honest to God—to his God, wherever he had gone—it wasn't.

The car was in some sort of gated development, but apparently the undeveloped part, where giant houses of stacked rock sat between long stretches of dense woods and thus the sort of fast-closing darkness that had the driver slamming the brakes—*shit, are you serious?*—as they entered yet another cul-de-sac marked only by a sign reading LOT 19 MINI-FARM.

Or LOT 12. LOT 11—*are you kidding me?* Nayma was in the back seat with Regan smushed in the middle, beside her a girl wearing a metallic choker Nayma recognized as that girl that was always staring out the window in third period Econ. Up front was Nayma didn't know who. Two boys, friends of Regan who swore there was a party somewhere in this neighborhood and yes of course they were invited, of course they knew where it was. Not like it was a formal thing, just some people getting together.

Nayma had been down Main Street, two tallboys of Victoria she'd bought (illegally) at the tienda in a paper bag, when her phone had started going off. Two texts from Regan she ignored and then a third *stop ignoring me.* When her phone actually rang she'd obeyed, answered, and five minutes later was in the car with Regan and the girl and the two boys.

"So," Regan said, as they circled out of yet another dead end. "Stinson Wood was in like jail."

"Uh-uh," said the staring girl.

"Like his ass was incarcerated."

"I heard not *jail* jail," said one of the boys up front. "Like some juvie shit."

"Still," Regan said, and leaned forward making plain the five stitches that knitted her eyebrow. "Hey, I think we're in like the wrong section or wing or whatever."

"It's around here somewhere."

"Like this is Phase 2 and we should be in like Phase 1?"

"Either stop complaining or make a donation to the I'm-driving-your-ass-around fund."

"In like your dad's car."

"On my gas, god. Just look for lights."

"Whatever."

Regan crashed back into the seat and nudged Nayma.

"Hey. Quit pouting. We won."

"I'm not."

"Like truth, justice, and the new American way."

"I'm not pouting," Nayma said.

But she was, or maybe not pouting, just stewing in her own self-pity, marinating, slow-roasting. Even when they saw the lights ahead signifying yet another giant house, only this one lit like a ship going down with all hands.

"Boom," said the driver. "I told y'all, did I not?"

They parked on the street, wheels up on the curb, lights out. Through a screen of crepe myrtles, they could see the back porch, the sliding glass doors beneath a rectangle of light.

"So we're approaching commando style," one of the boys said when they were out of the car. "Like quiet and all."

Regan stopped. "Why?"

"Because I heard maybe there's a grandma or something asleep upstairs."

"Seriously?"

"It's supposed to be a rager."

"A rager with like Grandma upstairs snoozing?"

"It's just what I heard."

"Fuck, Leo. Seriously?"

Not that Nayma cared. She had started walking before dusk, her abuelo sitting on the concrete stoop drinking his lone can of Victoria and staring out at the street, her abuela inside, tucked into the sheets and yet another *telenova.* Nayma had made it halfway across the parking lot before her abuelo asked where she was going. *Nowhere.* Just walking, and walking she had found herself in a sort of emotional fog, listless, indifferent. Only the movement registered, and walking she wondered if her abuelo had ever felt the same. But of course he had. He had never told her much about Immokalee, but she knew enough to imagine the circumstances of his life there. The town, to the extent that it was anything beyond an encampment of trailers and processing centers, was the hub of the tomato fields, the place from which migrant workers began the trek north, harvesting tomatoes in South Florida and then strawberries in the irrigated fields along the Gulf, finally peaches and apples in the Carolinas. It was an eight-month odyssey of endless indentured work. Slave work, if you got down to it.

Coyotes slipped the workers through the Sonoran Desert on foot and into Florida in the backs of U-Hauls. When they got out they owed fifteen hundred dollars for the transport and went to work paying it back, earning two or three dollars a day while living ten to a trailer in the windless fog of mosquitoes and heat and the powdered residue of insecticides so harsh they burned the skin. Of course you paid for that too, the privilege of the trailer costing, say, ten dollars a week, and transportation to the fields—that was another buck. Then, of course, you might one day decide to eat something, and there was yet another cost. In the end, it meant not only could you never pay off your debt—you actually wound up in greater debt. Which meant you could very easily spend the rest of your relatively short life never venturing a half mile beyond the fields. There were periodic raids by ICE or the DOJ but none of it added up to anything like justice. At best you were deported and what was waiting for you there? Work in a textile mill if you were lucky in the way her parents were lucky: making sixty pesos for ten hours of work, sewing collars and fostering arthritis. More likely, you would exist at the whim of a cartel. You might be a runner, a lookout, a mule. Until, of course, you weren't. Until, of course, a cartel bullet, placed neatly behind your right ear, pierced the growing tumor the insecticides had started years prior.

She followed the boys and Regan and the staring girl (her eyes had a sort of thyroidal distension Nayma hadn't noticed before, which maybe explained the sense of staring) out of the woods and into the edge of the backyard.

"Basement," the boy whispered, like this was some raid to be captured in the green luminescence of night-vision goggles.

"Jesus," Regan said.

Nayma said nothing, just followed.

She doubted there was anything she could experience that her grandparents hadn't already been through, and moved onto the uncut shoulder, the grass brushing her bare legs. One of the boys slid open the door and they followed him inside. Scattered paper plates. Pizza crusts and Tervis tumblers. On a giant television a raccoon-tailed glider was suspended mid-flight. LuckyVolcano842 had thanked the bus driver.

"Where are all the like..." the girl said, and one of the boys pointed upstairs.

"See," he said. "Told you."

Upstairs was some sort of living room rave. The couches pushed aside to make way for the dance floor. Post Malone cranked to an impossible volume and around a strobe light maybe two dozen bodies flashing in and out of the hypnotic glow. Regan spun into the crowd and after a moment pulled Nayma along.

But, no.

But please, just.

She slipped through the room, Regan hardly noticing, and stood on the edge of crowd, back to the wall. After a moment one of the boys wandered over to shout in her ear, *There's nothing to drink here* and then, *These are like a bunch of freakin' middle schoolers.* Nayma nodded. The boy shook his head and was gone. Nayma just stood there, the bass having sunk into her heart, her lungs, the pulse she could feel through her feet. Was it possible to walk home? Regan flashed by, illuminated and then not. Nayma wandered into the bathroom only to realize the movement behind the Grumpy Cat shower curtain was two bodies making out. She wandered back out and found a wall to lean against. It was only when she put her fists into her lower back that she felt the handle of the sliding glass door she was apparently slouched against. It was heavy but she managed to slide it open, slipped out, and shut it behind her.

It was quieter outside, the music no more than a dull roar through the double-paned glass. It was also dark, the porch vast, and she took no more than two steps before she bumped into what she identified as a wicker rocker. She sat in a porch swing and looked out at the yard. You could actually hear the crickets, no fireflies in sight but, yeah, crickets.

"I thought that was you."

She started at the voice.

"I'm sorry?"

"Nayma. I said I thought that was you."

The figure seated by the far wall coalesced into an identifiable shape just as the voice registered.

"Mrs. Greaves," Nayma said.

"Clara."

"Clara Greaves," Nayma said, not sure why exactly.

"I didn't know you were here."

"I just got here."

"You know my grandson Judson, I guess."

Nayma nodded and then, remembering the darkness, said, "Some friends do. I came with them."

Clara nodded too, or at least it seemed that way to Nayma. It was hard to see her there in the dark, but had she, Nayma would have seen Clara Greaves's eyes bright and wide with the narcotic glee that came from the lozenge that was pocketed in the corner of her mouth and only then degrading into a sliver of bliss.

"So loud in there," Clara said, "and so quiet out here."

"I can hear the crickets actually."

"That's something isn't it. Despite the noise, or the music, or whatever it is."

They listened then, or were quiet enough to listen. But what they heard was a clear bell, almost a gong sounding. When it sounded again Nayma realized it was Clara Greaves's phone.

"I'm sorry," she said, "I should take this, our neighbor…"

"Of course."

"I'm sorry. One second." She put the phone to her ear and Nayma watched her face contort. "You saw someone doing what?" she asked.

By the time Tom left the house to meet Brad Walters, the sky was hung with thunderheads and the wind was just beginning to skirt leaves up the sidewalk. Calhoun College was named for the worst of secessionists, John C., but in recent years the campus had acquired the luster of expensive progress, as cosmetic as it was sleek. But what was more interesting was the way it all glowed, the way the lamplight seemed to have followed him out of the basement and all the way here which, okay, was partly the edible, but also, at least partly, the world itself.

He wasn't sure why he was there.

Maybe because he didn't know what else to do or where else to go. He still hadn't said anything to his mom about his dad, and so far as he was aware, she didn't know about the FBI. But of course she did. Maybe not the particular federal agency or the particular crimes being investigated. But she knew, deep down—she had to know—that the check would eventually come due. The years of living with her husband and his moral shortcuts—wasn't it just a matter of time?

He paused on the front steps of the restaurant and let go a real, if somewhat theatrical, sigh.

Plums overlooked the lake, a giant farmhouse converted to a shabby chic bistro of Edison bulbs and craft cocktails served in copper cups. He found Brad at an upstairs table, the window up so that the breeze ruffled the cloth napkins weighed by cutlery.

"You made it," Brad said, half-rising and extending his hand.

"I did."

"No lady friend?"

"Flying solo, it seems."

"Too bad," he said, with what sounded to Tom like a bit too much in the way of disappointment. "I thought there was some Eurotrash girlfriend these days?"

"Afraid not."

"Something I saw on Facebook."

"No, just me."

"Some girl in Croatia or somewhere? Did I imagine this?"

"Maybe. I certainly have no idea what you're talking about."

"You have no idea?" Brad said. "Okay, my mistake. So, how are things, Tom?"

"Fine, the same. You?"

"Mom said you did some kind of ninja thing today."

"Did she?"

"So what's a ninja thing?" There was a decided smirk beginning to gather between the jowls of Brad Walter's face. "She said it was like an obstacle course."

"Something like that," Tom said.

"Drink some of that energy drink of yours before it? What's it called?"

"Ripcord."

"Ripcord! I remember now. With an exclamation mark."

"That's it."

Brad cupped his hands around his mouth.

"Ripcord!" he yelled.

"Yep."

"Ripcord!" he screamed, and somehow still managed to smirk.

"You seem to have mastered it," Tom said. "So tell me—"

"Ripcord! I love it."

"So tell me, Brad, how are the kids?"

"My kids? Christ," Brad said, and suddenly the smirk was gone. "My kids are needling. I've thought a long time about it and that's the word, needling." He put a hand up to signal the waiter. "I see them weekends, every other."

"They're like three and what, one?"

"Something like that."

"Still young and impressionable."

"Goddamn, Tom. You sound like their mother."

The waiter came over with his man bun and pandering smile.

"Do you happen to have any beet juice?" Tom asked.

Brad let go a low *Tooooooommmm* under his breath.

"I'm kidding," Tom said.

"No, you're not." Brad turned to the waiter. "We'll have two Old Fashioneds."

Drinks came out—"best between Atlanta and Raleigh, that, I promise you…"—and then a plate of pimento cheese and toast points.

Brad was getting remarried, had Tom heard?

"Middleton Place. Down in Charleston."

"The plantation?"

"*The oldest and most interesting gardens in the nation*," Tom said. "I'm quoting the Garden Club of America here. Which Miranda is always quoting so—"

"This is the girl."

"Miranda Colleton. This is indeed the girl."

"Colleton like the county?"

"They were all planters down around Walterboro, her family. Now all the money is in real estate. Time shares, mostly."

He went on while a storm blew up and out came two more Old Fashioneds. Tom watched the bridge over the lake turn. It was a swing bridge, and it rotated slowly on its center axis so that a boat could glide beneath. He was waiting on a sailboat, something sleek and masted, but what emerged was a barge hauling gravel, a swollen gravy boat lurching toward another unfinished construction site. The disappointment felt disproportionate, and he felt himself slumping into the evening while Brad talked about some mutual acquaintance, an old Calhoun classmate practicing maritime law in Savannah.

"Tom?"

"Yeah?"

"I was asking you about Harlow Pettis."

"Right." He had been. Only Tom hadn't been listening. There was the storm and there were the drinks, there was most certainly the edible. But mostly there was his utter and absolute disappointment with himself. Also revulsion, there was certainly revulsion, and for a moment he wanted nothing more than to go back. All his talk of moral clarity, his posturing, his philosophizing when maybe it was that simple: go back. Take responsibility. And then he thought: of course it's that simple. What else could it possibly be? He would have smiled had he not caught Brad smirking again. That Tom was the subject of gossip, this was no secret. The child of privilege and promise who in three decades of living had managed nothing more than the ability to scale a warped wall and then post it online. That in a few days people like Brad would be listening to his *SoulCast* implosion of profanity and preciousness, shaking their heads as much at his hazy logic as his crybaby entitlement—this was also known to Tom. The last decade of his life had been built around this awareness.

He felt his phone go off just as Brad downed the last of his drink.

"Let me just..."

He managed to make it to the bathroom before he planted one hand on the tile and took his phone out. It was something about the sudden standing, the Old Fashioneds, the edible, something about the message from Ivana—it had to be Ivana, didn't it?—that was vertigo inducing, the urinals rising up in a strange parabola before dropping back into place, all aglow. He shut his eyes, exhaled, and swiped the screen.

His message was right there:

I'm sorry, he had written. *I want to see you. I have to see you. Please. I made a mistake. I love you. I didn't realize this before but I love you.*

It was just as he remembered, except—this couldn't be right—the response was from not Ivana but Sherilynn which was—Jesus, which was Kneebrace! *Wow, Tom,* it read. *This is... this is a lot. We should probably talk.* But talking was the last thing he intended to do.

He was shoving his phone back into his pocket when it began to ring. It was his mom, and it wasn't so much the message as how she delivered it that frightened him. She was panicked and begged him to come home right now.

Someone was sneaking around behind the house.

Jack and Lana were in his truck when his phone went off. He passed it to Lana, not, it should be said, without some amount of frustration. She was silent and simmering and—Jack felt his heart break—ringless. That wasn't how he wanted it to be. The day, the Citadel game, it had all been a great success and he'd come home relaxed enough not to worry about things with his daughter or grandmother or the fact that the Financial Crimes Division of the FBI was after his dad.

Instead of worrying, he drank a glass of wine on the porch and had been on the couch with Catherine, her long legs across his lap, some house-trading show on HGTV, when Lana had come down and blown things up. Which is to say Lana had stomped down the stairs and demanded—there was no other word for it—*demanded* to be taken to her friend Christie's because *I've so got to talk to her right now, face to face*. Catherine had just stared at her but Jack, poor pitiful Jack, had hopped up so quickly he'd nearly knocked his wife off the couch (what was that about *a thing*? There was no *thing* here). He'd thought Lana might talk to him on the drive over, but Jack was just beginning to understand how little he actually understood about anything.

"What's it say?" Jack asked, since his daughter, having made plain her wishes, now seemed incapable of speech.

"It's Mom," Lana said. "Call your mom now, she says. All caps on the now."

"Call my mom?"

"That's what she says."

Jack took the phone back. "Did she say why?"

"You know what," Lana said. "I think I've changed my mind. I think I want to go home instead."

"Hold on one second, honey."

He dialed his mother and was about to start speaking when he heard the panic in her voice.

"Jack, someone's in the back pasture."

"Wait, what?"

"The back pasture. There's someone back there down in the trees. On four-wheelers, I think. I was at your sister's and then someone called and—"

"Wait, Mom, slow down, please."

"Tom says he thinks maybe they're poaching deer."

"Tom called?"

"No, the neighbor called and I called Tom, but please come over, Jack. Tom says he's going down there."

"Tom is going down where?"

"Into the back pasture. To confront whoever it is, which is absolutely crazy. Especially if they have guns."

"Did you call anybody?"

"Guns and drunk like they must be."

"Mom, listen to me. Did you call anybody? The sheriff? The game warden?"

"I just called Tom and he said not to. That he would handle it himself."

"Tom said this?"

"It's all I can do to stop him from going down there," his mother said. "I can hear them, Jack. They're drunk, I can tell. Tom says they're probably on meth."

"They're probably not on meth, but do not under any circumstances let Tom go down there."

"I'm trying."

"And call the sheriff's department."

He had no more than taken the phone from his ear when Lana started.

"I want to go home, Dad."

"I know. But I've got to check on your grandmother really quick."

"I thought you said for her to call the sheriff?"

"I did. But she's still scared."

"Take me home or I'm going to text Christie to come and get me."

He said nothing, and a moment later topped the hill where on the far rise of the pasture sat his parents' stone house, the two maples in front up-lit so that they stood like twin rockets waiting for launch.

He was slowing for the driveway when his phone went off again and he fumbled it out.

"Dad?" Lana asked.

"Please, honey. Give me just a…" Somehow he got the phone to his ear. "Hello?"

"Wassssup, mutha-fucka."

"Justin."

"What are you doing, fool?"

He was turning now up his parents' driveway, past the mailbox and along the white picket fence, the crepe myrtles flashing by.

"I can't talk right now."

"I pity the fool who can't talk right now."

"Listen," he said. "I'm serious."

"I pity the fool who's serious."

"I can't find my dad and there's some drunk assholes in the woods behind my mom's house, okay? I've got to go."

"Behind your mom's?"

"I'll tell you about it later."

"For real behind your mom's house?"

"I'll tell you about it tomorrow."

"The hell you will. We're on our way. Dad—" Jack could hear him speaking in the background. "Dad, we got to bounce."

"No," Jack said. "It's fine."

"We're on our way. Don't kick any asses without us."

"No. Not necessary. Please don't."

"We'll be there in thirty," Justin said. "Maybe forty since neither of us can remember where we parked. Your folks haven't moved, have they?"

"Please," Jack said, but the line was dead.

"I'm texting Christie," Lana said.

"What the hell!" he screamed.

"Dad!"

But he wasn't screaming at her: Tom was standing beneath the garage's motion light in camouflage coveralls, dark stripes painted across his face and their father's Remington 30.06 in his hands.

Jack threw open the door before the truck had actually stopped.

"What the hell are you doing, Tom?"

"Dad!" Lana yelled.

"Someone is down in the woods." Tom was defiantly, serenely, infuriatingly calm.

"Put the gun back in the safe," Jack said.

"Let me repeat myself," Tom said. "Someone is down in the woods. I'll add to that: Someone is down in the woods drunk and armed. I've already heard shots fired."

"Put the goddamn gun inside, all right?"

"Dad!" Lana yelled again. "Language?"

"Sorry."

"Lana," Tom said. "What did your friends think of today?"

"Oh my God," she said. "My friends were so totally blown away by it."

"By what?" Jack asked.

"Seriously, Dad?"

"Oh, right. You're talking about this ninja thing?"

Tom shook his head with a frightening slowness.

"Dad means well," Lana said. "He's just—"

"Yeah, I get it."

Jack pressed the heels of his hands to his eyes.

"The gun," he said calmly, and was about to say more when he saw his mother coming out of the house, barefoot with one hand clutched at the throat of the pink housecoat she had pulled tight around her.

"Jack," she said, "you're here. And, Lana, come here, honey."

His mother hugged Lana, and Jack waited impatiently for them to part.

"Tell me what's going on here," he said.

"Someone's down in the woods," Tom said.

"Yeah," Jack said, "drunk and armed. I got that. But I'm asking her."

"Well," she said, "it's just like your brother said. The neighbors saw lights and called so I came home from your sister's and sure enough."

"Headlights," Tom said.

"Let her finish," Jack said.

"No, he's right," his mother said. "Headlights on four-wheelers is what we think."

"And we're sure that's not Dad down there?"

"Your father?" his mother said.

"I'm asking if we're sure that isn't Dad down there. Maybe he kind of freaked or something, granny and all."

"It isn't Dad," Tom said.

"How do you know that?"

"First of all, we don't even have a four-wheeler."

"We have a Mule, don't we? That six-wheeled thing that's always broken?"

"It's not Dad. Dad's at the hospital."

"Mom?" Jack asked.

"No, it's not your father."

"You're sure?"

"She's sure," Tom said.

Jack glared at him before turning back to his mother.

"I just want some clarity here before we let Rambo go blasting away into the dark and stormy night."

"Oh, he is most definitely not going down there," their mother said. "Neither of you are."

"Mom?" Tom said.

"Did you call the sheriff?" Jack asked.

"They said five minutes but that was a while ago."

"Mom?" Tom cried. "I told you I'd handle this."

She turned to her youngest.

"I'm sorry, honey, but Jack is right. You said yourself they were probably on meth."

"I don't want you going down there, Dad," Lana said.

"I'm not."

"Well, I want another look," Tom said, and turned toward the fence and the back forty.

"Honey?" his mother called.

"Shit," Jack said, following.

"Dad!" Lana yelled.

"I know," he called back to her. "Language."

He followed Tom to the fence that ran behind the back porch that overlooked the field. To the left stood a series of ill-formed shapes it took Jack a moment to place as the obstacles in Tom's ninja course. To the right stood the barn, though not so much a barn as a tractor shed, a place to house the New Holland with its AC and radio, the Bush Hog, the disc plows and wheelbarrows. It was two hundred or so meters down to the tree line and sure enough, moving just within it, Jack saw lights. Two sets of headlights and what must have been a flashlight swishing through the boughs before flaring out over the grass where several bales were scattered like toys.

"See 'em?" Tom said.

"Yeah."

You could hear them too. Voices, though it was impossible to make sense of what they were saying.

"Poachers," Tom said.

"Very likely."

"Very definitely." He pointed just below what appeared to be a climbing wall, holds hand-drilled into the ply-board. "You've got to be pretty ballsy to drive two four-wheelers across the property line."

"Or pretty drunk."

They stood for a moment, forearms resting on the upper rail, the night cool and still, the air as crisp as it was clear. A breeze moved over the mown field and you could smell the drying hay. The sky was star-showered, so thick and deep you could discern the cloudy band of the Milky Way, the long sweep of its purpled arc above them like a distant ceiling.

When Tom spoke again he was whispering.

"Let's just walk down there," he said. "It's not a big deal."

"No."

"I'm not saying go down there all belligerent. We just walk down like, hey, fellas, what's up?"

"No way."

"I feel like some impotent child sitting here waiting on the sheriff. You think granddad would have waited for the police? You think he would have stood here and let a bunch of assholes fool around on his land in the middle of the night?"

Jack looked from the sky back to the headlights. He was

considering whether the question was rhetorical when he heard Lana behind him, calling his name.

"Dad," she said. "The cops are here."

A cruiser sat in the drive, lights off but engine running. Two deputies stood beside it, one skinny, one fat. His mother was hugging the skinny one. Jack approached and saw that it was a kid named Eliot who'd been in Jack's civics course half a decade ago. He wasn't a kid anymore, of course. He was six-three and had done four years as an MP in Korea before coming home to join the sheriff's department.

"Jack, look who it is," his mother called.

"Coach Greaves," Eliot said coming forward, right hand extended. "Good to see you, sir."

"Eliot. Thank you for coming out."

"How are your parents, Eliot?" His mother turned to the others. "We used to do children's church together, me and Glenda. We used to—"

"We should probably," Jack said, motioning toward the pasture.

"Yes, sir," said Eliot.

The fat deputy drifted forward like a zeppelin cut loose.

"You said lights?" he asked.

"You can see them from the fence," Tom said. "Four-wheelers."

"What do you know about the neighbors?"

"They're white trash," Jack said.

"Jack—"

He put a hand out to stay his mother.

"They have a good dad," Jack said, "but he's old and his sons—three of them—they take advantage of him."

"I heard shots fire," Tom said.

"You hear more than forty-six?" the fat deputy asked. "'Cause I'm, by God, walking down with fifteen in three magazines and one in the chamber and they don't pay me to bring 'em back."

"But I've known the Hamptons for years," his mother said. "You don't really think—"

"It's fine, Mrs. Greaves," Eliot said. "We'll just go down and see what's going on. We'll just talk to them."

"I'd prefer to go with you," Tom said.

The fat deputy shook his head.

"I'd prefer you to put up the deer rifle and wait inside." He turned to Jack. "Can we drive down?"

"It's flat all the way to the tree line. I'll open the gate."

"Dad," Lana said.

"Just the gate. Take your grandmother inside for me, will you, honey?" he said, and started down along the fence line. The gate was fifty or so meters past the barn in a gentle depression, the grass shin-deep and wet with dew. Walking down, the back pasture disappeared beneath the horizon but the corner of the house rose up like the prow of a great stone ship, two-storied, bright and leaning. Jack heard the deputy's cruiser, bucking its slow methodical way through the pasture, only its parking lights burning. He stood there until it passed and then swung the metal gate shut. There were no cows—there hadn't been cows for years—but the old habits remained. It's hard to quit the things out of which you'd built a life, he thought. The motions linger years past any sense of purpose. It goes away slowly, or if it's deep enough, maybe doesn't go away at all.

He heard something and froze, forearms resting on the gate.

The cruiser was halfway toward the tree line, but that wasn't it. The sound was closer, more human, and he felt the prickle of adrenaline and fear he'd last felt in the desert. The date palms and dead dogs, bombs stitched inside their guts. You didn't need caffeine because you couldn't turn your brain off. He crouched and turned and it was only then the figure came into focus: it was Tom, maybe twenty feet away and staring at him.

"Jesus, Tom."

"Scare you?"

"Surprised me."

"You shouldn't let someone slip up on you like that, old soldier like you."

"What are doing down here?"

"I'm going in," Tom said.

"You're doing what?"

"I'm going in."

"You really do sound like John Rambo."

"The allusion dates you, brother."

"You're an idiot, living an idiot's dream. You know that, right?"

"Be still for a second." Tom raised his nose to the night. "You smell that?"

"What?"

He put his nose to Jack. "It's you, actually. Are you wearing Dusk?"

"What?"

"By Herban Cowboy. I'd know it anywhere."

"I don't know what you're talking about."

"You are, aren't you? And here I'd always pegged you a Speedstick man. Sport Fresh. Maybe Wintergreen if you were feeling particularly virile."

"I don't know anything about it."

"Really?"

"Catherine bought it, all right."

"Go, Catherine."

"Look," Jack said. "You have any idea what aluminum chloride does to the human body?"

"I underestimated you."

"No one does. That's the point."

"Hey, don't apologize."

"I'm not apologizing I just—" He looked back in the direction of the house. "Let's just forget it, all right?"

"It's just deodorant."

"Oh for God's sake, Tom. Drop it, okay?"

"Delighted to." Tom rested his hands on the top of the fence as if testing the slat's stability, hopped over in one bound, and straightened his coveralls as if pulling at the lapels of a dinner jacket before zipping off toward the tree line.

"Tom?" Jack called, his voice half whisper, half pissed. "Come back here. Tom?"

When he saw the figure move again he lumbered over the fence and hurried toward it. He caught up with him in the pines along the pasture's edge. Ahead they could see the deputies out of the car, flashlights swinging between them, but no sign of the four-wheelers.

"Get back up here," Jack said.

"Are you panting?"

His brother was crouched in the darkness and, yes, Jack was panting.

"I thought you were an athlete," Tom said.

"You're gonna get shot."

"Get down."

"Old fatso's going to hear something and unload on you. Forty-six rounds he said."

"He's probably been saving that line up all his life. But seriously, you do realize you're silhouetting yourself, right?"

Jack kneeled and took a moment to gather his breath.

"You see they're gone," he said, still panting. "You had your fun. Now let's go back before Mom freaks."

"Mom doesn't know we're down here."

"Mom—"

"Look," Tom said. "Lights."

And he was right: the lights were just below them, down along the creek. When the breeze shifted, they could hear the low thump of the idling four-wheelers.

"They're looking for a way back across the creek," Tom said. "They're trying to escape."

"Let 'em."

"To hell with that. Armed poachers on our land? What would Dad say?"

"Dad isn't here."

"That's sort of my point, brother," Tom said, and was off

again, sprinting from tree to tree, and then Jack realized he was moving too, walking down the slope toward the creek, dry leaves crushing beneath his feet. He was coming down the hill like an announcement, a big circus bear of noise and disregard, and a moment later a floodlight swung up on him and he threw a hand up in front of his face.

"Turn off your light," he called, and staggered forward, blindly. "Get it off me, please."

In the glare he could see four or five men and two four-wheelers, tailpipes rattling with exhaust.

"Get your light off me," he said again, just as a second light burst to his right, a red flare that steadied into some impossible candlepower.

"All y'all motherfuckers, get down," said a voice to his right.

"Put down the gun," said another voice, this one to his left.

"Get on your faces," said the original voice to his right.

"Put it down," said a third voice.

Jack knew that voice as Eliot: he and the fat deputy were hustling in from Jack's left, flashlights wagging. The first voice was—oh, shit—the first voice was—

"Elvis!" Jack yelled.

"It's cool, brother," Elvis called back. "I got a bead on all these motherfuckers. You back out all smooth-like. I got you covered."

"You over there! Put down the gun!" This time it was the fat deputy and Jack detected the high strain in his voice that registered as fear. The man was afraid and with very good reason. Elvis was somewhere up on the ridge with the drop on everyone. He'd shot fedayeen snipers out of minarets in Fallujah, nine-hundred-meter shots with the wind rising and falling. Jack had heard the stories. He wasn't putting anything down. They could have his gun when they pried it from his cold dead hands.

"It's okay," Jack called. "Everybody just relax. It's okay," he called to the deputies. "I know this man. Elvis, put it down, please."

"You all right, Jack?" Elvis called back.

"Yeah, just put down the gun."

"I heard it come over the scanner and thought about your poor old mama out here all by her lonesome."

"I appreciate it," Jack said. "But it's fine. Please just put down the gun."

"I'm about to call the goddamn SWAT team," the fat deputy yelled. "I'm about to make a colander out of your ass."

"What'd he say?" Elvis called down.

"A colander," Eliot called.

"A what?"

"Like for draining spaghetti."

"I can't hear you," Elvis said.

"Like pasta?"

"Jack, what's he saying?"

"He said—" Eliot started.

"It don't matter what I said," the fat deputy called. "You just put the rifle down this minute."

Then Jack felt someone tug at his pant leg. He was standing perfectly illuminated—the spotlight from the four-wheelers, the flashlight from the deputies, some red glow issuing from Elvis's position—yet somehow Tom had slipped up beside him to lie invisibly in the undergrowth.

"Get," Tom said, "down."

"Christ, Tom."

"Now," his brother said.

"Elvis?" Jack called. "Eliot? Everybody please—"

Then he heard another voice.

"Jacky-Boy?"

And then another:

"Dad?"

"Jesus Christ," he muttered. "Lana! Justin! Do not come down here! You hear me? Do not come down here?"

"Jack," Tom said, "look out!"

"Do not—" Then Jack realized someone was charging up at them, barreling forward from the spot along the creek where the four-wheelers idled. "Stop," Jack yelled, "don't shoot. Nobody shoot! It's just a—" he said, but it was too late, and he swung forward to plant his fist square in the tiny face that was only inches from his own.

And then everybody started to scream.

The Germantown auditorium was broad and dim and, most importantly, packed.

Emily had lost count at around 120 people and guessed there must be 150 by now. The reunion, she kept repeating, a little more often than she intended, was a huge success.

But how could she not say it?

People kept coming up to her, thanking her, congratulating her while REM sang "Man On the Moon" and "Nightswimming."

Where is Knox? had quickly turned to, *Who is the bartender? Where did you find him?* they kept asking.

Actually not asking, *gushing* was the verb. Gushing about the bartender of dreams, Barry Read. And though it was no more than the great good fortune of having read reviews on Yelp, Emily was happy to take credit for it, to play it off mysteriously, as if she had some old and deep connection to Barry, something so intimate she could only nod demurely when someone mentioned his name.

It was, perhaps, a way to spite Knox, this almost nearly—but not quite—hinting at some other life. Stupid, yes, but she was a little drunk, and despite the turnout, a little sad. There had been no more messages and while it was childish, she was determined not to be the first to text. Knox was the one who had skipped out. He wasn't here for the play and he wasn't here for her reunion. He was the one *who wasn't here.*

What *was* here was the presence of the woman in the burn unit, her ghost, Emily thought, were it not for the fact that she was still alive. Ghost or not, she floated just above Emily's bare shoulders in a feathery cloud of gauze and grafted skin, IV lines tethering her like a float at the Macy's Thanksgiving Day parade.

Floating just above the woman was the prospect of Emily's return to work, the granular falling of hourglass sand which had, she realized, more or less run out.

She wandered over to the bar and plucked a glass of Yellow Tail, downed it quickly, and plucked another glass.

I'm not going back, she whispered to herself. But she wasn't so sure. It wasn't some abstracted sense of duty, at least not exactly. It wasn't an issue of pride. It wasn't an issue of money or ego or anger.

It was—

But then she didn't know what it was, which meant, perhaps, it was nothing. Only it wasn't nothing. It was her life, but also there was this whole other life, this world that was built around holding Kyle in the swing or marveling at Judson or cajoling Knox. There was this world where no one was raped or burned or shot in the parking lot of the Dollar General over a case of Natty Light.

Someone had once told her that the world was the manifestation of God's consciousness, and if that were true, if you believed it—and she thought, perhaps, that she did—you couldn't be disappointed by it. Yet sadly she was, because what was around her simply wasn't enough.

The emojis while the bombs fell.

Je suis Charlie! and a red, white, and blue filter on your profile pic.

This was life?

It was, after all. It is. At least a form of life, and she could drown in it, or she could go back to work because, honestly, what was the alternative? Get the kids into good schools while people rape girls in Nigeria? Put the vacation pics on Instagram while people throw acid in the faces of Afghan girls?

The lost ignored.

The lost a string of tears in a text message.

Not that any of it would touch the Rhett family. Their life was so safe, so cushioned, yet here was this sense of impending collapse that was held at bay only by…

So, Emily, said the burned woman floating above her, go home, retire, why shouldn't you? I would if I were you. Retreat behind the gate of your semi-posh neighborhood with its cart paths and boat slips. Get the Mexican yard crew. Get the Peloton bike. You've done your duty.

But what was this *duty* business? she wanted to know. This implication that you put in X hours or years toward the greater good and thereafter you were free to spend your days tightening your core at Pilates or sitting on the veranda at the Grove Park Inn, both activities, to be fair, that she very much enjoyed, but also felt should be judiciously rationed. But why? Why ration them? Why not simply live?

She downed her wine and moved around the edge of the dance floor.

Pray about it, Em.

And she was trying, she really was, but something wasn't connecting, though there was the very real possibility that it wasn't connecting because she was convinced it wasn't connecting, that if she could just change her mind or her attitude or her something, then she would feel that calming presence she had known as a girl.

It was possible this was all it took.

It was possible—

"Excuse me? Miss Rhett?"

She turned to find Barry Read, bartender of dreams, approaching her, one finger pointed skyward, a look of confusion on his face.

"Is this your doing?"

"I'm sorry?"

"This," he said. "Are you responsible for this?"

"Responsible for what?"

He pointed again at the ceiling.

"This quote unquote music. 'Have you seen her?' not by the Chi-Lites but by MC Hammer?" He was smiling, finger still upright. "This, ma'am, is an affront."

"I didn't even notice."

But she did now. Coming through the speakers the Hammer was crooning smoothly.

Barry cocked his head. "Really? The butchering of a Motown classic, and you didn't notice?"

"Actually, I notice now."

"Because I had hoped this little piece of blasphemy had been buried with Reagan."

"What if I said I specifically requested this version because, you know, Hammer time and all?"

"I think I'd have to walk out the door," he said, smiling.

"Without all your delicious Yellow Tail?"

"Without even collecting payment on our most low-rent package, yes, ma'am."

"Low-rent?"

"You telling me you didn't like the Cotes du Rhone?"

But Emily couldn't even remember the Cotes du Rhone. Then, like the music, it was present, and everything she had worried about didn't so much drift away as reduce itself. It was still there, but it felt so much smaller. Instead of abstractions like suffering and duty there was the wine, so cold you didn't notice it wasn't particularly good. There was the music, so nostalgic you didn't notice it wasn't classic Motown. There were her old friends, the people she had grown up with, who knew her—sweet, nerdy Emily, who had spent a single year at the Governor's School and then came home because she wasn't that sort of girl.

"I'm going to find the DJ," she said, smiling.

"And?"

"And thank him for his judicious and visionary taste in early '90s hip-hop."

Barry Read laughed a very beautiful laugh.

"I might even request Kid 'n Play," Emily said.

"You most certainly may not."

"Tevin Campbell."

"No, ma'am."

"Some Color Me Badd."

"I'm sorry, I have to draw the line at Color Me Badd."

"A little Def Leppard."

"Wait a second," Barry said, still smiling. "You just jumped genres on me."

"Keep your ears open," she said, a little more flirtatiously than she had intended, and again Barry laughed that beautiful laugh, and it was something in that laugh, the lightness, the kindness that led to her ask: "Hey, Barry. What's your position on burning beds?"

"Is this a band I missed?"

"No, I mean like 'burning beds.'"

"Some synth-pop outfit from 1986?"

"No, seriously, 'burning beds.'"

"You mean like 'burning bridges?'"

"I mean like literally. Like burning a bed. On fire. In flames." She hadn't realized how drunk she was.

"Like as a piece of what, of performance art?"

"Like with someone in it."

"Someone in it."

"Tied down, say."

His smile was still there, but only barely.

"Burning someone in a bed?" Barry repeated.

"Like flames, like a tampon."

"I beg your pardon?"

"I mean," Emily said. "I'm just… It's awful, right?"

"You're not making a joke here?"

"It's evil."

"It's inhuman, yes."

"Inhuman. Exactly." She leaned closer as if to whisper a secret. "Listen," she said, "do you know who Rachel Corrie was?"

"Are you okay?"

She stood there nodding, affirmed in something, though she couldn't say what.

"Are you—" Barry asked, but it was so loud.

She realized he was talking to her, his hand on her arm. He

had a look of concern now, and it pained Emily to see it. All that lightness, all that kindness—she had erased it.

"Let me get you some water," he said.

"No, I'm fine."

"It's no trouble."

And here she put her hand on his arm for balance. "I'm fine. Honestly."

"It's okay," he said, his eyes never leaving her. "I'll be right back."

When he was gone, she drifted around the room in an airy bliss of contentment and chardonnay that not even questions about Knox could pierce. She had stolen it, she realized. This sense of grace. She had stolen it from Barry and didn't care.

While he was looking for her, bottle of water in his hand, she stood by the bar and had her fourth—possibly her fifth—generous pour of Yellow Tail. She'd said a little prayer earlier in the evening, a simple *Lord, please help this go all right*, and what the Lord hadn't done, the wine had, or Barry had, or something. Or maybe that was the Lord? The way God worked in mysterious ways?

That she hadn't prayed in that moment for her marriage or her sons had weighed on Emily. But those worries had lifted.

It was okay, maybe, to simply not worry for an hour or two.

It was okay, maybe, to simply be happy.

She decided she was.

The DJ was playing Def Leppard and soon enough she was dancing, getting it on, singing along with the crowd that suddenly formed around her and not for a second did she think of the woman in the Georgia burn center or the flaming tampon dropped on her, not for a second did she think of her granny or her return to work on Monday or of how she would be leaving Kyle. Not for a second did she see her husband's face and think, What happened to us? That Which Cannot Be Named would not be named. It wouldn't even be acknowledged.

She just danced and danced until her face was soaked not with tears but with sweat.

And not for a second did she try to pray or think or reason.

Not for a second did she worry.

She just kept dancing, crying and sweating, but dancing.

Like she would never stop.

It's just a kid.

That was what Jack was about to say, his mind forming the words, though too late for his mouth to voice them. Now the kid had an ice pack over his right eye, and Jack leaned against the trunk of a sycamore beside Justin's dad. He held a second pack against his swollen fist. Elvis was over laughing with the Eliot and the fat deputy. *Third goddang infantry division,* Elvis was saying. *No shit. I ran cover for some of them boys.* Lana and his mom were on the pasture's edge, his daughter furious, he knew, because when she'd come running down to pick up the seven-year-old boy Jack had cold-cocked she had let Jack know just precisely how she felt. The stream of profanity felt oddly incongruous with the gentle manner in which she cradled the boy's head. But it also felt exactly right.

He didn't know where Justin was, down with the campers, he guessed—that's what they were, campers—trying to smooth things over. Two middle-aged fathers who appeared to be accountants or clerks, middle-manager types out camping with their four boys. Camping with permission, it should be said, Jack's father having invited them. Then the youngest, the boy who'd be wearing a shiner for the next week, had gotten homesick and they'd packed it in. Only they had gotten lost, and then stuck when they tried to drive the four-wheelers over the creek. Jack's father had told no one they were coming, of course. Not his wife and surely not his sons. One more mess, Jack thought, he was left to clean up. Except the mess was his doing.

"Don't be hard on yourself," Doctor Paulman Sr. said. "These things—"

"Yeah."

"They happen. Take some of this." He passed Jack the flask from which he'd been drinking liberally and Jack looked at it.

"Just a taste. Doctor's orders."

"Doctor's orders," Jack repeated, and took a small nip and then another. It was good bourbon, the only kind the man drank, golden and smooth. He capped it and passed it back. Loneliness, he thought. In the middle of a goddamn pasture of people. He put his hand out and Paulman passed back the flask and this time Jack drank deeply.

"You didn't happen to see if my daughter is still up there, did you?" Jack asked.

Paulman looked back toward the house where the lights burned like a ship going down.

"I did," he said. "She is."

"I guess you heard what she said to me."

"Enough of it."

"She's pretty angry," Jack said.

"She'll get over it." He passed Jack the flask. "People generally do."

"I didn't mean to upset her."

"You didn't?"

He looked at the old doctor, the corduroy jacket, the rimless glasses. He was sitting in the dirt, yet magnificently clean. The brushed silver mustache. The ivory fingernails.

"Of course not."

"Of course not," Paulman said. "So what are we trying to raise these days, harmless citizens?"

"That's the idea."

"Not the bold and the beautiful? First do no harm, right?"

"Are you asking me?"

"I'm telling you one fool can throw a stone in a river that ten wise men can't remove. You heard that one?"

"Not lately."

Paulman took back the flask.

"When he invited me—" He gestured down toward his son. "When Justin invited me I came. I'm seventy-three, Jack. My boy's forty-four, same as you. But that isn't the point. The point is, when your child invites you to go somewhere you go. And afterward you thank God for it. You know all my girls, Justin's sisters?"

"Of course."

"I always wished you'd married one of them. They've got bad husbands, every last one of them. Or maybe not bad, just not exactly good. They love me, my girls. But they love me the way you love a beautiful old hunting dog that's outlived its usefulness, good for nothing now but the memories. But such good memories. Take this."

Jack took the flask. "All I wanted to do is take her to the game today. Female cadets, you know? I wanted her to see that."

Paulman put his gentle papery hand on Jack's wrist and pulled the flask close enough to take it. "But why?"

"What do you mean why?"

"Why did you want her to go, to see what?"

"That's a good question."

"You got a good answer?"

"Can I have that back?"

"You'll be as drunk as me in a minute. Not as old, but just as drunk."

Jack nodded. "Did you ever know about the guy in our class at the Citadel that died in a bike wreck? This would have been our senior year. Justin ever tell you this?"

"I don't know. Why don't you tell me?"

"Well, senior year a guy in our class—I barely knew him—he was off campus riding his bike, going up one of those narrow little one-way alleys. You know how the streets in Charleston are. Tight, cobbled. Justin never told you this?"

"I don't think so."

"Well, he goes up an alley, a one-way alley, and turns out someone is coming down it the wrong way, absolutely flying. They hit him head-on and he goes into the windshield. He's wearing a helmet, but it's massive head trauma. His brain is swelling, he's bleeding internally, all the stuff you expect. They put him in the ambulance and within the hour some neurosurgeon is operating. It's bad news."

He looked at Paulman and down where Justin was still talking with the campers, the boy attended to, sitting up on a four-wheeler now, a cold gel-pack to his face.

"Anyways, they tell us in the afternoon that he's in bad shape and then that night in the mess hall his roommate gets up, walks up to the podium carrying his guitar. He was a good old boy, the roommate, and we figure we're all about to get an update and we do. Except what we find out is that he's dead. He's died on the operating table just a few minutes ago."

"Rough stuff."

"The entire mess hall went dead silent. Then the roommate sits down with his guitar in his lap and says he wants to sing a song. It was his buddy's—I swear I can't remember his name—but it was his buddy's favorite. Then he starts picking out that old Alabama song. 'Dixieland Delight' it's called."

"I know it."

"And thing is, I've always hated Alabama and I guess I still do. The songs are this clichéd Southern thing. Mama on the porch eating biscuits. Daddy walking in the traces of the mule. But I'm singing it along with him—spend my dollar, parked in a holler beneath the mountain moonlight—and then I realize the entire corps, every last cadet is singing it along with him, singing and crying, and what it felt like was we were one single being, this one single alive thing, all of us together, mourning. I'd like her to feel that just once in her life."

"Just once?"

"Once I think everyone deserves."

"But you don't want to be greedy."

"Grateful, not greedy."

Paulman passed him the flask. It was near empty now.

"You believe all that Dr. Phil bullshit?" he asked. "Grateful, not greedy."

"Should I not?"

"Hell, I don't know. Me, I'm greedy. Every second. That's what I've always wanted. To hold my children, to hold my wife, my friends—every second made beautiful. I didn't know it was greedy. I thought it was just being human."

"I don't know."

"I thought it was just being alive." He took the flask back, shook it, held it upside down. "We killed it."

"Sorry about that."

"Good bourbon ain't made to sit in the bottle." He tucked it inside his jacket. "Your granny still okay?"

"Seems to be."

"Incredible. How old is she?"

"Ninety-four, I think. Maybe ninety-five."

"One of the real old timers."

"Yeah."

"My daddy..." Paulman said. "We had a hog killing every year when I was a boy. Country folk, you know? It's the stuff of legend now. Black-and-white on the History Channel. But we did it every fall. Used everything but the squeal, and the squeal we sold to the Ford Motor Company to use in their trucks. That was my daddy's line. My daddy was a Chevrolet man."

"So's mine. Or was at one point, I guess."

"Is he down there with her, your daddy?"

"That's a good question."

Down below them, the four-wheelers began to move. They were nothing but lights and exhaust and they eased across the creek and started up the opposite bank along an old cow path.

"My wife said I'm going through a thing," Jack said.

"A thing? Are you?"

"Probably."

"Well, then. You know that line about when you're going through hell?"

"I don't think so."

"When you're going through hell the most important thing is to keep going. Something like that, at least."

Justin walked up.

"Look at you two," he said. "Laid up sorry, I'd say."

"The boy all right?" Paulman asked his son.

"All right enough. Lucky for us Rocky here isn't quite the hitter he used to be. Are you, dumbass?"

"I guess not."

"Agile, mobile, and embarrassingly hostile." He turned to his father. "We should go, Dad. Before they start air-dropping teams of lawyers. I mean if you can still walk."

"I can walk just fine," Paulman said, rising in a series of segmented motions, shifting onto one knee and then the other. He looked like a puppet raised to staggering life. "Carry your ass out of here like a piece of firewood if need be."

"Shit. I'll drive the car down."

"No need."

"Just sit still, old man. Before I have to call a real doctor."

When he was gone Paulman nudged Jack with his foot.

"Justin ever tell you how many babies I delivered before I retired?"

"Is this like your line from before?"

"No, this is different."

"'Cause it's a good line."

"I appreciate that, but this is different. Ask me how many."

"All right. How many?"

"No idea. That isn't the point. The point is, they needed me and I showed up. I was useful because I was there."

"You're telling me to get up, aren't you?"

"I think I am."

"Go find my daughter."

"That's about the gist of it."

Jack stood, his head a little woozy, his hand a little stiff.

"You know when I feel like I'm part of one single alive thing?" Paulman asked. "Every second of my life, son. Every goddamn second. You know why?"

Jack was silent.

"Because," the old doctor told him, "I decided I am."

Nayma was maybe, nearly, possibly, almost home when the lights crested the hill behind her. It was the first car she had seen since leaving the party and she watched it approach as if it carried some message. She wasn't exactly lost. Not that she was certain of her location either. There was an unfinished neighborhood deeper in the development, the roads paved and the occasional footings dug, but no houses yet, and she seemed to be in it. It was a cul-de-sac, or maybe a loop. Either way she'd wandered around it looking for something recognizable for a solid hour, passing the porta-johns on construction sites and pallets of cinder blocks before eventually exiting onto maybe White Cut Road but also maybe Pickett Post. Either way she had no idea where she was and wasn't about to reenter the maze that was BENTWOOD ESTATES.

Borgesian, Dr. Agnew would have called it, were Dr. Agnew here.

But of course, he wasn't.

Only Nayma.

Until the lights crested behind her.

There was a surge of adrenaline, and then slight confusion: hide, run, keep walking? Behind that came a brief flutter of fear, the desire to run into the woods, or simply duck down into the weeds. Hide, or, if that was what she was already doing—it came to her that maybe she was—then remain hidden.

Yet she didn't move.

Part of it was giving up, a form of surrender.

But it wasn't really that.

It wasn't really anything.

She simply didn't move.

Not even when the lights began to slow. Not even when the prickling along her legs registered as something beyond the brush of the grass.

It was a truck.

She could see nothing in the glare of its headlights, and then it eased beside her and though her eyes held a certain blinding brilliance, she knew exactly who it was.

When Elvis reached over to open the passenger side door she wasn't surprised.

"Hey, girl," he said, his hand out, as if beckoning to her.

And Nayma stood there, halfway between the road and the woods, halfway between school and home, trying to decide whether or not she was afraid.

"Hey, Nayma," he called, "you need a ride home or something?"

It occurred to her that perhaps she did need a ride.

That she was fully capable of accepting such.

She was, after all, a woman with a torch.

For a while it was just like before, or like before might have been had the world turned a little differently. Richard sat in the chair beside where his mother sat up in bed, talking, laughing, with not a thought of death or shame or the Financial Crimes Division of the FBI. They'd spent the entire day like that: no tubes, no subdural hematoma. Only the good times, only the best memories. All the trips he and Clara had made with his parents, riding up into the mountains when Jack was just a baby, and then when Jack was three or four and Emily was a baby. Gatlinburg. Pigeon Forge. Stopping down in Cade's Cove for the picnic where his own father—still alive, still strong—would unload a bounty of saltine crackers, sardines, and Land O'Frost ham while his ma took out the Bundt cake and the biscuits wrapped in tin foil, the loaf of Bunny bread because back then they still thought of sliced store-bought bread as a great luxury.

The food on the concrete table, the yellow jackets around the Nehi and Cheerwine.

The children barefoot in the creek.

This was years after Kennedy had been shot, years after Watergate and Vietnam, but they had somehow remained unscathed.

"Those were such good times," his mother said. "Weren't they, honey?"

They were. Good times, happy times.

It was embarrassing in its way, their easy happiness.

But Richard didn't regret it, because what is wrong with happiness?

Fishing off the dock. The swing set he and his father made out of crossties, the playhouse constructed from wooden pallets. Those days on the shimmery sand at High Falls Park, Coppertone and a thermos of Kool-Aid. And then years later the arrival of Tom, that late blessing they had experienced as a sort of silvering, as if the world was remade as not just newer but brighter too.

All these years he'd felt ashamed of Francis Gary Powers' refusal to take his shellfish toxin and with it his own life but Lord! how wrong Richard had been. What Powers had understood, and Richard was only now realizing, is how life is animated by hope. Hope—by God!

"Good times," his mother said, and fell quiet.

Richard sat by her as she drifted into the lightest of sleeps. And how lovely it was, the thin veil of her eyelids, her birdlike hands in her lap. There was no talk of Teddy going through the hay rake and beneath the tire and into the ground. No talk of Anson Greaves and his silence. Her fall no longer the tragic prelude it had appeared to be. Her fall now something to laugh about because guess what? Hope had pushed through.

When Richard woke he hadn't realized he'd been sleeping, yet it was dark outside. It was suddenly late, and he blinked the room into focus. He'd been sweating, could feel the bourbon still oozing its way out of him. He hadn't made it home, which meant no shower. He needed to wash his face and sat up quietly so as not to disturb his mother. Then he realized she was awake and staring straight ahead, all the joy from earlier erased.

"Ma?"

"I'm tired, honey."

"Get you some rest. It's late, I think."

And the way she swung her head almost imperceptibly, it almost seemed—

"Oh, honey," she said. "It isn't that kind of tired."

"Let me get you something to drink."

"I dreamed about your brother. I was standing in the kitchen. There was an ice cream sandwich out like we all used to love, right there on the counter, melting—"

"Ma."

"You know I was standing in the kitchen the day your daddy came up through the field, carrying him."

He moved to the edge of his seat and took her hand, but she slipped it away.

"Let me get you some ginger ale."

"I'm tired of it, Richard. Of all this."

"I know you've got to be sick of plain water."

"I went down to the basement looking for him," she said. "Ain't that crazy? But just for a minute it didn't seem so crazy."

"You know what we should get? It ain't but what, ten something? The Dairy Queen's still open."

"It didn't seem crazy at all. It was just like Teddy and your daddy, like they were waiting on me down there."

"We should get a Blizzard. Remember how you always loved a Blizzard?"

She took his hand now. "I did."

"Oreo."

"Oreo, that's right."

"I'll be back in fifteen minutes, Ma."

She put his hand between both of hers.

"I love you, Richard."

"I love you too. Give me fifteen minutes."

"I love you so much."

"Oreo."

"That's right, baby. Oreo."

The Dairy Queen was indeed still open, the parking lot crowded, the asphalt warm. Richard nearly danced inside to stand in line with the smell of fry grease and burgers and the girl handing an orange Dilly bar to a boy no bigger than Teddy. He got the two Blizzards and danced back to the car and all at once it wasn't just Richard who was buoyant. It was the entire world.

Sadness—never.

Death—no way.

The Financial Crimes Division of the FBI—absolutely inconceivable.

He was back on the Grand Strand, thirty years old and strong, his family around him. The Veil hadn't lifted because there was no Veil, and if there was no Veil there was nothing to descend, there was just Richard and his family, Richard and his life. All he had to do was face it. It was like Alphonse had said, there is another world, and it is this one. Which meant one world—which gave him hope! He had hope! The papers he'd taken from the Pioneer Stove were still beneath his shirt and he knew exactly what to do: give them to Emily! Forget acting solicitor Annie Smalls. Forget Jeff Duncan. He'd give the papers to his brilliant daughter and she'd fix everything! And even if she couldn't, he was alive, the people he loved were alive. The world—this one singular world—was all around him.

And she'd known it all along, his ma.

He sailed back to the hospital through the swishing door and into the elevator.

He was singing "Kokomo," he was fairly dancing.

Fifteen minutes, he'd told his ma, and stepping off onto the fifth floor it had been fifteen exactly. How was that for magic! How was that for the world being in sync! He thought he might have to slip the Blizzards in, kind of tuck them past the winking nurses—contraband! It would be a bit like a game, gliding quietly into the room to produce them with a flourish—tada!—and a little mock bow. *Guess what I got, Ma?*

But then something was—

Richard was halfway between the nurses' station and his mother's room when the chaos registered, the door open, people moving in and out. He had a Blizzard in each hand, fingers wrapped around the cold waxed paper cups, and all at once felt that cold move down his wrists and into some deeper marrow.

"Sir?"

It was a nurse, blocking the threshold.

"Sir? I'm sorry, but you'll have to wait out here."

Blocking the threshold where inside people were huddled around the large man who was shocking his mother's frail chest because—

Richard took a half step forward, not quite comprehending.

"Sir—"

And then that awful sound of the heart monitor flat-lining, shrill, insistent, like something not from this life but a movie about this life, the kind of thing that could never be real because, because…

Richard Greaves stood there, freezing from the tips of his toes to the top of his suddenly sweating head. Ma? If she would just look at him, if he could just get her attention. Ma, I wanted to tell you. He raised the Blizzards just a bit, as if to say, Here I am, I came to tell you, Ma. It's fine, everything's fine. There's another world, Ma. You knew it all along, didn't you? There is another world, and it is this one. I get it now, I do.

He tipped his head forward and no more than whispered.

"Ma?"

Sunday

IT'S LATER THAN WE THINK

Dawn and the yard was banked in a dense fog.

It was Sunday and, Dr. Elias Agnew realized, suddenly and decisively, fall. He stood at his study window with his cooling coffee and four-stoppered cane, searching. Somewhere out in the autumn cool were his mother's goats. He could hear them—their tiny brass bells cast in Poland and ordered online—and what they sounded like were the softest of wind chimes, so slight as to be apologetic. It was a sound he had come not so much to love—though he did love it—as to depend on. The promise that there was another living thing out there, and it wasn't simply Elias, alone inside what had become more mausoleum than home.

Which was all, he thought, a way of saying he was lonely.

He sipped his coffee and stared into the fog.

He could almost see something now, gray shapes in the gray dawn, a darker pattern within the granularity of morning. This was his favorite time, the time he waited for, when their presence was confirmed but not yet articulated. Like he was not quite seeing or was seeing ghosts. There was a certain promise in such, as if things were not yet certain, as if the past might not be as definite as it had thus far proven to be. He held on to the possibility.

Yet the light kept coming.

In another half hour the sun would rise over the pines that he and his mother had planted as a windbreak the year before she passed, and what he would see were the rolling fields that lapped down to the barn, the grass just beginning to yellow. What he would see would be the goats, bedded or grazing and now little more than shaggy pets. The world would be revealed. God's glory and so on and so forth, and, yes, it would please him in its simple way. And, yes, it would be lovely and precise. But though he had inherited every acre to the horizon, it would no longer be his.

It would be taken from him, or rather, he would hand it back over.

It was something he had never tried to explain to anyone, let alone himself.

After he had quit the ministry, after he had come home not exactly defeated, but certainly apologetic—though who could say to whom and who might ever say for what—*after, after, after,* he thought, he had imagined nothing but second chances. Then he came to realize there would be no second chances, just as he sometimes thought there had never been a first chance. He'd gone to college and graduate school and then divinity school, he'd taken a position at St. Matthew's, he'd lost his faith, he'd lost his way, he'd come home to his parents. And then his parents had died.

That was all, or seemed to be.

He walked back to his desk and sat before the open computer.

He had spent the last half hour of this morning, just as he'd spent a half hour every morning for the last several weeks, watching a YouTube video of the late soul singer Charles Bradley not so much singing as weeping/screaming/embodying the old Black Sabbath song "Changes." Elias had come across it by what appeared at first an accident, though was surely the will of whatever goodness was left in the world, and it had touched him deeply and immediately, much as the poetry of Franz Wright or the novels of Fannie Howe once had. It was a live performance, recorded just months before Bradley died, and Elias thought that he very nearly could sit and watch those eight minutes and fifty-nine seconds of raw emotion, possibly the most human thing he'd ever seen, every second for the rest of his life. Which was why he limited himself to a half hour.

But today he indulged himself, running the video forward to around five minutes where Bradley began to speak…*if you have a mama or a papa and had an argument and went away and never said you're sorry, brothers and sisters, it's later than we think…*

The bells brought him back.

He heard the bells, but softer still, moving away from the house and toward the barn. There was no seeing them, and he looked from the yard back to the room. There was his desk with the laptop and lamp, the open Bible, which—though he hadn't intended it—looked very much like a prop. There was the crucifix hung above the French doors. The walls were lined with the bookshelves his parents had installed decades ago for his fifteenth birthday—he was that sort of boy, and they were that sort of parents, bless them.

He dumped his coffee in the bathroom sink and walked through the house to the kitchen.

It was too much house if you got down to it, the square footage demanding children but there would be no children. Instead of children there were three dozen Oberhasli goats. As sweet as babies, his mother had said once. Aren't they, honey?

This was just after Elias's father had died, and it had been just the two of them, mother and son. *As sweet as babies.* It hadn't been intended as cruel, of course, it hadn't been intended as a judgment on his life, and he hadn't taken it as such, mostly he hadn't taken it as such. And who knew—did God know and if so, would He see fit to reveal such to His people?—perhaps it was a good thing that he had no children, no family, no wife or husband or mother or father. Maybe he couldn't have handled the crying and screaming and laughing. Maybe he would have melted in the face of all that life.

He hobbled from the kitchen to the bedroom, the bed unmade, his Waist-Relaxer Big & Tall trousers piled on the hope chest. Brushed his teeth in the bathroom, flossed. You flossed not for hygienic reasons, but because you could build a life out of such, the daily offices, the bedrock rituals. This was self-revelation. Yet another thing he had learned via God's silence. (He had to stop thinking like this.) Washed his face and finger-combed his hair. Thought he heard a car in the driveway but there was no car in the driveway. There never was.

What was wrong with him?

He looked at himself in the mirror.

"I'm going," he told himself, quoting Charles Bradley, "through changes."

Then he took his cane and walked back to his study, embarrassed.

He was almost to the kitchen when he heard what sounded like someone knocking.

Perhaps it had been a car, but at this hour, on a Sunday.

Who could it—

He opened the door on—

"Thomas Greaves," he said. "Child, what are you—"

He hadn't seen Tom Greaves in how many years he couldn't say. He had been one of Elias's best students, curious and quiet if always distracted, as if his spirit had already fled Germantown and was only waiting for his body to catch up. His presence had helped Elias through that first year back in Germantown. But that had been over a decade ago. Since then, there was the occasional email, the occasional update from this or that far-flung location, but in the actual flesh, no, not in more years than Elias could name. Now he stood on the porch, a backpack slung over one shoulder like a child waiting on the school bus.

"Good morning, Dr. Agnew. May I come in?"

They sat across from each other in the slanting light of the study. Coffee. Folded hands.

"I was going to say something like 'I didn't know where else to go,'" Tom said. "As stupid as that sounds. Then I realized it wasn't even true. I didn't have to go anywhere. I could just leave."

"And that's what you're doing?"

They were on their second cups, the first drunk while Tom made awkward small talk and Elias tried to read whatever lay buried in the shallow grave of Tom's face.

"My grandmother is in the hospital," Tom said. "Did you know this?"

"I did. I'm sorry. But she's well?"

"No."

"I thought I'd heard she was somewhat better."

"She was, they thought. Then she had a heart attack."

"Oh, Tom. I had no idea."

"She seemed fine and then… They're going to take her off life support today."

"I'm so sorry. I didn't—"

Tom unfolded his hands on the table, a little gesture that signaled dismissal as much as acceptance.

"She's lived a wonderful life, my grandmother. Is that a thing people say?"

"I think it is."

"She's lived a wonderful life. Is it okay to say something like that?"

"I think it is, certainly."

Tom nodded, his earnest head suddenly cast down at his hands.

"And now you're leaving," Elias said, "because of this, or because?" He waited. "Forgive me, but I'm not quite certain I understand. Is this because of your grandmother?"

"No."

"So this is?"

Tom shrugged, another gesture that seemed to drift toward certainty without ever quite arriving.

"I'm leaving because I'm going to be a father."

"A father? Well, how wonderful, Thomas. I'm delighted for you. I'm…" He stopped himself because something in the face now tilted from him had not quite assembled itself, and he realized it didn't know what to be. The almost smile that evaporated off the lips. "Are you?"

"Happy about it? I don't know. At first I thought it was some sort of trick, like a hustle."

"Is it?"

"I don't know, maybe. It doesn't matter though."

"And no one else knows?"

"It's kind of been a secret."

"I see."

"Do you know about secrets, Dr. Agnew?"

Elias studied him now. He had been looking at the boy—he could imagine him as nothing else but a boy—but now he watched with a new intensity.

"What sort of secrets?" he asked.

"They're all the same, aren't they?" Tom said.

"I'm not sure I understand."

"This woman, the mother. No one knows."

"And you're leaving, you're going to her."

"I am, finally."

"Where is she, Thomas?"

"Europe."

"I see."

"I left her there. I panicked," Tom said. "I guess I panicked. Tried to pretend it never happened."

"But now?"

Tom was silent and Elias felt himself leaning forward.

"And you came here to tell me?" Elias said.

"And to ask a favor."

"All right."

Tom looked up at him. "Could you take me to the airport?"

"This is the 'I didn't know where else to go' part."

"I mean I could have just gone."

"But you needed to tell someone."

"I guess I did."

"And did you, Tom?"

"Tell someone? No. I mean not besides you."

"Where is your family?"

Again that shrug. "Home. Maybe the hospital by now. I have a flight out of GSP at two."

"Two today?"

"Bought the tickets last night. Direct to Munich and on to Prague."

"I remember you made a pilgrimage."

"I don't really care for that word, pilgrimage."

"I'm sorry. I didn't mean—"

"No, Jesus, I don't mean to be rude. But it's embarrassing, the way I thought of the whole thing. Have you ever wished for moral clarity, Dr. Agnew?"

"I suppose everyone has wished for that at some point."

"Actually, I'm not sure everyone has, or maybe." He shook his head. "I don't know. I'm figuring that out a lot lately, how much I don't know. How naive I've been. A clear-cut right and wrong. I've wanted that all my life."

"And now you've found it."

"I don't know."

"Yet you must know something. You're going back, after all," Elias said. "To your child, to this woman."

"I got a message from her, an ultimatum, really. I'd been waiting on it."

"Do you love this woman?"

"We knew each other for like a matter of months. How do you know these things?"

"I don't know."

"I don't either. But I'm going anyway."

"Well, then." Dr. Agnew stood. Put his palms on the table and hefted himself skyward so that for a moment he looked down on the crown of Tom Greaves's head. It felt solemn, this rising. It felt formal. He hadn't meant it be so—it was simply a product of his immobility—but then having finally risen it felt proper, the theatricality of it all.

"I would be honored to drive you to the airport, Thomas," he said. "But on one condition: we go to the hospital and see your grandmother first, and—"

"I don't think—"

Elias stopped him with a hand.

"And," he said, "you tell your family goodbye."

The boy—no more than an eager child in Dr. Agnew's twelfth-grade English class—the boy stared up at him in fear, and then the fear was replaced by acceptance.

Elias put his hand on Tom's shoulder and gave it a single squeeze.

"It's late, Thomas. It's so much later than we think."

They drove the back way to Seneca, past the Wesleyan Church, past the county dump, past the Metromont #17 and past the self-storage warehouses with their orange U-Haul trucks. Past what was known and what was remembered and for Elias, it was all remembered. Twice a week his father had made house calls, visiting not only the old shut-in men and women with their strokes and space heaters, but younger folks too, the children, the new mothers. From the time he was six until the day he left for college, Elias had ridden with his father, both of them expecting, though never quite saying, that soon enough it would be Elias making those house calls, Elias replacing his father as the county's last country doctor.

That it had never happened wasn't the product of any immediate decision. It had simply never happened. Now there were no more house calls because there was no more father. There was no more mother either. An entire world was gone, not to be returned, and what, Elias sometimes wondered, would replace the old? The answer wasn't simply the new. Actually, it was. The new always replaced the old. But Elias was part of the old. And what is to be done with the old?

His parents were dead.

Who was left to raise them up?

Tom took his phone out and studied it.

"Everything okay?" Dr. Agnew asked.

"My mom."

"She's okay?"

"Yeah," he said, typing now. "She's there. They're waiting for everyone before they…"

The fog was gone from his yard, but it had not yet burned off the lake, and as Dr. Agnew piloted his Oldsmobile across the bridge, a single boat was visible in the water, drifting in and out of the mist.

Tom put his phone in his pocket and looked up.

"I used to jump off this bridge," he said.

"This bridge?"

"My misspent youth."

"I would imagine youth is meant for jumping off bridges, Thomas."

"You would imagine?"

"I don't…" Dr. Agnew said, because it wasn't, he realized, something he would know.

"You don't what?"

"I don't…I…" He looked at Tom Greaves across the wide bench seat and realized he could hardly see him through the tears that had suddenly welled in his eyes.

"Are you all right?"

"Yes." He smiled. "Of course."

"Are you sure?"

"I'm simply going," he said, smiling through his wet eyes, "through changes."

There was no one at the reception desk and they took the elevator up to the fifth floor in silence, walked past the nurses' station where a man stood hunched and whispering into his cell phone. Tom stopped, as if suddenly paralyzed, and then began to walk again. The FBI agent nodded at Tom as they walked past.

"A family acquaintance?" Elias asked.

"Soon to be, it seems."

They walked past him to the crowded waiting area where several large men stood near the magazine rack drinking vending-machine coffee. Several more bodies lay slumped on the couches in various states of consciousness. It took Dr. Agnew a moment to realize that one of the large standing men was Elvis Carter from the high school.

"Mr. Carter," he called.

"Hey, Dr. Agnew, good morning, sir."

"Good morning to you. Now tell me, is that Nayma?" He was pointing at the young woman asleep on the couch.

"Yes, sir. She was walking up the road and I stopped to give her a ride. This was late last night."

"And she's just been?"

"Just sitting out here." Elvis let his giant shoulders rise and fall. "I wanted to take her home but she wanted to come here."

"To the hospital?"

"Roger that."

"Did she say why?"

"I got the feeling she felt like somebody needed to be here. Her grandparents look after the Greaves woman some."

"Lord, that child." He looked at the two men standing by Elvis. "And these gentlemen?"

"Oh yeah, I'm sorry. Dr. Agnew, this is Stan van Gundy and this here is Jeff van Gundy."

"Actually, I'm Jeff," one said.

"And I would be Stan."

"The van Gundy boys," Elvis said. "They're looking to take over the basketball program this year."

"I see."

"Jeff here pretty much rebuilt the Knicks from scratch."

"Well," Jeff said, "I had a good front office."

"I see," said Dr. Agnew.

"Their sister's in here," Elvis said. "Poor woman was out mechanicking and had a car drop on her leg."

"A '57 Ford," Jeff said, or maybe Stan.

"A Fairlane," said the other. "Took the rear fin right above her knee."

"Goddang," said Elvis, shaking his head. "You ever see the fins on a Fairlane, Dr. Agnew?"

"I'd sooner face a bull shark," Stan said, or maybe Jeff.

"Brother, you got that right," Jeff said, or maybe Stan.

"Excuse me for one moment, gentlemen," Elias said.

Sitting on the opposite couch was Jack Greaves, Emily Rhett, and their snoring father, Richard. Spread on the coffee table was a black-and-white photo and what looked to be several spreadsheets Emily was slowly reading her way through.

Tom hugged his mother, who moved to stand behind the couch, eyes on the papers, her own hand gently on top of her husband's matted head. He opened his eyes and spoke to her, quietly, while she stroked his damp hair.

Dr. Agnew walked over to Nayma and sat gently beside her. The right side of her face was glossy and swollen not with makeup, but with what appeared to be a bruise. She stirred and he looked not at her but to where his hands rested on his cane.

"Dr. Agnew," she said, waking.

"Good morning, child."

"What are you doing here?"

"I was about to ask you the same thing."

"I got him to bring me."

"Elvis Carter."

"I was walking home and he passed."

"He told me. Only he didn't say why."

There was a moment of silence and Dr. Agnew looked from his hands over to the Greaves family, still huddled in quiet conversation.

"My abuela found her," Nayma said. "Then I came down here to pick her up and there was no one here. I saw her in there, in the ICU, alone."

"This is when you borrowed my car?"

"There was no one here and then last night it just hit me that someone should be. What are you doing here?"

"I had a visitor this morning who needed a ride. I brought him down."

"You know them, the Greaveses?"

"For some time, my dear. My father used to treat them."

"He was a doctor."

"He was."

"They have a whole family," she said, "all right here, together. I wonder if they realize how rare that is, how special."

"I don't know," he said. "But looking at them now, I think perhaps they do."

"Dr. Agnew? Excuse me."

Elias looked up to find Jack Greaves standing in front of him. Behind Jack, Richard Greaves stood resurrected and supported between Tom and Elvis. Clara and Emily stood with their arms around each other. Dr. Agnew thought of his own mother and his own father; he thought of so many people and so many things, all of them gone. He might have gone on thinking about them forever had he not heard Jack Greaves speaking to him.

"I'm sorry to interrupt," Jack said, "but they're about to let us go in to see her. Would you two...would you two care to join us?"

Dr. Agnew looked at Nayma.

"I think, perhaps," he said, "we should wait out here."

But Jack Greaves had already extended his hands, one to Dr. Agnew and the other to Nayma.

"Please," he said. "We're grateful for both of you being here."

"I think," Elias said, and realized Jack had taken both his and Nayma's hands and was pulling both to their feet and all at once he stood facing the Greaveses and facing Elvis Carter and facing even the van Gundy brothers, the morning sun coming through the window behind them, warm and brilliant. All morning he had dreaded its arrival, but that was only because he had forgotten the way it warmed the world, only because he'd forgotten—oh, how he'd forgotten!—the way it lighted the world, and all God's creation, and all God's creatures, and so on, and so forth, forever and ever.

Amen.

BOOK CLUB QUESTIONS

In what ways are the Greaves oblivious to their privilege? in what ways are they keenly aware of it?

Many of the characters struggle with a sense of "duty." How does this affect their decisions?

How does family history influence (or fail to influence) current behavior?

Clara Greaves believes it's "morally reprehensible" to be happy in such a violent world. Do you agree?

How do characters like Dr. Agnew, Nayma, and Elvis fit (or not fit) into traditional notions of "the South"?

ACKNOWLEDGMENTS

This is a work of fiction. And though the Germantown of the novel shares some superficial similarities with my hometown one is certainly not the other.

My thanks to so many good friends: the Lost Mountain Adventure Club, the Monday Night Sewanee Crew, Michael Denner, Pete Duval, Patricia Engel, Leigh Ann Henion, Matt Hrenak (Ripcord! maestro), Michael Nelson, Ron Rash, and, of course, all my family, especially Denise, Silas, and Merritt.

Portions of this novel appeared in different form in *Witness*, the *Oxford American*, and *The Other Journal*.